Watchfires

Also by Louis Auchincloss

The Indifferent Children
The Injustice Collectors
Sybil
A Law for the Lion
The Romantic Egoists
The Great World and Timothy Colt
Venus in Sparta
Pursuit of the Prodigal
The House of Five Talents
Portrait in Brownstone
Powers of Attorney
The Rector of Justin
The Embezzler
Tales of Manhattan
A World of Profit
Second Chance
I Come as a Thief
The Partners
The Winthrop Covenant
The Dark Lady
The Country Cousin
The House of the Prophet
The Cat and the King

Reflections of a Jacobite
Pioneers and Caretakers
Motiveless Malignity
Edith Wharton
Richelieu
A Writer's Capital
Reading Henry James
Life, Law and Letters
Persons of Consequence: Queen Victoria
and Her Circle

Watchfires

Louis Auchincloss

BOSTON

Houghton Mifflin Company

1982

Library of Congress Cataloging in Publication Data

Auchincloss, Louis.
Watchfires.

1. United States — History — Civil War, 1861–1865 —
Fiction. I. Title.
PS3501.U25W36   813'.54   81-2698
ISBN 0-395-31546-8   AACR2

Printed in the United States of America

S 10 9 8 7 6 5 4 3 2 1

For my good friend
RICHARD ROSSBACH
fellow pupil at Miss Bovee's School for Boys,
fellow actor in the Yale Dramat
and fellow trustee of
the Museum of the City of New York.

FOREWORD

I GOT the germ of this tale from an incident in the life of George Templeton Strong recorded in an unpublished section of his famous diary. I later developed it into an article which appeared in my volume of essays, *Reflections of a Jacobite*. My first attempt to fictionalize it was the short story "In the Beauty of the Lilies" that became a part of *The Winthrop Covenant*. This novel is my final development of the theme.

PART I

A Fiery Gospel

1

FOR ALMOST A YEAR Dexter Fairchild had been suffering from a growing discrepancy between the turbulence of his private state of mind and the continued placidity of his outward demeanor. If he remained faithful to the demands of his law practice, if he prepared his wills and trust indentures and performed his fiduciary duties as rigorously as ever, if he assisted his two young sons in their school work and helped them to learn their catechism, if he escorted Rosalie punctiliously to the social functions that their position in New York required of them, he nonetheless continued to experience a violent perturbation of spirits and, on occasion, to feel such palpitations of the heart that he would have to stand still and (if nobody happened to be noticing) close his eyes, for all the world like a man with cardiac pains praying that his seizure would pass.

He had, the winter before, passed the climacteric of his fortieth birthday, but everyone assured him that he did not look his age, and Rosalie had even suggested that he grow a beard, or at least a mustache, to disguise his smooth skin with the appearance of maturity appropriate to his standing at the bar. But Dexter preferred to be clean-shaven; he liked the well-modeled, if slightly too square, chin and the neat red lips that faced him in the mirror over his bureau in the morning. He flattered himself that they set off well his large, grave eyes, his straight nose, high forehead and curly chestnut hair. He liked to fancy himself a converted romantic, a poet who had seen that every man who was not an absolute genius had ultimately to adapt himself to the world of practical affairs.

The only bad thing about being forty would have been not to be where one should have been at such an age, and was he not the senior partner of Fairchild & Fairchild, a trustee of Columbia, of Trinity Church and the Patroons' Club?

No, it was absurd, it was mortifying, it was even shaming, but the stubborn fact remained that the commencement of his inner turmoil had coincided with his reading of Mrs. Stowe's vulgarly popular novel. He had scorned *Uncle Tom's Cabin* when it had first been published, eight years before, telling his enthusiastic wife that he refused to subject his emotions to the assault of an hysterical female romancer who, according to all unbiased reports, had painted the condition of slaves as a hell not even recognizable to an unprejudiced visitor to the Southern states. As Dexter had written at the time to the Evening *Telegraph*:

"One does not have to approve of slavery to disapprove of Mrs. Stowe's technique. Even if one grants that every incident in her story happened, or could have happened, this can hardly justify her stringing them together in a sequence that grossly distorts her image of the average Southern household."

But Rosalie's sister Annie, sometime in the winter of '58,

had prevailed upon him to read it. "I read everything *you* prescribe," she had argued. "So the least you can do is to look into the book you feel so free to denounce publicly." He had done so, and he had been stricken.

He had not, even to Annie, admitted this as yet. He had continued stubbornly to maintain his position that the novel's picture of Southern life was a fabrication. But what he could no longer get away from was his growing suspicion that Mrs. Stowe's distortion might have a valid purpose. If such things as she depicted actually happened, or even if they *could* have happened, was it not perfectly proper for an author to put them together in such a way as to show that this sort of hell was feasible under our laws?

And so had begun this curious dichotomy in his life, this inner fever, this seething unrest of his thoughts and feelings, under what he hoped was still the continued serenity of the attorney, the fiduciary, the family man. His mind throbbed with melodrama, with images of arrogant planters lashing the bare backs of male slaves and ogling the females. It was all of a vulgarity! And when he shook his head to clear it and to concentrate on the iniquities of his previous *bête noire*, the hysterical abolitionists of hypocritical Boston, it was, oddly enough, to find no diminution in his old animosity, so that his choice seemed to be, no matter which side he took, between poles of equal violence. It was beginning to be a question whether some of his interior commotion might not start to seep into his conversation, even his consultations, and mar the image that he had so long cultivated of the pre-eminently reasonable man.

He now began actually to perform exercises to try to control his demon. Standing before the full-length, mahogany-framed mirror at which he shaved each morning, he would address the Southern lawmakers from an imagined desk on the Senate floor:

"We are not contesting that the black man is your property. But we maintain that your ownership is analogous to that of the holder of real estate, which, by its very nature, cannot be transported to free soil. The slave who manages to make his way to New York should be entitled to his freedom there. His manacles must fall when he crosses our border. If you want him, you ought to keep hold of him. Is that so difficult? You argue that his lot is a happy one, that the workers in our New England mill towns are not half so fortunate. We cannot help wondering why slaves try to escape and workers do not. But we can promise you this. If a mill hand goes south to become a slave, not one northern hand will reach to pluck him back. There! Can we not live then in peace together?"

And now, recollecting Rosalie's abolitionist friends, he would tremble with a different ire and proceed:

"In solving our common problems we must learn to understand that we are each goaded by extremists. You have your firebrands, your secessionists, who seek to make slavery lawful throughout the union. We have our die-hard abolitionists who clamor to abolish slavery at whatever cost to our peace and world position. Somehow those of us, North and South, with a bit of sanity, a bit of good will to man, must try to save our union with a judicious compromise. It was worked out in 1820, and again in 1850. There is no reason it cannot be worked out again today."

On a cold December morning, after one of these now daily exercises, he sought, coming downstairs, to recover his equilibrium in contemplating the recently redecorated drawing and dining rooms. The former was as neat and still as he wished his heart was, with serene curtains of blue damask, a jewelry cabinet, papier-mâché tilt-top tables, delicate chairs of ebonized rosewood with ormolu, marble statuettes and a chandelier of crystal globes. The dining room was even more calming, darker and soberer, paneled in black walnut and hung with his collection of seascapes by Kensett, Heade and Lane. In its doorway he breathed for a moment in relief.

But Rosalie was already down, and he noted with regret the pink dressing gown that now seemed a fixture of the morning meal. He wished, if only for the boys' sake, that she would dress when she got up, but he knew that any suggestion to this effect would be taken as an accusation of general sloppiness and would involve an argument which he could only lose. He could hardly tell her, could he, that her large, strong features and firm, substantial figure needed the support of well-cut, perfectly fitting raiment and seemed to wander aimlessly in the trailing silks of the boudoir?

"I may have to go to Fifth Avenue tomorrow night," she observed, without looking up from her teacup. "Unless Jo gets back."

"Fifth Avenue" meant the house of Rosalie's father, Number 417, at Thirty-seventh Street. There Mr. Handy, a vigorous widower of seventy-five, lived in rather opulent brownstone comfort, attended by his maiden daughter Joanna and eight maids.

"I didn't know Jo ever left."

"She never does, poor dear. That's why we thought she ought to get away for a bit. She's been staying with a friend in Boston."

Dexter grunted. "Some abolitionist, I suppose."

"Well, what of it? Can't Jo, at forty-five, be allowed to choose her own friends?"

"I didn't question her right, only her discretion. Why can't Annie go to your father?"

"Annie's there now. But she can't stay. She's got some party or theater." Annie was the "baby" of the family, as well as the "beauty." She was only thirty-two and married to Dexter's cousin Charley Fairchild.

"And Lily's too grand, I suppose, to go."

"Well, isn't that what *you*'ve always said?"

Lily, halfway in age between Jo and Rosalie, had the gratification of being Mrs. Rutgers Van Rensselaer. Dexter, who knew Manhattan and Brooklyn society like a book, had tried to teach its subtleties to Rosalie, who, despite her birth, cared nothing for such matters and appeared to pay little attention. But she had the irritating habit of tossing his lessons back at him whenever he demonstrated any independence from or impatience with, his own deities. She had never forgotten, for example, that in a moment of connubial candor he had ranked the Fairchilds, who had been farmers in Yorkshire only three generations before, well below the Handys and Van Rensselaers, who went back to seventeenth-century Manhattan. In the game of genealogy a listless Rosalie had nonetheless learned to count her trumps.

"Lily has her social responsibilities, as you like to call them," she continued. "She's taken up with her New Year's Day reception. After all, it will mark a new decade as well as a new year."

"And pray God we all survive it!" Dexter exclaimed fervently. "But why does your father really need anyone?

He enjoys magnificent health, and he has a house full of maids."

"Somebody has to keep track of his social engagements. Without Jo he might go to Mrs. John Astor's on a night when the Hone Club was meeting at his house. You know how dependent he is on her."

"Well, why can't he stay home a couple of nights? Really, the pace the old gentleman keeps up! It's a wonder his heart can stand it. And the way you all bow and scrape to him! He might be King Lear with four Cordelias."

"Cordelia didn't bow and scrape," Rosalie pointed out. "That was precisely what caused all the trouble. And it seems to me not so terribly long ago that you were saying that my family was the only one left in New York with a proper respect for the older generation."

Dexter sighed. Of course, it was perfectly true. Indeed he had been drawn to the Handys, or at least to Mr. Handy, before he had even been attracted to Rosalie. The picture of this tall, broad-shouldered, silk-hatted gentleman with the magnificent aquiline nose and hawk eyes marching down Fifth Avenue to church followed by his four daughters, raising his hat to some, bowing to others, simply smiling to the barely recognized, yet always courteous, always affable, the president of the great Bank of Commerce, the chairman of innumerable boards, the friend of Seward and Sumner but also of Bryant and Greeley, the god of the Century Club, the former colonel of the state militia who had ridden by Lafayette's carriage on the old hero's triumphant return tour — yes, that had been the picture in Dexter's mind of what success should be. That was the image of what he had wanted for himself!

But, agreeable as Mr. Handy had proved himself through the now fifteen years of their close relationship, Dexter had discovered that, being married to Rosalie, he had become identified with her in her father's mind and was expected to be available as a kind of stagehand to the old man's glory. How did Mr. Handy do it? Rosalie was keenly critical of the smallest tendency to pomposity in Dexter, yet apparently indifferent to that quality when it peeped out behind the benign affability of her popular parent. She saw it — oh, yes, she saw it very clearly, as did her sisters — but their father was always immune from filial criticism. Somehow he had been smart enough to establish his infallibility ineradicably in the infant minds of his offspring. It might simply have been by canonizing his dead wife so that he could enjoy the undisputed glory of having been her choice.

"Shouldn't I go with you?" he asked.

"I'd rather you stayed with the boys. Besides, if Father is going out for dinner, I'd be expected to go in Jo's place."

"Will you like that?"

"Like it? I suppose it depends where we go. I certainly shan't like it if it's one of his pro-Southern friends. It's amazing how Father manages to keep in with everybody. But whoever it is, I suppose I can be a good girl and hold my tongue."

But would she with her husband's friends? It was much less sure. Dexter took a sudden gulp of black coffee to fight off the nagging reminder of Rosalie's discontent, but it was no use. Rosalie was not happy. She had not married the sort of man she thought she ought to have married. It was not that she ever complained. Whatever she had done, she had done of her own free will, and she would stick to it. But it was not always agreeable to be a husband whom a wife was sticking to. No, no, he reminded himself impatiently; he was not being fair. He took another gulp of coffee and almost scalded his tongue. Rosalie still loved him. What was wrong with their marriage was that she didn't *want* to love him.

"I'm jealous!" he exclaimed suddenly. "I've always been jealous of your father. I'm telling myself that you're going to 417 because you want to go there. Because you prefer it there! I know that's not true, but it's what I'm telling myself. That's my trouble."

Rosalie became inscrutable, as she always did when he took this petulant tone. "You're being silly. I'm perfectly happy in my home. And you know it."

"It's just what I *don't* know!"

"Ah, Dexter. Please."

"You basically wanted someone who would take you away from your father. By being a bigger man. You wanted a pirate. A rebel! And look what you got. A prim and proper New York attorney who passes the plate in Trinity to fool God so he won't see what goes on in Wall Street all week!"

"That's not how you see yourself at all," she retorted curtly. "You're just trying to convince yourself you're *not* that sort of man."

"And I really am? Is that it?"

"It's too early in the morning for this kind of talk. I'm perfectly satisfied with my life as it is, and so are you."

"You mean I'm too satisfied?"

Rosalie simply reached for the newspaper and declined to answer. But Dexter continued to be fussed. Somehow, he had failed her. That was why she came to breakfast in her dressing gown. It might be the beginning of a long deterioration. It might end with raids on the sherry decanter in his study. She had a loving, passionate nature that had shriveled in contact with his colder one. She had dreamed of a life larger than their petty routine existence in New York society. Perhaps she had been foolish even to have dreamed that Dexter Fairchild was going to give her such a life — if indeed she ever had. But he was still responsible because he had *known* that he wouldn't, and known that he wouldn't even if he could have! And why had he not warned her? Because he had wanted to marry Rosalie Handy, the daughter of Charles DeWitt Handy!

"Oh, my God, they really have hanged John Brown!" she exclaimed from behind the *Tribune*.

"Did you think for a minute they wouldn't?"

No, no, now he was not being fair to himself. He had *loved* Rosalie; he loved her still. The only thing that he couldn't bear was the idea that she was aimless, that she had found no real goal in life. He wanted to put his arms around her, cross as she was, and hug her and tell her that she didn't look awful in that dressing gown. "Rosalie!" he wanted to cry. "What have I done to you? What are you doing to yourself?" But he held his tongue.

The boys were heard, the elder chasing his junior noisily down the stairway. When Selby reached the dining room, which was sanctuary, he pulled himself up short and walked with elaborate casualness to his place. Fred did likewise, but glowered at his escaped victim across the table. Bridey, the waitress, irked by their lateness, set their glasses of orange juice heavily down before them.

"Fred said I was a traitor to my country for being sorry that John Brown was hanged!" Selby complained to his mother. He was a fat, bright twelve, with long dank blond hair and staring green eyes. Fred, fifteen, was darker and thinner. It was probable that he might one day be handsome.

"And he called me a Southern pig!" Fred snarled.

"Boys, must you be always fighting?" Rosalie protested. "Where did you hear it, anyway? I've only just seen it in the paper."

"We heard the newsboy in the street," Fred explained. He faced his father. "Wasn't it simple justice? He was a rebel, wasn't he?"

"Of course he was a rebel." Dexter turned to his younger son. "He took up arms against the government, Selby. Some of his men were killed. That makes it murder as well as treason."

"But that doesn't mean that Selby can't be sorry!" Rosalie exclaimed, flaring. "I too am sorry. I think every decent-minded man and woman must be sorry. Brown was expressing his outrage at intolerable injustice. He may have gone too far, but some of our early Christian martyrs went pretty far, too!"

"I have a friend at school who has an uncle in the Underground Railroad," Selby offered, sensing his immunity in the division between his parents. "Don't you think that's brave?" There was a silence around the table. "Well, I think it's brave!"

"Your friend's uncle had better watch out," Fred sneered. "He'll find himself being brave in jail one of these days. Runaway slaves are private property, and the law says they've got to be returned to their owners. Isn't that so, Dad?"

"That is so, Fred."

"Oh, Dexter, is that the sort of law you're teaching the boys?"

"It isn't a sort of law, my dear. It's *the* law. Don't blame me, I didn't make it. Blame the United States Supreme Court if you want."

"I *do* want. That court was packed by pro-slavery presidents."

"It's still the Supreme Court. And its law is still the law of the land."

"What about God's law?" Rosalie exclaimed fervently. "Surely it's not God's law that one man can own another? And sell him and beat him!"

"There are a great many Christians living south of the Mason-Dixon line who would dispute that."

"And I would dispute that they're Christians! I would say that their society is rotten to the very core!"

"But didn't we consent to slavery, Dad?" Fred demanded.

"Never!" his mother cried fiercely.

Dexter raised a hand in mild protest. "I'm afraid Fred is right, dear. We have to face facts. Slavery was the price we paid for our union. We wrote it, by implication anyway, into the Constitution. You can argue that we paid too heavy a price for union, but we paid it, and with our eyes open. How can we go back on our word now?"

"Oh, Dexter, there you go again with your sacred union! Why not let the slave states go? Certainly *I* don't wish to be associated with them. Why can't we simply say, 'Sorry, we thought we could stand the stench of your "peculiar institution," and we've tried, but we find it's too much for our nostrils! So can't we agree to disagree? Let us part company in peace.' And *then* we'd see how long they could stand alone as the only nation in western civilization that permits such barbarities!"

Dexter had become very grave during this speech. "I'm

sorry, my dear. I cannot allow disunion to be advocated in my house. The federal principle is more important to me than any question of slavery. Whatever our destiny, North or South, it must be an American one. And that is a principle, boys, for which I should willingly lay down my life!"

He knew that he risked seeming pompous and stagy, but it had to be worth it. Both boys remained silent, fixing their eyes, whether in awe or embarrassment, on the surface of the table. Rosalie said nothing and gave no indication of dissent, as was her custom when he took this tone with the family, but it was perfectly clear that her concession could go no further than that.

The short rest of breakfast passed in the same silence. Rosalie and Dexter read the newspaper, and the boys departed for school. Their father was about to rise to leave for his daily walk to Wall Street when Bridey hurried in with the unexpected news that Mr. Charles Fairchild was waiting to see him in his study.

2

"CHARLEY?" Rosalie asked in surprise. "Tell him to come in here."

"Please, mum, he said he wanted to see Mr. Fairchild alone."

"I hope there's no trouble with Annie or little Kate!"

"I'll let you know at once if there is," Dexter assured her.

He found Charley pacing up and down in his study, obviously in great agitation. Charley was Dexter's first cousin, as well as Rosalie's brother-in-law; he was also a junior partner in the family law firm. Having lost his father early, he had grown up to look upon Dexter, although only six years his senior, as a kind of guardian. Charley was handsome and blond, with soft blue eyes and curly hair, and, when he was not drinking, he seemed younger than his thirty-four years. But his marriage with the beautiful Annie Handy, promoted by Dexter, had not worked out as the guardian had hoped. Annie was spoiled and easily bored, and Charley seemed to be becoming dependent on parties and drinking.

"Will you read that!" he exclaimed shrilly, throwing a

piece of note paper at Dexter. "Will you just kindly read *that!*"

"What is it?"

"Read it! It came by hand for Annie last night. The writer obviously didn't know she'd gone to her father's. I opened it, thinking it might be something important. It was. But not the kind of something important that a husband can handle. Except by kicking his wife's ass the hell out of his home!"

Dexter put the letter down at once and stared coldly at Charley's flushed countenance. "I can imagine nothing that would justify such disgusting language about your wife."

"Well, read the letter, damn it! Judge for yourself."

Dexter continued to eye his cousin fixedly for a moment and then, slowly, took up the letter. He read the following in a flowing, thick script, not devoid of a certain showy distinction:

> Darling, what can you mean? You're not going back on your word? If I can't believe in you, what can I believe in? Tell me you're true! Your faithful, tortured Juley.

Dexter's left hand crept slowly up to his heart. Then, seeing Charley's red eyes fixed on him, he drummed on his chest with his fingers as if he were simply preoccupied. But there was an ugly pain there, and he swallowed hard.

"Juley?"

"Jules Bleeker. You know, the journalist? The one who writes society pieces for the *Observer?*"

When Dexter at last found his voice it was to exclaim, "But that man's the most obvious kind of bounder! We met him at the Van Rensselaers'. He's not even a poor excuse for a gentleman. I told Lily she was going too far."

"Oh, he gets around. Society has no standards anymore. People just want to be amused. And Bleeker, I suppose, can be amusing when he wants to be. I couldn't take the man seriously at first. When Lily's fat old mother-in-law tucked her lorgnette into her big bosom, he actually leaned over and murmured, 'Happy lorgnette!' He and Annie were always giggling together in corners. I never dreamed there was anything serious between them. He looked too much like a ladies' man to *be* a ladies' man, if you know what I mean. Big and dark and slinky-eyed."

Dexter shuddered. He brought back the image of Bleeker with an effort. Oh, yes, he remembered the man! Bleeker had even rather made up to him. He was intelligent, certainly, and curious, and polite, too polite. He was somehow soft as well as crude, with the affectations of a dandy and the build of a bull.

"And you deduce from this . . . ?" Here Dexter dropped the note on his desk as if it were something alive and venomous. "You deduce from this florid epistle that Annie has actually . . . ?"

"Fallen?" Charley finished with a sneer. "No, I don't go that far, though it's not her morals that would have stopped her. I just don't think they've gotten to that point yet. She's a terrible little prick teaser. She may have given him an assignation and then reneged. But the second time she may be more accommodating."

"And what are you proposing to do about it? What have you come to me for?"

"I want you to act as my lawyer. I want an instant and final separation!"

"Charley, don't be an ass! One doesn't break up a marriage

over a thing like this. Marriage is a sacrament. Do I have to remind you that you have a little daughter?"

"Remind Annie, I suggest."

"I will! And, of course, there can be no idea of my acting as your lawyer against Rosalie's sister. Entirely aside from my own affection for Annie."

"You were always soft on her," Charley retorted peevishly. "But you don't know her, Dexter. You think of her as a sweet, innocent thing."

"She was when she married you!"

"And do you know something about that?" Charley started charging up and down the carpet even more furiously. "We make a great mistake, bringing up girls as we do. We shield them from the world, but we don't shield them from their own filthy fantasies. It would be better to tell them what sex is about than to leave it to their imaginations. It makes things too hard for the poor bridegroom. He suddenly discovers he's got to be everything an ignorant girl has concocted out of dirty talk behind locked doors. Give me a professional from Mercer Street any night in the week! At least she knows what a man *is*. But these innocent debutantes! They smile and simper behind their fans. They blush crimson at the least impropriety. And then — bango — after a big society wedding, which hasn't tired them in the least little bit, they turn into fiends. 'All right, big boy! Show me life!' "

Dexter, during this harangue, was almost beside himself. He remembered Charley's wedding, only six years before, at Trinity, and Annie, dark, pale and beautiful, on the arm of her splendid old father. Now he couldn't avoid the horrid vision of her stripping off her veil and dress and pursuing, half-naked, her half-tipsy bridegroom about the nuptial chamber. At that moment he actually hated Charley. With a shudder he drew a hand over his eyes. Hated Charley?

"Let us get back to the point."

"By all means. I want a separation. If you won't get it for me, I'll go to someone else."

"Do you wish to advertise your shame to all New York?" Dexter cried sharply. "Do you wish to proclaim the fact that you couldn't satisfy your bride? For that's what everyone will say. Make no mistake about it, Charley!"

He saw that his point had hit home. As Charley turned away with a muffled "Damn you, Dexter!" he followed up his advantage. "A husband always comes out badly in these cases. Especially when he's been married only a few years. Annie has no reputation for philandering. People will say she must have had some cause . . ."

"Oh, everyone knows you've always had a thing about Annie!" Charley interrupted brusquely. "You should hear Rosalie on *that* subject."

"I have cherished and respected her as my sister-in-law and as the wife of my partner and cousin. I don't know what you imply beyond that. And I certainly conceive it to be my bounden duty to stand behind any member of the family who is resisting, and not advocating, a rift in the marriage bond. I think you will find both the Fairchilds and the Handys united against you in this."

"Despite that letter?"

"It is a letter *to* Annie, may I remind you? It is not a letter from her. If you can produce such an epistle penned by her hand . . . well, then, I'll listen to you."

"She's much too cunning for that."

"Charley, you malign her! I'll wager anything you like

there was nothing more between them than a silly flirt which this bounder is trying to take advantage of."

Dexter observed Charley closely as he made this last remark. Could it be disappointment that he made out in that pouting countenance? Was it possible that Charley, nostalgic for the freedom of bachelor days, had been ready to pounce on any excuse for a rupture? And that he now resented the preceptor figure of his older cousin who was, as always, intervening between him and his pleasures? The idea only confirmed Dexter in his resolution.

"I'll tell you what, Charley. Leave this thing to me. I'll send this letter over to Annie at her father's this morning with a note explaining how I happened to get hold of it. I shall also propose that I go there this afternoon to discuss the steps to be taken to put Mr. Bleeker in his place."

"Which is where?"

"Anywhere that he will not see Annie or bother you again. Don't worry. There are ways and means of handling cads like Bleeker."

"Suppose she refuses to give him up?"

"Give him up? Don't be ridiculous, Charley. She hasn't got him."

Charley at this muttered something about being treated like a child, and then strode abruptly out of the room. Still, he left the letter behind. Dexter looked at it balefully for a moment but did not touch it. Then he sat down to write his note to Annie.

3

WHEN DEXTER had been sixteen, an event had occurred that was to darken his life. His father, the Reverend Alexander Fairchild, rector of Saint Andrew's Church in Gramercy Park and, after the rector of Trinity, the most esteemed and influential Episcopal priest in the city, a preacher famed for his silver tongue and acclaimed for his charity and largeness of heart, had abandoned his wife and parish, his young son and daughter, his many relations and multitudinous friends, and decamped for the south of Italy on board the S.S. *Persia* in the company of Mrs. John Pettit, the neither strikingly young nor strikingly pretty wife of his oldest friend. New York and Brooklyn had shuddered with the shock at first, then cried to the heavens and, ultimately, chuckled. But something died in the heart of young Dexter that never quite came to life again.

His father, whom he was never more to see, he had simply worshipped. He had dreamed of following his example and of taking holy orders after graduating from Columbia. But now he turned away resolutely from all thoughts of an ecclesiastical career. He considered himself disqualified, contaminated. He knew that his reasons were emotional and not logical. He was bound to bear the stain quietly in his heart and to make his life a long reparation. He chose the law for his profession, as he was determined to preserve, and to help others preserve, what his father had broken. If he could not act within the church, he would act outside it.

His mother, a brisk, kindly woman of the world, took full advantage of the sympathy meted out by her rich friends and neighbors to secure favors for her little family without ever losing sight of the truth that if she allowed herself to become too much an object of pity she would become also an object of contempt. She was scrupulously careful to dress well and to live decently by judicious expenditure of her small means and by making herself useful to the leaders of Manhattan society. It was soon known that Millie Fairchild could be depended on to read to an old grandfather, chaperone a visiting niece, preside at a mission meeting, enliven a dull party or fill a box at the Academy of Music for the dullest opera. If her heart was broken, nobody was ever going to hear the jangling of the pieces. Dexter learned from her the quagmire danger of self-pity and the vital importance of concealing ill temper. He learned that it was more essential to be punctual and cheerful than to be witty or profound, and that society would not permit an impecunious young man even the appearance of dejection.

His sister Jane conned her lesson with a difference. She made what both her mother and brother considered the basic error of becoming a cynic. She decided that society cared for nothing but money and looks and that it should be her concern to be beautiful and marry a fortune. Dexter and Mrs. Fairchild never lost their faith in the fundamental good will of the small world they cultivated. Indeed, they regarded it as "vulgar" to lose faith. When Jane, who was two years older than Dexter, argued that the hollowness of the social world was manifest in the timidity of the more eligible bachelors towards her, that there could be neither valor nor truth in a community whose strong young men were put off by the mere sniff of a bygone scandal, Mrs. Fairchild would counter roundly that it was not the scandal that put them off so much as Jane's unladylike openness of speech and boldness of manner. And when Jane purported to solve her problems by marrying David Ullman, a rich, middle-aged Jewish banker who collected exotic art and anti-Semitic friends, her mother considered her daughter a failure, but, in her usual fashion, made the best of it. The Ullmans were not seen at the Peter Rhinelanders' or at the Peter Jays', but they were included in Lily Van Rensselaer's New Year's Day. As Mrs. Fairchild put it sourly, they were firmly attached — to the fringe.

Dexter, taking a different course, found his content, and ultimately a kind of happiness, in the study and practice of law. He subscribed fervently to the platonic theory of his Columbia dean: that judges "found" law by a kind of mystic deduction; that the principles of our jurisprudence resembled their divine counterparts as the earthly shapes of natural things resembled their ideal forms in eternity. Thus it had to be possible for each succeeding generation of lawyers to come closer to the absolute truth of an ideal system of law and equity. Feeling this almost made up to him for the memory of the priestly robe that he had missed, and he came in time to believe that if he should end his career on the bench, it might be almost as good for himself and his fellow mortals as if he had become their bishop.

After taking his degree he joined the firm of his uncle, a

brother of the former rector, and made himself an expert in wills and trusts. When the elder Fairchild died, only five years later, Dexter was already prepared to succeed to his practice, and he repaid some of his debt to his uncle by training the latter's son, Charley, and by taking him in as a partner to the small but now prosperous Wall Street firm of Fairchild & Fairchild. At the age of only twenty-five, Dexter felt that he had every right to consider himself firmly launched on the road to success.

His profession might occupy half, or even three-quarters of his life, but no more. Dexter was determined that his marriage should replace in the eyes of New York society the image of his father's shattered one. His choice of just the right bride would be made equally by heart and head. He had no desire to repeat the vulgar error of his sister, who had married for money alone; beauty, character, social position, health and fortune were all factors to be considered. Happily there were plenty of young women in his world to meet all these qualifications. As Dexter's mother used to say, why have second-class friends when it's just as easy to have first?

He was far too wise, however, to discuss his criteria for selecting a mate with others, even with his mother. He knew how quickly a young man could get the reputation of being calculating. Society expected its youth to be romantic, even if it deplored their acting romantically. The thing to do was to keep one's own counsel and *look* Byronic. Dexter rather fancied that he had a touch of the corsair in his brow and chin and fixed stare. If that made him an ass, well, what did it matter so long as he shut up about it? New York, no doubt, was full of asinine young men who considered themselves Byronic.

As marriage was to make him whole, it seemed logical to start his quest by filling the gap left in his life by his father, and what New York gentleman would make a better father-in-law than Charles Handy? Certainly few men were as much admired. Large, affable, venerable, he constituted a sort of unofficial host for distinguished visitors to the town. He encouraged the arts; he encouraged religion; he encouraged new business; he seemed to be always waving benevolent arms over the urban commotion below him. Without any elected position or published work, without even very great wealth, he yet wielded an astonishing influence. Dexter's mother used to say that Charles Handy was living proof that any man could be accepted at his own valuation.

Handy, a widower in his late fifties, had four daughters, one of whom, Rosalie, was of the appropriate age, even perhaps slightly over it. She was twenty-four. To Dexter, however, after careful observation, she seemed just right. If she was a trifle on the large side, there yet radiated from her creamy skin and china-blue eyes an air of health and vigor that promised to make her a good mother and a responsive sexual partner. If she was reputed to have a touch more than her share of temper and will power, would not love and children soften this? Many men had been fooled by this argument, no doubt, but many had not. A man had to take some chances.

He knew, moreover, that he would have more than a fair chance of acceptance. It was common gossip that Rosalie had lost her heart to a handsome and penniless adventurer who had ditched her at the last moment to make a richer marriage in England. She was supposed to have recovered from this misfortune, but it was still evident that she was restless at home, where her older sister Joanna presided over her father's rather stately household, and it might be presumed that even a Miss Handy, at her age, was beginning to worry about becoming an old maid. Look at Joanna, after all! But what gave Dexter his strongest encouragement was Rosalie's partiality for himself. She used to josh him about being conventional and stuffy, as girls of conventional and stuffy backgrounds always did, but he was nonetheless sure that she was attracted to him, and this, in his category of points, was the greatest of all in her favor.

For Dexter, despite all his calculations, was perfectly aware that he yearned for love. Everything in his heart was ready to beat with excitement the moment the choice should be made, and in the spring of 1843, just six months after his twenty-fifth birthday, he made it, and opened his campaign. He made his first move at one of Miss Joanna Handy's Sunday afternoon "at homes" at her father's Italianate brown box of a house on the corner of Great Jones Street and Broadway. After greeting his hostess and her distinguished sire he proceeded, with unconcealed directness of purpose, to take his place in the little group gathered around Rosalie in the conservatory. But instead of joining in the conversation he simply watched her intently. After some ten minutes of this she got up and asked him to follow her. In a corner, under a palm in a massive jardinière, she turned.

"Why do you stare at me like that, Mr. Fairchild?"

"Because I admire what I see before me, Miss Handy."

"Are you making love to me?"

"If you will allow it."

"Then you must do so in such a way that others will not notice. I do not like to be embarrassed in public."

"I promise that my conduct shall be exemplary. On one condition."

"Condition? You presume to set conditions?"

"One prayer, then."

"Let me hear it."

"That you agree to see me alone sometimes."

"Alone! Mr. Fairchild! You forget yourself."

"Oh, I mean only like this. Where we can talk without others hearing."

"But I should grant so simple a privilege to any gentleman on my father's visiting list!"

"Then that is all I ask."

Dexter, walking home that evening, felt elated. He knew that he had made a good start, although he perfectly understood that Rosalie did not consider him any sort of hero. Like so many of her contemporaries, nurtured in sentimentality, she was looking for Lancelot in every young lawyer or banker who made his appearance in her father's parlor. It was only to be expected that she should resist the fate that would fashion her future out of the materials of her past. She would find soon enough that there were no Lancelots. Not for Rosalie Handys anyway!

He even debated the wisdom of skipping his visit the following Sunday, to make her miss him, perhaps even to make her jealous. But on a careful review of his situation, he decided that he needed no such tricks. And, as soon as he next entered Mr. Handy's parlor, he saw he had done the right thing. Rosalie came across the room to greet him and led him to the potted palm in the conservatory where two chairs, placed conveniently for conversation, invited a tête-à-tête.

"Jo tells me that you teach a Sunday school for poor boys!" she began enthusiastically. "I had no idea you did that kind of thing."

"Yes, I've been teaching for six or seven years now."

"But that's wonderful!"

"Why wonderful?"

"Oh, because I was afraid you were concerned only with Wall Street and making money. Like so many of our men friends. With no concern for the less privileged."

"My boys are certainly among the less privileged. I've learned to take nothing for granted with them. I don't even assume they know about Adam and Eve. Or Noah's Ark."

"Is that what you teach them? The Bible?"

"Well, I figure they might as well get something out of the school. Even if they turn out to be atheists, there's always a value in knowing your Bible. Think of all the references . . ."

"So you hedge your bets with God!" she interrupted in a sudden change of mood. "If he doesn't exist, there may still be an advantage in knowing his myths? Oh, yes, let's not waste a thing!"

"What would *you* teach them?"

"Something about ethics. Whether it's ever justified to tell a lie. Or to steal. How you reconcile the commandment against killing with war. *If* you can. And slavery. What about slavery? Isn't that the great moral issue of our time?"

"I don't want to get into controversies with them. Who was allowed in the Ark and who wasn't is about as far as I care to go."

"You're like Pontius Pilate. You ask for a basin and wash your hands!"

Dexter burst into a cheerful laugh. "Don't you think, Miss Handy, that you're being just a bit rough on the poor Sunday school teacher? Blaming him for the Crucifixion because he teaches the Bible?"

She became angry with him then, and again on other

visits, but it was always evident that she enjoyed being angry with him. Their discussions were vivid, even heated. They argued about the position of women, the return of fugitive slaves, the wisdom of capital punishment, and invariably disagreed. But he was careful not to strike again the sentimental note for which he was reasonably sure she was waiting. There would have to be a concession, however slight, on her part first. Soon enough it came.

"I want to come to your law office," she told him one afternoon. "I want to consult you as a client. It will be all perfectly formal. I shall expect, of course, to pay your fee."

Without demurring in the least to her stated expectation, he made an appointment for the following day. When she appeared in his office, punctually on the hour, he enjoyed a novel sense of superiority. From her quick, shy glances at his sets of law reporters and at the sober lithographs of English judges, he took in that she was suddenly ill at ease. She was no longer Miss Handy in her father's formal parlor. She was a girl in a man's office, a seeker of advice, an amateur before a professional. She related her little problem diffidently, almost apologetically; she was embarrassed, she said, to take up his time with so small a matter.

It was indeed not a great one. She had recently received in the mail a copy of the will of a deceased cousin who had left her a legacy of five hundred dollars. But the estate had turned out to be much smaller than the decedent could possibly have expected. Should she renounce the bequest?

"What does your father think?"

"Oh, Father can't abide the widow. He says she's a hopeless spendthrift. He thinks I'd be an idiot not to take the money. But I am here because I want your advice, not his."

"Have you a copy of the will?" He took the document that

she handed him and glanced quickly through it. "I see the widow takes the residue. If you renounce the legacy, she'll get it. Is that what you want? There appears to be a daughter."

"Exactly. And she's my friend. But she's only the widow's stepdaughter. The widow would do nothing for her."

"Then take the legacy and give it to the daughter."

"But she wouldn't take it! She's too proud!"

"Then give it to me. I'll write the daughter and tell her I represent a client whom her father helped out, years ago, and who wants to make restitution to a blood relative. We can make it a slightly different sum from your legacy, an odd one like $521, so you'll never be suspected."

She clapped her hands in surprise. "What a perfectly brilliant idea! Thank you! We'll do it."

Leaving his office she asked him what she owed him. He proposed instead that they go riding together on the morrow.

"If after what I shall then ask you, you still want to pay me, I'll name you a sum."

Their eyes met in what became a rather solemn stare. Then she simply nodded and left.

On their ride the next day along the East River bridle path, as far north as Hell Gate, he asked her to be his wife. She did not accept him, but neither did she say no. It was finally agreed that he should visit her that summer in Newport, so she might get to know him better.

❖   ❖   ❖

Dexter was perfectly happy in his room at the Ocean House where he was staying, over an extended Fourth of July weekend, in deference to Rosalie's suggestion that it might be better if he were not her house guest. The traditional unease of the lover during the period in which his proposal was under consideration sprang from uncertainty as to the answer. As Dexter entertained no such doubts, he saw no reason that the periods when he was absent from his beloved should not be as pleasant as when he was with her. This equanimity was not due to any failure of his ardor. It was due to the failure of Rosalie's nerves. She, at least, was finding the period of decision a trying one.

He discovered that he loved everything in this new environment: the bright blue sky, the shiny green lawns, the mild sea breezes, the squawk of the gulls, the gaily painted, freshly preserved, fantastic summer villas. He loved the rocky coves and the vast, deserted, brown marshlands over which he could trudge for miles in the early morning without encountering a soul. He loved the cordial hospitality of his prospective father-in-law, who took him on tours of his new estate, Oaklawn, which occupied twelve fine acres at the beginning of Bellevue Avenue.

Mr. Handy was immensely proud of this new domain and relished personally supervising its continuing embellishment. A long, winding drive of soft red dirt made its picturesque way through noble lawns shaded by elm and beech, under a brown Gothic arch (a "folly"), past greenhouses and crenelated smaller buildings to the climax of the main residence. This was an asymmetrical structure of glazed chocolate-brown wood, with tiny bracketed windows in its mansard roof, two small round towers and a long, wandering wing. From every angle it presented a different countenance, almost a different style, which made it impossible to determine how large it was.

"Upjohn, of course, is primarily a man of churches," Mr. Handy informed his mutely gazing prospective son-in-law.

"One can see in the upper windows a touch of the Gothic. But only a touch, mind you. I told him I wasn't going in for derivative architecture. No, sir. I want a truly American house!"

Dexter thought, indeed, that the building was not unlike its truly American owner. Its massed strength had a way of dissolving unexpectedly into fine if rather fussy detail, as Mr. Handy's sturdy build and square chin seemed to be mitigated by his mellifluous, almost honeyed tone and in the charming politeness of his gestures. It was a relief to Rosalie's lover, anyway, that her father remained so impersonal in his discourse. Mr. Handy purported to mark out a broad area where men could talk as men, and from which women, with their petulance and perennial discontent, were firmly barred.

Dexter had little doubt as to the source of Rosalie's tension. She could not yet bring herself to accept the fact that she had fallen in love with a man who believed that the New York and Newport of the Handys and Fairchilds was a world in which a man could happily and high-mindedly live — and who was not ashamed to say so. The only difference between youth and age in their society, as Dexter made it out, was that youth was supposed to profess discontent with the existing state of society and only to *talk* of change and social betterment. Age, on the other hand, was supposed to have learned to appreciate the status quo, so why not skip the pose of youth? In any case, Dexter was convinced that the way to win Rosalie was not to pretend to be something he wasn't — that would be the way of a weak man — but to oblige her to take him as he was.

What did, however, finally begin to irritate him was Rosalie's resentment of his enjoying any pleasure offered by Newport that was not directly attributable to herself. She regarded with a jealous eye, for example, his long talkative strolls with her father, his mock gallantries to the giggling Joanna, his serious concentration on the inane gossip of visiting old aunts. But what she more particularly objected to was his relish of Newport social life. He allowed himself to be almost openly discountenanced when he discovered that Rosalie had excluded him from what promised to be a delightful Sunday picnic on the beach because she wanted him to dine alone with her at the little guest cottage at Oaklawn.

But how could a true lover refuse? He had to mutter something that at least sounded like gratification. In the cottage with the tall, narrow, spire-like dormer their dinner was ready at three o'clock. Dexter was surprised to note that the best silver and china had been brought out and that a bottle of champagne protruded its neck from the cooler. Rosalie picked up the cover of one of the hot dishes and sniffed.

"It's duck," she said with a note of defiance. Although he had said nothing, he was still under strong suspicion of pining for the picnic. "I remembered that you liked it. And I thought it would be more fun if we served ourselves."

He saw now that he might enjoy being mollified. She had done all this, after all, to give him pleasure. "It smells fine," he admitted.

She seemed for the moment disposed to accept his gesture and busied herself serving the dishes. She even insisted on uncorking the champagne and laughed heartily when it fizzed over her blouse.

"You're not going to tell me that you cooked all this?" he asked with a wink.

"I supervised it, anyway. I stayed in the kitchen all the

while it was being done. And I *could* have cooked it myself. I don't want to be one of those women who are the slaves of their servants."

"But you'll always have servants."

"Why do you say that?" The suspicion was back in her tone already.

"I thought girls who married successful lawyers didn't have to worry about such things."

"But I don't know that I'm going to marry a successful lawyer. I don't even know that I'm going to marry a lawyer."

He laughed at her earnestness. "Well, even if you don't marry anyone, I guess you'll still be all right."

"What makes you guess that?"

"Look, Rosalie," he retorted, with mild exasperation. "A man doesn't live like your father unless he has some kind of fortune. And who's he going to leave it to but his children?"

"Are you interested in my father's fortune?"

"Oh, for Pete's sake!"

"Are you, Dexter? I'd like to know."

"No! Not in the way you're thinking, anyway."

"In what way, then?"

Dexter felt, miserably, that he was making a mess of it. But why did she have to be so damned prickly? "I try to take an interest in the life of my city. What people do, how they live, what they talk about. I'm interested in their families, their houses, their politics, their parties. Even their fortunes. So there! I may write a book about New York some day."

"You mean about New York society?"

"Well, I'm not going to write a book about beggars and bums, if that's what you mean."

"You don't care about poor people, do you?" She stared at him intently. "I'm not criticizing you. Really. I'm interested, that's all."

"Of course you're criticizing me! You're trying to make me out a snob and a fortune hunter."

"I am not!" Tears suddenly filled her eyes. "You shouldn't say things like that, Dexter! I'm only trying to understand you. I want to know what sort of a man I'm thinking of marrying! I want to know the things you care about."

"I care about you."

"But what does that *mean*?"

"Oh, Rosalie, dearest, must you take everything so hard?" But she gave him no answer, and he sat in stupid silence, watching her lowered head, her shoulders shaking now in sobs. He knew that he ought to go over and put his arms around her to console her. Then the tears might subside, and everything would be all right. And yet he couldn't. He couldn't give in to her unfairness. If he did, wouldn't it be admitting that he was a different sort of man from what he was? And wouldn't that be a kind of suicide?

"All right, I'm being absurd," she confessed at last, wiping her eyes. "Let's not ruin our dinner. I'll pour you some more champagne."

"It's very good champagne," he said placatingly.

"Is it? I can't tell. But I suppose everything Father buys is good. They're only having white wine at the picnic, but he said *we* could have champagne. He even sent a little bottle to Mrs. Hill, our housekeeper. She's having her dinner at the big house, so we're not really alone."

"I had never imagined that the proprieties were being violated."

"They never are at Oaklawn!" Rosalie, in the volatile way of her sex, appeared suddenly to have recaptured her good spirits. "Oh, this *is* more fun than the picnic, isn't it, Dexter?" she almost pleaded. "You wouldn't really rather be talking to an old cow like Mrs. Coster, would you?"

"Of course not."

"What do you see in her anyway? She has false teeth and dyes her hair!"

"She's old, Rosalie."

"Old and false. Horribly false! I hope when I grow old, I won't fight it that way. I hope I'll leave my wrinkles and gray hairs as God made them!"

"Mrs. Coster is a personage. She knew Aaron Burr. She is supposed to have tried to make peace between him and Hamilton."

"Oh, stuff. I'll bet she egged them on."

"You have no right to say a thing like that!"

"Why not? What's she to you?"

"She's simply a lady that I admire. That I admire greatly."

Rosalie lifted her hands in disgust. "If you admire her so much, why don't you marry her?"

"Because she's eighty years old."

"Is that the only reason?"

"Yes!"

But Rosalie's utter gravity rejected his joke. "Tell me the truth, Dexter. Would you rather be at the picnic with Mrs. Coster or here with me?"

"You insist on putting me in the wrong. Can't a man enjoy two things? Can't he enjoy going to a picnic with a distinguished old lady, a kind of chapter of history, really, and having dinner alone with you?"

"But you'd *prefer* the picnic. That's the point!"

"I would not!"

"Oh, yes, you would!"

"If you keep on this way, you'll end by persuading me I would! You're simply ruining the afternoon."

She jumped to her feet in a fury. "Oh, go to your old picnic! I mean it. Go! There's still time. Go and make love to your old hag!"

Dexter rose in protest, only to discover that he was trembling from head to foot with anger. There was something like exhilaration in his erupting defiance. "Very well! I will!"

He left her without another word, without even looking back, and sprang onto his horse, which was tethered on the road by the cottage. He galloped furiously all the way to the beach. When Mr. Handy spotted him walking towards his party across the rocks, he rose at once and went to meet him. Dexter related in stammering terms what had happened, and his host took him firmly by the elbow and guided him down the sand away from the chattering throng.

"Let us walk until you have recovered yourself, my boy. Then we can join the others. You will tell them that Rosalie has gone to bed with a sick headache, which is probably no more than the truth by now. And perhaps tomorrow you had better go back to New York. Women take time. There's no point rushing things. Rosalie will come around, never fear. I'll keep an eye on her."

"But you're so good to me, sir. Why?"

"Because, my dear fellow, I think you're the right man for my daughter. It's as simple as that!"

Dexter for a moment was mute with emotion. When he finally spoke it was only to blurt out, "She may not ask me back!"

"Does Rosalie own the Ocean House? May you not come to Newport when you please?"

* * *

Dexter took the hint. When he came up again, in only two weeks' time, he stayed, as before, at the Ocean House. He wrote to Rosalie to notify her of his arrival and got, as he had expected, no answer. She must have communicated his presence to her family, however, for he received a note from Joanna bidding him to dine at Oaklawn. When he arrived, he found no Rosalie. She was at her cousins', the Kings.

"Albert King is very attentive these days," Joanna whispered to him archly. "A little bird tells me that Rosalie's trying to make somebody jealous!"

Dexter made no comment. Albert King was a slight, pretty, elegant young man, a great favorite in Newport society. He was not at all the sort to be attracted to his larger, graver cousin, but was sufficiently good-natured to lend himself to any game she might wish to play. Certainly at the archery contest that drew all Newport to Mr. Handy's lawns the following afternoon, King attached himself closely to Rosalie, carrying her quiver and offering her advice on which arrow to use. Dexter carefully avoided the appearance of watching them.

As he was leaving, Rosalie presented herself, resolute, in his path, without shooting equipment and without Albert King.

"Don't you think you're being rather mean?" she demanded fiercely.

"Mean?"

"Not even once to pretend you don't see through my shabby little game?"

"I wouldn't insult your intelligence."

"But a girl doesn't mind having her intelligence insulted by a man who's supposed to care for her!"

He looked at her sternly. "I love you, Rosalie. I see no reason to play games about that. It's too serious a matter for me."

"But you don't really love me!" she cried in near hysteria, and he glanced quickly about to assure himself that they were out of earshot. "You only *want* to love me. You want to love Rosalie Handy because she's the wife you've decided will suit you. And you're wrong! I have a temper that will spoil everything! Be warned before it's too late!"

"You mean you *would* have me? Oh, Rosalie!"

"I mean that I love you, God help me! I love you, and I don't want to. And you want to love me and don't. How can anything so crazy ever work?"

"Darling, you must try to rid yourself of this fixation. I may not be eloquent. I may not be glib. But when I tell you that I love you more than life itself . . ."

"Oh, it's false, it's false!" she almost screamed. "If you could only *hear* yourself!"

And she turned away and ran furiously into the woods, causing everyone to stare indeed.

Three hours later Dexter received word, in his room at the Ocean House, that Mr. Handy was waiting for him in the saloon. He found him very grave. Did Dexter know where Rosalie was? He didn't? Mr. Handy looked even graver. She had not been seen since she ran off the place. It would be necessary to notify the police, to search the beaches. In her state of excitement they could take no risks. Her friend Ellen Gray had drowned herself in Lily Pond the summer before, and Rosalie had brooded over the tragedy

. . . oh, yes, a thorough search would have to be made at once.

The next two hours were unlike any others in Dexter's life. When he later attempted to classify them, he found the courage to admit that a kind of horrible ecstasy had been mixed with the terror. Tramping with others across the rocks and the marshes in the cool twilight, against the blood-red of that setting August sun, he had felt a kind of exaltation at the idea that a girl might have taken her life because of an emotion aroused by him. Suppose he were to die now, with her. Would they not have reached an intensity of feeling, a summit of love, that could never be reached in the long after-years of a marriage of mere contentedness? The death of Rosalie would be a grisly thing, and to have been the cause of it an even more grisly thing, but was not life at this moment afire with gold and red as never before? Had he ever felt such a pounding of the heart? He was not Dexter Fairchild; he was something larger, something dark and violent and formidable. He walked on, so gripped by swirling thoughts and feelings that he hardly looked for clues upon the ground.

But when he saw her at last coming towards him on her father's arm, he felt as if his heart would burst with relief and happiness. He hardly minded that, pale and exhausted, she failed to respond in the least when he threw his arms about her.

"What a great to-do about nothing," she muttered in the flattest of tones. "Can't a girl sit by herself on a rock and look at the sea without everyone thinking she's going to jump in it?"

"Why did you want to look at the sea?" he heard himself ask.

She still held on to her father's arm, but now she looked at him. Her gaze was impenetrable. "I wanted to think. About whether or not I'd marry you. I think I decided I would." She raised her hand sharply to check any demonstration. "Please, Dexter, not a word. Not now. I've been through enough for one day."

4

NUMBER 417 FIFTH AVENUE, to which Dexter directed
his steps on the afternoon following his cousin Charley's
agitated and agitating visit, had been built by his father-in-
law only four years before, when the latter was seventy.
Mr. Handy used to retort blandly to those of his contemporaries who questioned the wisdom of creating so fine a
residence for a proprietor so advanced in years, that his
heirs would be able to sell it for many times his cost. It was
a square brownstone mansion with a four-window frontage
on the Avenue, and it boasted every modern convenience,
including a picture gallery. It was to this chamber, running
the length of the house, that Dexter was now admitted. But
to his surprise it was his sister-in-law, Joanna, and not Annie
who received him there.

"I thought you were in Boston!" he exclaimed.

"I got back this morning. It's lucky that I was here when
Annie got your note. She was very much upset."

"Did she show it to you?"

"Oh, yes. With the enclosure. She made no secret of it."

"Well, don't you think she should be upset? She has been extremely indiscreet, Jo, to put it mildly."

Joanna was the least attractive of the four Handy sisters. She had mild, gentle features and sad eyes that seemed to anticipate reproach, as did her constant gesture of holding her head slightly backwards. Her hair, brown and very straight, was parted in the middle, and she affected dresses of black or dark brown as if in unobtrusive mourning for the constantly dying old cousins whose passing her party-loving parent was reluctant to acknowledge.

"She's such a child, Dexter!" she protested, clasping her hands.

"A child? At thirty-two!"

"Oh, it's not a matter of age. And you and I both know that Charley has not been an easy person to live with. What's a girl to do if her husband's always at the Patroons' Club drinking wine and playing cards? Annie needs more love and sympathy than other people. Juley Bleeker was simply filling a void in her life."

"Juley! You call that bounder Juley?"

Joanna's expression congealed into stubbornness. Her timid eyes gazed at him now as through the grille of a barred gate that they both knew he could not batter down.

"He has been a guest in this house. Papa has received him."

"You don't mean he's called when Annie's been here!"

"You needn't shout, Dexter. As a matter of fact he was here this morning."

"And Annie received him under her father's roof? At a time when her husband was not present!"

"What's so wrong with that? *I* was present."

Dexter stared at her almost with incredulity. "After Annie had told you about my note? After you *knew* about her and Bleeker?"

His tone finally seemed to alert her at least to the possibility of something serious. "Oh, it was all just silliness."

"Silliness! What in the name of God is New York coming to?" He turned away in disgust from her expression of placid stupidity. "I give up. Tell Annie I'm here, will you?"

When Joanna, only too glad to be gone, had left the gallery, he sauntered nervously up and down the floor, casting restless glances at the pictures. For several minutes he did not distinguish among them, but then at last something struck him, and he drew up suddenly to regard more closely a large bright canvas over the legend, "The Abbess Detected."

It was one of those meticulously executed, brightly colored, anecdotal French paintings in which Mr. Handy delighted, showing a pretty abbess in a chamber more like a boudoir than a cell, sitting down to a delicious-looking repast of steak and red wine set out on a marble-topped *guéridon,* while two young nuns, unobserved, stifled their giggles behind a half-open door. On a calendar, over the abbess's head, in large print, was the word "Vendredi."

Moving down the wall, struck now with an idea, Dexter paused next before a large canvas showing Catherine de Medici, haughty and terrible in widow's weeds, emerging from the Louvre to make a scornful survey of the corpses of Saint Bartholomew's Day, followed by a reluctant troupe of younger ladies-in-waiting, whose averted looks and hands clapped to their lips offered a marked contrast to the phlegm of the ruthless queen-mother. But what Dexter particularly noted was the artist's sensuous treatment of the stripped corpses.

Moving to the end of the gallery, he paused finally before a canvas depicting a satyr teased by wood nymphs. One was pulling his hair; two others had hold of his arms; a fourth was propelling him from behind, apparently in a joint effort to plunge him into a sylvan pool. All the figures were nude. It was perfectly evident that the satyr, whose human torso was finely muscular, was only pretending to resist and that the game would end, the moment he chose, on a less innocent note.

He turned away abruptly from the picture, indignant that it should have so aroused his senses. Was there not a common denominator of fleshly appetite and lust in all of Mr. Handy's pictures? Might this not explain the blindness of Joanna, the giddiness of Annie? Might it not even be typical of New York society as a whole? What was their world but a bushel of lewdnesses tied together by a string of moral aphorisms? Did anyone but Dexter Fairchild really care about good and evil?

"Oh, Dexter, that *look!*" He heard Annie's cry, and there she was, absurdly beautiful, in a black and white dress, standing in the doorway. And now she was rustling towards him, too thin, too pale, too smiling, too laughing. Her hands gripped his shoulders as she held herself back to contemplate him. "Why, my dear, you're as grave as a Gothic tympanum of Judgment Day! Please! Can't you smile?"

"I don't consider this a smiling matter, Annie."

She dropped her hands at once to her sides and pouted, playing the little girl reproved. "Shall we discuss it, then, in sackcloth and ashes?"

"Try to be serious, my dear."

"This early in the afternoon? Can't I at least offer you a glass of wine?"

"This early in the afternoon? Thank you, no."

"Well, can I sit at least?" She dropped upon the ottoman in the center of the gallery and spread out her skirts on either side. Then she looked up at him with an air of wilful patience. "All right, then. Proceed."

"I'm sorry if I appear so lugubrious. But I'd rather make too much than too little of Mr. Bleeker's letter."

"This?" She produced it from somewhere, from a pocket, from under her belt, and tossed it, half-crumpled, on the divan beside her. "Really, Dexter. Do you think half the ladies in our benighted society don't receive such epistles daily? How else are the poor creatures to divert themselves?"

"You mean without love affairs?"

"Love affairs? Isn't that a pretty strong term for a common or garden flirt?"

Relief surged up suddenly through him, but he tried not to relax the severity of his countenance. "It may be just a flirt to you. I never really had any notion that it was more than that. But you must recognize that it will be a love affair to Bleeker."

"I don't think I follow that. How can it be one thing to a woman and another to a man?"

"I am speaking of intention."

"And I have none?"

"He has too much. A man like that, Annie, who has lived half his life in Europe, is not going to be content with chats in cozy corners. Or with writing throbbing letters. Or even with a snatched kiss."

"A snatched kiss!" Annie exclaimed in mock horror.

"A man like Bleeker — forgive my bluntness — is going to expect the ultimate favors."

"The ultimate favors!" Annie clasped her hands again. "I like that!"

"And even if he doesn't receive them, he's going to say he did. To protect his reputation as a lover."

"Heavens! And will people believe him?"

"People will certainly believe him if they know that you have received letters such as the one Charley discovered."

"Such as the one Charley *opened.* Knowing that it was addressed to me."

"He thought it might be something that had to be handled immediately. Something important."

"And it wasn't?" After a pause, her tone was suddenly dry. "Oh, never mind, Dexter. Of course, I know you'll always take Charley's side."

"I'll always take your husband's side. Isn't that a way of taking yours?"

"Are you joking? Charley hates me."

"Hates you? Oh, Annie."

"Face it, Dexter. God knows I have."

"Of course, in any married love there's bound to be a certain amount of jealousy and hostility."

"Right up to the brim!"

"But deep down . . ."

"Deep? What's deep in Charley but his thirst?"

"All right, Annie, we'll let that go. I came here to discuss your relationship with Bleeker, not Charley."

"And I came here to tell *you* that I won't have my flirtations interfered with. Everyone flirts. Everyone, that is, but Rosalie. Rosalie, of course, is perfect."

"Do *I* flirt?"

"Like mad! You used to flirt with me. And I loved it!"

Dexter turned nervously to walk to the wall. He was suddenly in danger of losing the whole battle. Carefully, he readjusted the mask of his severity.

"That was different."

"Why was it different?"

"You were a young bride, in love with your husband. Besides, you were my sister. In law, anyway. I knew that Charley could be difficult, and I wanted you to feel the support of brotherly love and affection. We were never seriously flirting."

"That's hardly gallant of you."

"But we weren't! You know we weren't!"

"Speak for yourself." A silence followed. "Besides, the only reason you stopped flirting was that Rosalie got angry about it."

Dexter reached about in his mind as if to pick up the pieces of his shattered dignity. "Anyway, I didn't write you silly letters. I didn't make declarations."

"No, you're too good a lawyer for that. Poor Juley, I admit, is indiscreet. But then perhaps his feelings are too much for him."

Dexter stamped on the parquet floor. "Damn his feelings! Annie, this thing has got to stop. I want you to give me your word that you will never see Bleeker alone again!"

"Not see Juley alone?" Annie's pout would have been an appropriate response to the request that she give up a night at the opera. "I couldn't promise you any such thing. Is a girl to have *no* fun after she's married?"

"Do you have any conception of the danger you're in?" Dexter demanded, exasperated by her lightness. "Charley was in an absolute frenzy of jealousy when he came to the house this morning. It was all I could do to get him to listen to reason. If he blows up again, I won't be able to contain him. This thing will be all over town, and you'll be ruined."

"Ruined?"

"Your reputation, I mean. And how do you expect to live in a city like New York without a reputation?"

"I was beginning to wonder how I could live in it *with* one. Have you any conception what it's like for a young woman with any spirit to live with a man as moody and thirsty as your cousin? Not to speak of the remorseless supervision of all the Handys and Fairchilds? With an aunt behind every tree and a sister behind every bush? And a brother-in-law to play the arch-snoop? What does poor little Annie have to live for?"

"You have your child."

"There are women, I suppose, who can live for their children. Rosalie, I dare say, is one. *I* am not."

Dexter paused to consider the threat in her tone. "What are you trying to tell me, Annie?"

She jumped to her feet in a sudden flare of temper. "Just this! That if you push me too far you'll wake up one morning to discover that Juley and I have decamped! That we've run off to . . ." She paused, and then flung her arms up as a destination came to her. "To Venice!"

Dexter was beside himself. "You'd do that!" he almost shouted. "You'd go off with that cad? That greasy bounder? You care *that* much for that scribbling climber? That pompous show-off? That . . . poetaster?"

"It would be you who had driven me to find out how much I cared!"

He saw that he would have to interrupt her game. She was having much too good a time provoking him.

"Let's sit down and discuss this," he said in a more reasonable tone, and they both sat, or rather perched, on the edge of the ottoman. "Let me draw you a picture of what your life would be like in Venice."

"Oh, I haven't settled on Venice."

"Venice, Florence, Paris, it doesn't matter. To begin with, you wouldn't be received by any respectable people."

"How dreadful!"

"You say that now, because you take dull, respectable people for granted. You can afford to despise them. But dull respectable people can assume a very different look when they slam their doors in your face."

"We'd see the real people. The artists and writers."

"You mean the would-be artists and writers. The hacks. The failures. The good ones are just as anxious to get into society as anyone else. But pass that for the moment. What would you live on?"

"Why, just what I mostly live on now, thank you very much. My own trust fund."

"Your father has the discretion to withhold the income. How much do you think he'd pay to support you in that kind of ménage? And what about little Kate? Do you think for a moment that Charley would allow his daughter to be brought up abroad by you and your . . . your . . ."

"My paramour!" Annie clasped her hands exultantly.

"I can't even utter the word. And how will Bleeker react when he finds out that his ticket to society, his greatest asset, has turned herself into his greatest liability? How long do you think he'll stick?"

"Longer than you think. You underestimate my charms."

"I have never underestimated your charms! But the combined charms of Cleopatra and Helen of Troy couldn't hold a man like Bleeker under those circumstances!"

"Ah, there you're wrong." Annie shook her head now with something like gravity. "Poor Juley. I think he really loves me. No, it would not be he who would be the first to crack." For several moments she contemplated her hands, folded in her lap. "You paint a dismal picture."

"I am only trying to spare you the cruelty of such an experience."

Suddenly, startlingly, she was weeping. Her head was bent forward, and her thin shoulders were shaking. Only the horrid vision of an embrace as Bleeker's way of comforting her kept him from putting his arms around her. And then she was suddenly on her feet again, striding rapidly back and forth across the gallery. Her voice was angry, cutting.

"My life is so . . . abject! So unutterably abject. What in God's name am I to *do*? It's all very well for you to lecture me about morality, but what do you do to help me? You talk about respectable people slamming doors in my face, but isn't that just what you're doing? Why should it matter to me whether they slam them in New York or in Venice? All I know is that that's what doors seem to be for!"

Dexter rose and held his arms out to her pleadingly. "Annie, listen to me. You have a mind. A beautiful mind. You've studied art and music. You've traveled in Europe. Just now you compared me to a Gothic tympanum. How many women in New York would even know what a Gothic tympanum is? Doesn't the life of the intellect offer you *any* satisfaction? You used to be a great reader."

"So that's what good people do? They read! And what do you suppose they read about? What the bad people are doing!" When he looked blank at this, she continued indignantly, "Well, isn't that what all those books were about that you used to give me? *Jane Eyre* and *Wuthering Heights* and *The Scarlet Letter*? Passion and adultery and bigamy?"

"But those novels all point out the disastrous effects of those things!"

"But the disasters come *after*. Maybe the passion was worth it."

Dexter stared at her in dismay. "Surely you don't mean that you have really so misconstrued those writers as to suggest that . . . ?"

"Let me change the target." Annie had no idea of being trapped in a literary debate. "Do books and art and music mean that much to *you*? Do Harriet Beecher Stowe and the Italian opera make up to you for the dullness of your life with Rosalie?"

Dexter turned away quickly. He did not even know quite whom he was protecting by hiding the pain that he knew must be showing in his face: Rosalie, himself or even Annie. All he was sure of was that it was somehow not to be borne that his life with Rosalie should be described in that way.

"Oh, Dexter, now I've hurt you! I didn't really mean to. But you put me in a position where I have no alternative. I *have* to make you see these things! You can put up with dullness at home because your real life is in your law office. *That* is where you live and breathe and have your being. But we poor wives don't have that. Rosalie and Jo are always talking about what miserable lives the slaves have down South, but they can't see that they're slaves themselves."

Now she took him by the elbow and turned him around to face her, so that he should see her mimic him as a lawyer. She coughed and frowned as she pretended to be studying a paper. " 'Let's see. What have we on the diary this morning, Miss Somers? Oh, yes, the Annie Fairchild matter. I'd better run up and see the little woman and put some sense in her head. This is not the kind of thing we care to see in court, is it?' "

He gripped her hands in his. "Do you think I see you as a case, Annie? Can you honestly look me in the eye and tell me that I see you as just a case?"

She broke away from him, shrugging impatiently, and walked to one of the two west windows. After a few minutes of looking down at the avenue, she turned to him with an air of embittered resolution.

"Very well, Dexter, I see it's no use. You're determined to win. I am not to be allowed to go on with my harmless flirtation. I am embarrassed to call it even that. So be it. Have it your way. But mind you, you will have to make it up to me! *You* will be responsible for seeing that I don't die of boredom."

"Oh, we'll see to that!" he exclaimed, exultant.

"We? I mean *you!*"

"All right, me. May I instruct Mr. Bleeker that I shall be representing you?"

For once he had surprised her. "You mean you're going to see him?"

"Certainly, I'm going to see him."

"And what will you say to him?"

"I think you can trust me with that."

"But, Dexter, you'll promise to be a gentleman!"

"Quite as much as he is, I promise."

"You look so fierce!" Suddenly she burst again into her high mocking laugh. "My knight! My white knight!"

He decided it was time he left. In another minute she might withdraw her commission.

5

DEXTER, in the years immediately following his marriage, used to tell himself that it had worked out a good deal more happily than he could possibly have anticipated from its start. In the first place, Rosalie had proved herself a better sport than most girls of her background. She seemed resolved to keep a guard on her critical tongue. If she would not go so far as to express enthusiasm for his enthusiasms, at least she would not openly deprecate them. Secondly, as Dexter had rightly suspected, the satisfactions of sex made up for a good many differences of opinion. And, finally, the arrival of children took up much of the attention that might otherwise have been directed to a husband's shortcomings. Rosalie was the kind of mother who adored babies to the point of cooling off a bit when time had made them less cunning, and Dexter had been free to work on briefs on nights when she fretted by the cradles of her sick children, Fred and Selby and little Charles, who, alas, had died in his first year.

But there was still no question that Rosalie continued to be irked that her life should so blandly follow the pattern laid down by her forebears. It was at times disheartening to a hard-working husband not to feel that his wife supported him all the way. There were even moments when Dexter contemplated with envy the image of the frontier wife, standing with shouldered musket at the stockade gate, happy to share the dangers of a husband off fighting the Indians. But, of course, he always recognized that he had no right to expect any such loyalty. If ever a man had walked into a marriage with eyes wide open, it was he.

A man, however, could not be always judicial. What did Rosalie *want*? he would sometimes testily ask himself. Did she want him to throw up his law practice and take her west in a covered wagon? Not at all. She was much too concerned about the health of her infants. Did she want him to eschew society and lead her into the paths of letters, art and music? Not at all. She was much too dutiful about her friends and relations and not in the least intellectual. What *did* she want then? Oh, she wanted, he supposed impatiently, to lead, more or less, the life she was leading, only for him to be less sure that it was the right one.

Early in their marriage, however, something occurred to convince him that, whatever Rosalie's evaluation of himself, she could still be intensely possessive. No part of Dexter Fairchild was going to be lightly relinquished to anyone else, particularly to her youngest sister Annie, who had been touring Europe with an aunt during the year of Dexter's courtship and who had returned just in time to be a bridesmaid.

Annie's birth had cost her mother her life, so she had never known but one parent, and that a too indulgent one. In looks, in character, in general demeanor she might have been a foundling, a strange little dark imp introduced by a not wholly kindly humorist as a contrast to her larger, more placid sisters. She was small and tense and bright; she moved in quick jerks that somehow meshed into gracefulness, and she constantly indulged in a high, sharp laugh. Whether because she had never known a mother's love or because her doting father and governesses had spoiled her, she never shared in the family's outward conventionalism. She was a rule to herself, and got her way by coaxing or wheedling or pouting or simply through a wicked display of caustic wit. When Annie was allowed to skip a Sunday service, it was less that she had made a point of freedom of religious thinking than that her father disliked her restlessness in the family pew.

She was exceedingly pretty, with large, mocking dark eyes and raven hair, and also exceedingly flirtatious, and it was generally assumed that she would marry early and well. But this did not happen. Annie never seemed to fall in love. She turned from man to man; she broke a few hearts, but her own remained intact. She read dozens of novels, attended every play and opera, and acted as a lively hostess for her father, who ruthlessly relegated poor Joanna to temporary shade whenever Annie was available. She did not appear to be bored with any particular part of her life, but she was certainly bored with the whole. Rosalie told Dexter once that Annie's problem was that she believed in nothing.

When Rosalie and Dexter were first married, Annie took a great interest in helping them to arrange their house, spending almost more time with them than at her father's. Lily's husband, Rutgers Van Rensselaer, was too much older to be a satisfactory brother-in-law for Annie, but what she promptly dubbed Dexter's "high seriousness" seemed to give her just the foil she needed. Annie loved to play the icono-

clast with him; she made a great thing of trying to shock
him with her agnosticism. On the subject of art, however,
they thought too much alike for dissension, and it was their
accord rather than their dissension that brought about the
first remonstrance from Rosalie.

They had been contemplating a little Kensett seascape of
the rocky coastline near Newport that Dexter had just purchased and hung in the dining room.

"It's absolutely fantastic how he combines the mist with
the clarity!" Annie exclaimed, clapping her hands. "It's just
that particular moment, early in the morning, when the last
bit of mist is about to blow away, and you know it's going to
be the most beautiful day in the whole history of the world!
And those sailboats . . . you can hardly see them. And suddenly, yes, there they are, tiny specks of white, almost in-
distinguishable against the sky. It's a *trouvaille*, Dexter.
You'll be a Maecenas!"

"Rosalie's not so sure."

"Oh, Rosalie's like Papa. She wants things to be just so.
'What does this man Kensett think he's painting? A clear day
or a misty one? Why doesn't he make up his mind?' "

Annie adopted so comically Rosalie's "Do you call that
art?" look that Dexter found himself bursting into disloyal
laughter. It was this that Rosalie heard from the hall and
that prompted her later to suggest to him that Annie should
spend less time in their house.

"But why, darling?"

"Do I really have to tell you why, Dexter?"

That was all that was said on the subject, but it struck
instant terror to his heart. Had he, without even being aware
of it, wandered *that* close to the primrose path that had conducted his father straight to hell?

At first he had tried desperately to close his mind to the suggestion. Rosalie, like most young wives, was absurdly jealous and suspicious. All the Handy sisters resented Annie. But his arguments simply fell to pieces before the continued image in his mind of Rosalie's pointing finger. How could he not look where it pointed? How could he any longer delude himself that his attraction to Annie was that of a normally affectionate man for a kitten, a puppy dog, a bunny rabbit, a darling little girl not quite nubile? No, no, it was a burning lust.

The only reason he had been able to cover this over with such ridiculous veils and rags, like a nude male statue in an artist's studio hastily draped before the advent of a ladies' class, was that he had never been visited by a burning lust before. And suddenly, shockingly, a thrilling vision of what the life of the flesh might have been had he married Annie burst upon him!

But this vision did not stay. There was a kind of arid consolation in his rapid recognition that he had *not*, after all, missed the bliss of such a marriage. For such marriages simply did not exist. The intensity of his attraction to Annie had its basis in her moral unavailability. She was forbidden fruit. His importunate physical need of her and his fear of hurting Rosalie were part and parcel of the same thing. Perhaps Rosalie's warning had come just in time. Putting his hands together in silent prayer, Dexter at last forgave his dead father.

Annie came to the house now only with Mr. Handy or Joanna. She made no reference to this change in her habits and seemed oddly subdued with Dexter. Had she felt some of the same attraction? He hardly dared hope so. He must have seemed too old to her. But he had been too scared not to be almost stiffly formal with her now.

"You've changed," she told him briefly. "I suppose that's what marriage does to people. Will I become as dull as you and Rosalie when I marry?"

He was afraid to answer her seriously.

Not long after this his cousin Charley, at one of their lunches downtown, asked him abruptly:

"Why do you never ask me to your house with the lovely Annie? Are you keeping her to yourself?"

Dexter, startled, stared at his younger partner as if he had just received a message from a higher sphere. Wasn't it plain enough? How could he have missed it before? Manifestly, it was his duty to foster a match between a sister-in-law so perilously at loose ends and this charming blond, blue-eyed, curly-haired cousin. A second Handy-Fairchild alliance — what could be more appropriate: physically, dynastically, morally? And if the vision of the mating of two such beautiful beings should cause the matchmaker a few hellish pangs, should he not grit his teeth and try to regard them as a solid down payment to redeem the mortgage on his soul?

That same week he arranged that Charley should dine at Mr. Handy's and be seated at Annie's right. The two young people had known each other for years, but never well, and now Charley, making the most of his opportunity, showed himself at his wittiest. Annie responded in like manner, and their end of the table fairly exploded with merriment.

Home with Rosalie, Dexter found her considerably less keen about the plan that he unfolded to her.

"Don't you think Annie needs someone stronger than Charley?"

"That's so like a woman! Just because Charley was a cut-up in his college days, he must be a rake forever. Can't you trust me that he's a reformed character? Charley, when you first knew him, was simply full of youth and high spirits!"

"He certainly used to be full of spirits," Rosalie observed acerbly. "But I don't mean to deny that he's done well under your tutelage. All the Fairchilds agree you've been the making of him. But if Charley has developed strength enough for one, does that mean you should shoulder him with the weight of two?"

"What makes you think Annie can't carry her own weight?"

"Annie needs a strong man," she repeated stubbornly. "A very strong man. One who might beat her occasionally. Or at least threaten to."

"Rosalie! You, who call yourself a modern woman!"

"Ah, but Annie's not."

"I consider Annie quite as modern as you."

Rosalie sniffed. "She doesn't think in those terms."

But events were soon beyond Rosalie's, or even Dexter's control. Charley and Annie were seeing each other regularly, and people were beginning to say that an engagement would shortly be announced. What match could be more suitable? The only surprising thing was that two such eligible and attractive members of society should have remained single as long as they each had. Dexter, to whom Charley confided the rapid course of his courtship, blessed them in his prayers at night and tried to convince himself that he loved Charley next in line after only Rosalie, his sons, his mother and Rosalie's father. Having guided Charley to the right bride would be, he promised himself, one of the triumphs of his life.

On Christmas Eve, at Mr. Handy's, the first party in his new house on now fashionable Fifth Avenue, Annie took Dexter to a corner away from the noisy crowd of relatives.

"Darling Dexter, you're the tower of sense in the family. I want you to tell me if I should marry Charley."

He looked with astonishment at those unfathomable eyes. Was she still laughing at him? "Annie," he said in anguish, "doesn't your own heart give you the answer?"

"No. Maybe I don't really have one. Is that my fault? Do I have to be an old maid because Jehovah, stingy old Jew that he is, cheated me in the heart department? How much of a heart does Charley have?"

"Well, whatever he has, it's all yours."

"Will it be enough for two?"

"If it grows. And why shouldn't it grow? You must feel something for Charley, or why would you think of marrying him at all?"

"Oh, I feel a great deal for Charley! I find Charley a very attractive man. How nice of you to wince, dear Dexter. Thank you! It's lucky for you that *you're* not eligible. Isn't marriage the only life for us girls? How else can we get out from under the paternal roof?"

Dexter's throat became thick. "Be serious, Annie."

"I *am* serious! I'm always serious. Haven't you learned that yet?"

"If you find Charley so attractive . . ." He paused.

"Yes. Go on."

"And if, as you suggest, you want to be married to get out from under the paternal roof . . ."

"I do."

"And if you think you can do your duty to Charley as a good wife . . ."

Annie laughed in delight. "I was waiting for you to come to my duty! I was about to look at my watch. You're almost a minute late! But, yes, I think I can be a good wife. As good as any of my sisters, anyhow."

Dexter decided to ignore the implied criticism of Lily and Rosalie. "Well, then, I see no reason you shouldn't marry Charley. I see no necessity for you to put your heart under a microscope. I'm sure, despite what you say, that you have as good a one as anyone else."

"That has sometimes occurred to me. I am simply more truthful, do you mean? Or perhaps simply more aware?"

"Well . . . there you are."

"So you advise me to take the great step? Think now, Dexter. Be sure of what you say! I have confidence in you. Only in you. I shall do just as you advise!"

The room around him seemed to darken as he looked into those smiling eyes. What did she mean? Could she be laughing at him *now*? He heard Mr. Handy announcing that he would read Mr. Moore's poem to the children in the parlor. "Yes, I advise the step," Dexter heard himself say.

He joined Rosalie's group in the new conservatory. In spite of the season they were discussing the slavery question with some acrimony. Rosalie in the past year had been devoting more and more energy to it. He wondered gloomily if she would find her "cause" in abolition and reflected, envious of Charley, that Annie had no need of such exaltations. She had enough of her own.

6

AT BREAKFAST in Union Square, the morning after Dexter's talk with Annie about Jules Bleeker, Rosalie was wearing the same pink robe, and Fred and Selby were engaged in their usual dispute.

"Grandpa Handy says that Mr. Buchanan is one of our great presidents. That he's saved the union."

"But at what a cost, Fred," his mother remonstrated.

"You think Grandpa is wrong?"

"I think Grandpa is getting to be an old gentleman. He has the ideas of his time. No doubt they were good ideas for then. I am sure he would think differently if he had seen the things I have seen."

"That you've seen, Ma?"

"Well, you know I used to visit my aunt Bella in Charleston. She could never convince herself that her husband's views were the right ones. She remained a Northerner at heart till the day she died. And she showed me some terrible things."

"But that was before we were born, Ma!"

Dexter remained hidden behind his newspaper, but alert to their talk. It struck him that it was not like Rosalie to support her arguments with evidence so stale. Was it possible that the "things" she had seen had been seen more recently? And how could that be unless she was engaged in some activity of which she had not told him? Abolitionism? It occurred to him suddenly that this might explain why she seemed to have spent so little money of late, insisting that her old dresses would last another year and that she did not need new curtains for the parlor. Was everything going to Boston? He gripped the paper nervously. Well, why not, why not? How could he expect anything else if *he* could not make her happy?

Selby seemed to have read his mind. "Mummy, would you help a slave to escape to Canada? If one came to the house at night and knocked at the door and begged you to take him in? Would you hide him?"

"Yes, Selby, I would."

"You see, Fred!" Selby cried in triumph. "I told you she would!"

"You'd be breaking the law, Ma."

"I'd be breaking a bad law, dear. And I'd do it willingly and cheerfully!"

"Would you be ready to go to jail?"

"If I had to." She glanced defiantly at Dexter as he now lowered his newspaper. "I'm glad to have the boys know that, Dexter. I'm sorry if it pains you."

"Your noble instincts could hardly pain me, my dear. I admire your courage and the strength of your convictions. But you must try to forgive a husband who cares, like your own father, about saving our poor old union."

"At any price? Would you save it at the cost of making New York a slave state?"

"My dear, you're being fantastical!"

"Am I? Mr. Lincoln, of Illinois, has said that the nation is bound to become either all slave or all free."

"Must I agree with a backwoodsman?"

"Don't be a snob, Dexter. There are plenty of Southerners who are insisting on the extension of slavery as the price of their remaining in the union. The *Scott* case gave them the territories, and that has only whetted their appetites."

"Very well, dear, I'll try to answer your question. No, I would *not* save the union at the price of making New York a slave state. I'll go even further. I wouldn't save it at the price of a single free state!"

Rosalie and both boys looked up at him with mild surprise.

"Sometimes I find your positions very hard to understand," Rosalie said with a sigh. "You sound almost with us this morning."

Dexter retired again behind his newspaper to read a summary of Southern editorials on the execution of John Brown. Their violence was shocking even in the violent atmosphere that had been created. Brown was epitomized as the incarnation of the Yankee spirit; his rebellion as a symptom of the murderous and cowardly Yankee mind; his punishment as the sign of what the North could expect if it continued its course of madness and folly. Dexter felt a sudden surge of hate so strong as to make him actually giddy. The yearning to join a crusade to free the slaves was now inflamed by a vision of Northern soldiers lashing overseers with their own whips, burning pillared mansions over the heads of white-bearded planters, marching to bugles across a liberated land.

He had to make himself swallow with an effort, to cough, to sit up straight, in order to dispel the absurd and exhausting fantasy. The union, the union! Remember the union!

"Why, Dexter, are you all right?"

"Quite all right, my dear. I must have swallowed something the wrong way. Boys, isn't it time you went to school?"

When they were gone, he told Rosalie that Charley was stopping in on his way to the office and that he was expecting Jules Bleeker at nine.

"Would you like me to stay and see Charles with you?" she asked.

"Do you mind very much if I say no? I hate to have the mother of my sons mixed up in a thing like this."

Rosalie laughed as she rose to leave the table. "See Charley alone, by all means. I don't even want to join you after that piece of sentiment!"

Ten minutes later he was sitting with Charley at the same table. The latter was very glum and drank his coffee thirstily.

"Bleeker should be here any minute," Dexter warned him, glancing at the clock. "I plan to give him one chance. If he will agree not to see Annie again — privately, of course — we shall take no further action against him."

"And if he refuses?"

"Then we shall simply proceed to destroy him."

Charley flung down his napkin with an angry snort. "In a duel? Thanks for that 'we.' Perhaps you don't know that Bleeker's a first-class shot. He fires his first bullet between the wife's legs and his second between the husband's eyes. Don't you give a damn about me, Dexter?"

Dexter asked himself with a sigh if he would ever come to the end of human vulgarity. "Of course, there'll be no duel," he retorted. "For what do you take me? Gentlemen don't duel in New York, and if they did they wouldn't duel with the likes of Bleeker. No, I mean destroy him financially and socially. I'll close every pocketbook and every front door in New York to him!"

"How?"

"You'll see, my boy," Dexter answered grimly, and then they heard the doorbell. He hurriedly conducted his cousin to the side door through the kitchen, to avoid a confrontation, and told Bridey to usher Mr. Bleeker into his study. When he arrived there he found the large, black-garbed figure of his detested visitor examining the Kensett seascape that Annie had admired six years before.

Bleeker turned to present his big features and florid countenance to his host with a smile as cheerful as if they were about to "go on" to some club dinner or convivial bachelors' occasion.

"Ah, there you are, Fairchild. I've been admiring your Kensett. Such a subtlety of coloring. It's hard to tell where the sea stops and the horizon begins. I can see why people speak of your tastes as advanced. While the rest of us are buying Italian peasant scenes and Turkish marketplaces, you're putting up your money for something as good as this. Congratulations!"

Dexter responded in the iciest tone he could muster. "Never mind the compliments, Bleeker. May we get right down to business?"

Bleeker nodded briskly, adapting himself at once and without the least apparent surprise to the quick change of atmosphere. "I'm at your service. I assume that you prefer to remain standing?"

"Much."

"Very well. Excuse me." Bleeker strode across the room

to crush out his cigar in a bowl. "Let us eliminate the last traces of conviviality."

But Dexter would not deign to notice the least attempt to place things on a humorous basis. "You are aware that your correspondence with Mrs. Charles Fairchild has been discovered?"

"Do you imply that it was concealed?"

"I certainly do. Your letter was delivered clandestinely."

"It was delivered through a servant. Let me ask you something, Fairchild. Whom do you represent in this matter?"

"The family, of course. The outraged family."

"I see. But do you represent Annie?"

"Do you refer to Mrs. Charles Fairchild? I do indeed. *And* her husband."

"You mean you are speaking to me this morning with Mrs. Fairchild's authority?"

"That's a bit of a shock to you, isn't it, Bleeker? Yes, I am speaking to you with her authority. I received it at her father's, just before she returned to her own house last night."

"Where she is residing, I gather, as the virtual prisoner of her husband. He had better remember there is such a thing as habeas corpus in this country!"

"Can it be invoked by the would-be seducers of married women?"

Bleeker took a threatening step towards his host. "It should be invokable by any man who champions the cause of a poor woman shackled to a swine like your cousin!"

Dexter held his ground without flinching. "I suppose we had better avoid epithets. Are you prepared to give me some assurance that you will have no further communication with Mrs. Fairchild?"

"Does *she* ask that?"

"She has placed her case in my hands."

"Then what assurance can you give me that she will be allowed to live a life free from the constant apprehension of violent abuse and drunken threats?"

"Do you presume to treat with me, sir?"

"And why not? Have I not enjoyed Mrs. Fairchild's confidence? Do I not have letters from her? Do you think that you are living in Turkey, where women are put in sacks and thrown in the river if they are disobedient? Let me disillusion you. The days are past when a married woman can be incarcerated while the family lawyer lays down ridiculous terms to her friends!"

"There is no more to be said, Mr. Bleeker. Kindly leave my house."

When Bleeker, seizing his hat from the rack in the hall, had stamped his irate way out of the front door, Dexter looked about for some way to vent his feelings. His eye fell upon the crystal bowl in which his visitor had had the impudence to deposit the ashes of his cigar. Hurrying to the table, he seized it and dashed it to pieces in the fireplace.

"That must have given you great satisfaction!" came a voice from the hall stairway.

It was Rosalie.

7

DEXTER SAT ALONE with his father-in-law after dinner
in the latter's library at 417 Fifth Avenue. The book shelves,
behind glassed doors and beneath flat tops on which rested
bronzes of stricken or striking animals — elk torn by wolves,
bear fighting bear, lions crouched to spring — gleamed with
the gold-tinted backs of old folios and volumes of prints.
The walls above were hung with dark Madonnas and dusky
biblical scenes, relics of Mr. Handy's "grand tour" in 1817.
The tables, under lace covers, were cluttered with baubles
and memorabilia: lapis lazuli, intaglios and daguerreotypes
of dim, dead Handys and Howlands. Dexter's eyes always
sought the charming miniature by Jarvis of Rosalie's mother
as a girl. Her large, haunted eyes and pale, heart-shaped
face suggested the premonition of early demise.

Charles Handy busied himself at the sideboard where a
flock of decanters, with silver labels hung about their long
necks, offered themselves to his choice. His roving, glinting,
staring gray-blue eyes were the features that redeemed —
or perhaps simply decorated, if ameliorated were too strong

a term — the sternness of his aquiline nose, square chin and thin, retentive lips.

"Joanna thinks it's hard on the ladies for the gentlemen to desert them when it's only a family dinner. But frankly, my boy, I feel the need to get away from her at times. She's been quite impossible ever since this last trip to Boston. Raving like the worst type of Yankee abolitionist! It seems she actually met Wendell Phillips. Some privilege! And when I ask her to kindly change the subject, she simply sits and stares at me with woebegone eyes."

Dexter always liked it when the old man abused his daughters. It made him feel intimate and preferred. But that night he was disturbed by the implications.

"Of course, she must hear some pretty dreadful stories from her friends up there."

"Those stories lose nothing in the telling; you can be sure of that. I'm willing to wager that ninety percent of the negroes in the South are better off than they would be in the jungles they were taken from."

"Did that justify us in bringing them over?"

"Us? Where do you get that 'us'? My dear fellow, no Handy, and no Fairchild, I'll be bound, had anything to do with such filthy practices. I'm proud to say that no Handy ever owned a slave, even in the days when half your old New York families did. Oh, our record is pure! But that doesn't mean that I believe in telling our Southern friends and neighbors how to run their lives." Here Mr. Handy, turning to his son-in-law, drew the lid of one eye slowly down over the eyeball, like a chicken. This stately wink, against a countenance of absolute sobriety, gave a ludicrous effect, perhaps intentional, to his irony. "Particularly when they command the loyalty of most of our army and navy!"

"The officers, I suppose you mean."

"Well, whom else would you count on in a showdown? What are your abolitionists going to fight with, besides their own bad breath? Some way to save a union!"

"It's another union that I want to discuss with you tonight, sir. I'm afraid there's bad blood between Annie and Charles."

"Tell me about it."

Mr. Handy seated himself and leaned back in his leather armchair, holding his head stiffly erect as he watched his interlocutor. He hardly twitched a muscle as Dexter related the sorry tale. Then he took a long sip of his brandy and wiped his lips carefully with a silk handkerchief.

"Well, it doesn't surprise me. No, I can't say it does. When they were married, I looked forward to having another Fairchild in my family. I hoped that Charley might be — well, not quite what you have been, dear boy — but something not too different. Yet it was not to be. Charley is weak, and Annie is flighty. The thing has been a failure from the beginning. I suppose we could patch this up, but doesn't there come a time when you wonder if it's worth it? I am not speaking precipitately, I assure you. Hasn't the moment come for a dignified separation? Let Annie come home to me and bring little Kate. She can go out socially as her old father's dinner partner. Joanna hates parties anyway and will be only too happy to be excused. Yes, I think it might really work out very well! We'll put the blame, discreetly of course, on Charley's bibulousness. I doubt that anyone in New York will dare criticize us." Mr. Handy cleared his throat now, almost menacingly. "What do you think?"

Dexter was stupefied. Did Mr. Handy see his daughter's dangerous situation only in the light of his own social convenience? Was he, Dexter, the sole man left in the city who regarded the marriage vow as binding? But his shock was quickly smothered in his new concern for the implied risk to Annie. For, deprived of even the dubious protection of Charles, living in the house of a preoccupied widower and subject to the amoral gushings of a sentimental old maid sister, what was to save her from the impetuous and importunate Bleeker?

"I hate to think we have come to that, sir. I should like to believe that, with Bleeker out of the picture, Annie and Charles would be able to put together some semblance of a decent life."

"And how do you propose to eliminate Bleeker? He's not altogether a bad chap, by the way. He has an eye for a picture. He gave me a tip on where to buy a fine Landseer. It's called *Missing the Hunt*. You haven't seen it yet, Dexter. It's being framed. It shows a foxhound, with lugubrious eyes and a bandaged foot, sitting with its head in the lap of a dear little girl who is consoling him."

"I don't address myself to his taste in art," Dexter replied, trying to keep the disdainful pucker from his lips. "I am concerned only with his taste for married ladies in a social sphere above his own. I see, sir, that I shall have to dot my i's and cross my t's. Do you realize what this man will tell the world if Annie moves in here?"

"What?"

"That she went to her father's house to be able to receive her lover!"

Mr. Handy sat immobile in his chair. The hand that lowered the brandy glass moved almost imperceptibly. Something glacial seemed to be forming over his countenance. Yet when he spoke, his voice was soft.

"Are you implying, sir, that I encouraged his attentions to my daughter?"

"Surely, Mr. Handy, you know me better than that! If you have a greater admirer in all New York, I should like to know who it is. But Joanna, I fear, has been indiscreet. She has countenanced Bleeker's visits to Annie. Yes, sir, in this very house! And take my word for it, he is a man who will stop at nothing to enhance his reputation as the Casanova of Manhattan!"

"And what, may I ask, do you propose to do about him?"

"I propose to ostracize him. I propose that we strike the first blow. Once people see him for what he is, his spite will be harmless. I have already given him his chance to clear out. But the cad openly proclaimed himself your daughter's champion!"

"Let me see." Mr. Handy leaned forward now, seemingly staring at the floor, as he was apt to do when thinking hard. "He's on the staff of the *Observer*, is he not?"

"Have we any weapons there?"

"Silas Cranberry's store is their biggest advertiser. And we hold a lot of Silas' paper at the bank. I'll give you a note to Nicolas King. See him the first thing in the morning. Something may be done there."

Mr. Handy rose and went to his desk to write the note. He scratched away for several minutes, then folded the notepaper, placed it in an envelope and silently handed it to Dexter, who jumped up to receive it.

"I hope you won't be too hard on Joanna, sir," Dexter murmured.

The old man gave him a cold glance for an answer as he passed from the chamber. It boded ill for poor Joanna.

*   *   *

The Bank of Commerce squatted on lower Broadway, its fat round yellow dome seemingly resting on its street portico of six Corinthian columns. Nicolas King, bald, mild-mannered, with thin blue veins lining his bluish cheeks, sat at his roll-top desk touching his fingers together as he listened, inscrutably, to Dexter.

"Insofar as Mr. Cranberry is concerned," he said at last, in a tone as dry as the crackle of autumn leaves, "there is no particular trouble. It is simple enough for me to convey to him the views of your distinguished father-in-law with respect to Mr. Bleeker's character. I shall be seeing him, as it happens, this very afternoon. I do not know why Mr. Handy feels as he does, but he has written me that he has excellent grounds to think ill of Bleeker, and there is no reason that I should not instruct Mr. Cranberry of his feeling, and no reason why Mr. Cranberry should not take such action as he deems fit. But there is another aspect of this matter that concerns me more personally. Are you aware that Bleeker has been proposed for the Patroons' Club?"

"Good God, no!"

"As chairman of the Admissions Committee I can hardly be in doubt. His name comes up this week."

"Then I'm just in time!"

"Wait a second, my friend. Your father-in-law's opinion on a moral question may be controlling with me. I have worked with him intimately for thirty years. He and I accept each other's verdicts without question, because we know each other to the roots. But the Admissions Committee of the Patroons' is another matter. It is not enough for me to call the man a cad. I must cite chapter and verse."

"Would it not be enough to tell them that he has attempted the virtue of a married woman of spotless reputation?"

King's almost hairless eyebrows became pointedly arched. "Ah, my dear Dexter, if we were to limit ourselves at the Patroons' to gentlemen of your and my domestic virtue, we might have to give up some of our most convivial — not to say some of our most distinguished — members!"

"Would it alter your mind if I were to tell you that the lady was a member's wife?"

King frowned. "That is a good deal worse, I concede. Though even there I fear we are not without precedent. There is a certain solidarity among men in these matters. Still — I don't know. I should certainly have to have the member's name."

Dexter hesitated. "The member is my cousin, Charles Fairchild."

King's sigh was high and windy. "Oh, I'm afraid Charley's name is not going to have all the effect you hope. He is not in very good standing at the club. There was that business of his being so intoxicated at the new members' evening, and then, only last month, he was posted."

"I took care of that with my own check."

"Oh, *you*, my dear fellow, everyone respects you. Some of us hope to see you president of the club one day. But your cousin is another matter."

"Surely, sir, the Patroons will rally to defend the threatened honor of a fellow member, even if he's had a drink too many and let a bill slide!"

King seemed a bit shocked at this outburst. "Well, of course, if you put it *that* way."

"I *do* put it that way! Will it be necessary for me to produce the letter that Bleeker wrote to Mrs. Charles Fairchild?" Dexter looked down at the floor as he said this. He was taking a chance, for he could not possibly surrender a letter so compromising to Annie.

"No, no, your word will be quite enough," King said hastily, and Dexter breathed in relief. Now that King had been convinced that he was in deadly earnest — and had his father-in-law behind him — there should be no further trouble. A man like Bleeker, after all, was hardly worth a scuffle with the Fairchilds and Handys. "I'll take the matter up with Bleeker's sponsor. No need for it to come before the committee. I'll simply suggest that he withdraw the candidate's name."

8

ROSALIE FAIRCHILD had at first been amused at her husband's lively concern over her sister's "flirt." Then her amusement had turned to irritation. And finally, as she took in the full dimensions of his campaign to destroy Jules Bleeker, she became disgusted.

It was the first time in their married life that her husband had seemed mean to her. They had both been interested in the recent discovery of Mayan pyramids in Yucatan and in the speculative piecing together of an ancient civilization dominated by priests who sacrificed human beings on these high altars. Now she seemed to see Dexter, in a tall cap and green robe, standing over a dazed, bullied, sullenly watching crowd, preparing to plunge his obsidian knife in poor Bleeker's exposed, hairy chest. Ugh!

It disturbed her to find that there was something close to actual dislike in her reaction. She had often disagreed with Dexter; she had frowned on him and even downright disapproved. But she had never before felt this particular chill. To her there had always been an essential attraction, almost a charm, no matter how sharp her exasperation, in the integrity of his naïve good citizenship, of his passionate determination to be a good husband, a good father, a good lawyer, a good neighbor. Just as his smooth, tightly coordinated body, always so neatly dressed, or undressed, had once dominated her senses, so had his orderly mind and habit of cubbyholes, his secular God and cabined idealism, impressed her as a personality stronger than her own. He might have been misguided; he might even have been the tiniest bit crazy, but there was a power, or a fanaticism, behind his attitudes that had saved them from smallness. But now! What was happening now but the possible confirmation of the long-repressed suspicions of her ante-nuptial days?

As a girl Rosalie had always believed — unless hoped were a better term — that the day would ultimately come when she would realize a special destiny. She did not know at all what that destiny would be — a family, a child, an art, an occupation, perhaps even a tragedy, a martyrdom — but it would be distinctly "other" than the enveloping silks and tassels, smooth, but tough, not to be torn, of the rigorous love and fluffy duties of the Howland and Handy tribe. The ailing mother, Joanna Howland Handy, whom she had lost so young, the endless Howland aunts and great-aunts and cousins, once or twice removed, had seemed united in what she came to think of as the family formula: a cheerful, chattering insistence that they were not like other people, however much they might have seemed so — no, they were "nicer." The Handys and Howlands went to Newport, yet they weren't "social"; they descended from early governors but they weren't "stuck up"; their dresses rustled freshly, all buttons buttoned; their talk was sanitized and their giggles

only slightly suggestive; their "at homes" were lively, almost
festive, full of laughs, too many laughs, almost screams
really, and it was all supposed to be consistent with a philosophy of informality and simplicity, nay, of downright
coziness. Rosalie had fitted herself into this atmosphere with
some difficulty and a history of mild resistance, much as she
had forced her strong figure into whalebone and her large
feet into tight slippers with heels that turned her natural
lope into a mincing walk. But she always felt that in time,
enough time, she would somehow be able to establish her
own independent relation to it all.

Yes, that would surely be permitted her, would it not?
They were not tyrants, nor did they wish to be, not even her
father, who might have been thought by those who did not
know him to have offered such an image. But that was only
because, dear kindly soul, he really *was* all the things that
his women folk simply tried to be. He was natural; he was
the thing itself — whatever the thing was.

On her eighteenth birthday Rosalie had been allowed to
read a letter that her late mother had written for her guid-
ance:

> Always remember, dear child, that it is not absolutely
> essential for a woman to marry. She may be as useful in the
> house of a father or married sister as in her own home. Do
> not marry unless you are fully convinced that you will be
> able to love your husband with all your heart and revere
> him with all your mind. This is all that matters; wealth and
> ancient lineage in a man are nothing if he cannot be loved
> and revered.

Rosalie felt a chill as she read this, as though a long white
arm had reached out from the tomb to check her anticipated
liberation. For there was something about the heavy abso-

lutes of true love and reverence that seemed to block her path. They stood, like granite posts, on either side of the road to individuality, supporting a grilled gate that was not going to open to any key that *she* could provide. Was life really so closed in? Just as she thought the moment might have come to elude the eternal "niceness" of the Handys, the major virtues loomed up to act as the stern guardians that the minor ones had failed to be.

As time passed, she strove to reconcile herself to the precepts of the dead. Would it be so difficult, after all, to love a man and to revere him? Might it not even be that for which she had pined? Wasn't what was wrong with the Manhattan of the Handys and Howlands precisely that there was no real love, no real respect — because there was no one worthy of *that* much love, that much respect? Except, of course, her father.

And then she had met Philip Hake. Although a native New Yorker he had lived in England half his life, while his father had been consul in Liverpool, and had gone to Oxford and, more importantly, to Rugby, where he had fallen under the spell of the great Dr. Arnold. Philip was a big sturdy man with a red beard and fiery eyes who wanted to start a boys' school in New England on the model of Rugby and who was calling on financiers in Boston and New York to raise his capital. He had come in due course to Mr. Handy, who had been struck with his force of character and vigorous Christian idealism, and who had invited him on several occasions to the house. On only his fourth visit he had asked Rosalie, to whom he had devoted his very direct attentions and compliments in the first three, if she would have any insuperable objection (in principle, that was) to being the wife of a schoolmaster. On learning that she would not be so averse, he called the next day on her father to present himself as a suitor for her hand.

Her father, like all the rest of the family, had divined that poor Rosalie, who had no experience in hiding her emotions, was already in love with the handsome newcomer, but he was by no means anxious to accelerate the affair. Summoning Rosalie to his study, he was very blunt about his reservations.

"Your young man may be impetuous, but he is by no means reckless. He seemed a bit dashed when I told him what there was in the Howland trust that you inherited from your mother. And he seemed even more concerned when I informed him that you could never touch the principal. He then wanted to know if I was prepared to invest in his school, and I told him frankly that I wasn't, that I have three other daughters and many charitable commitments. I don't blame a young man for wanting to get ahead, but he must understand the facts."

Rosalie's mind reeled at the sudden, hateful juxtaposition of love and money. She took a deep breath as she told herself that she must be understanding, that Philip *had* to take such things into consideration.

"Couldn't you help him, Father? I mean with your friends? Wouldn't they be willing to back a school if you recommended it?"

"I think they might. Particularly if they knew he was engaged to my daughter. I told him as much. But I told him something else, too. I told him that I wanted you to have the summer to think it over. That under no circumstances would I sanction an engagement before the fall."

"But he's going to England!" Rosalie cried in anguish. "He's going to spend the summer in England to interest his friends in teaching in his school. I thought we might be married in June and go together!"

"Much too precipitate. If you are married in the fall, I shall arrange for you to go to Europe on your honeymoon. And I shall also undertake to endeavor to raise some of his needed capital." Her father's thin lips came together in a long tight line. "I think that is handsome enough, eh? If you marry now, you'll have to do it on your own."

"Oh, Father!"

"My dear, you must remember that I stand in the position of mother as well as father. I think you can oblige me in this. A summer is soon past. All right? Don't turn away from me. Give me a smile. A little smile? You'll do as I say?"

"You give me no alternative."

"There's a sensible girl." Mr. Handy always accepted a surrender, wisely ignoring the manner in which it was rendered. "And now let me give you a piece of advice. It is customary, when a young lady requests a period of time in which to consider a gentleman's offer of marriage, for him to consider himself unilaterally bound. If I were you, I should be more magnanimous. Tell him that he is to be free in the interlude. He will appreciate your largeness of spirit."

Rosalie did as she was advised, and Philip took it all well, too well. He made no rash suggestion that they elope. It was his opinion that they should do just as her father said, and that, considering all the circumstances, Mr. Handy was behaving handsomely. Rosalie had a horrid feeling that he was looking forward so much to going back to England and discussing the plans for his beloved school with other inflamed disciples of the late Thomas Arnold that he did not much care whether she went with him or not. It was all agony for her, but an agony that she dared not show.

The long hot summer in Newport was a dismal one. She suffered from a fixed premonition that she would never see Philip again. She busied herself with the usual social activities, but only to avoid the questions that would have followed her abstention. She took long walks alone down the rocky coastline and read Rousseau's *Nouvelle Héloise*. In a mood that strangely mixed the darkest realism with the filmiest fantasies, she decided that Philip would never love her and that she could still be happy as his wife.

When they returned to New York in September she found a letter from him that had just arrived. In it he announced his engagement to Miss Lucy Taylor, daughter of Sir Ernest Taylor, baronet and M.P. They were to be married in London before Christmas. He wrote:

> I'm afraid I was hurt and bitter last spring, at your coolness and doubts, your insistence on keeping my manly ardor at bay. But now, dear Rosalie, I understand the full extent of your wisdom and intuition. It may even be that God had a hand in it. For my beloved Lucy not only has always wished to share in a teaching life; she owns a large Tudor house in Dorset that will make an ideal central building for what, within a scant year's time, should become The Taylor School for Boys. We are giving it that name in honor of Lucy's father, who is not only paying for the remodeling of the house and grounds, but who has consented to act as first chairman of our board of trustees and who has promised to interest his parliamentary friends in the project. I am sure you will rejoice in my good fortune, and I eagerly look forward to the day when you will come to visit our mother country, perhaps on a happy wedding trip of your own, and journey down to Dorset to see our institution and meet my Lucy to whom I have talked so much of you.

When Rosalie, ashen pale and trembling, showed this letter to her father, he grunted as if not in the least surprised.

But when she accused him, with muffled sobs, of having ruined her life, he took his loftiest tone.

"I forgive you your violence, my dear; you are understandably agitated. I have no doubt that in a very short time you will recognize your injustice to me and be properly sorry for it. Philip Hake is a man who is never going to love anything but his school. I discerned that after our first conversation about the extent of your fortune. Yet he is not, fundamentally, a mercenary man. He is simply one with a mission — a bit of a fanatic, if you like. He believes that his rather shabby means are justified by his noble end. I did not foresee that he would enter into another engagement quite so expeditiously, but I certainly recognized that he was a man who would better himself if he could do so without positive dishonor. That is why I wanted you to leave him free. I make no secret of my delight that it is Miss Taylor and not you, who is to be sacrificed to his academy. English girls are brought up to expect that. Americans are not. For surely you will not tell me that you still want this man, *knowing* him for what he is?"

Rosalie fled from the presence of her terrible, unanswerable parent, and the name of Philip Hake was never mentioned again in her presence.

For two long years she was convinced that she would never marry. She would stay at home with her sister Joanna and lose herself in the ministrations that attended her father's days and nights. She would visit the poor; she would do sketches and water colors; she would teach in Sunday school; she would play the piano. She would keep killing time until time killed her.

But the ticking clock brought her a surprise: not death but ennui. And when the Sunday afternoon came around, in the third year of her abandonment, that brought Dexter Fairchild's abrupt declaration of his courting attentions, she was startled by the similarity of his approach to that of her erstwhile suitor. Curiously enough, it amused her. And what was even more curious was that she never once considered that this strange, intense young man might treat her as his predecessor had. No, if there were going to be coolness in *this,* it would come from a different quarter!

And then, very soon, on only his second visit, it began to be evident that she was not going to be as cool as she had thought. A part of her that she had believed dead, or at least numb, began to stir again. She was not at all sure that she wanted it to stir; she was even inclined to regard it as a betrayal of the nobler emotion she had initially felt for Philip. She had certainly never pledged herself to be true to her betrayer, but was it not somehow incumbent upon her to preserve the capacity for so bright a flame for a greater man? Greater than whom? Well, greater certainly than Dexter Fairchild!

She had always thought of a husband as someone to look up to, and he was actually smaller than she, though only the tiniest bit. Their eyes met at the same level. And then he seemed so finely made, as of choice materials skillfully put together. He stood, or sat, absolutely immobile, but when he moved, it was quickly and agilely, like a cat. She was intrigued by his white smooth skin, his clear blue-green eyes, that he would fix upon her, his sartorial elegance. She even liked his faint whiff of eau de cologne.

It was impossible to dismiss him as a dandy. He was a serious, hard-working lawyer. It was equally impossible to discount him as a worldling or even a snob; there was a suppressed intensity about him that made her uneasy but that commanded her grudging respect. She could not quite laugh at the violence of his need to say the right thing, do the right thing, *be* the right thing. If his values were wrong, his passions gave him a kind of dignity.

It also gave him a kind of strength. She faced the fact that she was drawn to him. Her sister Lily, in the expansiveness of her own conjugal satisfaction, had hinted of undreamed delights in the arms of Rutgers Van Rensselaer, and now Rosalie could not help substituting this elegant young man for the image evoked of her portly, bewhiskered brother-in-law.

After Dexter had made his proposal, and she had retired, as once before, with her family to Newport, her real troubles began. It was not that her relatives talked to her about Dexter. They saw no need to. It was entirely taken for granted that he represented the obvious solution to all of her problems and that it was only a matter of time — and very little time at that — before she should take her proper place in Manhattan society as Mrs. Fairchild. She could tell by the easy way in which her father referred to Dexter, or failed to refer to him, that he saw that young man not only as a desirable son-in-law, but as an inevitable one.

She thought a good deal of her mother's dying injunction, but she began to wonder if it had been reasonable or even quite honest. Where in her world was the man going to be found who could be totally loved and totally revered? Did he exist? Had her mother felt that way about her own father? Really and truly? Weren't there aspects of the personality of Charles Handy that were at least analogous to some in Dexter Fairchild? Or perhaps even less admirable?

Dexter's enthusiasm for Newport was almost unbearable to her. In New York he had been partially protected from her criticisms by the armor of his profession: it might have been a risky, even a dangerous business to shoot too many darts at a clever lawyer. And then there was always the thick, the rather cloying atmosphere of public duty constantly performed that emanated from the more prosperous sections of the Manhattan bar. But Dexter in flannels, in blazers; Dexter sauntering down the beach or singing a bit shrilly at a picnic; Dexter rising to offer her father an unctuous toast at dinner, seemed the very spirit of the summer community. He was just as gay, just as ornamental, just as frivolous as Newport — no more so, no less. And she had never liked Newport.

On the other hand, he showed himself to an unexpected but undeniable advantage in summer sports. Watching his trim figure move rapidly past the breakers in a spirited crawl out to sea, observing how deftly he handled the tiller of her brother-in-law's sailing yacht, seeing him score a near bull's eye in archery, she could not but admire his masculine agility and competence. Obviously, he had prepared himself for these activities with some of the same conscientiousness that had guided his preparation for law. He was certainly a man determined to fall behind in nothing, and when warm thoughts came to her of how he might perform acts much more personal, her cheeks would become flushed indeed. Yet all she could guess of these was from his kiss, firm, quick, discreet, rendered suddenly behind a door, or a garden bush, when Joanna was not looking, or pretended not to be looking.

After her explosion at their private supper party and his abrupt return to New York, she was abjectly miserable. She could still, however, be irritated when she found that her father had advised Dexter to come back to Newport. Mr. Handy took his usual high tone in response to her complaint.

"Do you think you own that young man? Do you think he cannot have an independent relation with another member of your family? With me, for example?"

"Yes, but he doesn't. You just want him for me. You think I'm incapable of catching another husband!"

"I think you're incapable of catching a better one."

"Must I have one at all?"

"Of course not. It's perfectly open to you to live with me and Joanna and Annie. You will always be welcome to do so. But remember that I shan't be around forever. The day may come when you'll bitterly regret having let Dexter Fairchild go. He'll be snapped up soon enough by some lucky girl. Be sure of that!"

On the morning before the archery contest, which she knew Dexter would attend, Rosalie had a rather desperate discussion with her sister Lily in the rose garden. Rutgers Van Rensselaer always lived on his boat during his annual visit to Newport, but his wife preferred the comfort of Oaklawn.

"All of you think I ought to marry Dexter," Rosalie began sullenly.

"Ought? Don't be silly, Rosey."

"Well, of course you don't *say* it to me. You don't have to. I suppose I'm always saying it to myself."

"But you like him?"

"Oh, yes."

"Perhaps you love him and don't know it."

"I don't know." She faced Lily almost with defiance. "I like it when he kisses me."

"Well, there you are!"

"But, Lily, I don't know if I respect him!"

"Respect him? Why, he's the most respectable man in the world!"

"Maybe that's just it. I guess what I really mean is, do I revere him?"

"What an odd term. Do I revere Rutgers? I hope not!"

"You're so practical, Lily. I wish I were as practical as you."

"No, you don't! You're *proud* of being romantic. Just don't let it lead you to Joanna's condition!"

But Rosalie was determined not to submit to a lecture on old maids. "Tell me, Lily. Frankly. Do you think Mother felt that way about Father?"

"What way?"

"Well . . . that he was physically . . ."

"Attractive? Of course."

"Yes, but more than that. Overwhelming!"

Lily looked startled. "Overwhelming what?"

"Let's say, her better judgment."

"You mean, so that she . . . she . . ." Lily gaped.

"Married him."

Lily's relief was lost in perplexity. "I don't follow you."

"I mean married him without really respecting him."

"Certainly not! I think we've said enough on this subject. You're working yourself into a state of nervous prostration. I suggest you go in now and rest until our guests come."

Rosalie, in her room, was alone as never before. Now that she had permitted herself to question the integrity of her mother and the ultimate nobility of her father, she had no allies. None of her sisters was going to follow her into *those* uncharted waters; she could drift as she chose out to open sea.

Later that day, when she had fled the house and the archery contest, sitting on a rock and looking out to the actual ocean, she made her decision at last to make an anchor out of the very cause of her aimlessness. She would accept this man whom she certainly did not revere and perhaps did not even quite love — at least as her mother had used that term. Yet she clung to her new suspicion that she was probably only doing as her mother had done, as her sister Lily had done, as any woman would do who did not insist on becoming a Joanna. There had to be a price for everything.

9

Rosalie had made it her rule, in sixteen years of marriage, to avoid, wherever possible, direct confrontations with her husband. Silence settled a hundred differences of opinion in minor matters. But now she decided that her silence in the case of Jules Bleeker was showing signs of malignancy. It was only fair to Dexter himself to give voice to her opinion, and she waited one morning at the breakfast table until the boys had departed for school.

"Are you sure, Dexter, that you're justified in what you're doing to Jules Bleeker? It strikes me as a kind of persecution."

"Persecution! You know what he's done!"

"Yes, but didn't Annie lead him on?"

"You've never been fair to Annie!"

"Someone in the family has to balance your extravagant admiration. Tell me this, then. Do the men you're talking to go along with you of their own accord? Or do you have to bludgeon them into it?"

"I wouldn't call it bludgeoning. I *have* run into some resistance, I admit. It rather surprised me, actually, considering how clear-cut the moral issues are."

"And that doesn't give you pause? It doesn't make you reflect that you just *might* be wrong?"

Dexter stared at her with something like bewilderment in his clear gaze. "How can I be wrong, darling? This man has been urging your sister to commit adultery. Can he be fit for our society?"

"But does that mean you have to ruin him?"

"I gave him his chance. He refused to give her up. Either we are Christians, who are prepared to protect the sacraments, or we're not."

"Perhaps we're not. Perhaps that's what you're not willing to face. That you're swimming against the current."

"So I should just give up? Is that what you mean? Give up and let Bleeker continue his vile game until he wins it?"

"You don't show much confidence in Annie."

"How can I have confidence in a young woman who is bored with her home life and has nothing else to distract her? I'd be a fool, Rosalie!"

But she was determined not to let him escape her, as he so often had, with emotional formulas. "What I think I mean is this," she said firmly. "I have a theory that men, like women, have been basically the same through history. The majority, that is. The average Roman, the average Greek, wasn't he pretty much like the average American today? What makes one era different from another is its dogma, not its people. And isn't its dogma always made up by the small, busy group we call priests?"

He stared. "And I'm a priest? Is that what you're getting at?"

It occurred to her that he did not altogether object to the idea. "Yes. A priest doesn't have to be a clergyman. He's simply a person in charge of the mysteries. Whether they're religious or political or what have you. His job is to keep the others in line. He has to use prayers and miracles and magic." She paused now, watching him carefully. "He may even have to fake them. He may even have to use . . ." Again she stopped. She had never gone so far with Dexter. Could one go too far with Dexter? What would happen?

"May have to use what?" he demanded. "Force? Torture? Autos-da-fé? Go ahead, Rosalie. Say it. You think I'm treating Bleeker the way the Inquisition treated heretics!"

"Yes, I do! That's just it. That's just exactly it."

He laughed. So that was what happened. "Well, you'll be relieved to learn I'm not planning to burn him. Though I'm not at all sure I wouldn't if I could!"

Rosalie picked up her newspaper to hide what was almost embarrassment. She remembered with a faint shudder her image of the Mayan on the pyramid with the obsidian knife.

10

Rosalie and Dexter were lunching at her father's, as they did every Sunday after church. As they came in, she watched her husband's eyes scan the little group assembled in the front parlor, all standing, as if to avoid the uninviting, tall-backed Italianate chairs of black walnut. She knew he was looking to see if Annie was there. Joanna had told her at church that Annie was professing a cold, but she had not told Dexter. He made no effort to conceal his disappointment, because he did not know that she was watching him.

"I suppose Annie's cold is diplomatic," she said to Joanna. "Too much family here today."

"She's had rather a nasty row with Father. About Jules coming here while I was in Boston."

"I thought Dexter had that all under control."

"But you know Annie. Just because a matter seems to be settled is no reason not to make a scene. I wish she wouldn't, because Father takes it out on me." Joanna burst into one of her high nervous giggles. "He practically accused me of running a disorderly house!"

Rosalie regarded her sister with faint surprise. It was not

like Joanna to use such a term. She seemed to be trying to demonstrate a sudden, rather febrile independence.

"Well, Mr. Bleeker has certainly given us all something to talk about."

"Father treats me like a child," Joanna continued petulantly. "One of these days he may find out that I'm older than he reckons."

"Who is that minister he's talking to?"

Dexter, coming up to them, heard the question. "Don't you know him? That's Francis Halsted. The author of *American Slavery Justified by Natural Law*."

"That horrible man!" Rosalie exclaimed in disgust. "How *can* Father! Is there no limit to his cosmopolitanism?"

"It's an interesting book, darling. You should read it before you condemn it. Halsted maintains that slavery is a natural step in the evolution of a race. He puts it in historical perspective with Rome and Greece, and he has a fascinating chapter on the Justinian Code . . ."

"Oh, Dexter, you're hopeless the moment anyone mentions anything about law!" Rosalie interrupted him sharply. "You think any statute, passed by no matter what barbarians, is a justification for damming up the smallest trickle of Christian charity!"

Both Joanna and Dexter looked shocked at this unwonted acerbity. There was a moment of silence.

"Well, you'll have a chance to convert Mr. Halsted from his views," Joanna informed her. "I've seated you next to him."

"Jo, how could you? I thought you were a good abolitionist!"

"Don't mention that word before Father!" Joanna ex-

claimed with mock terror. "Anyway, I want you to listen to
Mr. Halsted."

"Whatever for?"

"It helps to know how the enemy thinks."

Joanna seemed to be trying to look mysterious. She crossed
the room to speak to the minister. Rosalie could see by their
glances that they were talking about her.

The dining room doors were now opened, and the guests
went in to lunch. Rosalie observed that her clerical neighbor
closed his eyes devoutly while her father said grace. But
with the "amen" he came awake with a spring, and delivered
an elegant little speech about his admiration of Mr. Handy.
It was impossible for her not to respond to this politely, and
she found herself engaged in a benign discussion of the
blessings of the relationship between fathers and daughters.

He was certainly amiable to look at. He had gentle eyes,
sky blue; they peered at her with diffidence, almost with
timidity, as if they hoped, or even suspected, that she might
be amused, sympathetic, or even downright funny, but as
if, too, they were ready to take flight and bound away like
a bunny should she prove in the least bit unfriendly. His
skin was light and his hair blond; it was only in the two
long concentric lines on either side of his very red lips and
in the darkness under his eyes that she could tell that he was
in his middle, perhaps even late thirties. It was extraordinary
that a doctrine so repellent should be lodged in so fair a
form.

Suddenly he changed the subject and looked at her with
an anxious expectancy that she was at a loss to interpret.

"Your sister tells me that you disapprove of me."

"Oh, we'll never get on if we discuss your book, Mr.

Halsted," she assured him hastily. "I suggest we talk about the aims of the French emperor in Italy."

"But I don't mind people disagreeing with me. I don't mind at all."

"It would be more than disagreement, I'm afraid. I might even forget I'm a lady. So please. Do you think we can trust the Emperor Napoleon?"

"You mean you might become abusive?"

She had certainly not anticipated such insistency. "Feelings run high about slavery. As you, of all people, should have discovered, Mr. Halsted."

"But can't we still love each other?"

"Love each other?" She allowed her tone to be startled. There was something in the softness of his voice that seemed to suggest a more than Christian warmth.

"Doesn't Christ tell us to love each other?" he asked.

"I might find it difficult to love a priest who preaches that Christ preaches slavery."

"Preaches it? I never suggested that. I said that slavery was not abhorrent to nature. That it is the way in which a weak and undeveloped race may be usefully employed by a stronger one. In an ideal society slavery would disappear. And it *will* disappear, dear Mrs. Fairchild, believe me. It *will*." As she stared at him, half-hypnotized by his gentle, persevering tone, she made out two yellow gleams in the center of his eyes. "In the meanwhile, so long as the slave is loved by his master, I believe that Christ condones his condition."

"And how many slaves are loved by their masters?"

"More than we know of, I hope. More than we know of, I pray."

"Well, you had better pray long and hard, Mr. Halsted!"

Rosalie exclaimed, giving vent at last to her swelling anger. "And may I remind you that I am doing my best to behave like a lady in my father's house? Don't try me too hard!"

"I have no wish to try you. I feel as strongly as you about the humane aspects of the question. I deem it a mortal sin to beat slaves or to break up their families. I believe that a slave-owner has a duty to treat his slaves exactly as he would his paid employees."

Rosalie turned now in her chair so that they regarded each other face to face.

"That's all very well, sir, but it misses the point altogether. Let me put it this way. If *all* the slaves in the South were totally content with their lot; if they all had the mild and loving masters that you so fantastically suppose, and if all the laborers and mechanics in the North were as downtrodden and wretched as *I* happen to believe the slaves now are, I should still be dedicated with all my heart and soul to the abolition of your peculiar institution!"

Once again she thought she could make out the yellow gleam in his eyes.

"I like the way you talk, Mrs. Fairchild. Do you think you could convert me?"

"I am afraid you're not convertible. Anyone who has written a book!"

"Ah, you give me up!" he exclaimed, with a little wail and a smile, as she turned abruptly to her other neighbor.

❀   ❀   ❀

That afternoon Joanna called for her in their father's carriage to drive her to the new park at Fifty-ninth Street. Dexter and the boys had gone for a hike along the East River. But Rosalie was surprised when the carriage pulled up before the parish house of the marble Gothic church of Saint Jude's on Fifth Avenue and Forty-third Street.

"You didn't know we were going to call on the Reverend Francis Halsted, did you?" Joanna asked, with an arch smile.

"Joanna Handy, will you please tell Tom to drive on! Do you think I'd set foot in that man's house?"

"It's not his house. It's God's house."

"Then there must be two gods. Mine doesn't believe in slavery."

"Rosey, you made a great impression on that man. He wants to go on with your lunchtime discussion. I think you've converted him."

"You can't be serious!"

"I swear!" And Joanna at this piously crossed her heart. "Come in for a minute. As a favor to me. Please!"

Rosalie, utterly bewildered, at last shrugged her shoulders and descended from the carriage. They were ushered into a high-ceilinged office on the ground floor with tall Gothic windows that looked out on a green yard. Halsted was standing behind his desk wearing a beaming smile as they entered.

"Welcome, Rosalie Fairchild!" he exclaimed. "Welcome to the Trinity Station of the Underground Railway!"

Rosalie sat down suddenly on a chair by the desk. She was conscious only of Joanna's vivid pleasure at her shock.

"So it was all a front?" she gasped. "Even the book? You wrote it as a cover?"

"No! It was genuine enough when I wrote it. I was very deep in error. I cannot describe to you adequately what it is like to be so deeply in the clutches of the devil. For I have no doubt now that such was my unhappy state. I was possessed. It was like a dream, not a dream of frustration where everything is constantly escaping or eluding you, but a dream where everything seems to fit exactly into place, like magic. And magic it was. Black magic.

"My experience in writing the book was the strangest part of it. Always before, writing had come to me with difficulty, even with agony. But then the pen seemed to race over the paper as if guided by another hand. Even my style seemed more formed and mellifluous. One of my reviewers who had read an earlier work of mine about the desert fathers remarked that I seemed to have developed a totally different style, and a better one at that. I greeted my new fame humbly, reminding myself that I was simply the instrument of a greater force, that I might be enjoying the blessing of having been chosen as the tool needed by the almighty to prevent a terrible war, just as Mrs. Stowe had been chosen by Satan as the tool to bring that war on.

"And then came the experience which I no longer think it is irreligious to compare to Saint Paul's on the road to Damascus. I was preaching one Sunday morning, right here in Saint Jude's, and I saw our great west window suddenly irradiated by sunlight through a break in the clouds, and I heard a voice crying out the same question: why was I persecuting him? That very night I went to a friend, a holy man, and he told me how to become a member of this great movement."

"And he advised you not to publish your change of view?" Rosalie asked.

"Yes, that, after a fashion, was to be my penance. To give up the balm of recantation. To provide a station in the Underground that no Federal or Southern agent would ever suspect. The top floor of this parish house has been used for more than a year now as a place where escaped slaves can rest and recuperate and receive medical attention. Joanna has been with us for three months. She tells me that you can nurse and cook and give us money. She assures me that you are totally discreet. As to your views on slavery, I can testify myself as to their soundness! Will you join us?"

"But my coming here to work — which is what I take it you want — won't it give you away?"

"Because of the supposed divergence of our philosophies? I think not. You are identified with your husband's political conservatism, as Joanna is identified with your father's dislike of abolition. Neither of you has made any public denunciation of me. It would not seem strange for a lady of your station to come to a parish house for volunteer work."

Rosalie felt an odd tingling that seemed to emanate from deep within her. She did not know if it were thrill at the honor of being called to such a task, or simply relief that she should have so unexpectedly found a seeming answer to her inner problems.

"Of course, I'll do it!" she exclaimed, jumping to her feet. "I'll do anything you need!"

Joanna got up, too, and kissed her, and Halsted, smiling benignly, led them off to a tour of the house.

At the top of the second stairway he opened a door to a long attic room, dimly lit by low dormer windows and two large candelabra set on what appeared to be trunks. Rosalie first thought that the chamber was empty, until, following her sister in, she saw five negroes, two men and three women, seated on a rug, in a circle, with cards in their hands. They looked up silently at their visitors, without surprise and without greeting.

"Please go on with your game, my friends," Halsted enjoined them, which they thereupon did. "Harris here and his wife will leave for Portland tonight on the S.S. *Atalanta*," he told Rosalie. "With a cargo of textiles. They should be safe in Canada in three days' time. The others are going via Buffalo and Lake Erie. We can only be sure of absolute security for two on the *Atalanta*."

"How do you get them in here?"

"They come in coffins to the church funeral parlor."

One of the women turned around at this. She told Halsted with evident apprehension that she didn't want to leave the parish house that way, that it had scared her "worse than the bloodhounds."

"No, Amy, you're going on board as a lady, in deep mourning with black gloves and a veil. I shall escort you myself."

"But don't they suffocate in the coffins?" Rosalie asked in alarm.

"They have holes in them," one of the men answered cheerfully. "I was even cold!"

Halsted now led Joanna and Rosalie to the other rooms on the attic floor. There was a dispensary, a kitchen and four bedrooms. He explained that during the hours when the ordinary parish activities were conducted on the floors below, everyone had to talk in whispers. One of the bedrooms was occupied by a man who had contracted pneumonia hiding in a swamp. His case was grave and required nursing at all times. Rosalie offered to start her turn the very next day.

As Joanna was taking hers that same afternoon, Rosalie came home alone in the carriage.

"How was your drive?" Dexter asked her.

"Delightful," she responded firmly. "I really think Central Park is going to be as fine as anything in a European capital."

In her exultation she thought she might even forgive him what he was doing to Bleeker.

"On our way home Jo took me to Saint Jude's," she continued. "She's trying to persuade me to do some work with her at the parish house. I might run the sketching class."

"Saint Jude's? But that's Halsted's church!"

"Yes, but I won't have to see him. There's no necessary relation between his views on slavery and the work at the house."

He looked at her in surprise. "Did you see him this afternoon?"

She hesitated. "As a matter of fact, I did."

"And you talked with him? Despite the row you had with him at lunch?"

"Well, I guess I owed him an apology. After all, he was Father's guest."

Dexter whistled. "That fellow must have the silver tongue he's credited with. To get *you* to come around! I guess we could use some of his forensic talent at Fairchild & Fairchild!"

Rosalie turned to her work bag. She had a long way to go, she decided grimly, in the art of deception. But she would get there.

11

ON NEW YEAR'S DAY of 1860 Dexter started his long walk north, with its pleasant if arduous prospect of some dozen house calls, at Broadway and Canal Street. He proposed to end it by six o'clock at his home in Union Square where Rosalie would be giving her reception. It was a bright, cold day, and his spirits were high. The frigid air seemed to clean the city, to intensify its colors, to make the whites more white, the blacks more richly black. The white-blue sky was so clear that the taller buildings as far north as Fourth Street seemed an easy walk, and the great cast-iron stores along Broadway, with their walls of curve-topped windows separated only by their frames, suggested to him the Venetian palaces along the Grand Canal that he had only seen in pictures.

The campaign against Bleeker was proceeding apace. Dexter had prepared his ground carefully, and now it was time to call in his loans. He proposed to speak to some seven or eight important persons in the course of his visits. Only a few words should now be necessary to close the iron wall that he had been building against the intruder.

Everything, personal as well as national, seemed suddenly to point to hope. Mr. Lincoln, of Illinois, whose speeches he had been carefully following, appeared to be offering a feasible compromise between slaveholders and abolitionists, if the two sides would only accept it. Dexter was convinced that if a resort to arms could be put off, the Northern states, with their bursting populations and growing industry, would find themselves ultimately in a position to dictate abolition without bloodshed. If they would but have patience! And they might yet; they might . . .

His first call was on old Mrs. Verplanck, who still lived in the red brick house on Canal Street where she had been born eighty years before. She wore a lace cap and powdered her hair in what some persons called an affectation of the past, but which devoted antiquarians, like himself, cherished for its reminder of a more elegant day. He never tired of hearing her tell of how she had been taken to the White House as a little girl and presented by her father to President Washington. Dexter relished his popularity with the old; he was proud that John Church Hamilton, son of the great Alexander, had said of him, "That young man knows more about us than we know about ourselves!"

As Mrs. Verplanck's first caller, he was free to discourse on the abominations of his enemy.

"Dear me, isn't it lucky that you told me!" the old lady exclaimed. "Mrs. John Hone was going to bring Mr. Bleeker here next week. Apparently he has shown a great desire to meet me. He seems to think I can give him some background for an article he wants to do on 'old New York.' But now of course I shall tell Mrs. Hone that it's quite out of the question."

"I promise you, ma'am, you'll never regret it."

"Oh, my trust in you is complete, dear boy!"

Dexter felt that his heart was full to bursting as he continued his northward trek. Did it not do him a bit of good, subject as he was to the muffled criticism of his home, to feel appreciated, once in a while, if only by a dear little old lady? And why, after all, should not a dear little old lady be able to evaluate his character as well as anyone else? Better even? Had Rosalie known George Washington and Chief Justice Jay?

It was three o'clock when he entered the great marble house with the tall fluted white columns and Corinthian capitals that formed one unit of the noble arcade at Astor Place. It was here that Silas Cranberry, amid his fantastic collection of modern Roman statues, entertained as many of the social world as one so newly rich could induce to visit him. Caesars, Huns, martyrs and gladiators stood on pedestals above the multitude of his chattering visitors. Dexter, glancing around the principal chamber, suspected that the crowd was largely drawn from the staff of his host's great emporium.

He spotted Cranberry, bald, heavy-jawed, with tiny glittering eyes, standing, thumbs in his vest pockets, amid a respectful circle of younger men who fell back as Dexter came up, recognizing that their function was only to provide an audience until the advent of a real guest.

The roughness of Cranberry's greeting was only slightly mitigated by his perfunctory smile: "So you'll come to my house, Fairchild, when you want a favor from the lowly storekeeper? Is that the size of it?"

"So it might appear. But it also happens that I was planning to give myself the pleasure of calling on you and Mrs. Cranberry before I needed the favor."

"Without your Mrs.?"

"My wife happens to be receiving today."

"How would I know? She didn't ask me."

"She will next year. I have her word for it."

Dexter's gentle tone at last placated his brusque host. "Well, I guess I shouldn't be too rough on a man who comes to bid me a happy New Year. But this business of Bleeker sticks in my craw. What's it to me if the man's a bounder? Is that a reason to tell his newspaper I'll pull out my advertisements?"

"We hoped that you might regard our cause as yours. And that you might agree that such a wrong inflicted on a gentleman like my cousin affects all the leaders of the city."

Cranberry pursed his lips to emit a low whistle. "I ain't in your crowd, Fairchild."

"Isn't that your choice, sir?"

"*My* choice! Are you telling me I could get into the Patroons' Club?"

"I'm not telling you that. That would be a question for the Admissions Committee. But I am certainly telling you that I should be glad to write you a letter of endorsement."

Cranberry snickered at this, frankly uncivil. "Oh, I know that dodge! 'Dear Board of Admissions: I promised Mr. Silas Cranberry that I would write a letter for him. This is the letter.' "

Dexter tried not to look too exultant. "I cannot conceive, sir, what there may have been in our past relations to justify your impugning my honor. If I were to write for you, it would be to endorse your candidacy heartily. After what you've just said, of course, there can be no further question of that."

He turned to stride away, but just slowly enough to allow his host to catch him by the sleeve.

"Don't take offense, Fairchild. I was too hasty."

"I'm afraid you were."

"Maybe one day I'll ask you for that letter. In the meantime, thank you. God knows, Jules Bleeker doesn't mean a tinker's damn to me. He's probably a horse's ass, anyhow. When do you want his head?"

By five o'clock Dexter had penetrated the world of the chocolate brownstone and was ascending the high stoop that led to the porticoed entrance and fine mahogany double doors of the Rutgers Van Rensselaers. These opened before him without need of a bell, and he gave a friendly New Year's greeting to the old butler who welcomed him. Lily Van Rensselaer, larger and more stately than her sister Rosalie, stepped out of the receiving line to take him to a corner for a private word.

"Annie's here," she said in a low voice. "That man Bleeker called, though I left strict orders he was not to be admitted. He refused to take a 'no' from a servant, and Rutgers had to go to the door to speak to him. There were raised voices. It was very awkward."

"Lily, the worst is over. By next week nobody will have heard of Jules Bleeker."

And then he saw her. She was standing alone, in a black dress, at the far end of the room, looking directly at him. Without another word he crossed the floor to her.

"I come to report to Queen Guinevere," he announced with mock gravity. "My mission is accomplished."

Annie stared back at him with an air of equal sobriety. "You mean that the damsel in distress has been rescued?"

"Just so. A certain gentleman — if that is not too polite a

term for him — is going to find New York a rather difficult place in which to earn a living."

Annie's brow was almost puckered in a frown, a rather arch one. Then she shrugged. "Was that what all the hubbub in the hall was about? Poor Juley! How brave you all are! And, now, having removed one pernicious influence from the damsel's life, are you prepared to supply her with another? For I don't suppose you intend to leave a defenseless damsel without a single pernicious influence?"

"I thought I should leave that task to Charley."

"My King Arthur? Some saint! But if I'm to be stuck with an Arthur, I must still have a Lancelot. Are you prepared to be my Lancelot, Dexter?"

"Lancelot's mission has just been accomplished."

"Lancelot's mission is just beginning!" Annie exclaimed sharply. Her tone was almost menacing. "Do you really think you can walk out on me now, Dexter Fairchild?"

He stared back at her, dazed. "What . . . what are you suggesting?"

"Suggesting? I thought I was shouting it to the rooftops! As evidently a woman has to, in this new year of 1860! You have removed Juley from my life. Very well! I accept it! Isn't it up to you now to take his place?"

"Are you trying to tell me . . . are you trying to tell me . . . that you care for me? In *that* way?"

"Oh, Dexter, what a fool you are! The gentleman is supposed to take *some* lead in these matters."

But Dexter was still in his daze. "And what about . . . Bleeker?"

"Do you think for a minute I'd have let you *touch* Juley if I'd really cared about him? You don't know me!"

He wanted to fall to his knees. "Annie, I adore you!" he murmured.

The next minute he heard her high, excited laugh, and she had left him. It was time to go home. Rosalie's reception would already be drawing to a close.

12

THE OFFICES of Fairchild & Fairchild, at 57 Wall Street, occupied the second floor of a pleasant green three-story building that presented three white-shuttered windows to the street. Dexter's own chamber was hung with prints of English judges and contained, in neat stacks rising to the ceiling, the firm's small library. The heavy figure of Jules Bleeker moved slowly back and forth before the desk at which his unwilling host was motionlessly seated. The visitor spoke in a cold, speculative tone.

"My first impulse was to call you out, but I knew that would do no good. You burghers don't fight. Then I thought of coming to your office with a horsewhip. But that would have been playing into your hands. Your friends on the bench would have had me in jail for a year or more. And finally, thinking it over, I began to cool off. I began to be even interested in what had happened to me. What sort of a man are you, Fairchild? Or are you a man at all?"

"What I am need not concern you."

"Oh, but it does concern me. I find myself without a job and without a friend in a city of locked front doors. How the hell did you do it? And why? You're not her husband. You're not even a blood relation." Here Bleeker paused to stare at his adversary. "It couldn't be that you're in love with her yourself?" He shook his head slowly as Dexter failed to move a muscle. "No, that would be impossible for a snowman like you."

"You have lived too much abroad. You can't be expected to understand the motives of a simple American gentleman."

"Maybe you're not a snowman, after all. Be frank, Fairchild. If you did it out of jealousy, I'd forgive you. I might even shake your hand!"

Dexter rose, to terminate the interview. "We could talk all night and never understand each other. What's the use of it?" He paused briefly. "There is, however, one more thing. If you are in possession of any letters from Mrs. Charles Fairchild, I should be willing to pay a good price for them."

Bleeker stared. "You think I'd *sell* them?" Then he laughed bitterly. "Oh, of course. The bounder is beaten, so he's supposed to crumple. Or, like Shylock, to renounce his faith. Only you have the wrong script, Fairchild. In mine, the villain turns on his prosecutor with a splendid defiance. You can take your proposition and cram it up the aperture — if indeed a snowman has one — in the nether part of your frozen body!"

Dexter sniffed in distaste. "I suppose I should expect such talk from you."

"You will be relieved to hear that I am removing myself from your city. I have had a standing invitation to come to Richmond and write a column for the *Enquirer*. It will be pleasant to be among gentlemen again. Perhaps I can warn them about what they are up against. They think, because they know how to fight bravely, that they will prevail in a struggle with men of straw and men of ice, such as I have met up here. But they may be wrong. If your millions of labor-slaves are ever harnessed into an army and sent into bloody battle by such remorseless bigots as you, who can tell the outcome?"

"Who indeed? May God preserve our union! *Keep* your letters. Annie can't be hurt by the likes of you!"

Jules burst into a harsh, raucous laugh. "Annie! That teasing, tantalizing little bitch? Do you honestly think she'd give one holy goddam if I told the world she copulated with sailors every Saturday night on a public pier?"

"Get out of my office!" cried Dexter, livid.

"You don't know her, Fairchild!"

"Get out of here!"

"I can't go fast enough."

※　　※　　※

When Dexter left his office, shortly after Bleeker had gone, it was to make his weekly call, on his way home, at his mother's house on Fourteenth Street. Mrs. Fairchild lived in a tiny brownstone, with only two round-topped windows to each of its four stories and with a snug but cluttered interior in which the handsome, austere Federal pieces of her prosperous days were fitted in among the beaded curtains and strewn shawls and tasseled cushions of her widowhood. But its small, vivacious, chattering proprietor, whose lips seemed to keep time with the eager fingers that darted at her needlepoint, managed to dominate and somehow harmonize the scene.

"It's this business of Aunt Serena's will. I know you're sick and tired of the subject, but I want you to listen to me. There are seventeen residuary legatees, including myself, all nephews and nieces. But the bequest of the Alberta Mine stock to the three Stocktons, who are only the remotest sort of cousins, comes to as much as the whole residuary estate. Now you *know* Aunt Serena never intended that! Besides, she was eighty-nine and thoroughly addled."

"Are you trying to tell me, Mother, that she didn't recognize the natural objects of her testamentary bounty?"

"What do you mean? Don't push your legal jargon at me!"

"The law has its tests for testamentary competence. Did Aunt Serena know that she had an estate to dispose of and who were her closest relatives? I suggest she did."

"But it was all so hazy to her!"

Dexter closed his eyes. He was in a cool green forest by a sylvan pool. He was a satyr, tawny and strong, his lower regions clad in shaggy pants which might and probably would, with a little pulling, slip off, to expose him, erect, splendidly prepared, to the naked wood nymph, all pale, shimmering skin and loose, damp dark hair, who cupped her little breasts in her hands and hooted at him with mocking laughter.

"Dexter, are you listening? John Hone was in to see me this afternoon. He says that if the seventeen residuary legatees get together and allege that Aunt Serena didn't know what she was doing when she signed that will . . ."

"Even when she named you as her residuary legatees?"

"Well, John says that if we knock the will out, we'll take the whole estate. By the law of . . . what do you call it?"

"Intestacy. And you won't mind going into court and stating under oath that Aunt Serena was insane?"

"But it's just a *formality*, Dexter!"

The nymph was now accompanied by other naked nymphs, but his eyes were only for her. Laughing, shrieking, they surrounded him to push him in the pool. They pulled him and pushed him, and he felt her fingers under the belt of his shaggy pants . . .

"I'm sorry, Mother, but I can't represent you in this. I believe that Aunt Serena, if a bit vague, was nonetheless essentially of sound mind."

"But, Dexter, you know I won't go to court unless you represent me! This is *too* mean of you!"

The pants suddenly swooped to his ankles, and slowly, menacingly, he stepped out of them. The other nymphs fled away screaming, but she remained. She cowered against the damp black rock where a water slide fed the little pool, her bent back and pinched buttocks before him, her head turning slowly around . . .

"When the good lord distributed consciences, my boy, he gave you more than your share. But it's your old mother who has to pay the price for it!"

Dexter, looking up at his mother now, felt a strange immunity to her reproaches. All his life he had been afraid of disappointing her, as if her image of him had been a kind of ideal that he could only live by constantly aspiring to. She was the brave little woman who had battled for him in adversity, who had cadged his tuition expenses from richer relatives, who had sold her last bits of family jewelry to dress him like a gentleman. It was true that he had paid it all back, and more, but what were such payments, made when he was established, in contrast to what she had given him through the sweat, so to speak, of her social brow? No, the very essence of a debt to a mother was that it was unredeemable, like the pangs of childbirth. And now he no longer cared to redeem it. That was the difference.

"You know you don't really need that money, Mother. Jane and I will always look after you."

Where was the nymph? He felt a sudden shocking sense of loss. Ah, there she was! She had laid herself down, stretched out on the bank, bold as brass, shameless, smiling provocatively up at him. Now she was slowly raising her knees . . .

"Oh, Dexter, go home! You're not paying any attention to what I'm saying."

He left his mother without regret, almost without apology, and that same evening he was aware of a similar independence with respect to his wife. They were at dinner at Mr. Handy's at Number 417, as they so often were, a family party consisting of the old man, his four daughters and three sons-in-law. Dexter noted that Rosalie kept glancing at him with annoyance as he stared down the table at Annie. And he hardly cared!

"The Democrats are bound to split," Mr. Handy was saying. "There's no other way. The Southern Democrats are intransigent. I assume the Northern party will nominate Senator Douglas. And I shall certainly vote for him. To avoid certain warfare."

"I'm not sure I shan't find myself casting my vote for the Southern candidate," Rutgers Van Rensselaer stated with much throat-clearing. He was stout, bushy-haired, with a dangerously scarlet complexion. "You'll probably all call me a Simon Legree, but I can't see it's any affair of mine what they do with their niggers."

"Rutgers is thinking about his phosphate mine in Georgia," Charley Fairchild observed with a wink. Everyone at the table was surprised to hear him speak, as he had seemed absorbed in his wine glass and in signaling to the waitress to keep it filled. "We don't want that confiscated, do we?"

"Well, some of us at least have property to worry about!"

"Don't mind him, Rutgers," Mr. Handy cautioned his oldest son-in-law. "Charley is only trying to get your goat. What about you, Dexter?"

"I'm keeping an eye on Lincoln, sir."

"Bully for you!" Joanna exclaimed with a little clap of her hands.

Her father glared at her. "The election of Lincoln will lead to secession," he announced solemnly.

"Not necessarily, sir," Dexter objected. "He is pleading for moderation. It is true that he once invoked the God of Hosts, but recently he has been toning down his speeches." He turned now to Annie. "What about you? Who are you for?"

She answered his gaze with the same directness. "What does it matter? I have no vote."

"You might influence one."

"Whose? Charley's?" She laughed bitterly, without even looking at her husband. "Why should I care about slaves? I'm one myself."

"A slave with a rather long chain," Charley sneered, and there was a moment of general constraint.

"You should be for helping the slaves if you *are* one," Rosalie reproached her.

"And you, my dear, who are *you* for?" Mr. Handy asked.

"Oh, I think the time has passed for talking," Rosalie replied with a sigh. "We've talked and we've talked and we've talked, and where has it got anybody?"

Dexter reflected that the slavery question had destroyed

all good conversation. One knew how one's friends stood on every point; dinner parties were like endless dress rehearsals for a dull play. Nobody had any true objectivity; they simply took the point of view that answered their immediate needs. Rutgers cared for his mine; Joanna needed a cause to make up for the lack of a husband; Charley sided against anyone he disliked; even Mr. Handy was devoted to his own image as a peacemaker, operating with the cigars and brandy behind the social scene. And wasn't Rosalie looking out for her soul? And Annie? What was Annie looking for?

As he looked at her again now, she seemed the only real person in the room. Her white skin, her dark eyes and hair, were real. Her marriage, which he had patched up, seemed as shabby and rotten as the union of North and South. Who had cared about it but he? Had not all New York, *his* New York, been willing to wink at adultery and accept the separation of spouses? It had been only when he had raised the banner of the sanctity of marriage that the others had reluctantly fallen into line. Once the sacred words had been spoken, the revolt had been quelled. But did he want to do it again? Did even *he* care anymore?

That night, when he and Rosalie were back in Union Square, he asked her to come with him for a moment to the library. As if she had anticipated some such move, she went at once to the fireplace and, sitting on a stool before the grate, leaned forward to apply a match to the prepared paper and logs. Standing behind her, he watched the slow start of the fire.

"I know that you are doing something that's probably illegal," he began. "I don't want to know about it. But I'm willing to pay for it. I shall give you five thousand dollars for anything you like. And there will be more later."

She did not turn around; she did not answer him for at least a minute. Then she asked, "Is this a bribe?"

"You may call it what you like. It has no strings attached."

"You mean it's for your conscience? Very well. I'll take the money. You're right about my doing something. It's in a good cause."

"Don't tell me about it! Let me simply say that I admire you."

She was silent, as if thinking this over. But he was not to have her comment. "Why don't you go to bed, Dexter?" she suggested at last, still facing the grate. "I think I'll sit and watch by the fire a bit."

13

THE AFFAIR started a week after his silent compact with
Rosalie. Leaving the office early one afternoon he told
Charley that he was going to his house to discuss Annie's
new will with her. Charley, who started his drinking now at
noon, looked up from a desk bare of paper to give his cousin
a long stare and then, quite deliberately, winked.

"Put in a nice little trust for me, will you?"

Dexter did not deign to answer him.

The Charles Fairchilds' house stood directly across Union
Square from their cousins'. Dexter, standing in the bow
window of Annie's blue drawing room, done in the latest
deuxième empire style, looked down to where a nurse was
departing for a walk with little Kate. Then he glanced across
to his own abode. Its blank façade seemed to proclaim that
Rosalie was not in. Where was she? At some secret meeting
in an abandoned warehouse? He shrugged. Annie's voice
came from the sofa behind him.

"I knew my will bored *me*. But it really must be very

boring if it bores you. Or are you lost in the arcane mysteries of a distribution *per stirpes* and not *per capita*?"

"I'm not thinking of your will. I'm thinking about you."

"Well, that's better. I like that much better. Tell me what you're thinking about me."

"I can't see you this way anymore. You've got to be all mine or none. Charley doesn't care. And I've squared Rosalie."

Turning now, he caught the flicker of triumph in her eyes. But it was only a flicker. Nothing could take the place of her curiosity for long. "How on earth have you squared Rosalie?"

"I've given her money for her causes. Whatever they are. Whatever she wants."

"And she let you off for that? How curious! You don't suppose *she* has a Juley concealed somewhere?"

"Please don't speak of her that way."

"I'm not good enough? Is that it?"

He took a step towards her but stopped. "It's not that. It's just that she has nothing to do with you and me. Nobody has. But I can't make love to you in Charley's house."

"Actually it's mine. You should know that. You drew the deed. I can make love to anyone I choose in it!" She stretched her arms out invitingly along the back of the divan. "But I think I'm going to have to give you some lessons first. You're too intense. Not that it isn't a good way to start. But after a bit of it a lady likes something gentler. Come and sit by me."

He shook his head gravely. "I can't even touch you in this house. It's Charley's home, whoever owns it."

"What are we to do then? Take to the streets?"

"Have you ever known me to be unprepared? I've rented a little house in South Vesey Street. I've engaged a discreet, decent sort of woman as housekeeper. I've hired a cab that can meet you any time outside Grace Church, take you to the house, wait and bring you back. The driver won't even know where you live. The woman at the house won't even know who you are. You can be veiled. There'll be absolutely no risk."

Annie's eyes were fastened upon his as he told her this, her lips parted in a half-smile. "It seems to me that you take me rather for granted. Imagine going to all that expense without even asking me if I would come!"

"Do I take my life for granted? What's the expense to me? What have I to lose? If you don't come, I shan't care about anything."

She brought her hands smartly together. "Oh, let us hope you won't be reduced to that sorry state! Of course, I'll come. Shall we say tomorrow? I know you like to do things formally. Good! Have your cabby parked across the street from Grace Church at two o'clock. Right? Tell him to pick up a lady in a blue hat with a veil." She threw back her head and burst into her high laugh. "I hope it will be the right one!"

When she came to South Vesey Street the next day, as agreed, tightly veiled and clad in a long blue coat that covered all her dress and presented a vertical line of pearl buttons from her neck to her ankles, he found himself as shy and awkward as a boy of twelve at his first dancing class. Annie, without taking off her veil, perched primly on the edge of a chair.

"Aren't you even going to show me your face?"

"Is that all you want to see?"

"It might do for a beginning."

"You men are so crude."

Was she joking? He had no idea.

"Perhaps you will allow me to raise your veil?"

She moved back in alarm as he approached. "Don't touch me!"

"I'm sorry."

She relaxed, and he sat in a chair beside her, but at a respectful distance.

"May I hold your hand?"

She stretched out a small black-gloved hand which he took in his. After another moment she allowed him to remove the glove. But when he reached for the other hand she drew it sharply back.

"Maybe this is enough. For the first day, anyway. You must learn to be very gentle with me!"

Dexter felt almost sick with frustration and disenchantment. Was this the bold dryad of his fantasies? Should he be firm with her? Should he even be rough? But no, no, perhaps all women were like this in the beginning. He would have to play it her way.

But as soon as he rose, to conclude the interview, she raised her veil. Her eyes were laughing at him.

"Where is the bedroom, Dexter?"

When, trembling with apprehension and desire, he opened the door to it, she turned to bar his entrance. "Come back," she said softly. "In exactly fifteen minutes. You needn't knock."

"My darling!"

She snickered. "Lucky Rosalie! Fifteen years of a husband's total fidelity! How many wives can boast of that?"

His hand held the closing door. "How do you know I've been so faithful to Rosalie?"

"In affairs we can make statements. But we never ask questions! Remember! Fifteen minutes exactly."

And then, firmly, she closed the door.

*　　*　　*

It seemed to Dexter, in the weeks that followed, that his life had simply erupted, like a rocket on the Fourth of July, into bright little pieces, yellow and blue and fiery red, all over a black and starless sky. It was not only that he seemed never to have lived before those passionate encounters in South Vesey Street; it was as if he no longer lived anywhere else. He went through his days like a somnambulist. He got through his work at the office adequately, but very slowly. He found that he was more patient with subordinates, caring less as he did now, about the results of their labors. He was able to talk at breakfast with his sons on general matters and on their personal ones, and he could chatter away with his lady companions at dinner parties. The eternal topics of slavery and secession seemed to him like the banal, tinkling music of a hotel band playing behind potted palms while the customers dined. Existence was a comedy, a rather dreary comedy pacing its slow way through a second season. Life had reduced itself to South Vesey Street.

Annie's emotional life was less constricted by their new relationship. If she enjoyed their lovemaking, as she certainly did, she enjoyed the drama preceding it and the drama following quite as much. She liked putting on her veil and making her mysterious way to Grace Church; she liked making friends with the dazzled old housekeeper of the rented house; she liked dressing herself in shawls that only partly covered her nudity and approaching Dexter like some Eastern princess. She liked to undress him and to say obscene things and laugh at his shocked expression. The act of love that was so completely, so almost stunningly satisfying to him, was only a climax to her. Whereas he wanted to be either in bed with her, in the closest embrace, or altogether away from her to think back on it, she wanted to linger and dally, to lie naked on the bear rug, to talk and giggle and sip wine. When she taxed him with being a brute who wanted only one thing, he admitted it freely.

"But it's because you're so consummate an artist in the rites of love! You make everything else seem trivial."

She did not appear to consider this altogether a compliment. "Maybe that feeling is a family characteristic. Charley is a bit that way. Oh, I don't really compare him with you, darling. He lacks your forcefulness. But he does have a way of rolling off into a snoring sleep after he's satisfied himself."

Dexter jumped up indignantly and tied the ends of the belt to his silk robe tightly together. He averted his eyes, in frank distaste, from her sprawled nakedness.

"I beg you not to talk about Charley. The subject revolts me."

"Really, darling, at times you can be an awful prude."

"I am what I am. Our room here is sacred to me. I don't see how you can bring in such thoughts, such images. Charley snoring! My God, Annie! Have you *no* sensitivity? Or no respect for mine?"

"I don't ask about you and Rosalie. Oh, la, la!"

"Annie!"

"All right, all right. Don't look at me that way. I know you don't like me lolling about in the nude." She sat up in a pet and slipped into her dressing gown, buttoning it care-

fully up to her neck. "There! Am I decent enough? Now
that his lordship has taken his pleasure?"

"Annie, I *am* a brute. Forgive me. Take it off, and we'll
make love again."

"No, no! Enough is enough! I don't want you to have a
heart attack. Not here certainly. Besides, I know you want
to get back to your office. And I have a fitting at four-thirty."

"You say *I'm* unromantic. How can you think of a fitting
at a time like this?"

"A woman can always think of a fitting. And do you know
something else? I hate the huggermugger of all this. I'd like
to flaunt you to all New York!"

"Dearest, you know, we've had all that out. We can't do
it to our children, our spouses, your father . . ."

"Father!" Annie gave a little scream of laughter. "He's
probably smelled us out long ago, the old fox. How you
worship him! But no, I don't mean for you to go over all those
grounds again. I've accepted them! Still, a girl can dream,
can't she? I like to dream of being a courtesan in Paris."

"I guess lots of girls dream of that. But it's a rotten life,
really. Those poor creatures may have jewels and carriages,
but they end up in the wards of public hospitals."

"Oh, a truce to your public hospitals! I want to tell you
about the dream I had last night. You were a duke or a field
marshal or something frightfully swell, and I was a *grande
cocotte* who was costing you millions. Yes, darling, millions!
Not just a little house in South Vesey Street that you'll relet
for a spanking profit the day after you tire of me. And I rode
through the Bois at noon with diamonds bigger than the
Empress's! I was the toast of the Jockey Club! Oh, yes, I was
ruining you, the way I ruined all the men I loved. The way

I should probably even ruin the muscular little dancer with the beautiful thighs from the opera ballet, whom I saw on weekends when you were off with the Emperor at Compiègne!"

He placed his hands over her lips.

"Annie," he pleaded. "Is nothing sacred to you? Nothing at all?"

"Don't you know what's sacred to me, silly? Let me go now. I have to get dressed."

14

HE FOUND ROSALIE a continuing enigma. He had no idea
whether or not she had divined the existence of the house at
South Vesey Street. On the day after she had accepted the
five thousand dollars she had complained of a cold and had
suggested that he avoid contagion by sleeping on a cot in
his dressing room. He observed that she manifested no signs
of illness and made no move to reinstate their old sleeping
arrangements after her supposed indisposition should have
run its course. A separation from bed, if not from board, had
been effected, and without the exchange of a single reproach.
How many lawyers could have accomplished that?

Her daily manner with him was carefully natural, a bit
matter-of-fact, perhaps a touch dry. She would discuss household and family plans in front of the boys and the maids, but
when they were alone together she always had a book or a
newspaper or a work basket and did not try to make conversation.

Their arrangement, if arrangement it could be called, was
at once a relief and a torture to him. He wanted to ask her
what she was really feeling. He wanted to explain to her

that what had happened was perfectly consistent with his love for her. That it might even be consistent with continued sexual relations. But how could he say anything at all without revealing the existence of a relationship of which she might still be ignorant? And how could she, if it were flung in her face, not resent it? Not denounce it? All she seemed to be asking of him was that he should maintain the appearance of decency, and how could he refuse a betrayed wife that?

It helped, anyway, that she was so busy. He suspected that she was somehow breaking the law, and although he had lost most of his interest in national events in his absorption with South Vesey Street, he almost felt that he would welcome an exposure, even an arrest — any incident that would give him the chance to stand out publicly as Rosalie's supporter and to share her punishment. It might make the load of his debt to her less intolerable.

One day when he happened to be uptown in the middle of the morning and had gone to Union Square to spend an hour in his library between appointments, he had an experience that made him think that such a crisis was not entirely fantastical. He had let himself into the house with his latch key, so that his presence at his desk was presumably unknown to the household. Hearing a step in the corridor he called out:

"Is that you, Bridey? Don't worry. It's only me."

As total silence followed, he walked to the door and found himself facing a negro boy of some fourteen years of age. For a long moment the two simply stared intently at each other. Dexter observed that the boy was dressed in one of Fred's suits. It was obviously too big for him.

"And who may you be, my lad?"

The boy without a word turned and fled upstairs. It was as if history had broken rudely into Dexter's personal pre-occupations. He promptly quit the house and passed the balance of his hour walking rapidly on Broadway. That evening Rosalie faced him with a different expression, one that almost suggested contrition.

"You saw that boy today. I'm sorry. It won't happen again. He and his mother were in a place that had become suspect. I had to take them in here for the day."

"Please, Rosalie! Do it again! Do it whenever you want."

She glanced at him with a faint smile. "Dear me, are you as guilty as all *that*?"

"I only want to help!"

"Very well. I accept your help."

Charley was almost as enigmatic as Rosalie. He had developed what to Dexter was the odious habit of addressing him in the office in a half-bantering, half-sarcastic tone, always implying that Dexter, whenever he left the office earlier than usual, had a "secret conference" with an "important client uptown." Dexter would stolidly ignore his implication and give a coldly literal construction to everything his cousin said. He no longer tried to moderate Charley's drinking or to stimulate him to greater industry. He simply saw to it that his partner's legal duties were fulfilled by associates.

Did Charley know? Did Charley even care? Had Annie thrown her infidelity in his teeth? She was quite capable of it. She was beginning already to be careless about her trips to and from South Vesey Street. Once she had come in her own hired cab without waiting for their private one.

"Do you know something?" he asked her, after they had made love and were having the now customary glass of wine. "You didn't have your veil on when you got out of that cab."

"You were watching for me from the window? I like that!"

"But you were exposing yourself. Supposing someone saw you?"

"Oh, do let's suppose it! What do you think would happen?"

"I'm afraid it might be the end of the world. Our world, anyway."

"Would it be in all the papers? 'Adultery in Manhattan society!' 'Insular incest!' "

"Charley would certainly divorce you. Rosalie would probably divorce me. My law practice would be ruined."

"Decidedly, I must remember to don my veil!"

But something in her tone made him now wonder if he, too, might not try to see their situation in terms of high comedy. Was it really essential to be so grave? Might he not learn from her not only the delights of love but a more balanced view of the universe?

"Maybe I'm worrying about the wrong thing," he mused. "Maybe such a discovery would help to liberate us. We could snap our fingers at the world and say: 'All right! So we *are* lovers. Do your worst!' "

Annie still smiled, but her eyelids just flickered. "What has made you so suddenly bold?"

"You!"

"I promise to be more careful."

But her hesitation had only the effect of making him more precipitous. He saw his whole life collapse under a raging, cleansing stream.

"We could go abroad! I could learn to practice international law. We could live in Paris. Oh, Annie, we'd be free to start all over again!"

She made a little face. "How can you forget all the things you told me about that? People slamming doors in my face? The misery of second-rate acquaintances in third-rate watering places? Is that what you're offering me now, Dexter?"

"But it would be different with me!" he cried indignantly. "I'm no Jules Bleeker! You and I would have the kind of life together that would make serious people respect us. In time, anyway. And while we were waiting for that, we'd have ourselves. My boys will soon be old enough to make up their own minds about what parent they'll see or not see. I'm sure I could persuade them to accept our love!"

"And what about my Kate, who's only five?"

"Well, why wait till we're discovered? Why not go off now? Then we could take Kate with us!"

Annie rose and firmly took his glass away from him. "I think we'll go on as we're going, thank you very much. I have never heard a better argument for a clandestine affair!"

Deflated, he managed nonetheless to continue their talk on a joking level. But he was aware that he had been bitterly hurt. It was a distinct shock to have to recognize that just as he was making, however tentatively, the emotional preparations to build their affair into an independent universe, she was making hers for keeping it well within its original bounds. If he had begun to be ashamed of treating her as something private, something secret, something "owned," it was a dubious solace to his conscience to discover that she was perfectly content to go on treating him the same way!

When she had gone he chose to walk all the way home, although the day was overcast and drizzling. It gave him the opportunity to assemble and analyze his impressions of himself. The strange new heaviness at the bottom of his heart, as he now began to make it out, was the result of his recognition that his asylum from the world was no asylum at all. In the very violence of his physical satisfaction he had been professing, paradoxical as it might have seemed, to perceive a kind of spiritual rebirth, at least in the sense that it had created a new Dexter Fairchild, who existed apart from the tensions and frustrations that had beset the old. And Annie had seemed a kind of goddess, embraced by a mortal, having no existence, at least for him, outside of South Vesey Street. The love between them had been an entity complete in itself, existing, so to speak, in a void, a love that knew neither jealousy, nor falling off, nor bickering, nor even simple ennui. But now the doors of his foolishness, his stubborn, deliberate foolishness, had been thrust apart, and he was back again with all the misery of a merely human relationship.

On Monday, the day of their next appointment, Annie did not come at all. In an agony of jealousy and resentment he broke one of their primary rules and called at her house in Union Square. Word was brought to him that Mrs. Fairchild was resting in her room, but when he insisted on seeing her, she came down to the drawing room, irate, in a dressing gown.

"Will you kindly tell me why you have taken leave of your senses?"

"You didn't come!"

"I had a headache. There was no way of sending you word."

"You could have had a nap in our house. I wouldn't have

disturbed you. As it is, I've been half-crazed, wondering if anything was wrong!"

"But that's perfectly ridiculous. You've got to get hold of yourself. And now you must go. I'm going out to dinner tonight, and I have to rest."

"Where are you going?"

"I don't know why that's any affair of yours. But, as it happens, I don't mind telling you. I'm going to the Fearings'."

"The Henry Fearings?"

"Yes."

"That . . . that *ogler*! Is Charley going?"

"As a matter of fact, he's not. He'll be at the Patroons'. Charley and I have been rather going our separate ways these days. As you, of all people, should know."

"Well, I suppose it's all right. Mrs. Fearing will be there, of course."

"No, she won't. She's with a sick aunt in Trenton. Henry has asked me to be a good friend and act as his hostess."

"But that's not decent!"

"Dexter, you're being absolutely idiotic. Henry and I are second cousins. One does that sort of thing for cousins."

"Not for second cousins. I can't allow it."

"*You* can't allow it! Go home!"

She turned away abruptly and hurried upstairs. To have followed her would have been to create a scandal, and Dexter had no alternative but to leave.

He was horribly afraid that she would not appear at their next appointment, but she did. She made no reference to their argument until after they had made love and he was pouring their wine.

"We have to get something straight, my dear. Outside this house you are to have no say whatever over my actions. It's bad enough to have one husband. I have no idea of being saddled with two."

She smiled as she said this, but her tone had a touch of frost.

"How can you expect me to turn my love on and off?"

"That's your business. All I'm telling you is that if we are to continue meeting, we are each to have complete freedom of action, except under this roof."

"You don't love me!" he cried in anguish.

"Did I ever say I did? What I feel for you you should know by now. There is no point in giving it a name. I don't think I could ever feel anything for a man at the cost of being his slave. That was one of my troubles with Charley. I shall certainly not make the same mistake with another. Particularly not with another Fairchild!"

"You want to go to parties! You want to flirt with men!"

"Certainly. If I choose."

"You want to make love with them!"

"No, you are quite enough for that. Almost too much, if anything. You may rest assured that you will be my only lover."

He reeled under the unexpected shock of this reassurance. "Always?"

"Always? What rational human being could promise that?"

"Well, for how long, then?"

"Until I tell you. I shan't deceive you. So you see? There's nothing to be jealous about. Nothing even to worry about. And you, of course, will have the same freedom."

The more that Dexter thought about this, the less he was able reasonably to object to it. The only trouble was that it had nothing whatever to do with passion. And now he discovered that he had a new dread: not that Annie would tell him a lie but that she would tell him the truth. Every time that she appeared, or failed to appear, in South Vesey Street, he would wonder if she was about to greet him, or send him a note, with the news that she had found another lover. It began to seem to him that his whole existence had come to depend on silence: Annie's, Rosalie's, Charley's, the world's. Words had become thunderbolts, and speakers avenging gods. He made love to Annie with a fierceness that seemed almost a revenge that he was only a fantasy to her.

He knew that she was bound to tire of her fantasy, because she was bound to tire of the few little facts that constituted its base. But he had never really fooled himself that his dream was going to last forever. Everything in Annie's nature from the beginning had bespoken her essential fickleness, and some of the drive with which he thrust himself into her arose from his need to make her a more lasting part of himself. Yet he knew that this could never be done, just as he knew that the very transiency of her passion was part of its appeal. There was even a kind of horrible relief in his knowing that this madness had its own finale built into it, and some of the violence of his passion went into a kind of cold storage to be used for consoling memories on the day that the affair should end. He lived on two levels: one where everything yielded to his senses and another where he measured those senses with the eye of an observer who knew that never again would such heights or such depths be achieved. He was like a Faust who had sold his soul to the devil, but who would carry with him to hell a diary of his days of bliss.

15

THERE WAS NO WAY that Dexter could get himself invited without Rosalie to the parties that Annie was attending, and it was too much, even for a man as disturbed as himself, to expect Rosalie to go with him to spy on her sister. But when Annie let fall at one of their meetings that she was going to a ball to be given that night by his own sister, he privately determined that he would present himself there.

Jane Ullman did not ask her brother and sister-in-law to all her parties, or even to all of her larger ones; a coolness had long existed between her and Rosalie. The latter had made it a bit too clear that she had no wish to be used as a knight or bishop, or even as a pawn, in the Ullmans' social game. She was perfectly happy, she had told too many persons, to accept everything about David Ullman but his aspirations, and Jane, like many of those married to social climbers, having had to accept her share of snubs, was all the more sensitive to even a fancied one in a relative. So the two families met mainly on family occasions.

David Ullman had purchased a large corner brownstone

at Twentieth Street and Fifth Avenue, and had encased it in white marble and added a ballroom in the rear. It was universally known as the "marble brownstone." Jane had packed the long hallway to the ballroom with potted plants and banks of flowers so that when Dexter saw her, tall, blond, straight and very thin, standing under the arched doorway in white satin and diamonds, she might have been a fairy princess. Only on closer approach, as he recognized the middle-aged squareness of the Fairchild chin, was the image blurred.

"I thought you might need an extra man for your dance," he said, as she presented, rather gingerly, a cheek for his fraternal kiss. "Rosalie's away somewhere, and I was lonely sitting home."

"I'm delighted, my dear." Jane's tone a bit reflected the marble of her mansion's exterior. "You shall be my partner in the cotillion. David never dances."

"That's very kind of you, but I'm sure somebody more important should be so honored. Don't you think I ought to ask my sister-in-law? Charley's not here, is he?"

"No. Charley is not here."

"Then shouldn't I keep an eye on Annie?"

"Is she inclined to misbehave?"

"Not at all. But a girl so young and lively, going about without her husband . . . well, some young blade might get the wrong idea, mightn't he?"

"Might he? When she's chaperoned by her sister's husband — unaccompanied by her sister?"

Dexter ignored her irony. "Well, that's just it. She needs a chaperon. Rosalie's been worried about her."

"So Rosalie sent you tonight, did she?"

Really, she was as spiteful as when they were children!

"It's not Annie's fault. She has a hard time with Charley, you know."

"No, I don't know, Dexter."

"Well, he drinks."

"Dear me!" exclaimed Jane, who was perfectly aware of Charley's habits. "What a pity she didn't marry a Jew. That's so rarely a problem with them."

Dexter left her at this and moved into the ballroom where a waltz was in progress. Annie, in a golden dress, was dancing with great animation with his eighteen-year-old nephew, David, Jr., who was obviously entranced with his vivacious and sophisticated "older woman" partner. She evinced no surprise when she spotted Dexter, giving him only a brief "family" smile. But its very briefness seemed to indicate that she had no intention of confusing South Vesey Street with Fifth Avenue. Determined to dance with no one but her, he walked past the mirrored doors crowned with ivy to the table where champagne was being served to the gentlemen. As he sipped from his glass and gazed about the room, he suddenly froze at the vision of a large, hulking figure in black bowing to their hostess.

It was Jules Bleeker.

What was almost as unsettling as the hated sight of his former rival was the latter's behavior. Recognizing Dexter across the room, he simply raised a heavy arm in casual greeting and turned back to the group with whom he had come.

Dexter, beside himself, hurried off in search of his brother-in-law. He found the latter standing alone in an alcove, smoking a cigar and watching the dancers with a rather supercilious air. David, who had been anxious enough in the earlier days to have people come to his parties, had now, at sixty, achieved a sufficient social security to permit him to condescend to such frivolities as dancing. His concentration was more on the inner world of power. He would, for example, have given much to belong to the gentlemen's discussion group known as the Hone Club that met at its members' houses for monthly dinners. But Mr. Handy, the chairman, still drew the line at Jews.

"Good evening, Dexter. I'm surprised to see you here. I thought you were too serious a man for these affairs. Your sister seems to take a perverse pride in assembling under one roof the heaviest jewels and the lightest heads of the city. But perhaps you view it all as a student of manners, eh? Good! These idiots should be put to some use."

David was a fine-looking man for his age, with a good strong figure and smart, if slightly too elegant clothes, a noble brow and jaw and dark, receding hair, but he was just a bit too cocky, just a bit too sure that the sharpness of his intellect and the power of his money would awe his fellow burghers. Dexter, who liked to think that he had no prejudices, was yet troubled by the fact that he was most conscious of David's Jewishness when he dwelt on David's defects. He wondered if even Mr. Handy was not basically more tolerant than he. The latter was frankly anti-Semitic until it was to his smallest interest to cultivate a Jew, and then he would drop his animus as easily as a ship captain might dispose of surplus cargo in a storm.

"I certainly share your opinion as to *one* of your guests," Dexter replied. "Only that if he's an idiot, he's a rather dangerous one. I had thought that every decent door in New York had been closed to Mr. Bleeker."

David's eyebrows were arched. "My dear fellow, where have you been? All that is quite forgotten. Jules Bleeker is the chairman of a committee of Richmond businessmen who have come to New York to explore the ways and means of preserving the union. There's a meeting next week at your own father-in-law's."

Dexter gaped. "At Number 417?"

"Yes, sir! At the sacred 417. I'm going there myself. You weren't asked?"

"Perhaps it's because I told him I was for Lincoln."

"Or perhaps because Mr. Handy thought it might be a bit embarrassing for you and Bleeker to meet! After all, you did make the town rather hot for him."

"But I still can't understand it. Mr. Handy knows all about Bleeker!"

"You mean about that business with Rosalie's sister?" David, however lofty, liked it to be known that he was abreast of every piece of scandal in society. "Evidently he regards Annie as being in no further danger."

"Did she know Bleeker would be here tonight?"

David burst into a rough laugh. "My dear Dexter, do you think even an international banker can read a lady's mind?"

Dexter left him, fuming at his own indiscretion. Did all New York know about him and Annie? The idea made him suddenly reckless, and he approached the group where Annie was standing. It was during an intermission between dances.

"May I have a word with you?" he asked loudly.

Nobody looked surprised. It was a brother-in-law's prerogative. Or *was* that the reason? Annie raised her eyebrows slightly and moved with him to a less crowded part of the dance floor. "You're not very discreet."

"Discretion be damned! I came to tell you that if you dance with Bleeker I shall strike him in the face!"

Her eyes glittered. "You wouldn't dare!"

"You'll see."

"You're going to be sorry about this."

"That's my affair."

"I warned you that I should not tolerate any interference with my social life!"

"You are absolutely free. Except with that bounder!"

"Some freedom! Very well. I shall go home. Not, let me make it entirely clear, for *your* sake. But for Juley's. I want to spare him the embarrassment of having to knock you down!"

She turned and walked in rapid short steps to the doorway and disappeared. He simply stood staring stupidly after her until he felt his sister's presence at his side.

"You're making an absolute spectacle of yourself!" she hissed. "I'll thank you not to use my house as a *maison de passe!*"

❖   ❖   ❖

Annie did not appear in South Vesey Street at their next appointment, but this came as little surprise to Dexter. He waited until five and then went uptown to pay his weekly "business call" on his mother.

"Please put away those papers, Dexter. I have something much more important to discuss with you today. You know I've never been one to beat about the bush. How long is this shocking business between you and Annie Fairchild going to continue?"

Dexter seemed to be seeing the incensed little woman before him with the drowsy, half-curious eyes of a man who is being shaken out of a deep and absorbing dream.

"I suppose Jane made a great thing about that little scene at her house."

"Jane is not my only source of information!"

"Well, you know how people gossip."

"Does that mean you're going to deny it?"

"I don't see why I should dignify such an accusation with a denial. You lay a grave charge at my door. What is your evidence? Have I been seen with Annie in some place we shouldn't have been? Have we been spotted slipping in and out of doorways in shady parts of town?"

"Do you presume to act like a defense lawyer with your own mother?"

"Certainly. When she acts like a prosecutor."

Mrs. Fairchild's fingers worked furiously with her needlepoint. Her brow was puckered, and she kept her snapping eyes directed at her work. His attitude, so different from his customary deference, had evidently taken her aback. "I simply say that your intimacy with your wife's sister — not to mention that she's the wife of your own first cousin and law partner — is on its way to making you the talk of the town. I don't presume even to suggest how far this intimacy may have carried you. In these things the appearance is quite as good as the fact. You're sitting on a barrel of dynamite, my son. Be warned!"

Dexter reflected that if his mother had had wind of the house in South Vesey Street she would certainly have mentioned it. She had never been one to hoard her trumps. But it was also more than possible that Annie had been indiscreet. Could she have resisted hinting of her affair to some of her girl friends? It would have been too humiliating to have them believe that she was without consolation while Charley made love to a bottle.

"Have any of my in-laws been complaining?"

"No, I'll say that for them. The Handys have been perfect.

But then what else could they do? The scandal of a thing
like this would be more than any family could bear, even
one of their station. No, they must sit on their tempers and
smile at the world. Trust old Charles Handy to keep them
in line!"

"In that case, what is there to worry about?"

"Dexter Fairchild, I can't believe it's you talking!" She
stared at him in total exasperation. "One can sit on a thing
like this just so long! When it blows up, my boy, it will blow
away your marriage and your whole life! It will be your
poor father all over again, except worse. Much worse!"

"I admit to nothing, Mother. Nothing whatever. In a
matter so serious I must insist on a little hard evidence. But
I will tell you one thing, for whatever slight consolation it
may afford you. I am not engaged in any activity the con-
sequences of which, should it become generally known, I
am not entirely prepared to face."

"And what consolation is there in *that*?" There were tears,
rare tears, in his mother's pleading eyes. "What consolation
is it to me that you're willing to destroy yourself?"

But his only reaction to her tears was astonishment at his
own lack of feeling. Never had he dreamed that such a
demonstration, which would have shattered him as a boy,
could leave him so unmoved. Was he a monster? Or was he,
at long last, simply a man? He rose to walk to the window
and stood, looking down at the street, with his back to her.

"Suppose, Mother — just suppose, mind you — that what
you suggest is true. And suppose further that everyone concerned — Charley, Rosalie, Mr. Handy, the other daughters
— had their reasons for not wishing to be involved. Not just
to avoid scandal, but for some . . . some deeper indifference. Where would be the harm? Who would be hurt?"

"Society would be hurt! Do you think you can flout the most sacred rules of Christian ethics and get away with it? Do you think you can pull away the foundation stone of our whole civilization and not hurt people? Why, why . . ." She paused before this yawning nadir of infamy. "Why, God himself is hurt!"

They faced each other in their common surprise that she should have introduced the deity. It was not only unlike her; it rang a note that was utterly false. Between them seemed to lie the ruins of a culture somehow betrayed. But betrayed by which of them? By both? What would be the fun for his mother of living in her intensely personal world, a world of gossip elevated and of gossip murky, of an endless murmuring over the teacups and against the gentle clash of silver, if there were no accepted moral judgments to tag to every recounted misfeasance?

"Oh, Dexter, you don't know what you're doing to me! All your life you have stood for the good, right things. More so than the child of anyone I knew. There were even times when you seemed to go too far. Jane used to say you were a bit of a prig. But I see now how much we both depended on you. Oh, yes, from the very beginning! It was you who got me through your father's terrible desertion. It was you who gave me the strength to go forward and make a go of my life. Because I believed in you! And because I believed that you believed in the right things: goodness and kindness and decency and keeping one's word and being true. And that was what made those things real to me again. You see, I gave up God when your father left me!"

"Oh, poor Mother." He went over to the sofa to take her hands in his. "I'm so sorry. But I can't be other people's religion. Even yours."

She pushed him away angrily at this. Then she took a handkerchief from her workbag and vigorously wiped her eyes.

"You came to discuss the renewal of the lease on this house. I suggest we get on with it."

16

ROSALIE found her reaction to her husband's affair confusing. There were times, usually in the morning after he left for the office, when she was seized with spasms of anger. How dared he presume, after years of sanctimoniousness, to turn his back on all the sacred lares and penates that he had so long and proudly displayed on his family mantel, and embrace, without the least apparent qualm, the twin sins of adultery and incest? Did he care nothing for the scandal that hung over the heads of her old father, whom he had always so tiresomely professed to revere, and of his sons, whose future he had sworn to keep unstained from the very crime that had reduced his own youth to dust and ashes?

And then, by the time she made ready to go to her work at Saint Jude's parish house, she would be calmer, more judicious. Was it not, after all, a bit her own fault that he had waited so long for a truly reciprocated passion? Had not her initial doubts about him created doubts in himself about his love? Was he not simply enjoying what every man basically wanted? Was it not possible for her to rise above smallness and jealousy and try to see him for once as he really was? And as she too — ah, there was the rub! — had always, deep down, wanted him to be? A Dexter dedicated to the passions of the flesh, a seeming contradiction in terms!

Besides, had she not been bought? Had she not sold her neutrality for five thousand dollars? With the assurance of more to come? And had she not found peace and a sense of mission? Was not that worth a little humiliation?

"If I were you, I shouldn't care what Annie was up to!" Joanna told her hotly. "You and I are engaged in work that makes her little flirtations seem simply vile!"

"Please, Jo! I don't want to talk about Annie."

It was true that Rosalie found her work at the parish house engrossing. At times she nursed the ill; at times she played games with the children; at times she simply listened to the fugitives' tales of their lives and escapes. She was struck by how little bitterness the victims of slavery seemed to show; they tended to accept what went on in the South as something decreed and inevitable that they had simply been blessed enough to get away from. They were more interested in the future than in the past and asked eager questions about life in Canada. It did not occur to them that the slave states would ever submit to emancipation; on the contrary, they appeared to view the might of their old masters as so great that no one in any part of the United States was safe. When Rosalie suggested that the day might come when the Northern states would be able to enforce emancipation by statute, they simply gazed at her in polite silence.

Frank Halsted fascinated her as much as his refugees. He seemed never to tire, never to falter, never to show the smallest sign of impatience or frustration. To her he glowed, like the figure of Christ in a Rembrandt etching, in a world of shadows. And he had time for everybody. No matter what his schedule he could pause to talk with her, giving her what seemed the very core of his attention. And yet she saw him do exactly the same thing with others.

"Do you know what I was able to do with that wonderful gift of five thousand dollars?" he asked her. "It supplied the down payment and first two trips of a vessel I've chartered to make a regular run between here and Montreal. And all thanks to you, dear Rosalie!"

"I'll get more!" she exclaimed. "I *know* I can get you more."

"You mean your husband has become a sympathizer? I hadn't dared to hope for that."

"Not exactly. Let's just put it that he owes me something."

One Sunday morning after church Mr. Handy walked up Fifth Avenue with Rosalie to his house, while Dexter and Joanna strolled on ahead of them. Directing a level stare at his son-in-law's back, Mr. Handy remarked that he felt as if they were all living above a cellar packed with dynamite. Rosalie was surprised, not only at what he took for granted, but at what he assumed that she did.

"What makes you so sure that Dexter is misbehaving?"

"What makes *you*? Do you think your loving father can't tell when there's that sort of trouble in his family?"

"I don't know what I think. I have no facts."

"What facts do you need? Haven't you and Dexter talked about this thing?"

"Not a word."

"Unimaginable!"

"Well, what could I *say*, Father?"

"You could tell him to behave himself or you'd go with the boys to my house. You know how much I have cared for Dexter. But if he were my own son and you my daughter-in-law, I'd take *your* side in a case like this!"

"And supposing I threatened to leave him? Supposing he took me at my word? Supposing he and Annie flung their intrigue in the face of New York?"

Mr. Handy pursed his lips in a silent whistle. "He has us there, I suppose."

"Of course, he does! You must leave it to me, Father. You must trust me to work it out."

Her father squeezed the hand under his arm. "My own dear girl. Do you know you're a heroine?"

"No, I'm not. But I know what a heroine is. And I didn't always."

"And what is she?"

"Every female slave who flees her master!"

"Good heavens!" Her father threw up his hands in disgust. "You sound just like Joanna!"

But there was another reason that Rosalie wanted to leave her husband alone, and one that she was not going to impart to anyone. An ambivalence had crept into her feelings for Frank Halsted. He was not only the leader of the parish house; he was becoming for her a romantic figure.

A romantic figure to a plain, otherwise sensible woman of forty-one, the mother of two schoolboys? Of course! Was not such a woman just the sort to be moved to folly, or at least to the dream of folly? She knew that what she had to fight was less the emotion than the shame. Her first reaction to libidinous thoughts was always shame of it. But she had learned through the years that such fantasies were basically harmless and the shame quite unnecessary. Was it not, after all, partly Halsted's fault? He was always talking of "love." He called the volunteers, including herself, by their Christian names, usually preceded by a "dear" or "dearest."

"We really have done very little for the poor slaves," he

told her. "It is ourselves whom we've benefited. For we have learned to love. Before, we lived in a loveless city. But now we have been brought closer together. I love you, dear Rosalie, and I am not ashamed to tell you so. I love Joanna, and I am not ashamed to tell her so."

"I think, if I may make a suggestion, Frank, that it would be wise not to overstress that tone. My sister is, after all, something of an old maid, and it might excite her unduly to be so warmly approached by a handsome young clergyman."

"Rosalie! What a suspicion. For shame!"

"But I know whereof I speak."

She reflected afterwards, in a talk with Joanna, that she did indeed.

"Isn't he adorable?" Joanna asked, in a kind of ecstasy.

"He's very sentimental," Rosalie retorted tartly. "He's even rather slushy."

No, the shame was not downed yet. The roughness of her tone showed that. She had still some arguing with herself to do. She conducted an inner debate: if she chose to imagine herself as young and desirable and coveted by an adoring Halsted, all the more charming for being embarrassed by his uncontrollable passion for her, what harm was there in that? To her sons or family? She certainly did not have to concern herself with the adulterous Dexter.

She and Dexter, a few years back, had fervently admired the great Rachel, who had brought her French repertoire, including *Phèdre*, to New York, and now she found herself indulging in a game of mental play-acting. She would recite to herself the famous declaration scene, just as it was written, except that Hippolyte, when confronted with his stepmother's passion, instead of rejecting it with scorn, would stammer out his own reluctant reciprocation. But on what followed next she would drop her curtain. She would close her fantasies on the ultimate scene, for she had an inner censor that forbade her from going too far.

"I wonder what you are thinking of now, dear Rosalie." Frank had silently entered the dispensary to find her looking out the Gothic window at the rain. What was *that* scene but a sentimental print?

"I was thinking what a great actress Rachel had been."

"Wasn't she! So full of passion. Did she express your soul, Rosalie? Is that what lies under the placid exterior of good women? Do you seethe inwardly?"

"That's it. We seethe."

"You seethe at injustice! You seethe for the cause!"

"Exactly."

"God bless you, Rosalie!"

She was honest enough to admit that her little game preempted her from too rigid a condemnation of her husband.

"After all," she told herself, "do I know how *I* should behave if Frank were to approach me, as my little slut of a sister undoubtedly approached Dexter?"

But didn't she in fact know? She would have spurned him, as the real Hippolyte had spurned the real Phèdre! For if the old puritanism of the Handys and Howlands had been diluted in her to the point of excluding the sin that existed only in the mind, or at least of ranking it as less culpable than its robuster brethren, the ancient sense of guilt had been replaced by an equally sharp horror of seeming ridiculous. *That* was the real reason that her censor lowered the curtain on her tumbling mental pictures of an abandoned cleric and a matron who had put by her staidness. Oh, yes, she was safe enough, even against the unimaginable! She was the victim, even in fantasy, of her own steely sense of what was fitting. And she always would be.

The little game, in any event, was not destined to last. As the wet dreary winter dripped into spring, she began to apprehend that her minister was not the man she had pictured. A romantic fantasy could not exist independently of its too much altered model. Rosalie could adjust for minor differences, but not for major ones. Just as the imagination would not put hair on a bald model, or teeth on a toothless one, so it would not provide sense and balance where there was only extravagance.

She was beginning to suspect that she was working with a fanatic. Halsted never spoke or thought, so far as she could make out, of anything but slavery. What she had at first deemed a fine, even a holy ideal, began to emerge as an obsession. And she discovered that his love of the enchained was more than balanced by his hatred of the enchainer; that the former might not have even existed without the fire with which he nourished the latter. She had spent a morning listening to the tale of an intelligent and beautiful negress from a plantation near New Orleans, and she was too full of her story not to bring it to Frank. "It's unimaginable!" she exclaimed. "That girl was the daughter of her own master, and he was going to *sell* her!"

"I'm afraid that's only too easily imaginable."

"But how could a man have *no* paternal feelings? He was going to sell her to his own son! A young man whom she had every reason to suspect of having improper feelings for herself. His half-sister!"

"They don't see their slaves as human beings. That's the curse of the South. In Catholic countries, where slavery existed, the church always insisted on the equality of souls. But our Southern Protestants see heaven as an extension of earth, with the same class divisions. If the slaves are permitted eternal life, it is only that they may continue to serve. And if a brother and sister commit fornication and incest, don't forget that it may result in a valuable asset!"

"They manufacture their own slaves!"

"Exactly. It is the blackness of the slaves and the whiteness of their owners that gives the institution its peculiar horror. In Rome, where slaves were often of the same color as their masters, and frequently better educated, they could be treated almost as equals. But when slaves are brought here black and ignorant, and kept in ignorance, they become degraded in mind and soul as well as in body. Can you think that the men who have done this to them will escape eternal damnation?"

Rosalie was startled. Even her grandmother Howland had never talked about damnation, and she had been about as stern on the subject of morals as one could imagine. "Damnation? Oh, I don't like to think that anyone is really damned. Punished, yes, if you like. For years and years, maybe. But how could anyone, in one mortal lifetime, do enough evil to deserve everlasting retribution? No, not even Simon Legree!"

"Oh, but I believe they can, Rosalie! I believe in hell. Eternal hell! Remember, I've been there!"

She turned away from the glitter in his eyes. "If you got out of it, it can't have been eternal."

*　*　*

One morning Joanna called in Union Square in a great state of agitation. Halsted was transferring the refugees at the parish house to other hiding places. He had received a warning from a friend in the police force that Saint Jude's had fallen under suspicion at last. Someone had chattered.

"Be sure not to go there!" Joanna warned her. "It may be that they don't know who Frank's volunteers are, and you may be needed to hide somebody."

"I suppose I can fix up the attic," Rosalie mused. "I'll see to it right now." But she paused, as a thought struck her, on her way to the stairway. "If Frank is suspected, can he drop his disguise? Can he come out now and tell the world where he really stands on slavery?"

Joanna clapped her hands. "Oh, my, yes! He's going to do it on Sunday. Right there in the pulpit at Saint Jude's. It will be a tremendous moment. You'll go with me, of course? Or will Dexter insist that you go with him to Trinity?"

"He may make a little scene, but I shall ignore it. Certainly, I shall be with you at Saint Jude's."

Rosalie was good as her word, and that next Sunday at eleven she and Joanna were seated in a front pew at Saint Jude's. Frank, radiant in his glistening surplice, spotted the sisters as he took his stand in the pulpit and did not hesitate to send them his warmest smile. It was plain that he was intensely happy. The delights of his forthcoming revelation must have been actually sweetened by a year of odious pretenses. He had earned his reward at last. Now he would enter into the kingdom of God on earth.

He started his confession so softly that for a while his congregation did not realize that anything out of the usual was happening. As he gradually made it clear what he was about to say, a profound silence settled over the church. He told his parishioners, just as he had told Rosalie on her first visit to the parish house, how he had been possessed by the forces of darkness, and how he had been redeemed by a vision of the light, right here where he was now standing, and while he had been delivering his Sunday sermon. His voice began to soar as he developed his new concept of the sacred duty of every Christian to fight slavery. This duty, he maintained, was not confined to opposing the spread of slavery in the territories or newly admitted states; it embraced the march of abolition right into the heart of Southern strongholds. This was to be accomplished by law if possible, but if it could not be done by law, then with God's will, it would have to be accomplished by force of arms!

At this a quarter of the congregation arose and filed indignantly out of the church.

Rosalie felt alone and bleak. She had yielded up her fantasy. It was as if the attracting male force of the man in the pulpit had escaped from his body in the silver words of his impassioned oratory and left him now, another angry priest. And she had had her fill of priests.

17

DEXTER, on a warm May afternoon in 1860, attended a meeting of his father-in-law's "Save the Union" committee. Some fifty gentlemen, including the delegates from Richmond and Atlanta, were seated in double rows of gilt chairs facing each other across the floor of the picture gallery to discuss the crisis created by the Republicans' nomination of Lincoln. Dexter had come in late and had not been introduced to the visitors. He sat near a partially opened window to enjoy the gentle breeze from the avenue, only half attentive to the speechifying. His eyes took in the painting of Catherine de' Medici inspecting the corpses of Saint Bartholomew's Day. So, he reflected grimly, might some Northern dowager, in a year or more, stroll forth to inspect the toll of war. The queen-mother's widow's weeds showed that she had survived her husband; the dead were all young males. Who said it was a man's world?

Mr. Handy was on his feet now, addressing the group. He did so gracefully, mellifluously, forcefully.

"There are those who claim that we men of affairs are

concerned only with profit. That is not so, but if it were, would it be so bad a thing? What makes for profitable banking and commerce? Peace and harmony! Who profits from war? The suppliers of arms and munitions, admittedly. But they are only a minority among industrialists. Most of us are hurt, if not actually ruined by it. I retort, gentlemen, to the yellow journalist who wrote that our organization was motivated by greed, 'Aye, but what kind of greed? A good greed. A divine greed! We are puffed with a greed for all the good things of this life: rich crops, warm houses, sound currency, happy men. We wish to live at peace with our neighbors and with good will to all!' "

Dexter's eye caught the satyr teased by naked wood nymphs, and he half closed his eyes to dream of Annie. But would she ever come to South Vesey Street again? She had missed their last appointment and never explained. Would he have to crawl to her on his knees? And accept the probability that she was seeing the wretch, sitting in that chair by Mr. Handy, from which he kept his eyes rigidly averted? Yet to observe whom else had he come?

His attention was now attracted to his brother-in-law, who took the floor.

"We have had the Compromises of 1820 and 1850," David Ullman was saying. "Is there any valid reason that we should not work for the Compromise of 1860? I propose settlement of the slavery question in the territories by vote of the settlers." David was leaning back against the wall, his long legs, clad in spotless, neatly pressed light gray, casually crossed. There was a protesting murmur from some of the men. "But isn't that the democratic way? Aren't the settlers the people most concerned? And I propose in return a compromise of the fugitive slave question by a statute of limitations. One year after a slave has come to live in a free state he should be a free man!"

Dexter fumed. How could a poor negro hope to hide out for a whole year? He would be bound to be run down, caught and sent back to his master. Was there nothing that David would not advocate to curry favor with Mr. Handy's friends and save his own loans to Southern businesses? Dexter was about to raise his hand to ask a biting question when he saw his father-in-law's meditative glance upon him, and he was stilled. Was he in any position to irritate Mr. Handy?

In the intermission period, while the delegates were helping themselves to drinks at the long bar table put up at the east end of the room, Dexter, who had remained alone by his window, stiffened suddenly as a stocky figure in a black coat with a big dark head and tousled hair approached him. The man was actually holding out his hand in greeting! Dexter put both of his own behind his back.

"Very well," Bleeker said, coming to a halt. "Just as you wish. I only thought that the principle of this meeting was to bury hatchets, not to brandish them."

"Are you a Southerner now, Mr. Bleeker?" Dexter asked coldly.

"You might almost say so. I've developed a good deal of sympathy for their point of view. In fact, if it weren't for slavery, I'd say Virginians were the most civilized people I'd ever known."

"Rather a big 'if,' isn't it?"

"Perhaps." Bleeker shrugged. "Yes, I agree that's a tough one to swallow. But all your screaming abolitionists aren't making things any easier. Anyway, I'm a great admirer of your father-in-law. He's doing all he can to avert disaster. How's Annie?"

"Mrs. Charles Fairchild is well, thank you."

The wretch actually winked! "Do you remember what I told you at our last meeting? That I'd almost forgive you if you'd done what you did to me out of passion? Well, it looks as if I'm going to have to almost forgive you."

"I have no idea what you're talking about."

"You don't? Well, the reputation of your prowess has traveled farther than you think. She's a dish for the gods, isn't she?" Dexter had to shrink back before what actually threatened to be a nudge in the ribs! "Does she still cry 'Bully Boy' when she 'comes'?"

The only thing that kept Dexter's hands from flying to Bleeker's throat was the sudden vision of his father-in-law, across the room, over his adversary's shoulder, watching the two of them intently. But he trembled all over in a surge of conflicting impulses. The hands that wanted to strangle his adversary were now clenched so tightly that the nails bit painfully into his skin; his temples throbbed. And then, as the idea of all he owed to Mr. Handy flickered and jumped before him, he knew, with a sigh of utter exhaustion, that he must do nothing.

Without a word he turned from Bleeker and strode to the door. He was already in the corridor at the head of the dark stairwell when he heard his name called. It was Mr. Handy, who had followed him out to the landing.

"What's come over you, my boy?"

"I'm sorry, sir, I couldn't take it any longer. David and that man Bleeker and all their damnable Southern sympathies. I can't wait to vote for Lincoln!"

"The South will secede."

"Let them try!"

Mr. Handy pursed his lips. "You would force them into it?"

"If they insist on being forced, yes!"

"You seem under a strain, dear boy. You've been working too hard. Go home and rest."

Dexter clutched the old man's hand in silence and bounded down the stairway. He had walked all the way from Thirty-seventh Street to Union Square before he realized that he had left his hat. Running up Annie's stoop he pressed the bell hard. She was in the hall, dressed to go out, and opened the door herself. She at once took in his discomposure.

"Don't talk here," she murmured. There was a maid standing in the hall. Annie brushed quickly by him and went down the stoop. He followed her out into the square.

"You were Bleeker's mistress!" he cried as they faced each other.

Even in his excitement he could wonder at her coolness. She hardly blushed. "You ought to know. You took me from him."

"But you told me he was nothing to you!"

"It was true. He meant very little to me." Her eyes narrowed; she was actually angry! "But you're teaching me to appreciate him. Charging into my house without a hat and shouting all over the square!"

"You're a brazen . . . a brazen . . . hussy!"

"And you're an ass. What earthly business is it of yours what lovers I had before you? How could it possibly hurt you?"

For one wild moment in the tumbling red of his thoughts he remembered his own argument to his mother. Then he brushed it aside. "Because it does. You know it does!" When she simply shrugged and turned to walk a few paces away, he cried, "You came to me already contaminated by his lewd embracements!"

"They were no more lewd than yours!"

"Annie!"

"Oh, let's stop this foolishness, Dexter," she said in a drier tone, turning back to him. "I think we both realize that things have been cooling down in the last weeks. Let's not spoil what we had. I've made love to nobody but you since Vesey Street. Not even Charley. That was all you were entitled to. Indeed, it was more."

"I loved you, Annie!"

"Not really. I was a habit, and a lady should never let herself become that."

Dexter collapsed on a bench, his head in his hands. "How can you say I didn't love you? You didn't love *me*."

"I fancied you. Which is just as good. And now let us try to end this decently. I was planning to do so, anyway, before I went to Newport. These things shouldn't be dragged out. It's a good idea to make a clean cut. Particularly when we have to pick up an old relationship. For don't forget, my dear. We have to go back to being proper in-laws. You won't be able to glare at me that way at Daddy's! You can't afford to behave like an ex-lover."

"The ex-lover will soon be replaced, no doubt," Dexter said bitterly.

"I hope so!"

He rose and stared at her as if he were seeing her the first time.

"Don't *look* at me like that, Dexter. I hope you will find somebody, too."

"Never!" he cried hoarsely. "Never!"

She simply shrugged and turned back to her house where her landau was waiting. Dexter watched her drive away and then walked numbly to his own abode.

Rosalie was not home; Bridget said she would not be in until late. The boys had gone to a birthday party in Brooklyn Heights and were spending the night. He ate a cold supper and spent the evening in the library brooding over a bottle of brandy.

If the shock of the day's events had brought him abruptly back to his old reality, dull and dreary and sickeningly familiar, the image of Annie, in reverse fashion, seemed to be retreating into the realm of fantasy, like some disembodied siren, some enchantress of legend, someone swathed in veils, with large dark eyes peering at him lewdly, her hips moving in a slow, circular, oriental dance, Circe, Medea, Salome. Could one love a phantom in Union Square? Could one love anything but a phantom in Union Square?

As his lonely evening wore on, and he meditated on the folly of this infatuation, it occurred to him that he had not only forsaken his duty to his wife and to his family, but to the sacred union of the states. Had not his inertia, his passivity to moral issues, already plunged him into a nest of incipient rebels? Had he not even exchanged words with the abominable Bleeker? Clenching his fists he leaped to his feet and declaimed aloud to a wall of books against the horror of the slave-owning aristocracy.

When he went at last upstairs, his heart was still beating rapidly, despite all the brandy that he had consumed. Lying in bed in the dark he stared up towards the ceiling and prayed aloud.

"Dear God, I know we should allow our Southern states

to live in peace. But if in your infinite wisdom, and through the mediation of your servant, Abraham Lincoln, you should see fit to permit *them* to strike the first blow, if you should turn your eyes away from them in their unholiness and allow them the sin of secession, will it be wrong if we leap to arms with joy and jubilation? If we bring the devastation of your anger to their fair land? If we burn their plantations with cleansing fire and chastise their rebel people with the sword? Or even worse? Will you blame us if their women are raped by the very slaves we have freed, if . . ."

He must have fallen asleep because he awakened to Rosalie's voice from the door of his dressing room:

"What is it, Dexter? You're making the most terrible racket. Are you having a nightmare?"

18

Mr. Handy looked grave. He moved the heavy little statues of dogs and wolves that he used for paperweights about the surface of his desk. He pursed his lips into a kind of ball so that hollows appeared in his cheeks. He stared up at the rows of leather-bound sets on the wall. Yet Dexter had the distinct impression that the scene had been prepared.

"Would it be appropriate for me to make a confession to the assembled family?" Dexter asked.

"What do you think that would accomplish? Are you under the illusion that they don't know?"

"No, I've been appalled at what they all know. Why did nobody warn me, sir?"

"We were waiting for you to come to your senses. We were afraid that if we so much as murmured a word of reproof, you and Annie might take off to foreign parts."

"Indeed, we might have!"

"So you see."

Dexter rose to pace the room nervously. "Why are you so merciful? I've violated the most sacred laws of human society.

How can you sit there and tolerate my presence? Why don't you kick me out into the street?"

"You almost want me to, don't you?"

"I deserve it!"

"You will be punished enough, my boy. Don't worry about that. We can leave that business entirely to you. I am sure that your standards of penitence are strict. All I ask is that you keep your remorse to yourself. It can create almost as much scandal as sin."

"You mean I should just go on, as if nothing had happened? Practicing law with Charley? Sitting down at your dinner table with him and Annie? Making small talk with Lily and Joanna?"

"That is precisely what I mean. You are not to betray, by so much as a sigh, that you have the smallest feeling of having been guilty of any impropriety."

"Even to Rosalie?"

"Ah, as to Rosalie, I give you no counsel. That is a matter between man and wife. My advice goes only to your conduct with the rest of us. So there! We need say no more about it."

But Dexter could not bear to close the subject just yet. "You may think me greedy," he pursued, "and no doubt I am. But can you give me some little assurance that if I do as you say . . ."

"You mean if you *don't* do as I tell you not to!"

"Very well. If I refrain from any reference to the past, if I measure up to every last one of your requirements . . . is there any hope that I might regain some part of your esteem . . . even . . ." Agonized at the void that dipped around him, he had to risk it. "Even some part of your affection?"

"You have never lost it, my boy. I always wanted a son, and you have been it. I understand the difficulties you suffered with your own father. Perhaps your ideals, your standards, were a bit too high. Very well; you slipped. Now you have steadied your step. Go forward, my boy. My son!"

As the old man rose, Dexter leaped up impulsively to embrace him. When he stepped again into Fifth Avenue, he knew that he was the slave of Charles Handy for life.

❋   ❋   ❋

At breakfast in Union Square the next morning he faced his two sons and Rosalie after a sleepless night. For once he was glad she was wearing her pink dressing gown. It seemed appropriate that she should not be dressed as he wished her to be. It underscored the propriety of his repentance.

"I want you boys to know that I have changed my political principles. I am now a member of the Republican party! I have decided to work for the election of Mr. Lincoln. I believe with him that our country must one day be all slave or all free. I have determined that it must be all free."

"You'll be driving the South out of the Union, Dad," Fred warned him.

"Then we must fight to retain them."

"And blow them to bits!" Selby cried enthusiastically. "While their soldiers are fighting ours, their slaves will rise up behind them. Miss Nesbitt at school says they will!"

"Don't bet on that, Selby," Fred snapped. "The slaves have no arms and no training. They have no leaders. They'd be slaughtered to the last man."

"You're all so bloodthirsty," Rosalie said with a shudder. "Can't we just let the South go? Why keep people in a union they hate?"

"But you're always talking about freeing the slaves, Mum!" Selby exclaimed. "How are you going to free them by letting the South go?"

"And creating a huge slave state?" Dexter interposed.

"Because I don't think it would last. I think it would fall of its own weight. Who in the civilized world would care to be allied to a slave state? Spain and Dahomey and Turkey!"

"I'm afraid you're dreaming, my dear," Dexter warned her. "The Southern belligerents want to take over Mexico. They talk of a vast and powerful slave state that will dominate two continents! They . . ."

"Boys, it's time for school," Rosalie interrupted impatiently. When they had gone, Dexter announced solemnly that he had another confession to make. Her opaque glance seemed to indicate that she might even prefer to go on with his discussion of the slave state.

"I saw that fellow Bleeker at your father's yesterday."

"That must have been a disagreeable surprise."

"But one that may have helped to bring me to my senses. The swine is acting as a kind of lobby for slaveholders." He paused, but as she gave him not the slightest lead, he had to blurt out, "It's all over between Annie and me!"

Rosalie's expression was very cold. "And why should Mr. Bleeker have that effect on your intrigue?"

He winced at her term. "Perhaps he made me realize how far I'd strayed from where I ought to be."

"Or perhaps you didn't like the idea of standing in his shoes?"

"I suppose that's one way of putting it."

"You felt that having taken his girl friend, you might be exposed to taking his political views?"

"Oh, no. But put it that I felt . . . well . . . contaminated."

"I fail to see why."

"He's pro-slavery, damn it all, Rosalie!"

"You needn't swear at me."

"I'm sorry. But I should think you might be glad that I'm coming over to your views."

"I'm not sure that you are. Why do you have to be against everything that Bleeker is for? Isn't he as much entitled to his opinion as any other gentleman?"

"Bleeker? A gentleman! Rosalie!"

"Well, he is. More than you, anyway. He didn't hound you out of your job because he wanted your girl, did he?"

"But I didn't do that because I wanted Annie!" he cried in dismay.

"Didn't you? Perhaps you didn't know you did."

"I had hoped you might forgive me. I was a fool, of course."

"I might forgive you the intrigue. I'm not so sure I can forgive you the exultation."

"Over what?"

"Over your own redemption! Oh, don't think I'm being superior, Dexter." Her tone changed suddenly from exasperation with him to impatience with herself. "I can face the fact that I haven't been the wife you need. The wife, I might even say, you deserve. In many ways you're a very good man. You're kind and patient and dutiful. You're an excellent son and father. It's not your fault that our values are so different. It's not really even your fault that you irritate me so. And, believe it or not, there have been moments, during your affair with Annie, when I've admired

you more than ever before. When you've seemed . . . well,
more of a man."

"But not more of a gentleman," he added bitterly.

"Oh, I don't think you really go in for being a gentleman.
I don't think many people in New York do. It's not our kind
of thing."

Dexter remembered the days when Rosalie's tears, like his
mother's, had been very terrible to him. But now her tear-
lessness was something worse. Was it possible that she could
no longer be reached by a genuine remorse, a renewed exclusive devotion? She who, however stiff and critical and
standoffish, had always struck him as basically, almost pa-
thetically, needing and wanting his love? Hadn't he, even
in the wildest moments at South Vesey Street, had in the
back of his mind the sense of a refuge, an oasis, when all
the madness should be over, in the rescuing arms of Rosalie?
But now, bleak and gray, a world spread out before him in
flat squares, where there was neither passion nor love — only
a mild tolerance that scarcely veiled contempt. And what
man had ever deserved it more richly?

"I hoped that it might help me to retrieve myself in your
estimate if I could share your beliefs."

"It might, if I thought you had changed your opinions for
humane reasons. But you're like so many abolitionists. You
don't love the slave. You hate the slaveholder. There's only
death and destruction in your heart."

"We have to be ready for death and destruction."

"But it makes me shudder when people like it!"

"I don't like it. I try to face it. And when the time comes
I shall be willing to do my part. In any way I can be of most
service. With a rifle or bearing a stretcher or whatever they
ask of me!"

"Oh, I'm sure." Her shrug deprecated his patriotism. "It's not your courage I question. You'd kill for the love of Annie, and you'd kill for the hate of her." She rose to shut off his protest. "I'm sorry. I don't want to discuss this anymore. I find it too agitating. Let us go on with our lives as we have been. I'm glad it's over with Annie. For all our sakes. Not that I think it will save her marriage. That I fear is rotted to the core. As to our own . . . well, let us see."

"You will find me humble, Rosalie! You will find me ready to help you in any way you want!" He paused, disheartened by her continued impassivity. "I love you! But I shall understand if you can never forgive me!"

"Forgiving is not my problem. Or even forgetting. I am going to see Bridey now about the order. Talk doesn't really help. As I say, let's just go on."

"That's what your father told me. Only he gave me hope."

"Of what?"

"Of the return of his affection."

"Oh, but it's easy for *him*," Rosalie retorted with something that sounded almost like a sneer. "He owns you."

"I guess he owns us all."

"He doesn't own *me*," Rosalie asserted with emphasis, and then at last she left the room.

PART II

His Terrible
Swift Sword

19

THE RUSH OF EVENTS that followed the election of Lincoln was like a clattering new train on the New York Central tracks. Dexter found himself suddenly alive and awake as he had not been in the moments of greatest ecstasy in South Vesey Street. The secession of South Carolina, the assault on Sumter, the calling up of volunteers, seemed once more to match the public excitement with his own pre-Annie internal commotion. Leaning out the window of Union Square to watch the enlisted soldiers parade past, mingling with the crowds on Broadway that applauded the return of Major Anderson, standing with his father-in-law on the dais in Washington Square while a Tiffany stand of colors was presented to the commanding officers of the Sixteenth Regiment, he felt himself at one with the whole big, shouting, hustling, flag-waving city. The God of Hosts had called forth his troops at last!

Purpose came back into life like a spring flood; direction filled up the summer void. Rosalie, already qualified as a nurse, was kept from rushing to the aid of the still non-existent wounded only by the more urgent demand for her administrative talents in the organization of the Sanitary Commission. Dexter knew that she would have been embarrassed to admit that war had brought her cheer, but her heightened color and the warmer note in her voice as she hurried to and fro to her meetings betrayed her. Fred and Selby were at last united in patriotic fervor, and the little household in Union Square seemed to glow with a fine new harmony.

Dexter, at excited family gatherings at Number 417, noted Annie's obvious boredom with the national crisis and could not help reflecting that it made her less alluring. There was something petty, almost mean, in such a resolute separation of self from the popular enthusiasm. It made a sorry contrast to Rosalie's emulation of the great gray lady of the Crimean War.

But the most dramatic change of all was in Mr. Handy. No sooner had word come of the first shell fired at Sumter than all his doubts and hesitations had vanished. There was no longer any question about business interests or the market value of peace. In one bound he went further than Joanna or even Rosalie. He would pound his dining room table now and proclaim that the rebel states should no longer have the option of re-entering the Union at the simple price of abandoning the principle of secession. No, sir! They should be readmitted only when their slaves had been emancipated! And for no compensation! They had had their chance for that. Now they would have to fight, not only for their enchained blacks, but for their cotton, for their plantations, for their very lives!

Mr. Handy proceeded, with other prominent men of affairs, to organize the Union Defense Committee of the Citizens of New York, which met and worked, day and night, to provide uniforms and arms for the New York regiments. When Dexter told his father-in-law that he had joined a group of gentlemen who were drilling in the evening to qualify themselves for this new army, he was treated with a firmness and a severity that he had not encountered before.

"Drill as much as you want, dear boy. It may be necessary for every able-bodied man in the North to be ready to fight before this trial is lifted from us. But there can be no idea of your joining up now. I'm going to need every minute you can spare from your law practice — and a good many you can't."

"But that, sir, is work an older man can do. Or one who is not physically qualified to fight."

"Don't fool yourself! You'll need every ounce of strength you have before I'm through with you! The great lack in this war is not going to be manpower. It's going to be brains and administrative ability!" Mr. Handy shook his head emphatically. "When I think of all those fine generals siding with the South, it makes me fairly ill. Lee! If we ever catch the scoundrel, we should string him up!"

Dexter was disturbed. The emotion that had filled him to the brim, as from a gushing pipe, each morning that he had awakened since the firing on Sumter, seemed to necessitate some physical outlet. Could he survive his own inner tumults at a desk?

"How will I look to my sons, sir? I, who urged everyone to vote for Lincoln and bring on the war?"

"The times are too grave for that kind of petty consideration. We can't just think of ourselves and how we're going to look in what sort of silly hat. I need you, Dexter, in the most important work of this struggle. To raise an army! You say you're willing to give up your life? I take that for granted. I'm asking you to do something harder. To put your country before your vanity!"

Dexter was astonished to find that the old man had just as much force and penetration as he had always pretended to credit him with.

"I suppose we must agree to disagree in this matter, sir," he suggested desperately.

"Not on your life! I think you owe me something, son." In the pause that followed Dexter dropped his eyes before Mr. Handy's long yellow stare. Noting his concession, the latter nodded. "Very well. Let there be no more talk of enlisting. You shall be my number-one man. And when we've got the army raised and equipped, *then*, my boy, and only then, you may go!"

The only remedy that Dexter could find for his frustration was in hard work. When he was not in his office, he was calling on businessmen, raising money and soliciting supplies. It did not take him long to observe that the spirit of patriotism and sacrifice were close to the surface of national events and that after the first explosion of enthusiasm, the old goals of profit and pleasure as usual began to reassert themselves. He sometimes discussed this with Rosalie, whom he rarely saw now except at breakfast. But when they did talk, it was with a mutual interest in what each was doing that was novel in their relationship.

"Do you suppose the Rebs find it as hard as we do to rouse their people to any action?" he asked.

"Probably. Wars are started by very few people. They must be carried on by very few."

"You mean most people don't care?"

"Well, isn't that what you've just been telling me?"

He looked at her with suspicion. "Do you imply that the few people who started this war were Northerners?"

"Well, didn't you all really want it?"

"Oh, Rosalie!"

"You know I've always felt that. Why fuss about it now?"

"Because I don't think you're honest when you imply that *you* don't believe in the war. You're as busy as a bee, and you love it!"

"But my business will be casualties! One can't love that. And, besides, I'd be just as willing to look after enemy casualties as our own."

"You mean you're neutral?"

"Oh, I don't *know*, Dexter. What does it matter? Why can't you be like Father? He has no doubts. He's not always pummeling people with suspicious questions. He likes the glory, and he likes the gore!"

Dexter thought of this interchange a week later when he stood with Mr. Handy and some dozen members of the Union Defense Committee in the White House, listening to his father-in-law expound the problems of raising regiments to the new president. It was his first glimpse of Lincoln, and he studied the chief executive with intense curiosity.

The president was leaning forward over his desk, his chin resting on his fists. His long plain face was lined with seeming exhaustion; the half-closed eyes indicated only a forced attention. From time to time he nodded. Mr. Handy now paused, as if not sure that his message was being conveyed.

"I hope you don't mind, sir, if I put what I have to say in plain English?"

"Oh, no. That's what I like."

"The fewer intermediaries between us and your administration, the better."

"Yes, Mr. Handy. We must avoid seesawing."

Mr. Handy resumed his eloquent flow. What he had to
say about the necessity of raising further regiments and the
obligation of Congress to pay, no matter what revenues might
be lacking, was cogently, even dramatically put. There was
something rather splendid in the sight of this large, vigorous
old man devoting his energies to his nation's cause. And yet
Dexter could not quite dispel the suspicion that there was
something faintly out of key, something almost stagy in the
presentation. Mr. Handy and the other gentlemen from New
York might have represented justice and the necessity of
force. The president somehow represented the cost. Cost in
what? Well, perhaps, simply the cost in blood.

"He's a well-meaning man," Mr. Handy said afterwards in
the bar of Willard's Hotel. "And I think, on the whole, an
honest one. But it's a tragedy that he doesn't know more of
military affairs. And that General Scott is so ancient. We have
a president who tells yarns and a chief of staff who's older
than the capital he defends!" He raised his glass to the
others. "Well, God help us, gentlemen! We'll have to do the
job ourselves!"

Back in New York the following night, at another family
party at Number 417, Dexter was able to measure the full
extent of his reinstatement in the clan by the fact that he was
allowed to sit by Annie.

"I am sorry for what Charley told me before dinner," he
said to her.

"That I've seceded at last? Yes, I've walked out on him.

Rebellion seems to be in the air. You can't have been much surprised."

"I hate to think what'll happen to Charley."

"Oh, he'll probably drink himself into a cocked hat. But he'd do that if I stayed."

"And what will you do now? Will you live here with your father and Joanna?"

"You've always been determined that I must bore myself to death, Dexter! Even during our . . . how shall I call it . . . our interlude? You always insisted that I should be as dull as possible when I was not in South Vesey Street. The great lover was to be my sole diversion! Like an odalisque in a harem, I had to wait patiently for my brief moment of bliss."

"Please, Annie!" he cautioned her, glancing over at her father.

"Oh, silly, do you think I don't know how to moderate my voice in this house? The only reason Daddy has any idea of what we're talking about is that nervous look you just gave him. He could hardly miss that."

"Well, then, where will you live? All alone, in Union Square?"

"I'm going to Paris with my daughter. I'm going to rent the flat over Lizzie Osborne's in the Rue du Bac. I shall try it for a season, anyway. And don't tell me that nobody there will receive a 'separated' wife. Lizzie writes that I may even be presented at the Tuileries!"

Dexter, looking into those animated eyes, had a vision of Napoleon III, with lascivious lips and a shiny goatee, leaning over to kiss Annie's little hand. He coughed to dispel the vision.

"I don't see how you can leave at a time like this."

"What can I do about the war? Can I fight? I've never been able to do anything with my hands, so pity the poor soldier who has to wear my bandage." She laughed her old high laugh, but now he did not join her. "Oh, you're all so serious! Frankly, it bores me. You're so holy and grave. At least the Southern cavaliers have a dash to them. But I don't care to be hanged as a Confederate sympathizer, so I'd better clear out."

"I wonder if you'll ever come back."

"If you lose your war, maybe. Then you might all be fun again. But if you win it, you'll be impossible! And you will win it, I suppose. Dull, pompous people always do. No, I'm not coming back!"

"Has your trip been arranged?" he asked, with a more formal politeness. "Can I help you with tickets and passports?"

"Oh, Daddy's arranged the whole thing at the bank," she replied easily, and he realized that he was still under the Handy surveillance. Normally, such a chore would have been sent to his office. No, he was not quite trusted yet.

This was even more deeply emphasized when he discovered, a month later, that Jules Bleeker had been sent to Paris to write for the Richmond *Inquirer*. The Handys all knew, but nobody had spoken of it. They had given Annie up, but they were hanging on to him.

20

IT WAS EARLY on a July morning, outside Willard's Hotel,
and Joanna Handy was supervising the loading of the picnic
hamper into the double-seated open carriage with two horses
that Dexter had engaged for the day to drive his father-in-
law out from the capital to Centreville to watch McDowell
trounce the rebels. He and Rosalie stood on the curb and
watched.

"You won't change your mind and come with us?" he
asked.

"I've got to be at the Sanitary Commission, thank you very
much. Some of us have to work to win this war."

"I suppose it does look rather awful," Dexter admitted as
a boy came up with the champagne bucket. "But your father
has set his heart on it."

The sight of the wine turned Rosalie's sarcasm to sharp
disgust. "Awful? It's absolutely bloodthirsty! All these carriages and ladies with parasols." She turned scornfully away
from the line of vehicles where similar preparations were
being made. "Do you really want to see our boys killed?"

"I doubt there'll be much killing today. It should be a rout. McDowell outnumbers the enemy three to one."

"Well, I don't think one should even go to routs. Here's Father now. Goodbye. Happy hunting!"

Mr. Handy, in a light brown suit with a tall silk brown hat and a pearl-handled cane, appeared in the hotel doorway and bowed to them solemnly. Rosalie, raising her hand, hurried off. The damp air, the whitening sky, the mild mist, foretold a scorching day.

"We'd better get started," Mr. Handy announced.

They slowly followed the long line of traffic, carriages, cabs, army wagons and equestrians. Washington seemed to Dexter a study in white and brown. White was in the government buildings, some still unfinished, stark Greek temples, and brown in the military personnel and equipment that everywhere abounded. It was as if the capital, a pale virgin, had fallen into the hands of dun-colored, hirsute barbarians. As they crossed the Long Bridge into Virginia, Mr. Handy and Dexter compared bits of information about the relative deployments of McDowell's and Beauregard's troops. They agreed it should be only a brief encounter. Joanna was silent and moody.

"Rosalie's right," she said once. "We shouldn't have come."

After an hour of jolting Mr. Handy fell asleep. His head was tilted back, his mouth open, and he snored loudly. Joanna watched him until she was sure that he could hear nothing.

"Dexter, I want to ask you something. Don't you think I should be doing my part in the war, too?"

"But you're doing it. You're looking after a great public servant."

"Any maid could do what I do. Or maybe a paid companion. I want to be a nurse."

"You're too old."

"I'm not! I've asked Rosalie. They're *supposed* to be old. She says she can arrange it easily. But she told me I'd have to tell Father. Dexter, please! I want you to do that for me."

"Jo, you can't leave him now. A man of his age who's taking on the load of work he's taking on? Where's your sense of perspective?"

"Where's yours? Must I always be the one who's sacrificed? Oh, don't you see? It's my one chance to live!"

"Think of all the young men who are being given their one chance to die."

"I know I sound selfish. But I'm not, really. I only want to help. To do my part!"

"Well, look at me. I gave up the army to work for your father."

"But that's different. He needs you."

"He needs you, too."

"You just say that because you don't want to cause him the slightest annoyance. You all defer to him so! And nobody ever thinks of me!"

Dexter frowned. "These are not times for thinking of ourselves."

"There are never any times for thinking of Jo Handy! That's for sure!"

She flung herself back in her seat to pout, and the journey, which had started so gaily, proceeded in a rather sullen silence. Far to the west they heard the rumble of gunfire.

Dexter was to remember afterwards that the first ominous note was the approach of a group of soldiers, ambling along in no kind of order, followed by a cart pulled by one old horse and containing a pile of packsacks. Mr. Handy, waking with a start, ordered the coachman to stop.

"Aren't you fellows going in the wrong direction?" he called out benevolently.

One of them, who had been drinking, put his hand familiarly on the side of the carriage. "Not us, pops. We signed up for three months, and three months is up."

"But there's a battle going on! Don't you hear it?"

"All the more reason to get the hell out of here, don't you agree?"

Mr. Handy became magisterial. "What is your regiment?"

"The Sixteenth New York."

"Good God! One that I helped organize! Young man, you're a disgrace to the cause! And so are all the rest of you!"

Dexter, fearing violence, called to the coachman to drive on. As they trotted ahead a loud burst of jeering came from the men, and Dexter had trouble restraining his father-in-law from standing up in the carriage to shout back at them.

"After all, sir, it's their right to leave."

"You talk about rights? In *these* times? There are no rights. We must have a draft! Of course, we must have a draft."

As they approached Centreville, the sound of gunfire was now constant, and Dexter climbed up to the driver's seat to help him to decide which of the hills looking down on the little stream of Bull Run would provide the best observation post.

"Look there, sir! It looks as if those people were coming over to us!"

And, indeed, across a field an open carriage was approaching them rapidly. Dexter had just made out a lady in white in the back holding tightly to a wide-brimmed hat when the man beside her half rose from his seat and hollered:

"Our boys are licked. It's going to be a stampede!"

But it was by no means clear from what direction the stampede would be coming. Every horse or vehicle in sight seemed to be headed in a different direction. Two army officers cantered towards them down the road, and Dexter cried out:

"Is the battle really lost?"

"Thanks to you blasted tourists!" one of them shouted back as they sped past.

Dexter was to recall afterwards what the next sight had reminded him of. As a boy he had once gone camping with his father in the Adirondacks, and they had stumbled upon and startled a huge herd of deer. Traversing a long valley of high grass between two hill ranges, they had happened upon a splendid grazing stag surrounded by his bodyguard of lesser males. The big buck had reared up his head and departed at a gallop, while his guard had scattered to give the alarm. Dexter had never forgotten his amazement at seeing the whole valley suddenly turn brown as hundreds of deer had leaped into sight and poured away from him in opposite directions in two tumultuous streams. So now did the few carriages and carts that had been visible seem suddenly to be converted into wild caravans as from every point, on the road and across the fields, hustling carriages and creaking carts and running figures appeared.

"Get going!" a gentleman on horseback shouted at them. "Johnny Reb is only a mile back!"

The driver did not wait to be told twice. Lashing his horses he turned the carriage around so abruptly that Mr. Handy roared at him to mind what he was doing. Dexter shouted questions to any who came near, but nobody heeded him. At the first turn on the way back they encountered soldiers, mud-covered, shuffling, running, in total disorder.

"Oh, look!" Joanna cried. "There are two who are hobbling. We must take them in! Driver! Stop!"

The driver did not do so until Mr. Handy had stuck his cane hard into the middle of his back.

"Did you hear my daughter, rascal? Pull up!"

Joanna was out of the carriage in a second, and she and Dexter helped two dazed youths in ragged blue into the back seat on either side of the compliant Mr. Handy. Joanna wanted to take more, but at this the driver protested vociferously that it would be too much for the horses, and Dexter persuaded her to give in. He resumed his former seat beside her, and the long ride back to the capital began.

Nothing on the road could move at more than a walk, and the slowest pedestrian could keep abreast of the horses. Dexter, after the first hour, considered getting out and walking to make room for another exhausted soldier, but he decided, on due consideration, that it was his duty to stay close to the old man and his daughter. The traffic ahead seemed more orderly now, as the carriages and vehicles that had led the retreat were those in better condition.

Silence had fallen over their little group. Mr. Handy stared disconsolately at the countryside, and Joanna watched the two soldiers, one of whom was asleep. The distant rattle of gunfire continued. From time to time an officer would gallop past them along the side of the road. People would shriek questions at him, but they could never hear the answer.

It was as if the bowels of the earth had moved to eject dust and darkness over the somber fields. All that had been green and fresh was brown and spent. The war seemed to have reached into the very afternoon sky to cover it with murky clouds. What was the chairman of the Union Defense Committee now but a poor old King Lear, stripped of his crown and knights, seeking with his poor fool of a son-in-law the warmth of some wretched hut against the horror of a pounding storm?

Oh, they had talked and talked, of freedom, of union, of sacraments, of duties, but what were those things when the real wind blew but the big floppy hats and parasols of the ladies of their excursion lost in the muds of Virginia? There had been tongues, silver tongues, in the North, in the South, the tongues of Mr. Handy, of Garrison, of Sumner, of Phillips, of Webster, of Calhoun, of Davis, but what were they all but the dangerous whistles that could only, in the end, shiver the giant ice bank and deluge the land in avalanche?

"Mr. Handy, is that you, sir?" A young cavalry officer had pulled up beside the carriage. "I'm adjutant to General Miles of the Seventh. He told me to keep an eye out for you. Are you all right?"

"I am fine!" Mr. Handy exclaimed sharply. "Kindly tell your general that he should not be wasting his concern on civilians. It's very kind and polite, I'm sure, but I'd rather have you after Beauregard!"

"We'll take care of him, sir. Never fear."

"The day is not lost, then?"

"The day may be lost, sir. But it's only a day."

"God bless you, my boy! Give 'em hell!"

The adjutant cantered off towards the sound of gunfire, and Mr. Handy waved after him.

"Your spirit is wonderful, sir," Dexter observed.

"I trust that you don't mean yours isn't?" Mr. Handy demanded, aggressive from his encounter with the adjutant.

"I confess I feel a bit down."

"It's only a battle, you know. It only means that the war will be longer. For we're going to win, my boy. By God, we are going to win!"

Dexter regarded his father-in-law with a faint surprise. Had *none* of the old spirit of compromise been revived by the day's events? Apparently not. Wotan with his spear had thrust Talleyrand to the side. Charles Handy would fight rebellion to the death.

It was after midnight when they recrossed the Long Bridge. Rosalie was waiting in the throng before the door of the Willard. She hurried to the carriage as soon as she spotted it, and she and Joanna, without a word, supported their father into the hotel.

Upstairs in Mr. Handy's suite, when he had been put to bed and Joanna had retired, Rosalie, pale and tired, joined her husband in the little parlor. She left the door of her father's room ajar.

"Well! You had a memorable day!"

"Don't mock me, Rosalie. It was hell."

"And what will happen now? Will Beauregard take the capital?"

"General Scott has two regiments. He should be able to hold the city."

"And if he can't? Could the South afford to capture him? Would even the rebels be stupid enough to deprive us of our beloved chief?"

"You seem to take it very lightly."

"How else do you expect me to take it?" she demanded in

a sudden, startling burst of anger. "How do you think *you've* been taking it?"

"What do you mean?"

"Traipsing over the countryside with bottles of champagne! Making a *fête champêtre* out of a bloody war! It's like your attitude about the slaves. All fine gestures and phrases!"

"Don't kick a man when he's down, Rosalie."

"Down? You should see yourself!"

"I've changed. Today has changed me."

"And how many boys in blue had to bite the dust to accomplish that?"

"You're very cruel."

"Am I very unfair?"

"I guess not. But is it ever too late to change? Won't you help me to *stay* changed?" He could see now that she was really very tired, as much as he was, but he couldn't let her go to her room quite yet. "Oh, stay for two minutes! Maybe Beauregard *will* take the town, and then it will be too late. All I want to say is . . ."

There was a snort from the other room. "Ah, you've awakened him!" she whispered in distress.

"Is that you, Rosalie?" came her father's voice.

They both went in and stood at the end of his bed.

"Go to sleep, Daddy. Dexter thinks even General Scott can hold the city."

"Of course, he can. Don't be disrespectful! What happened today only means that the war's going to be a little longer." He stretched his arms, yawned and then closed his eyes serenely. "That's all, my children. A little longer."

21

ROSALIE could hardly bring herself to speak to Dexter on the train ride back to New York. The more she thought of his ridiculous expedition, with the champagne and turkey sandwiches, the more it seemed to her that he was making as much of a travesty out of war as he had out of peace. But the god of battles, she reflected grimly, whom he had invoked with such pompous solemnity before the outbreak of hostilities, had looked as foolish in Virginia as in Union Square. At least it might be possible now for him to learn to face a few facts.

She realized that she was not being fair in putting it all on him. Her father had been the true inspirer of that jaunt to Manassas. But her father was an old man, and Dexter should have talked him out of it. Charles Handy in his day, after all, had been a hardheaded and realistic man. *He* had not suffered all his life from the memory of a libidinous parent whom he had ended by imitating!

One resolution that she had firmly made by the time she set foot on the station pavement in New York, was that she was going to accept the offer of the Sanitary Commission to serve on board the hospital ship, *Franklin Pierce*. This vessel would travel between the port of New York and the Chesapeake Bay area to transport the wounded to Northern hospitals. Most of the ship's nurses would be males, but the great Doctor Gurdon Buck wanted six matrons, or nurses-at-large, as he called them, to supply a note of feminine attention and consolation on what would be for many poor wretches a long, painful and perhaps fatal voyage. Rosalie had mentioned the possibility of this job to her sons, who had thoroughly approved of it, and then to Dexter, who had simply declined to believe that she was serious, and she had temporarily dropped the idea. But now she had the ammunition she needed. Now she was steeled.

At family breakfast the next morning in Union Square, Fred and Selby were in a great state of excitement. They wanted every detail from their father about the disaster at Bull Run. Dexter, before their mother's glacial silence, was obviously embarrassed.

"Was it really a rout, Dad?" Selby asked. "Would you call it a stampede?"

"Close to it, I'm afraid."

"Are the Rebs really that much better fighters than we are?"

"Let's put it that they were last Sunday."

"What I can't see," Fred contributed, "is why old Scott didn't send relief from Washington."

"He didn't want to lose the capital!"

"Well, I think it's an outrage. Their running away like that! I hope it won't be over before I have a chance to get in. I'd like to see how *my* friends behave. They couldn't do much worse, I guess."

"Oh, Fred, darling, don't say that!" Rosalie cried in dismay. "You couldn't possibly get in before you're eighteen. Can anyone imagine the war lasting that long?"

"Not at this rate," Fred retorted. "Jeff Davis should be sleeping in the White House in a few weeks' time!"

"Did you see many people getting killed, Dad? I mean, actual corpses?"

"I really don't want to talk about it, Selby. It's a national tragedy. Let us mourn it in silence."

Rosalie decided that she could not let this pass. "It's all very well for you to say that, Dexter. But you were there and saw it all. It's only natural for the boys to ask questions. Even if it was, as you say, a national tragedy."

But Dexter disarmed her with immediate capitulation. "You're quite right, my dear. Boys, ask me anything you want."

Both, however, were embarrassed by the sudden passage between their parents, and in two more minutes they were off to school.

Rosalie contemplated her husband over her newspaper. If she were going to speak, she would have to do it now. He was folding his newspaper. In another minute he would raise his almost empty coffee cup for a final sip. Then he would cough, rise and carefully brush any bread crumbs from his waistcoat and say, "I'll be off now, dear." She spoke up quickly.

"Dexter, wait. You remember our talk about the hospital ship? I've told them I'll go!"

He stared down the table, his lips parted, the perpendicular line of his frown bisecting his smooth forehead. "Are you telling me that you're going to leave me?"

"Leave you? Don't be melodramatic. It's only for a tour of duty. Dexter! Don't look at me that way."

"I'm sorry. I suppose I'm hopelessly old-fashioned. I thought a wife's and mother's place was in her home."

"Normally it is. But there's too much at stake now. You were perfectly willing to join up and sacrifice your own life, if necessary, until Father persuaded you it was your duty to help him with the regiments. If you can give a life, surely you can loan a wife. For a few months, anyway."

"Is that what it will be? A few months?"

"Of course, it's hard to say. I'd be going back and forth. I'd be in New York some of the time. And naturally, if you or the boys were ill, or anything like that, I could always get leave. Or even quit, if necessary. I wouldn't be enlisting, after all."

"The boys need more than a nurse. They need a mother."

"But it isn't as if I were never going to see them! And they're in school all day, anyway. Actually, they're very keen about the idea. They think it would be wonderful to have a member of the family where the fighting is."

"A fighting mother," he said bitterly. "While their father stays home. What sort of position do you think that puts me in?"

"Oh, Dexter, don't take it like that!"

"How else can I take it? I'd much better sign up right away. Even if it's too late for me to get a commission."

"Please, dear, don't be self-pitying. You're a million times more important to the Union than a silly old nurse. The boys know that. Everyone knows that!"

"*I* don't know it. The job with your father is about done, anyway."

"But there'll be any number of others! You're going to be needed here desperately. And I've arranged to have that nice Mrs. Lindley — the one you liked so much when I was sick two years ago — live in and keep house for you and the boys. You'll be perfectly comfortable." But she saw by his deepening frown that this was not the position to take. It would be better to emphasize his sacrifice and inconvenience. "Oh, I know it will be difficult for you. But we all have to give up something to win this war. I expect you to be generous enough to let me do my tiny bit while you do your big one."

"War is a man's job."

"It's everyone's! Didn't Bull Run convince you of that?"

He was still watching her with that steady, thoughtful gaze of his. He had hardly moved a muscle since she had told him her news. "You'll never forgive me that little episode, will you?"

"You must think me very petty."

"You haven't forgiven me Annie, anyway."

"Oh, forgiven. What does it really mean? I've put it aside. It doesn't exist for me anymore."

"But I find it hard to believe that you'd be doing what you're going to do if I'd never been unfaithful."

"How do we know? Let's not go back into the past. Maybe some day, if this terrible war is ever over, we'll sit down and hash it all out. What I'm trying to tell you now, darling, is that I need your help. To do the things I know I ought to be doing!"

She was instantly ashamed of her "darling." It had been meant to have the appearance of falling without premeditation from her lips; it was the purest guile. Dexter's eyes cross-examined her. But his tongue did not. What he said was mild enough.

"You're right about other jobs turning up. They want me on your Sanitary Commission."

She hit the table with her palm in surprise and delight. "Oh, Dexter, how wonderful! It's just the kind of work you'll be best at. Pulling order out of chaos. You'll be the most important man in the whole business of health care! And here was I, thinking I was so grand with my silly old boat!"

"I haven't decided about it yet. But let me tell you what I've been thinking. The army wasn't the only thing that took a licking at Bull Run. Your husband did. I've felt such an ass ever since, Rosalie! I've seen the scorn in your eyes and known it was wholly deserved!"

She was startled at his sudden change of tone. "But that was all just foolishness. You mustn't dwell on it. You . . ."

"Oh, but I must!" he insisted. "It's the only way to redeem myself. If I can be clear in your eyes, I'll be on the right track. So tell me one thing — in all honesty. If I take the Sanitary Commission job and make a go of it, and if I look after the boys while you're gone, have I a chance of regaining your respect? I don't ask for your love. That would be too much, in view of all that's happened. But if you can respect me, I think I can live with myself."

"But I've always respected you!" she almost wailed.

"I'm sorry, dear. That is simply not so."

Oh, he still had his old power of turning the tables on her! She, who had yearned for the high seriousness of a role of her own in the war, basing the shedding of domestic duties on the seemingly solid ground of his inconsequence, was now faced with a situation where the sacrifice was all on his part and her mission turned into a kind of joy ride.

"I shall most certainly respect you as a commissioner," she said in a low voice from which she attempted to strip the bitterness. "You shall have all the respect at my disposal. All the respect and admiration."

"Then that is settled. We'll tell the boys tonight. But, no, you've already told them of your plans. Is that right?"

"I'm afraid so."

"Then I suggest you get in touch with Mrs. Lindley today, so that she may learn her new job as soon as possible." He rose at last. "And one other thing, my dear. I suggest you take Joanna with you. She's pining to serve."

"And Father? What about Father?"

"Oh, I'll manage to keep an eye on him. Never fear."

When he had gone, she simply burst into tears. Was it conceivable that his gallantry had been cruelly intended? But no, she was not even to have that comfort. He had meant every word of it. The only thing to do now was her duty. She would go to sea. What did it matter if it was not going to give her all the satisfaction she had so foolishly anticipated?

22

Rosalie thought of the voyages of the *Franklin Pierce* to the South and to the North as a preparation and an actuality. Preparation was in the sailing from New York to the Chesapeake on the big, throbbing paddle-wheeler, cleaned and scrubbed and sometimes even freshly painted, with its huge saloon full of neatly made empty camp beds and its decks bare except for the few sailors on duty and the doctors and male nurses lounging in the long chairs, watching the blue Atlantic and the whitecaps and the wheeling gulls. Preparation was efficient, even cheerful: counting stores, filing records, with time to pace the deck, facing the exhilarating breeze. She thought of it as somehow akin to her own protected girlhood, neat, compartmental, guarded snugly by the ship's sides and bottom from monsters of the deep and by the sea itself from the ravening shores with their forests and beasts and wild men. Even after she knew what to expect on their arrival at Virginia shores, Rosalie still loved the voyage out.

Actuality was the trip back, with every available square foot of deck space covered with stretchers and mattresses and cots, occupied by bearded, bandaged young men, most silent, some at times groaning, and every now and then one poor soul hideously shrieking at an amputation that could not be postponed till docking. The six matrons, including herself and Joanna, worked on watches, three at a time, four hours on and four off, doing everything that was asked of them. They stood by the doctors in operations; they assisted the male nurses in changing bandages and linen; they served food on trays; they talked to the men and helped the disabled with their correspondence; they circulated among the beds to answer queries or receive complaints.

Rosalie was surprised at how valuable the discipline of her background proved. She had anticipated just the opposite. She had feared that she might seem remote, awkward, "standoffish." But she discovered that the habit of deference enabled her to fit easily into a military hierarchy, and that it did not surprise her, as much as it did others, to find idiots in high rungs of the ladder of power. She also learned, although she had always been one to deprecate invidious class distinctions, that she had been brought up in so rooted a conviction of her family's superior position that she had no fear of "demeaning" tasks. She and Joanna would cheerfully help the black boys in the galley when the other matrons wouldn't.

But there was also a more personal preparation, afforded by her own sentimental history. She wondered if she were not at last beginning to find that elusive "life of her own" that she had so long assumed would be provided, if at all, only by a husband. She had not, God knew, been a warmonger, and she had been revolted by the cheers and grandstanding that had accompanied the war's outbreak, but was it wrong to feel elevated — even purified — by ministering to the casualties of Armageddon? Was that, too, a kind of false patriotism?

She had always speculated that, when Christ had bade his disciples to give up all — family, friends, property — to follow him, there might have been an actual relief to some in letting go the domestic packs so firmly strapped to their shoulders; that what was being given up might have provided as much motivation as what was to be striven for. Was she now in danger of that kind of backward approach to the light? How little she thought of Union Square and Fifth Avenue. How little she even thought of her own two boys! She was guilty, perhaps, of the hypocrisy of exaltation at her own sacrifice — when that sacrifice had really been a kind of cheerful bonfire.

Work was the obvious answer to such doubts and questions. They occurred only when the hospital had been emptied. When it was full, there was little time for self-evaluation. Even when she sat with the dying, with no duty but to hold a hand, she trained herself to step outside of Rosalie Fairchild and be only a calm, consoling presence. She had learned that at the end men hated any show of tears or pity.

She could even be efficient now at the actual moment of death. One night she sat up till dawn with a Vermont boy — he seemed no older than Fred — who was dying of a head wound. He thought she was his mother and talked in a sibilant whisper about his plans for the farm: the purchase of a new mule team, the development of an apple orchard, the sale of timber. There was something almost unbearably pathetic about such a multitude of detailed plans on the very threshold of extinction. Yet when death came, just before dawn, she heard herself say to the doctor approaching with his lantern:

"This bed is available now, sir. Shall I move the sergeant from the stretcher on the port side? He's been very restless and uncomfortable."

Sometimes there would be a domestic note. A young man, who had had both legs amputated and who was still the most cheerful member of his compartment, asked Rosalie if Miss Handy were a member of the Newport family that lived in Oaklawn.

"Why, indeed she is!" she exclaimed in surprise. "And so am I. We're sisters. Are you from Newport?"

"I worked as an assistant gardener for your father when I was in school there. I thought it was the same Miss Handy, but she looks so different in her uniform. I think it's wonderful of you ladies to do this kind of drudgery!"

"We consider it a privilege to help boys like you."

His eyes just flickered as he promptly changed the subject. "And how is your wonderful old father?"

"Working hard. At supplying the New York regiments."

"At his age! How terrific! But it must be a great hardship for him, having two daughters away at sea. Ask your sister if she remembers Joe Brest."

"Oh, I know she will. I'll send her right over."

She left him, appalled that a man who had permanently lost the use of two young legs should pity an old one who had temporarily lost the use of two middle-aged daughters.

The Joanna Handy of the *Franklin Pierce* was a very different woman from the Joanna Handy of 417 Fifth Avenue. She was still inclined to simper and gush, and she kept her old way of looking at people as if she feared they were going to strike her unless she could disarm them with a desperate giggle, but her fussiness and nervousness seemed to be co-ordinated now in a kind of steady flurry of hard work. The soldiers smiled at her, but it was always clear that they liked her. With her unsmotherable good will and her happy way of joining in any laugh against herself, she had become a kind of ship's mascot.

Aboard a strange ship, without other members of the family, Rosalie was not surprised to find herself developing a new relationship with her sister. What did surprise her was the extent to which Joanna, formerly so meek and self-effacing, except for occasional flaring tantrums, seemed to take the upper hand. It was not that she was in the least bossy or officious. On the contrary, she was the soul of consideration and helpfulness. But she was quicker at adapting herself to shipboard conditions than Rosalie. She seemed to need to be told everything only once, and was always on the alert to add to her knowledge. Rosalie found that, when she had forgotten an instrument or had left something off a doctor's tray, Joanna was often silently at her elbow to repair the omission. And she seemed to do it, too, as much for her as for the doctor. Rosalie was aware of a deeper sisterly affection than she had ever suspected in the past. Poor Jo! They had all taken her so much for granted!

Jo, however, had not taken any of *them* for granted. How well she had observed her younger sister came out in a talk they had on the long, tense morning when the Confederate iron-clad *Merrimack* steamed out of Norfolk harbor to challenge the tiny Federal *Monitor* in Hampton Roads. The *Pierce* was far off, anchored off Fortress Monroe to await the shipment of wounded, but they could hear the distant firing to the east, and all hands stood on deck facing anxiously in that direction. It was a mild, misty morning, and the sun streaked the light clouds with a tawny orange and cast a muffled sparkle on the slaty waters of the quiet Chesapeake.

"If that big gunboat licks the *Monitor*, what do you think will happen?" Joanna asked Rosalie.

"I suppose it'll sink everything in sight. Nothing can stand up to it, they say."

"You mean it could sink our whole navy? Ship by ship?"

"If it could ever find them all."

"And break the blockade? Do you mean the Rebs might win the war with a single boat? Oh, Rosey, what a fantastic world we live in! Would it sink the *Pierce*?"

"A hospital ship? No! Or would it? Maybe there are no gentlemen on ironclads. Maybe they went out with sails."

"And it's all being decided right now, over there!" Joanna faced towards the distant booming and shivered.

"Are you frightened? I know *I* am."

"Do you know something?" Joanna turned to her sister with glittering eyes. Then she giggled. "I'm not. Not a bit!"

"You're very brave!"

"I'm not a bit brave. I'm simply happy. Isn't that an awful thing to say? Happy when we all may be blown to bits? But I am! I've never been happy in my whole life. Never, until I came on board this ship. Is that very wicked?"

Rosalie was moved by this echo of her own thoughts. "Why should it be wicked? Mustn't God want us to be happy every minute, if we can manage it? Even in the most awful times? Didn't we used to hear in Sunday school of whole families of martyrs singing their way happily into the arena?"

"But I never believed any of that. I didn't, really. I believed in God, but I didn't believe he believed in me. Is that heresy? I don't care. I've always thought of God as someone like Father. A person you had to do things for, but who would never do anything for you."

"Why, Jo!"

"Well, it's true. No one's ever done anything for me but you. *You* were the one who got me on this ship. You were the one who shamed Father into letting me go!"

"And you were never happy at home? Really never?"

"Did you think I was?"

"I suppose not, really. But I thought you just wanted a husband."

"Of course I wanted a husband! But that was only *one* of the things I wanted. I could have made do with anything or anyone if I'd only felt *needed!*"

"And you didn't feel that with Frank, at Saint Jude's?"

"I was beginning to. That was the beginning of *this*, really. But this is the real thing!" She stopped again to listen to the firing. "They must be so close together." She shuddered. "Tell me, Rosey. You liked Frank, didn't you? Oh, I don't mean wickedly, like Annie. But in a dreamy kind of way?"

Rosalie wondered at her own total ease at such a question. "Yes. In a dreamy kind of way."

"I have lots of little private 'affairs' like that. I don't suppose there's any harm in them, really."

"Unless you're married."

"Oh?" Joanna looked startled. "You mean there's a wrong? To Dexter?"

"Yes."

"But if he doesn't *know*, Rosey? And if there's nothing to know, anyway?"

"It's what it does to him. In my mind. These little affairs, as you call them, have a way of tweaking a husband's nose. When they're over, he doesn't look quite the same to you."

"You mean he's *worse?*"

Rosalie smiled. "No. Just a mite smaller."

"And that's not so good, is it, if he wasn't too big to start with?"

They looked at each other in surprise and then both laughed. A sailor ran up to give the report that the two iron-clads were actually touching. But the *Monitor* was holding her own!

"I feel as if we were present at the end of the world!" Rosalie exclaimed. "And I'm as calm as if it were Sunday afternoon at Oaklawn!"

Joanna laughed bitterly. "Better the *Merrimack* than that! Oh, Rosey! Have we ever been like this before?"

And the sisters turned again towards the distant firing, gazing across the gray, untroubled water, their arms about each other's waists.

23

DEXTER had never experienced such frustration as he met working for the Sanitary Commission. Now that the first enthusiasm for the war had spent itself, it was proving more difficult to induce people to contribute, even the things most sorely needed. He spent his days and nights calling on businessmen, railroad officials and politicians, arranging for the contribution or purchase of medical supplies and their expeditious passage to the fighting fronts. As men of affairs began to take in the likelihood of a long, hard war, and even of possible defeat, they were less inclined to forgo a profit or incur an inconvenience. Dexter felt at times as if he were hauling a heavily laden barge down a canal. It was impossible to get any way on; the barge would stop dead in the water the moment he relaxed his pull. The war began to seem to him like the ocean in a storm; the commotion was all on the surface, and in the dark deep below the wide-eyed fish poked about the rocks and rushes as usual.

There were some bright spots. His cousin Charley, in what seemed a miraculous change of habits, gave up drinking and began to work hard at the office to save the practice that

Dexter had had largely to give up. Fred and Selby turned into model sons, cooperating with Mrs. Lindley, the house-keeper, to make the house function without Rosalie. And there were the sweet moments when other members of the commission congratulated Dexter on some job particularly well done. But he nonetheless found that he had to keep fighting a growing vulnerability to dark depression.

It seemed to him that his lights had gone out, that he was laboring now, so to speak, for mere survival, rather than for the attainment of any high goal. Always in the past he had worked towards an ideal. He had been on his way, or so he had fancied, to becoming a great lawyer, maybe even a great judge, in a system of jurisprudence that every decade, if not, indeed, every year, brought a step closer to the ultimate coincidence of the arcs of ideal and practical law. He had been on his way to founding a family that would carry on the highest traditions of good citizenship and public leader-ship. And, finally, if war should prove inevitable, he had been looking forward to playing a major role in the attain-ment of emancipation and the guarantee of permanent union.

But what had happened instead? All his ideals seemed to have been blown away in that terrible stampede from Bull Run. The government was vacillating; the military, incom-petent; the business world, greedy. The only persons who really cared were the young men sent off to die uselessly. The war would end in a draw; slavery would survive; the law would be tarnished; the Fairchilds would remain a dull, ordinary, middle-class family. And Dexter himself? Well, what was he *now* but a forgiven adulterer whose wronged wife had taken such glory as was left off with her to a ship on the Chesapeake, leaving him to the bleakness of a mother-less home and a city that cared only for profit?

He would tell himself that he was being absurd. New York was full of people who cared about the war. Did not his own son Fred talk passionately about enlisting as soon as he was of age? Did not Mr. Handy organize committee after committee? Should he not take into consideration that a beggar (and that's what he was, a beggar for the commission!) was bound to be confronted with the worst side of the people he had to approach? Come now, Dexter Fairchild, he would tell his image as he shaved in the morning, you must pull yourself together!

But nothing seemed to work. He made his hours longer, and he simply found himself more tired at night. When Rosalie wrote him about the Vermont lad at whose deathbed she had assisted, he replied bitterly:

> It makes me wonder what right we have to ask young men who lack three hundred dollars to buy a substitute to lay down their lives. I suppose in all wars the young and strong have died for the old and weak, but I wonder if even in Nero's Rome people were not less indifferent to the legions fighting for them in distant Gaul than our New Yorkers are to the boys dying in Virginia.

Charley Fairchild, with whom he sometimes lunched at the Patroons', began to be worried about him.

"You're going to wear yourself out, Dexter. You should bear in mind that it may be a long war."

"How can I complain? Nobody's amputated *my* legs on a rolling hospital ship."

"Is that what Rosalie writes you about? I think she ought to come home. I think you need looking after."

"I might say the same about you and Annie."

"But I don't *want* Annie back! Annie and I are through. You know that!"

"But you're not divorced."

"Dexter, do you honestly think you're the one to advise me about my marriage?"

"Forgive me! I don't seem to know what I'm saying these days."

"Forget it. Annie writes that she's decided to live permanently in Paris. She'll bring Kate up as a French girl. That's all right. If the war's ever over I'll go across the ocean and see my little mademoiselle. And maybe one day buy her a nice French husband. American girls are always happy in Paris."

"What about Bleeker?"

"Oh, that's bust up already, hadn't you heard? He's gone to London. I think he has a position on the *Times*. Annie should be able to be at least half-respectable. You can manage that in Paris. She will be *cette charmante petite Madame Fairchild*, with an always absent husband, who is *just* discreet enough about her admirers to keep her from becoming a demimondaine. In middle age she will have a recognized, accepted liaison with an elderly duke. And when she's old she'll play cards and be converted and become a *dévote*."

"Charley, what have I *done* to your life?"

"What have you done to your own, old man? *You*'re the one I'm worried about!"

Later that same afternoon Dexter was scheduled to meet with Silas Cranberry at the latter's great department store on lower Broadway. He had a splitting headache and felt faintly feverish, but would this have excused a soldier on the eve of battle? Promptly at four o'clock he presented his card at the information desk of the emporium.

Cranberry liked marble, in his store as in his mansion. The huge square building, which covered a whole block, boasted

a white marble façade, and in its center, a white marble
courtyard, filled with ferns and palms and covered with a
giant skylight. In the middle of the courtyard was a fountain
surrounded by marble-topped tables, one of which was permanently reserved for the coffee breaks of the proprietor
himself, who liked to mingle with his customers at fixed
points of the day. It was here that he received Dexter.

"The Edgeworth property runs along the Sound near Ros-
lyn," Dexter explained. "It's the perfect site for a sanitarium.
The buildings are easily adaptable for public use. I figure
that we could put up five hundred convalescents and fifty
cases of permanent disability. Colonel Edgeworth is willing
to donate the entire hundred acres, with all buildings and
furnishings, plus a starting endowment fund of a hundred
thousand dollars."

Cranberry's eyes, small dark spots in a moon of white,
blinked. "I suppose he can afford it."

"No doubt. Nevertheless, I am overwhelmed."

"I thought you were too used to picking the pockets of the
rich to be overwhelmed by anything, Fairchild."

Dexter smiled carefully. He had learned to check his feelings at the gate when he came for money. "I still feel that
Colonel Edgeworth has shown himself a great patriot."

"He inherited half his money and married the rest. Why
shouldn't he give it away?"

"Not all in his position feel as he does."

"Colonel Edgeworth's a member of the Patroons', ain't he?"

"He is."

"How do I know he isn't the member who blackballed me?"
There was an ominous pause. "Well, you knew I'd been
blackballed, didn't you, Fairchild?"

"How could I not? It was as great a humiliation for your sponsor as for you."

"But you didn't resign, did you?"

"No." Dexter moistened his lips as he prepared himself for the ultimate concession. "I can't propose you again unless I'm a member, can I? I'm afraid there was a bit of old-time prejudice against storekeepers in your case. But that sort of thing is rapidly disappearing. A year or two more and we shouldn't have any trouble."

Cranberry broke into a jeering laugh. "You must be planning to ask me for something awfully big, Fairchild!"

"I care for our wounded, sir."

"Of course, of course. But will you assure me that Colonel Edgeworth was not the man who blackballed me?"

Again Dexter hesitated. He was perfectly willing to give the assurance, but it was unwise, in soliciting, to seem too great a toady. "I'm afraid that would be violating the confidence of the club. You might in that way go through the whole membership, one by one, until I was obliged to be silent about a name."

"Well, I guess that's the right answer," Cranberry said in a more relaxed tone. "I wouldn't really care to have you betray a confidence. What's on your mind, Fairchild? Shoot."

Dexter told him that the commission wanted to establish four such convalescent homes and that he had sites in Putnam, Suffolk and Westchester counties under option for the remaining three. Would Cranberry consider buying the Suffolk site and endowing it with $100,000?

"I'd consider it, yes."

"Would you more than consider it?"

"Let me see the papers and the plan, Fairchild. I'm not a

man to waste your time. If I agree to study something, I'm serious about it."

Dexter, fatigued but elated, rose. "I'll be back in the morning with all the documents."

"Wait just a minute. What do you propose to name this convalescent home? The one in Suffolk. *My* home."

Dexter reseated himself. "How about the Silas P. Cranberry Refuge for Soldiers and Sailors?"

Cranberry grunted. "I don't know about the wording. But the idea of putting my name on it is all right. I think the man who puts up the cash should get the credit. What's Edgeworth's place going to be called?"

"Well, the Colonel happens to be a great admirer of General McClellan, so we're naming it for him."

"I hope it cures more soldiers than he wins battles! And the other two, what will they be called?"

"Well, one hasn't a donor as yet, and the other will almost certainly be given a saint's name. The probable benefactor is a very devout Catholic."

"I see. And how will that make *me* look, when your announcement is made — the only one of the four with the egotism to insist on the use of his own moniker!"

"I don't think anyone would give it a thought. We needn't make simultaneous announcements of the four grants."

"But people will be bound to associate them!"

Dexter was nonplused by this wholly unexpected objection. "I'll be glad to do anything you suggest to avoid it."

"I don't suggest, Fairchild. I stipulate! Here are my terms. My funding of the Suffolk home will be subject to this double condition: not only must it be given *my* name; the other three homes must be given the names of *their* donors!"

"But, my dear Cranberry, that may cost us the Colonel's grant! I had already suggested that his home be named for him, and he said it was against his principles."

"Then you'll have to persuade him to change his principles."

"And if I fail?"

"Then you'll have one less home, that's all."

"But, really, I cannot see how the others will affect you. I beg you to consider . . ."

"You have heard my terms, Fairchild. Good morning. If I see you back here tomorrow, I shall assume they have been met."

Dexter felt dazed as he made his way out of the store. He could hardly believe that he was actually going to have to go to the other donors with so unbecoming a proposition. And would they be big enough to make such a sacrifice? Did he even *want* them to? The counters that he passed seemed to be overflowing with luxuries; the well-dressed female customers pushed past each other to be the first to buy. He thought again of Rosalie's letter about the Vermont boy. What *right* did they have to ask mere boys to pour out their young blood on the red dirt of Virginia while these sharp-toothed old harpies jostled each other in the hunt for silks and satins? He felt his fingers tighten on the handle of his cane. If he didn't get out of there soon, there might be a scene like Christ with the money changers in the temple.

He decided to call at 417 Fifth Avenue and ask Mr. Handy's advice. He had not seen the old gentleman for a week. Perhaps *he* would be able to persuade the Colonel to allow his name to be used. But Mr. Handy, when met, was not in a mood to talk about anything but his remarkable experience over the preceding weekend. He had been just going out when Dexter rang the doorbell, but he immediately turned back into the house, guiding his son-in-law by the elbow to the billiard room, where he made him sit down and listen.

"So delighted you called, dear boy! I came up from New Jersey this morning after the most fantastic weekend I've ever had in my life. I've been dying to tell someone about it. You know my cousin Rusty Hatch. Well, only last Sunday he made Ward McAllister a bet of twenty-five hundred dollars that he couldn't take a deserted country house in Bernardsville and fix it up in five days' time so that he could entertain a house party of twelve for the weekend. And it had to be a weekend, too, with all the trimmings: service, horses, food, wines, music, the works. The loser would pay all expenses, in addition to the bet. Well, Rusty should have known Ward better. McAllister went to work, and, by Jove, a magic castle materialized! I was lucky enough to be one of the favored guests. Lily and Rutgers were there, too. You should have seen it, Dexter! On Saturday afternoon there was a drag hunt for the younger fry, and that night a dinner of eight courses and six wines followed by a string quartet and then dancing! Rusty didn't even wait for Sunday before conceding. At midnight, as we all cheered, he raised his champagne glass to toast Ward and write him his check."

Dexter gazed at the old man as if seeing him for the first time. "I must write Rosalie about it," he said in a flat tone. "I'm sure she'll be amused."

Mr. Handy coughed. "Of course, it might not seem as amusing to someone on a hospital ship," he cautioned. "One tends to lose one's perspective in the face of so much suffering."

"You don't think, sir, that Mr. McAllister may have lost some of his?"

"And your father-in-law's?" Mr. Handy's temper had immediately exploded. "I assume his is gone, too! Well, let me tell you, young man, that you don't win wars by pulling long faces. I've done my share in this conflict, and if I choose to relax over a weekend I think I'm entitled to do so without being made to feel a heartless old fool by my own family!"

"Mr. Handy!" Dexter exclaimed, jumping to his feet. "Let me apologize, sir. Please! I don't know what's wrong with me. I'm tired. Perhaps I've been working too hard."

Mr. Handy, immediately mollified, rose to place a pardoning hand on his shoulder. "I think you have, dear boy. Now I really look at you, you *do* seem a bit peaked. Go home and get some rest. Go to a music hall. Remember what makes Jack a dull boy. It must be lonely for you at home without Rosalie."

"The *Pierce* is due here tomorrow."

"That's fine! We'll have a party! Do you meet her at the dock?"

"No. She likes me to wait till all the patients are disembarked."

"Very well. Give her all my love. And bring her to dinner here tomorrow, will you?"

Dexter returned to his office, where he had supper at his desk, working late. By the time he got home, both boys were already in bed, so he retired, but could not sleep. Lying awake in the dark he could make no sense out of an image that kept coming back and back to him. It was of himself, alone, standing on top of one of those strange pyramids discovered in Yucatan. He seemed to be arrayed in a robe of some stiff outlandish cloth and to be waving his arms to a multitude below. He shook his head repeatedly to dispel the crazy vision.

And then, suddenly, sitting up in bed with a start, he recalled the talk with Rosalie in which she had likened him to a high priest. So that was the image! Of himself, at the top of the steps of the pyramid, swaying in a sort of crazy dance, brandishing a knife, calling for human victims. But none would come. He saw that as he lay back on his pillow. The people below were united now. They would creep slowly up the pyramid stairway, step by step. And when they had reached the top, they would throw him down, so that his body, like a big floppy doll, would turn over and over, bouncing from step to step, his skull crushed, the poor rag piled at last in a little heap at the bottom, to the squeals and laughter of all.

Exhausted, he fell asleep.

24

THE *Franklin Pierce*, white with tall black funnels and the red sign "U.S. HOSPITAL" painted on her fender, lay lashed to a narrow pier, like the carcass of a leviathan. Dexter could discern no sign of life on board except for a sailor on guard at the gangway, and he deduced that the sick and the dead had already been removed.

"Oh, yes, Mrs. Fairchild's aboard," the sailor answered him. "Miss Handy went ashore an hour ago, but your wife says she can never get her paperwork done until the ship's cleared. May I say that we're all great admirers of Mrs. Fairchild, sir?"

"No more than I!"

He was directed to a passageway at the end of which he found a small office and Rosalie, dressed in gray, working at her desk. She turned around without starting when she heard him, but as she took in his pallor she jumped up with a little cry.

"Dexter, you look done in! Are you ill?"

At this he felt at last the full impact of his fatigue. "I

guess I'd better sit down." He seemed to drop into the chair
by her desk. She scanned his countenance anxiously.

"Can I get you something? What's wrong?"

"No, no." He held up a hand to stay her ministrations. "I'll
be fine. I'm a bit tired, that's all. I think it's the shock of this
business about your father's weekend."

"Father's weekend? What on earth are you talking about?
Don't tell me the old boy's been kicking up his heels!"

Dexter, frowning at her lightness, proceeded gravely to
relate the story of the McAllister-Hatch bet and how it was
won. He thought that she looked at him rather strangely as
she listened.

"And that's what's upset you?" she asked.

"Well, doesn't it *you*?"

"Oh, I'm used to Father. You should be too, by now."

"But in wartime, Rosalie!"

She shrugged. "What can you do about it? He's a pretty
old dog to learn new tricks."

He thought he detected a totally new tone in her voice in
so referring to her parent. "I suppose you're right. But it
seems to have knocked the stuffing out of me. Last night I
kept dreaming about it. Waking up and then dreaming about
it again. I saw myself somehow stretching my arms out, and
reaching and reaching, and I seemed always just about to
snatch the laurel of victory from the hand of a kind of marble
effigy — the statue of a woman, I think — a Mrs. Stowe or a
Mrs. Howe perhaps — and then suddenly there was a jerk
at my jacket, and there was your father, with vine leaves in
his hair and holding a jug, a veritable old Bacchus, pulling
me back and crying, 'You'll be late for the party, my boy!'
And then I'd snarl at him, like an angry dog, but he'd just

cackle with laughter and make me feel a fool. Oh, such a fool! The last time I actually woke up sobbing!"

"Poor Dexter. Imagine! Mrs. Howe holding the laurel. What a picture! But you shouldn't have made such an idol of Father. You forget, he's an old man."

"So was Cato."

"Yes, so was Cato. Well?"

"But don't you *care* if the war is lost?"

"Will that be the result of Papa's weekends?"

"I suppose I must seem half-crazy to you," he said, with a deep sigh. "But then you never believed in the war."

"I didn't, in the beginning. But I think I've changed."

"You have?"

She seemed to be considering how to put it. "I guess I don't know just what people mean by believing in it. I believe we had better win it."

"What has changed you?"

"The cost of it. The ghastly cost. I can't bear to have it all in vain. I had thought, if we could only avoid bloodshed, the Southerners themselves might ultimately see that slavery wasn't going to work. But now, with all the bitterness of the war, who knows? And when I think of the thousands of young men butchered and worse than butchered . . ." For a moment she closed her eyes. "No, we can't go back to slavery after all that. We *have* to go on." Her voice rose to something like a wail. "Even if Fred has one day to be part of it!"

He gazed at her admiringly. "Well, nobody can say *you've* lost your nerve." And then, suddenly the room seemed to spin. "What's going on? Are we . . . are we under way?"

"Dexter! You *are* ill!"

When he recovered consciousness he was lying in a bunk

in a semidarkened cabin, aware of being clad in pajamas. Next, he became conscious of a small porthole just above his head. Then he heard Rosalie's voice at his side.

"You're going to be perfectly all right, dear. You're in one of the *Pierce*'s cabins. You fainted, and we put you to bed. You may have a mild case of pneumonia. You're going to stay right here where I can look after you."

He turned his head to look at her. "Won't the ship sail? Won't I be using a bunk needed for a soldier?"

"She won't sail for at least a week. By then you'll be ready to go home."

"But won't I be interfering with your work?"

"A husband comes first. Even in wartime."

He closed his eyes, with a feeling of blessed relief, and slept again.

The next day passed in a kind of euphoria. Being on a vessel gave him a sense of utter remoteness. He was detached from work, from war, from friends and family, from everything and everyone but Rosalie. And she was a different Rosalie, stronger, firmer, more solicitous, kinder. He basked in rest and coolness. He would lie happily alone, when she was busy elsewhere, and listen to the slap of water against the ship's sides and the cry of the gulls. He almost felt that he did not want to get well.

They began to talk more as his health improved. They discussed the trips of the *Pierce* and his work on the commission. Would the war be the making of Joanna? Might she even yet marry? She told him that Jules Bleeker was writing a pro-Confederate column for a London newspaper and that he and Annie had split up.

"Yes, I heard. Charley told me. She'll never stay with any man."

"She's as giddy in love as Father is with his parties!"

"Ah, but your father works for the cause." After a pause, he continued in a different tone. "Rosalie?"

"Yes, dear?"

"May I ask you something serious? Do you think you and I could ever go back?"

"To where?"

"To the way we were when we were first married."

She gave the sheet she was folding a sharp pat. "Should you really want to? Were we so fine then?"

"Of course, I know you never really approved of me. Not from the very beginning. You thought I was worldly and snobbish."

"You were certainly worldly. I'm not so sure you were snobbish. And I think I might not have minded your worldliness — after all, my background was not exactly ascetic — if I had thought it was sincere. Like Papa's. But there was always something . . . well, artificial about it."

"You mean I put it on?"

"In a way. As if you were under some kind of a dark duty to be worldly."

"But that sounds crazy!"

"Maybe you were a bit crazy. I was even sometimes half-afraid you might convert me! Because there was something fanatical about you. Everything had to be so black or white."

"Well, you won't have to worry about my blacks and whites anymore," he said ruefully. "They have all blurred."

"No doubt you'll repaint them again neatly enough when you recover."

"Oh, Rosalie! You're laughing at me again."

"Not really. I'm laughing at both of us. My blacks and whites were as bad as yours. Worse! Oh, *I* was such a prig,

Dexter! So sure of my sincerity, my honesty, my deep, *deep* heart! But I've learned on this vessel that nobody needs my silly heart. I'm just as useful as I am competent, not a whit more. And that made me do some thinking about hearts. What right did I have to think I had any more than you? Any more than Annie?"

"Oh, you have more than Annie."

"Annie started life with a heart. Only perhaps it got smothered somewhere along the line. Yours, my dear, is fine. You mustn't worry about it."

"I'd like to think we *could* go back."

She rose. "I think that's enough for now. We must remember you're still a convalescent. I'll put this quilt over the porthole. You should rest, my dear."

When she had done this, she leaned down in the semidarkness to kiss him on the forehead. It was more than the kiss of a devoted nurse, if perhaps less than that of a devoted wife. But he felt that it might do — and certainly that he would try with everything he had to make it do. When the door was closed behind her, he smiled to himself at the idea that his old ego was coming back with his health. He was going to insist that she love him at least as much as she had loved the war!

25

ROSALIE was discouraged about Dexter's convalescence. He remained for five days on the *Pierce* and then spent a week in bed at Union Square. The pneumonia seemed to take care of itself, but his spirits continued low. When he got up he would amble slowly about the second story, standing for minutes on end staring down into the street. His doctor told him that pneumonia was a well-known depressant, but even so, his languor and apathy gave her concern.

Dexter himself insisted that he was perfectly all right and that she could now return to her vessel, but she suspected that he dreaded her going. She discussed this with Charley Fairchild one afternoon in the front hall, as he was leaving, after visiting Dexter upstairs.

"You're really going back?" he asked in dismay.

"Well, not till Dexter's well enough, of course. But in time I think I must. Don't you?"

"I'll be perfectly frank with you, Rosalie. I don't think Dexter can manage without you. He doesn't seem to be able to organize himself. He's been working much too hard. None of the other commissioners put in the hours he does. They all have their own businesses to carry on. But Dexter doesn't even come to our office anymore."

"I thought you didn't need him," Rosalie responded in surprise. "I thought you were handling everything so beautifully! And let me say at once, Charley, that I consider that the men who are keeping the businesses running for their partners in war work, are contributing just as much to the cause! *They* will be the unsung heroes of the war."

"That's all very well." Charley showed little enthusiasm for her endorsement. "And I know Dexter likes to think I'm carrying his load. But the truth is, I'm not. He's a far better lawyer than I. The clients will stick along with me for a while, but if it's a long war, we're going to lose a lot of them. Dexter owes it to himself and his family not to let the practice he took so many years to build up go to ruin."

"But what can *I* do about that?"

"If you're home, you can make him go to the office at least two or three days a week. That should do the trick. I've tried, and he won't listen to me. But he can't disregard you, when you're pleading for yourself and the boys!"

Rosalie felt the coils of his argument closing uncomfortably around her. "But how can I use a selfish argument in times like these? Besides, would it be fair? I can't pretend that the boys and I depend altogether on his law practice. Dexter knows I have substantial expectations."

Charley frowned, as if to shield her from embarrassment. "That may be more questionable than you think. As a member of the firm that represents your father I should not make any disclosure of his affairs, but I think, under the circumstances, I may be justified in telling you that he has made some unfortunate investments in the past three years and that he is living well beyond his income."

"But that's terrible! You mean he might die and leave Joanna strapped?"

"It's nice of you to think only of Joanna."

"Well, she's the one who'd be worst off. She has no trade, unless she goes in for professional nursing. There really ought to be some way that parents who accept the sacrifices of grown-up children should obligate themselves to look after them!"

"You mustn't be too hard on your father. He's always been an optimist. He has no concept of how much he's spending."

"Then someone should tell him!"

"Who? A daughter who's off at sea? But the really important thing is for you to get Dexter back to work. *Both* at the Sanitary Commission *and* at his law office. Forgive me for saying it, Rosey, but I can't help feeling that a man of Dexter's capability is going to be more valuable to the Sanitary Commission than one more nurse. Valuable though I'm sure that nurse is."

"Oh, of course, I know that," she conceded gloomily. "He can build a hospital while I'm nursing one soldier. But I still can't see why I'm that indispensable. Must Dexter be *made* to do two jobs? Can't you, really and truly, hold the office together? I'm sure, dear Charley, you underestimate yourself!"

"Don't forget I have a problem. I'm on top of it now, but you know what they say about alcoholics . . ."

"Oh, hush up!" she cried in dismay, hastily putting her fingers over his lips. "You're going to be just fine! But, all right — I'll think about it."

"Poor Rosalie." He shook his head sadly. "I see how much you want to go back."

"Oh, run along now, please!" she exclaimed sharply, afraid

that she was going to weep. "You've done your job. Enough for one day, anyway!"

But as soon as Charley had gone, she remembered her own trust fund. Surely, *that* would always be hers, no matter what her father lost. And couldn't she live on it? Well, of course, she could live on it, and so could Dexter and the boys! It wasn't much, but at least they would be housed and clothed and fed. How absurd were the expectations of New York society! If you couldn't keep a carriage and leave town in the summer, people thought you might as well turn your face to the wall.

All that night she kept dreaming of the *Pierce* and waking up. *Why* was she really needed at home? The boys were exuberantly healthy and totally occupied with school and sports. Mrs. Lindley had the household under perfect control. Dexter was in poor spirits, true, but there was nothing *physically* wrong with him. And the agreement of his three big donors to go along with Silas Cranberry's outrageous condition had been a great feather in his cap. He was the hero of the Sanitary Commission! How could that not cheer him up in time? Was it not even possible — just barely possible, that he was putting his gloominess on a bit? To hold her back? Might he not even be *jealous* of the *Pierce*?

The next morning, when Dexter's mother made her daily call on the patient, Rosalie was struck with a brilliant idea. Following Mrs. Fairchild on her way out to the front hall, she asked if she might have a word with her.

. "Of course, my dear. You may have two. What are the old for but to listen?"

"I was wondering, when I go back to the *Pierce*, if it would be possible for you to move in here and keep an eye on Dexter. I know that's a great imposition, but Mrs. Lindley would do everything for you. She would make you thoroughly comfortable. And it would be so nice for Fred and Selby, having their grandmother here when they come home!"

Mrs. Fairchild searched her daughter-in-law's eyes carefully, as if looking for hidden traps or motives. "Don't you think Mrs. Lindley would resent having someone look over her shoulder? For that's what I'd be doing. You can't trust that breezy type. Always so enthusiastic and busy, busy. But when they catch colds — and they always do (maybe it's from their own breezes!) they tend to go to pieces."

"Well, I should tell her, of course, that you had complete authority."

Her mother-in-law grunted. "That never works. No, dear, I think I can do better for you by just checking in every day, as I have been."

Rosalie reflected bitterly that it was probably her own fault that Mrs. Fairchild was not more obliging. Her relationship with her mother-in-law had never been warm. Her appreciation of the latter's rule of never interfering with her or the children had been tempered by her suspicion that it had as much the taint of indifference as the merit of policy. And she had never been able to bridge what she deemed the gulf between their values: Dexter's mother, to her view, was worldly to the marrow of her being. Living all her life on the fringes of wealth, she had been obliged to cultivate its possessors, with the inevitable result that she had become more conservative than they.

Rosalie supposed now that Mrs. Fairchild's reluctance to move into her house sprang from a desire not to appear to condone the "folly" of her marine nursing, and she prepared herself for a lecture on her own domestic duties. But it was not forthcoming.

"How soon do you think you'll be going back?" she asked instead.

"Well, how soon do you think I can safely leave Dexter?"

Mrs. Fairchild grunted again. "So long as you ask me, I think it's better to take the bull by the horns."

"Meaning?"

"Meaning that if you're going, you'd better go."

"And just leave him? Ill?" Rosalie contemplated with surprise the restless little woman before her. Mrs. Fairchild had a way of fiercely shaking her head and shoulders when she had a point to make. She would continue these gesticulations even after she had made it.

"Dexter's not going to die," his mother observed bleakly.

"But I assume that a wife's duties are more than merely mortuary!"

"He'll get along."

"You have more confidence in him than Charley does." Rosalie found it odd to be taking sides against herself. "He thinks he'll work himself into a crack-up and ruin his law practice if I'm not around to direct him."

"Charley just wants to be free to go back to his bottle."

"Oh, Mrs. Fairchild! What a terrible thing to say!"

"It sounds terrible, but don't forget my long experience with the male members of the Fairchild family. You know how my husband treated me. And how Dexter has treated *you!*"

Rosalie was startled by a novel, vindictive gleam in those small glittering eyes.

"But that is all over, Mrs. Fairchild!"

"Over! A man does that to you, and you can call it over? When it happened to me, I had to slave to make ends meet to bring up my children. There were no hospital ships for me!

But I tell you this, Rosalie. If I'd been off on a boat with a life of my own, I'd have never come back! Never!"

"Of course, you would have! For the children's sake."

"Maybe I'd have taken them with me. I don't know. The times were different, then. But of one thing I'm certain. If I'd had what you have, I wouldn't have given it up for any man under the sun!"

"If Dexter could hear you!"

"Would you like me to go upstairs and tell him to his face? I'd be glad to!"

"No, no, in the name of God, please!"

All she wanted now was to get the terrible little old lady out of her house. How was it possible that, from all the cards and card parties, from all the gossip over the needlepoint, from all the evenings on gilt chairs watching the young fry dancing, from all the murmured condolences and festive congratulations of a New York social life, should have sprung this maenad! Was the war going to tear every mask from every living countenance?

But Mrs. Fairchild was leaving now; she was assuring her, in her old, brisk tone, that she would call regularly to be sure that Mrs. Lindley wasn't getting sloppy.

"I know she's *started* well. But don't forget they get colds!"

Rosalie accompanied her to the stoop, nodding dumbly at her injunctions. But when she had closed the door behind her mother-in-law, she stretched her back up against it tightly and searched the ceiling with wild eyes, as if seeking a remedy there for her desperation. Even Dexter's mother had never loved him! The boy must have been included in the abounding wrath against his sex aroused by his father's desertion. And how could she now leave a man whom nobody loved and when she alone had promised to? How could she

leave a man who, with her help and support, and a semblance, maybe, of love, might build hospitals for the wounded
and a great law practice for her sons? While she indulged
her silly fantasy of being Florence Nightingale? "O God, I
have no choice!" she cried harshly aloud. "None at all!"

* * *

Joanna came for dinner that night; Mr. Handy had gone to
a party. Dexter retired early; Charley Fairchild took the
boys to a dramatic version of *Uncle Tom's Cabin,* and the
sisters passed the evening in the parlor together. Rosalie told
Joanna of her present resolution to quit the *Pierce,* and they
heatedly argued the merits of her decision for an hour. When
Joanna at last appeared to have accepted it, she then told
Rosalie that she had made the same decision for herself.

"Oh, Jo! No!"

"I'm perfectly calm about it. You needn't worry about me.
I've had my cry, and it was a good one. I've faced the fact
that so long as I'm doing this of my own free will, so long
as nobody is *making* me do it, I can live with the fact."

"But it's too absurd! You're not in my fix. Father's perfectly
all right. Look where he is tonight! And, anyway, I'll be here
to keep an eye on him."

"You'll have your hands full with Dexter and the boys.
And Father is *not* perfectly all right. He is rapidly losing
the sight in one eye. He fell on the stairs yesterday and only
by a miracle didn't break anything. Doctor Strong tells me
he thinks he's had a small stroke and that we must expect
more. He may become totally incapacitated at any time. Of
course, he could live for years, but he is definitely going to
need someone to look after him and run the house. The
place is a mess. I'm going to have to fire three of the maids,

as it is. No, Rosalie, I must do it, that's all. It's hard on me, and it's hard on you. The war's hard on everyone."

"But, my dear, we could get a housekeeper and a nurse, if need be . . ."

"No, Rosey." She had never seen Joanna so calm, so firm. "He needs a daughter, and I'm going to be that daughter. I shall go back now. I don't want to talk about it anymore. And, of course, there will be hospitals where I can work here. Father won't require all my time. Not yet, anyway."

"And I'll work with you!"

"Yes. I shall like that." Joanna peered out the hall window and saw that her father's carriage was there. Rosalie helped her into her coat and tied the strings of her bonnet under her chin. Joanna kissed her. "Good night, dear."

"I wish to God we were back at Fortress Monroe!"

"Listening to the gunfire? How bloodthirsty you are, Rosey! But so am I. Is this our penance?"

Rosalie, watching her sister lift her black satin skirt as she descended the stoop to take the proffered hand of the coachman and step into the landau, wondered if it could be the same woman who had cleaned the deck of the *Pierce's* galley on her hands and knees and had helped the male nurses with the chamber pots.

PART III

In the Beauty of the Lilies

26

ON NEW YEAR'S DAY of 1868 the sky was white and clear, and the long icicles that hung down the windowpanes outside the dining room on Union Square made Dexter think of the diamond pendants that his brother-in-law, David Ullman, had bought for Jane to celebrate his firm's purchase of a million acres of phosphate mines in Georgia. After reading Horace Greeley's passionate call for the impeachment of the President, he glanced up at the impassive brown countenance of his son Fred bent over the financial page.

At last those slaty gray eyes were lifted to meet his.

"Something in your mind, Dad?"

"Just that everything seems to point to a rather exciting new year."

"Well, it should be one for me. If the old Commodore makes good his threat to grab Erie."

Fred worked for Bristow & Mayer, one of the brokerage firms associated with the "Vanderbilt crowd." Bristow had married the old man's niece. Fred was totally absorbed in his work.

"Oh, I wasn't referring to anything as earthshaking as

that," his father retorted with rather labored sarcasm. "I was thinking of this proposed impeachment."

"Do you suppose they'll really go through with it?"

"I'm betting they will."

"And you think it a good thing? You want to see Ben Wade President of the United States?"

"It's not that," Dexter retorted with a grimace. He paused to consider his words. He knew that he tended to become highly agitated at what he considered the outrage of the South's regaining in peace what it had lost in war, and nothing irritated his son more than what Fred called "waving the bloody shirt." Fred was still, at least to his father's eyes, the lean bronzed hero of the Wilderness Campaign, the youngest aide on Grant's staff, whom a year of horror had changed from a meticulous, almost prissy youth into a cynical and hardened veteran. After three years of peace, during which he had rather grudgingly lived at home, Dexter was still afraid of him. "Let me put it this way. I do not believe that Andrew Johnson has so purged his heart of Southern sympathies as to be able properly to administer a reconstruction program to which he has been overtly hostile."

"He doesn't have to administer it. The army does that."

"But he's working against it, Fred. He's undermining it!" Again Dexter paused, aware of his now more tensely beating heart. He could not seem to subdue his indignation. Were four years of holocaust to have been in vain?

"By firing Stanton?" Fred demanded. "Isn't it going a bit far to impeach a President for removing a contumacious member of his own cabinet?"

"That is only the legal reason."

"Is it even legal? Isn't there a serious constitutional question there?"

"Undoubtedly." Dexter snatched at the temporary calm of legal analysis. "Johnson may have power under the Constitution to rid himself of his secretary of war. The true question is whether he is unconstitutionally opposing the reorganization of the rebel states. That is how the article of impeachment should be drafted. Do you believe, Fred, you, who have put your life on the line for our union, that those states should be readmitted before they have genuinely accepted the principle of negro suffrage?"

"But is military occupation going to make that acceptance any more genuine?"

"General Grant seems to think so. Isn't he your hero?"

"He *was* my hero. I'm not sure one should have heroes in peacetime. Anyway, I'm glad I have nothing to do with the occupation. It's always a shabby business, and brings out the rats."

"But if it's necessary, Fred?"

"Maybe it is. Maybe it isn't."

"If it's shabby, it's because all the right young men, like yourself, have left it to the regulars."

"Well, what are we supposed to do? Stay in uniform forever? I did my stint, Dad. As you have said, often enough."

Fred went back to his newspaper, and Dexter tried to do the same, but he found he could not read. Fred was always so prickly about anything concerning the war. Sometimes it seemed impossible for his family either to speak about it or be silent. Dexter would never forget the terrible time, in '64, when Fred had been hospitalized with a head wound in Alexandria, and he had taken advantage of a business trip to the capital to make a flying visit to his son's bedside. He had been struck by the remarkable alteration in Fred's looks. Pallor and emaciation had brought out the fine, strong lines of his bone structure. The shining gray eyes, the rich chestnut curls of his hair seemed to give life to a beautiful marble mask. Dexter had allowed himself to go overboard in an editorial for the Sanitary Commission *Gazette*. He had ventured the opinion that the phoenix of American youth would arise triumphant from the ashes of war, that young men like his wounded son would be better citizens for the stress they had undergone. Fred, unfortunately, had seen the article and had bitterly resented what he had termed his father's "capitalization" of a minor discomfort.

"I guess you're not really out of uniform when you're working for old Vanderbilt," Dexter ventured now, hoping that he was moving to a safer subject. "Is Harlem-Central really going to make a grab for Erie?"

"Everything points to it, Dad." Fred again put down his paper. "Central needs a line to Buffalo. Look at a railway map. It fits like a piece of a jigsaw puzzle."

"Dan Drew is going to be a hard man to take over. And I hear those youngsters, Gould and Fisk, are the trickiest things in town."

"True. But Vanderbilt knows all about them. They're out for money and nothing else. They've been milking Erie dry. They're too greedy for their own good, that's the point. I'm sure we can take Erie, if we go about it right."

"You really admire men like the Commodore, don't you?"

"There aren't any men like the Commodore! He's unique. You should watch him in action, Dad. For seventy-four, he's astounding. You talk about heroes. Well, he's the Ulysses S. Grant of 1868!"

"Who's the Ulysses S. Grant of 1868?"

Rosalie had just come in to take her place at the end of the breakfast table. She no longer appeared in the dressing gown to which Dexter had privately objected some years before, but he sometimes now missed it. For if she had then seemed inclined to linger too long in the house, to dally overmuch in facing the demands of her day, she now had the air of being ready to sally forth too early, to leave behind the domestic hearth too cheerfully, even too ruthlessly, in order to offer her brisk attention and alert presence to friends — or opponents — who might assail her on her very stoop. This morning she was arrayed in sober gray and had on a box hat that seemed to deny every principle of femininity. But the large troubled eyes, the brief, deprecating smile, were all of the old Rosalie.

Fred explained his reference.

"That old pirate! Really, Fred, I don't know where your values have gone. Isn't it bad enough to have you working for him without singing his praises under our roof?"

Her words were wormwood to Dexter, though of a wormwood that now seemed to be part of a daily diet. If he stood too much in awe of their oldest son — and he admitted such a tendency — surely Rosalie erred in the opposite extreme. She loved Fred, certainly, but on her own terms. She had worried about him desperately in the last year of the war, but now that he was home safe she seemed to have put that behind her. She knew as well as Dexter that Fred was paying marked attention to his boss's daughter, Elmira Bristow, a great-niece of Commodore Vanderbilt, but did that induce her to moderate in the least her strenuous language about the tycoon of Central? And the extraordinary part of it all was that Fred, however openly resentful of his mother, seemed to care for her approval more than that of anyone else, including Elmira Bristow.

"I have noticed, Ma, that people who are concerned with

civil rights tend to assume omniscience in all political and financial matters. You might find it helpful to face the fact that you know nothing whatever about the business world."

"I know it's dog eat dog, and that's enough for me."

Dexter could never seem to stand apart in these mother-son confrontations. He suffered from an uneasy compulsion to run between the bristling opponents, for all the world like some silly Sabine woman, a babe in arms, thrusting herself between the pikes of her embattled kinsmen. "I suggest, my dear, that Fred views these things in a somewhat different light," he observed mildly. "He sees Mr. Vanderbilt, if I take him correctly, as a creative force — perhaps a rough one, but still creative. When the Commodore marshals his millions to some vast acquisitive end — as, say, purchasing control of the Erie line — it is with the purpose of imposing order on chaos."

"You mean a monopoly."

"Well, what's wrong with a monopoly, Ma?" Fred demanded hotly. "If it's in the right hands?"

"I'd like to ask the poor men in Erie that question."

"The poor men in Erie!" Fred turned to his father, in a hopeless appeal from female obtuseness. "Do you think, Dad, Mother has any conception of how corrupt and rotten a man like Gould is? Of course not! Where would she have met such a type?" He faced his mother again with a pitying condescension. "Take it from me, Ma, the objects of your sympathy are the vermin that come in through the drains."

"I suppose that's just your opinion, Fred. There could be others, couldn't there?"

"Not about Jim Fisk, anyway."

"Well, I don't presume to have any informed judgment about the directors of Erie. But I do note that in your attitude these days, my boy, there seems to be a considerable dose of Number 417."

Dexter was startled to hear Rosalie, for the first time, refer to her father's general philosophy simply by his address. Did this represent some ultimate step in her long emancipation from the paternal authority? And might not Union Square be lumped in her mind with Fifth Avenue? Was not his own tense concern with the rivalry at that very breakfast table underlined by a fear that it might be the embryo of a more domestic conflict?

"Grandpa has probably seen more of the leaders of our business world over a longer period of time than any man living," Fred retorted. "I imagine that he has attained some degree of wisdom."

"Does the Commodore go to Papa's now? I remember when he was considered beyond the pale."

"Mr. Vanderbilt doesn't go about in society," Fred replied with dignity. "He keeps a kind of court of his own."

Dexter fixed his eyes upon his plate for a breathless moment, waiting to hear if Rosalie would now attack the Bristows. But no, even she had her limits. He seized the chance to shift, once again, from a dangerous topic.

"Speaking of your father, Rosalie, will you be going there today? I shall start my calls at noon, and I expect to end at Number 417 about five." He was relieved to note that Fred had already returned to his newspaper.

"I'm afraid I shall have to work on my agenda for the Equal Rights Association."

"Oh, darling. On New Year's Day?"

"Particularly on New Year's Day. If I want it to be a good year. Anyway, I don't care to mingle with the Radical Republicans that Papa cultivates these days."

Dexter frowned. What was irking her so? For months her temper had been steadily shortening. There was always the excuse of menopause, but that was supposed to be over. Sometimes he wondered if she did not still begrudge him her hospital ship. He was the one who had benefited by her renunciation, becoming almost famous, after recovering from his pneumonia, for his work on the Sanitary Commission. Whatever he might argue, the fact would always remain that his war career had waxed as hers had dwindled. But whenever he tried to induce her to discuss this frankly, she would brush him off with an "Oh, it's nothing, nothing. Only nerves. Face it, my dear. You're saddled with a nagging middle-aged wife."

"You weren't always so down on Radical Republicans, Rosalie. Not in the days when we used to call them abolitionists."

Rosalie glanced up sharply. "That was before they were trying to tear up the Constitution!"

"But I thought you were against the Constitution. You used to say it tolerated slavery."

"I should know better than to get in a legal argument with you, Dexter. But very well. I amend my statement. It was before they were trying to pull down the government! Men like Charles Sumner and Thaddeus Stevens think the President should be their flunkey."

Fred rejoined the discussion at this. "How is it, Ma, that you are now so against negro sympathizers?"

"Because they're *not* negro sympathizers!" Rosalie's voice rose to near shrillness. "They want to drag poor illiterate blacks from every pig farm in the South to make them state senators! And why? To help the black man? Not on your life.

They want to punish the old planters! It's all hate of white men for white men, the way it was before the war. Stevens doesn't care if he starts a race war in the South. If the whites are all killed, he has his revenge. And if the blacks are all killed, he's solved *that* problem!"

"I don't see how you can say that Stevens doesn't care for the black man," Dexter interposed. "He has made public his wish to be buried in a negro graveyard."

"And that's the only place he'll ever meet one!" Rosalie retorted.

"Happy New Year, everybody!"

Dexter's eyes softened as he smiled to welcome the moderating influence of his younger son in the doorway. Selby liked to affect the amiable appearance of the artist he had not yet quite become. He wore a purple velvet jacket and a white shirt with lace ruffles. He looked like nobody else in the family, except that his round, clear, rather fleshy face seemed a faint caricature of his grandfather Handy's, and the constant smile in his wide, staring blue-green eyes might almost have been a mockery of his mother's worried gleam. His hair was blond and straight and would have been more appropriate to his brother Fred's serious brow, as the latter's chestnut curls would have better suited the would-be painter.

"How nice that none of you has to work today!" Selby continued, taking a seat and helping himself to a muffin. "I wish *I* had a job so I could have a holiday. What are all your New Year's resolutions? I suppose, Dad, you have vowed to eat a rebel general *sauté* for dinner every night until January 1, 1869. And Mamma has resolved to have women in pants by the same date. And Fred — what about Fred? But of course!

He has sworn to make his first million in time for the announcement of his engagement to a certain grand-niece of a certain railroad magnate!"

Fred glowered at his younger brother, while both parents beamed. "As long as we're predicting the impossible, how about this one?" He raised his coffee cup in a mock toast. "I drink to the first job of Selby Fairchild!"

"You're always sneering at me, Fred. Why don't you get me a job?"

"Are you serious?"

"Perfectly serious."

"What about *Lucrezia Borgia Presiding at the College of Cardinals in the Absence of Alexander VI?*"

"That immortal masterpiece was torn to pieces last night on the stroke of midnight!"

"Oh, darling, no!" Rosalie cried.

"Selby! Why?" Dexter demanded.

"I had a New Year's Eve party in my studio, Dad. For three painters whose work I thoroughly admire. One was your young Newport friend, La Farge. We had a good deal of champagne, enough, anyway, to ensure the veritas in the vino. Then I made each of them solemnly pledge to tell me the truth about the painting I was about to show them. I warned them that it would be cruel to allow a young man who had already invested two years in art to pursue it further if he had no real talent. I swore that I was in no danger of suicide or even depression. I pointed out that I had other aptitudes and other opportunities. That if I were to get started in a trade it was high time I did so. All three vowed to be honest. I then pulled the sheet from Lucrezia."

Dexter listened intently. Since he had sent Selby to Paris, just after the war, to study art in the atelier of Carolus-

Duran, he had suffered from doubts as to the boy's capability. Rosalie and Fred knew nothing about painting, and they took opposite sides as to the desirability of having an artist in the family. Rosalie had reached the point, in her violent reaction to the world of her forebears, where she seemed to prefer any alternative to law and business, while Fred did not regard "daubing" as a fit occupation for a man. Dexter, on the other hand, cared deeply for art and for his own growing collection, but he suspected that Selby's talent was merely a "pretty" one, that it would be dedicated, if at all, to derivative and conventional art. And yet he could hardly bear the prospect of Selby's disillusionment. His younger son had too keen a mind and too fine a taste for the merciful anaesthesia of fatuity. Whatever Selby became, Selby would know.

"Joe Husted was the first to give his opinion," Selby continued. "He said that if I were willing to accept a place in the second or third rank of artists, I might live to make money as a portraitist and to give pleasure with historical scenes. Ted Bush was kinder. He thought there might be a future for me as a muralist in public buildings. But La Farge went straight to the point. In art, he said, there is no middle class. There is a small upper, and a large proletariat. 'You would never be happy among the latter, Selby,' he told me. 'My advice is give it up!' It was almost the new year. On the stroke of midnight I cut Lucrezia to ribbons with a carving knife. The other two were horrified, but La Farge, in true La Farge fashion, embraced me."

"I never liked him," Rosalie declared indignantly.

"But you can paint it again," Dexter insisted. "Better than ever."

Selby smiled at his father, as if he knew just what he was

thinking. It was of the essence of Selby's kindness never to oblige anyone to express a thought that would cause pain to him who uttered it or to him who heard. "But it's just what I'm not going to do," he insisted. "I'm going to give up painting. Why do you all look so blue? Even you, Fred. Come now! I can always go back to it. But doesn't it make sense that I should try something else for a while? Doesn't it, Dad?"

"If you want to, my boy." Dexter was only afraid that there might be tears in his eyes.

"Well, there we are! Pour me some coffee, Ma. And now, Fred, what about that job you were talking about? Have you got one for me? Do you think I could sell stocks and bonds?"

"As a matter of fact, I think I *may* have a job for you. Just the kind of thing, too, that you could do to perfection. Mr. Bristow was talking only yesterday about sending someone as a passenger — or at least to look like a passenger — over all the Erie lines. His job would be to keep a sharp eye open for defective material, sloppy service, inaccurate timetables, anything to build up our position that the directors are looting the railroad. It's not a question of fact. We have that. It's a question of proof. We want to be able to go to the public, or the legislature if necessary, and explain why it is essential that Central control the line. An elegant gentleman like yourself would make the perfect spy!"

"And I can see the world at the same time!" Selby exclaimed with enthusiasm. "I've always loved travel."

"Well, you'll see New York State, anyway."

"Something Manhattanites rarely do. I'm your man, Fred! If you think you can sell me to Mr. Bristow."

"But, Fred, you just finished telling us how badly the Erie

is run!" Rosalie protested indignantly. "And now you propose to risk your brother's life on rotten rails and creaking cars!"

"I'm not asking him to take any risk the general public isn't taking, Ma."

"Why should the poor boy take *any* risk?"

"Now, Mummie, don't embarrass me!" Selby leaned down the table to give her hand a pat. "After all, I was too young to fight in the war." He turned to wink at his father. "This may be my chance to be a soldier at last. A soldier for Central!"

Selby could always handle his mother, and Rosalie, having finished her two morning sips of coffee, nodded, satisfied, and rose to go to her association's headquarters across the square.

"Give Father my love," she admonished Dexter as she left the room. "And tell Jo I'll go over the list with her tomorrow. She'll know what I mean. But don't tell her in front of Father."

It was not considered necessary to keep Mr. Handy instructed of his daughters' work in behalf of votes for negroes — and women.

Fred followed his mother, muttering something about its not being too cold for a ride in Central Park and promising Selby that he would speak to Mr. Bristow that afternoon. Dexter welcomed the immediate drop in tension in the room as his wife and oldest son departed.

"I think I can get you a better job than Fred's," he suggested.

"Oh, but I like the idea of his!"

"Why should you do anything? Why shouldn't you take your time for a little rest and what the French call *recueillement?*"

Selby laughed cheerfully. "Don't you think I've had enough of that? Two years of *recueillement!* I can't kid *you,* Pa. You know as well as I do that all that time in Paris wasn't devoted to hard work. And even here in my studio I've spent half my day reading novels. No, it's high time there was a little discipline in my life. And, all joking aside, I was half serious about what I said about the war. I *have* a kind of thing about being the only member of the family who did nothing in it."

"But you were a child!"

"Oh, I'm not saying it was my fault. Or that taking a job with a shifty old sharper like Bristow is any kind of a substitute. It's just that I have a bit of a sideline feeling that needs balancing. Maybe it's time I started to be something besides the son of Dexter Fairchild, the great Sanitary Commissioner who bossed Lincoln and Grant around and who had the eye to pick up the first painting of Jimmy Whistler's in New York . . ."

"Selby! Cut it out!"

"Or of Rosalie Fairchild, the Florence Nightingale of the Chesapeake. Or the brother of Fred, the hero of the Wilderness!"

"But how many people do we know who can paint well enough to get even the compliments you despise? How many have heard of a painter called Whistler?"

"And how many care?"

"*I* do. And anyway, it was you who called my attention to *The Rialto in Moonlight.* It was you who kept me from buying that Cabanel and gave me the idea of keeping the collection wholly American. And what was the use of all the slaughter and horror of the war if it wasn't to make a world where young men like yourself could create beautiful things? Or even simply appreciate beautiful things?"

"Dad! Is that *you* talking?"

"I know it sounds like drivel, coming from a hard-bitten old Wall Street lawyer." Dexter paused and stared down at the table until the lump in his throat dissolved. It suddenly seemed to him that any failure in Fred's career on the stock market, or in Rosalie's causes, or even in the orderly return to the union of the rebel states, would be as nothing compared to the prospect of pain and bitterness in the round face of this mildly overweight young man. For Selby was so much nicer than the world he lived in. "I've fussed all my life about doing my duty. And now it sometimes seems to me that my life has contained nothing better than the pictures in this room."

"Well, they're very fine. You've always had an eye."

"Somebody else once told me that. In this very room, too. A man I hated. Now I wonder if he was quite as bad as I thought. Anyway, I wonder if the pleasure I get from these paintings may not be just as big a thing as anything I did for soldiers in the war. As important a thing. Is that what I mean? That passive things rank with active things? Or maybe that there are no passive things. That receiving and giving are the same."

"You don't really believe that, Dad!"

"Maybe I just believe it for you, my boy. Maybe that's it. Don't go to work for Bristow!"

Selby laughed at the sudden anguish in his father's tone, but he also came over to put an arm around the paternal shoulders. It was his way of telling him that he had made up his mind. He had given up painting for good.

27

On his way up Fifth Avenue to Number 417, late in the afternoon of the same day, after making four New Year's Day calls, Dexter felt his ego, so deflated in the morning family conclave, almost restored to its usual buoyancy. He had learned not to blush at the flutterings of his own conceit, so long as he kept them in his private domain. It was undeniably agreeable to receive the flattering attentions of the social world, to note the half-step a hostess would make from the receiving line on seeing him and hear her "Ah, dear Dexter, we *are* honored!" And then, as had just happened at the Rutgers Van Rensselaers', to overhear a man murmur to his wife, "Look, there's Mr. Fairchild! *He* gave that big dinner for General Grant at the Patroons' last fall."

At the end of the long gallery, standing in the midst of a respectful group of gentlemen, Mr. Handy greeted him with a beckoning wave.

"There you are at last, my dear Dexter! We were just speaking of you. Come and give us your opinion about the impeachment."

Mr. Handy, at eighty-two, was a trifle stouter, a trifle

whiter, a good bit more forgetful, but he still exuded the same ebullient, almost aggressive hospitality. Dexter noted among the group around his father-in-law, David Ullman, Charley Fairchild, Nicolas King and the marble features and large stern nose of William Maxwell Evarts. He was a bit dashed by the great lawyer's presence. His "genius" was rebuked by Evarts', he liked to imagine, as Antony's had been by Octavius'.

"What should be our first toast of the year?" Mr. Handy pursued, without waiting for his unneeded answer. He raised a cut-crystal champagne glass. "To President Wade?"

But this was going a bit far, even for a group so staunchly Republican. Old Mr. King coughed; Charley Fairchild smirked; Mr. Evarts looked coldly away.

"I think he might be an adequate caretaker until we have had the opportunity to nominate and elect President Grant," Dexter observed tactfully.

"We mustn't let the rebels win in the White House the war they lost in the field!" cried Charley, echoing what he had heard Dexter say so many times in the office.

Dexter frowned at the violence of his cousin's tone. There was no doubt that Charley was beginning to drink again. It had taken a war to cure him once. What cataclysm would be needed to stop him a second time?

"These are solemn times, Mr. Handy," Evarts now affirmed. "But I am not convinced that they justify so drastic a remedy as impeachment."

"What is our alternative?" Dexter asked him. "It seems to me that we must strike while our iron is still hot. Proper Republican sentiment is slackening everywhere. People are getting sick and tired of Southern problems. If Johnson has his way for the rest of this year, we may never be able to make the rebel states accept negro suffrage. They claim the negro is illiterate. Well, whose fault is that? Let them educate him!"

"With an army on their back?"

It was David Ullman who had asked this. There was a gasp of indignation in the group at so brazen a note of dissent, and from a Jew, too! Ullman stood, his hand folded on his chest, erect, superior, supercilious, addressing his glance solely to his venerable host, for all the world as if he had been the guest of honor and not one who had just recently been admitted to the privileged gathering at Number 417. "I suggest," he continued in the same bold fashion, "that we are still under — and never have been out from under — a constitution that forbids any combination of states to impose military rule on the others. And what is more, I am rash enough to believe that this is the practical as well as the constitutional answer to our problem. A confederacy that had the determination and the guts to hold off opponents twice as populous and many times as rich, will yield more easily to persuasion than to bayonets."

Dexter, glancing from face to face in the listening group, had the distinct impression that if a joint response could have have been articulated, it would have been, "If you don't like this country, Ullman, why don't you go back to Hamburg?" The only exception was Evarts, who now struck Dexter as tending to reconsider just how much Republican loyalties might require of him.

"I wonder if you, as a lawyer, Dexter," Evarts remarked, ignoring the incendiary tendency of Ullman's speech, "won't agree with me that what is going on in Washington is a rather dangerous bid by one branch of our government to dominate the other two."

"But if Congress is simply filling the vacuum created by the refusal of the chief executive to carry out its mandate?" Dexter protested. He was beginning to feel that dangerous tingle in the back of his neck. He bit his lip in the effort to remind himself that he must not lose his temper in an argument with a man who never lost his. "Just as Mr. Lincoln had to suspend habeas corpus, so we may have to suspend states' rights. And to rid ourselves of a President who refuses to do so!"

There were murmurs of "Hear, hear," but Evarts glacially shrugged. "It seems to me that you are begging my question," he retorted.

"Well, I guess Evarts isn't going to join in our toast to President Wade," Mr. Handy remarked with a snort. "Nor you, either, Ullman. But what about the rest of you fellows? I'd rather drink to a new President than to an impeachment. Somehow the latter doesn't seem quite the right note for New Year's Day, no matter how much we may be for it. So no, I shall *not* propose that we drink to the impeachment of poor Mr. Lincoln."

Embarrassed glances were exchanged.

"My father-in-law meant to say Mr. Johnson," Dexter observed quietly.

"What's that?" Mr. Handy asked testily. "I think I know who the President of the United States is. Even if he's a railsplitter or a tailor."

"You meant to say Andrew Johnson, sir," Dexter insisted politely. "Not Abraham Lincoln."

"Johnson, of course. Didn't I say Johnson?"

"A mere slip of the tongue, sir."

"I wonder if it was," volunteered the ever-objectionable Ullman. "I wonder if a great deal of the sentiment against

Johnson isn't simply a hangover from what people felt about Lincoln. And never dared express."

"I bow to nobody, sir, in my reverence for our martyred President," Mr. Handy said severely, and David Ullman, with an impudent little bow, moved across the room to join his wife.

Mr. Handy took his son-in-law by the elbow and propelled him down the gallery to where Jo was standing by the punch bowl, indulging as he went in a series of *ad hominem* arguments.

"The trouble with Evarts is that he can never stop being a lawyer. He's not like you, dear boy. He doesn't know that there is a time to be disputatious and a time to be sincere. I daresay that Evarts is at heart a good Republican and basically on the side of the angels, but he can't resist taking the opposite side of an argument, just to show the room how smart he is. One of these days that habit of his will get him into serious trouble — mark my words. He doesn't even mind siding against his friends with a man like Ullman. Now, of course, I know Ullman is your brother-in-law, but you and I can still agree, I hope, that he isn't even a poor pretense of a gentleman. I only asked him here today because he's married to your sister."

Dexter did not bother to point out that his relationship with David Ullman had lasted for twenty-five years and that the latter's recent profitable deals with Mr. Handy's bank were much more likely the cause for his belated invitation to Number 417. He turned to Jo Handy as the old man stepped away to greet his mother. Mrs. Fairchild, in black beads and black sequins, small and tense, had been watching her host eagerly for a chance to pounce.

"Here is Rosalie's 'list,' whatever it is," Dexter said to Jo, placing an envelope in her hand. "I hope you two are not plotting a revolution."

"It's a list of people we can count on at the meeting at Mr. Cranberry's."

"Count on?"

Jo glanced at her father to be sure he was out of hearing. "You'll see," she said mysteriously. "You're coming, aren't you?"

Dexter felt a sudden depression at his sense of female conspiracy. Could nothing be as it used to be? "Your father seems in fine fettle," he observed, with a touch of belligerence.

"Oh, he gets on very well. Only he forgets things. I have to write everything down. And it's becoming a bit difficult for me to secure all the invitations he expects. He can't believe he's not as popular as he was ten years ago. But there does come a point when people are less keen to invite an old gentleman to dinner who forgets his hostess' name and dribbles soup down his shirt front."

Dexter was distressed by the candor of this evaluation. Jo was beyond praise as her father's companion and household manager, but hadn't it been a finer, more "old Roman" day when the vestals had worshipped at the shrine to which they ministered?

Mr. Handy turned now to include Dexter and Jo in his talk with Mrs. Fairchild. "I was just telling your mother, Dexter, that my spies inform me that Fred's courting old Vanderbilt's niece. You needn't look so startled. If I waited for you and Rosalie to tell me the family gossip! Of course, some years back . . ." here the old man lowered his voice and winked slyly at Mrs. Fairchild — "such a connection would not have been considered very advantageous. Except, of course, to the Vanderbilts. But we must keep up with the times. Oh, yes! Do you know that story about the daughter of Madame de Sévigné who found herself obliged to replenish the family coffers by marrying her son to the heiress of a wealthy farmer? She went about the court telling people that old fields need manuring!" Even Mr. Handy seemed now to recognize that this was going rather far. "Not, of course, that I mean to bring the Bristows or Vanderbilts into so odious a comparison. But you see what I mean."

"Perfectly." Mrs. Fairchild sounded grim. She placed a small, black-gloved hand on her son's arm. "Dexter, I want to talk to you."

He followed his mother to the ottoman in the center of the room. Clasping her hands together and thumping them against her knees, she made no effort to pretend to anyone watching that they were having a party conversation.

"Then it's true what I've heard about the Bristow girl! She won't do at all. She's not the thing."

"I understand she's charming."

"They always are. But the mother's vulgar and the father's a charlatan. And don't count on the great-uncle. Vanderbilt has a dozen children of his own without worrying about grand-nieces. They say it'll all go to the eldest son, anyway. He wants to establish a dynasty."

"Maybe Fred doesn't care about the money."

"I thought that was exactly what he *did* care about!"

"Let us at least give him the benefit of a doubt. He cares about making it, not marrying it."

His mother shrugged, half scornfully. "Those are male distinctions. Money is money to us women. All I can do is warn you. It's bad enough to marry a parvenue when you get a

bundle of greenbacks. But to marry one with nothing . . .
well, what are we coming to?"

"Don't you think Fred can look after himself?"

"Of course not! No man understands how society operates.
A man expects rules, and there are no rules. But there are
partialities and prejudices, and Fred had better learn about
them."

"All I can say, then, is you'd better tell him yourself. He
won't listen to me."

"Will Rosalie listen to you?"

"On the subject of Fred?"

"No, on the subject of *herself*. For that's my second little
New Year's offering, dear."

Dexter sighed. "All right, Mother. Let's get it over with."

"Rosalie is going entirely too far with her women's rights.
There may be some of us who support a betterment of the
condition of women in factories. And there are even those
who would like to see a few women in the professions. After
all, there's no reason why *all* the old maids should have to
look after aged parents, like poor Joanna. But this business of
votes is going too far. Rosalie is counting on the general letting down of standards in the war. She thinks a woman can
get away with anything today. But she's wrong! Things are
beginning to swing back. I've heard considerable talk that
Rosalie's going too far!"

The mere idea of people being down on Rosalie took Dexter back at once to his old vision of her, as somehow vulner-
able, sitting at the breakfast table in that pink dressing gown
with her hair undone. His heart ached with all his old need
to protect her. But then he recalled her sharpness of that
morning, not unlike his mother's sharpness of this afternoon.

Did the women in one's family have nothing better to do than cut one down to size? What did it profit a man if he gained the whole world and lost his domestic peace? And what was left *now* of the matutinal glow of being Dexter Fairchild, citizen of note?

"Maybe it won't be so bad if things do swing back a bit," he muttered. "Maybe it would be the best thing for Rosalie herself."

28

ROSALIE AND JO were riding down to Lafayette Street in Mr. Handy's landau to attend a meeting of the New York Committee of the American Equal Rights Association at Silas Cranberry's marble Corinthian-columned mansion.

"I hate going there," Rosalie observed bleakly. "I hate the man, and I hate his vulgar house."

"Is Dexter coming?" Jo ignored, as usual, her sister's intense reaction.

"He says he will."

"And will he support us?"

"It's asking quite a lot. Mr. Cranberry became a client of his after that matter of the rest homes for soldiers. A very important client."

"But surely Dexter is in a position not to have to kowtow to clients."

"All lawyers seem to have to kowtow to clients," Rosalie responded with a sigh. "Sometimes I think the more successful a man is, the more he has to kowtow. We have nothing in New York like the indomitable British peer. Or the proud old Southern planter, for that matter."

"You know, Rosalie, you strike me as almost sympathetic to Southerners these days. Must you always be swimming against the current?"

"I guess I have a weakness for lost causes. I hated Southerners when they had slaves. But now . . . well, they strike me as showing a rather forlorn dignity. It's more attractive than what I see in Papa's friends. And Dexter's." But she pulled herself up at this. "No, I mustn't be down on Dexter. It's very good of him to come today. I'm just afraid he'll be horrified."

"If Cranberry is intractable?"

"If the meeting is intractable."

"Will you really walk out?"

"Yes! And hope and pray that every woman in the room will follow!"

Jo considered this a moment. "Well, I will, anyway."

"Oh, I count on *you*."

"And maybe enough others will. To form a women's movement. If that's what we really want."

"It's the only way we'll ever get anything done."

"It doesn't scare you a bit?"

"Do you know something, Jo? Do you remember what you told me that day on the *Pierce* when we heard the cannon fire of the two ironclads? You said you weren't afraid. That you actually liked it! Well, that's the way I feel now. When I think of the frustrations of my life! The things I've started and never finished. The underground railway and the nursing and now this." She stopped suddenly as she realized that Jo, too, had been involved in these things, without even the cloudy satisfaction of a home and two sons, and that Jo bore her lot with patience and equanimity. "Oh, my dear, look who I'm talking to! But maybe you have the same feeling.

That it would be exhilarating to be out in the open, to spit in the eye of the world! There isn't that much time left, after all. We've passed fifty . . ."

"But that was only a week ago for you."

"Still, I'm there, and what a marker it is! I'd like to feel there's time for one good job really well done. Would you join me?"

"I don't think I can leave Papa. It would hardly do to walk out of one job just to do another, would it? But you're not going to emancipate women in a day. And Papa won't live forever."

"Don't be too sure!"

It was a mark of how far they had come together that they could both laugh.

"I'm better off that way than you are, I suppose," Rosalie continued more pensively. "Dexter and the boys don't really need me now. But why should Papa be any more your burden than mine or Lily's or Annie's? That's another thing we must establish. That a woman shouldn't have to marry to be taken seriously!"

"I suppose you wives save the race from extinction."

"And it's a great question if it's worth it. Sometimes I wonder, Jo, if I don't go in for causes just to give myself something to do. That I may care more for the fight than the victory. That I'm basically no different from the old abolitionists who used the slave to smite the master."

But Jo had no patience with this recurrent mood of her sister's. "You're discontented because you've never been given a proper chance to exercise your talents, and you've never been given that chance because you're a woman! Maybe that's too simple. Maybe I'm too simple. But I continue to see it that way."

Sitting, an hour later, beside Jo on a little gilt chair in the meeting at Silas Cranberry's marble hall while their host discoursed on the continued wrongs of the black man, it occurred to Rosalie that he would have been perfectly cast as Simon Legree in the stage version of Mrs. Stowe's novel. He had small red eyes, a bald head and a round belly under a scarlet vest that he constantly stroked. The statues of ancient Romans with which he had filled the chamber seemed to represent his rather desperate effort to reduce their ordered world to a frozen catacomb under the dominion of the storekeeper.

"The articles of impeachment have now been drawn," the nasal voice droned on. "We may shortly expect to see the machinery of our government go into action. Let Andrew Johnson be a lesson to posterity of what happens to the politician who stands between the black man and the voting privilege that three hundred thousand of our boys in blue perished to give him!"

Rosalie found herself speculating on the origin of the anti-Southern fury in this small unlovely man. Had the stately wife of some great Southern planter, sweeping through his store on a Manhattan visit in ante-bellum days, treated the proprietor as a mere salesclerk? Or had he found himself, on some trip to Atlanta or Richmond to establish a branch store, treated as a Yankee drummer? On such incidents did history depend? She noticed now that the six portrait busts on the shelf to her right were not, like the larger statues, modern Roman pieces romantically inspired, but genuine products of what she took to be the Augustan era. And it struck her that the heavy, jowly look, common to all six, the suspicious eyes, the disapproving frown, were traits of the American business male.

"Who would have dreamed," the voice continued, "when a small, select assemblage of Southern aristocrats built the institution of slavery into the scaffolding of an apparent democracy, that in less than a century the day of equal opportunity would dawn?"

Rosalie saw her husband slip into the room by a side door and take the nearest empty chair. Was he, too, a Roman? She recalled how irked he had been, some years before, when she had observed there were no gentlemen in New York society. The men were all burghers, as the Romans had been burghers: their features proved it. And that might have been the reason that women had played as small a role in American as in Roman history. There were no Nell Gwyns, no Madame de Pompadours; the men cared only for money. Well, women, too, could enter the money market!

"There are those who say the war is over, so why should we not have peace? But, ladies and gentlemen, the war is *not* over. We are merely in a state of truce, a cessation of hostilities, that began on the fatal day at Appomattox when our otherwise glorious General Grant, in the exuberance of his dearly earned victory, granted such fatally lenient terms to the foe. The war is not over, and will not be over, until every black male in the former rebel states is free to cast his vote without fear of intimidation!"

Rosalie jumped to her feet amid the applause that followed.

"May I make a motion, Mr. Chairman?"

"What is your motion, Mrs. Fairchild?"

"I move that this committee pledge itself to promote the right to vote of the American female, whether black or white, or of any other color, with the same vigor as it does the right of the American negro male!"

The room was silent for a moment. Then the women, who constituted a third of the assembly, began to applaud, at first lightly. Finally a minority of them began to call out their approval. Cranberry raised his arm for silence.

"I agree that the right of women to vote should receive our serious attention. But the motion is premature. Neither this committee, nor the national association, has yet decided that women should vote at all. Even if we anticipate an affirmative answer on that issue, we are not yet in a position to promote it. Why should implementing the vote of the negro male, which now has the approval of the entire association, be delayed? Let us not divide our forces. Let us stay together and strike our blows in order!"

"But what assurance do women have," Rosalie protested in a louder tone, "that their rights will ever be considered? We have known too many delays before."

"It is not unreasonable to ask you women to delay the issue for a bit. You have not suffered as the negroes have. You have not endured the ultimate indignity of slavery."

"Have black women not suffered it? And have not all women, of every color, been denied their elementary rights from the very dawn of what you men call civilization? Before slavery ever existed?"

Cranberry began to show his ire. "We fought the war to abolish slavery! Not to give women the vote!"

"I had hoped we had fought the war to abolish the exploitation of one human being by another. Why do you wish to give the vote to some black man who cannot sign his name, who very possibily cannot distinguish between New York and China, and deny it to me?"

"Because he doesn't talk me to death!"

There were cries of "Shame," and Rosalie saw Dexter leap to his feet.

"I say, Cranberry, that won't do!"

"All right, all right, I apologize. But really and truly, are we to have the fruits of our victory snatched from our hands by women who invent new aims that the war was fought for? Suppose Mrs. Fairchild were now to suggest that the war had been fought for unwed mothers, could those unfortunates muscle in on the black man's struggle for the ballot?"

"Mr. Cranberry has no concern with how the black man votes," Rosalie exclaimed, addressing herself now to the room. "He knows that those votes will be cast in states where he does no business. But he cares a great deal how *women* may vote, should they be enfranchised. Because he knows that his hundreds of peons, his half-starved female clerks, would soon be voting for a minimum wage!"

At this there was an uproar. Half the audience jumped to their feet, mostly declaiming against Rosalie, but several women began shouting in her favor.

"There is a motion on the floor!" a woman cried at last over the din.

"But not seconded," retorted Cranberry.

"I second it!" The voice was Jo's.

"All those in favor raise their right hand."

Barely a quarter of those attending complied, and the motion was lost. Rosalie noted with bitterness that Dexter sat grimly in his seat, both hands in his pockets.

"I resign from this association!" she announced, rising again to her feet. "And I hope that every woman in this room will follow me out!"

Going to the doorway she turned to face the chamber. Jo

was already at her side. Dexter was with them, but she noted that he was concerned only with retrieving his coat from the butler. Of the thirty women present, some dozen moved to join the sisters. Rosalie solemnly embraced each one of them.

✿   ✿   ✿

Dexter took Rosalie home in his coupé, Jo having taken her father's carriage. He did not say a word all the way up Broadway. As they passed Grace Church, she broke the silence at last.

"Oh, go ahead and say it, Dexter! That you're horrified."

He looked with pained surprise at Rosalie's angry profile. Had she lost *all* sense of a husband's prerogative? Because he had leaned so far backwards to go along with her activities, was he now "estopped," as one might say in law, from making any protest at the prospect of his home being turned into a permanent club for noisy women? He had been disgusted by the scene he had just witnessed, appalled by the clamoring females and half-sympathetic even with the loathsome Cranberry, who, in his opinion, had been unreasonably hounded into losing his temper.

"You planned this whole thing in advance," he protested. "Don't you think you might have warned me what I was going to face today?"

"What would have been the use? I knew you'd be opposed to it. And, I'd already made up my mind."

"Let me get it straight, Rosalie. Is it your position that I should accept the almost certain loss of one of my biggest clients and the conversion of my domestic peace into a hideous uproar, without a murmur?"

"It's my position that in the biggest decision of my life you might have supported me!"

"I didn't vote against you." He was too appalled at her identification of the "biggest" decision to comment on the lesser one that it uncovered.

"You abstained. It amounted to the same thing."

"But, Rosalie, you know I back you in everything you do! That doesn't mean I have to *agree* with you, does it? I haven't yet made up my own mind how I stand on votes for women. Am I to be stampeded into it?"

"I suppose I'm showing the weakness of my sex," she replied bitterly. "But, yes, I *did* want you to vote with me. Regardless of your convictions. I wanted you to stand with me in my moment of crisis. I gave up my hospital ship for you! Oh, I know you never asked me to, but I did. And I forgave you your affair with Annie. I suppose it's unworthy of me to mention that, but I did. And I've entertained your clients and raised your children. I've been a good brownstone wife. And now that at fifty I begin to see at last how to work for a cause in which I passionately believe, now that I want this *one* thing for Rosalie Fairchild, all you can talk about is your domestic peace!"

"You know I love you."

"But what will you *do* for me?" she demanded passionately. "I guess I'm sentimental enough to have wanted you to make *one* gesture for me! Regardless of your prejudices!"

Dexter looked out the window at the dripping iron portals of a store front in the gas light of a street lamp. It was raining. He felt the old urge to surrender to her, the old need to comfort and console her, to protect her from the pain that seemed to throb in every pore of her large sensitive body. But now the image of those shouting women intervened. Was a man to be left with nothing — stripped, castrated, flung out in the dark wet street? He closed his eyes and almost groaned with the difficulty of *not* giving in.

"I'm sorry, dear," he murmured. "I do not see how I could have behaved differently. You ask too much."

"Well, I shall ask for nothing more," she retorted, turning to show him eyes filled with tears. "And I warn you, Dexter, nothing is going to stop me now! I'm going to speak out for women's votes at every street corner of this town. I'm going to campaign throughout the state. Who knows? Maybe throughout the nation. I may be hissed and booed. I may be tarred and feathered. I may even be jailed! But I know now what I am and what I shall be!"

"Rosalie," he begged her, "even if you don't care what you do to me, can't you think of the boys?"

"Fred won't give a hoot. He's completely obsessed with his sordid Erie battle. And Selby approves of me!"

Silence fell between them, and he found it in him, even now, to wonder if it wouldn't be more fun to be on her and Selby's side. But staring down, fascinated, into the black, eddying gulf of his self-pity, he knew that he was not going to resist the impulse to plunge.

29

Selby Fairchild, on a clear, cold Sunday afternoon, paused in Madison Square to contemplate the house at which he proposed to call. It was spandy new, midway between a standard brownstone and a mansion, an oblong standing clear of other edifices, yet designed so as to fit as neatly as a brick into a box, should the owner be required one day to sell its yard to a builder. Yankee foresight, Selby reflected. The front that faced the square was of brownstone with four tiers of windows, three to a floor, and a grilled doorway, but the long side that presented itself to his view was painted pleasantly red with the same number of windows and several bricked-up frames. Seth Bristow had bought the house only six months before from the man who had built it but lost his fortune before moving in. Such was the history of Manhattan real estate.

The front door opened at his approach, and he passed, after surrendering his coat and top hat to a footman, down a dark corridor to the darker parlor in back. The curtains had been drawn for Mrs. Bristow's reception, though it was only three o'clock, and the gas lights and candelabra were aglow as for an evening party. Behind his host and hostess was a huge canvas on which the Vestal Virgins of ancient Rome were seen turning thumbs down in response to a red-faced, hirsute gladiator's call for their verdict as to the victim sprawling in the arena sand under his heel. The curtains of the Bristows' great chamber, the rugs, the coverings of the chairs and ottomans, were all of the same dark, murky red. Mahogany, wherever it peeked out, was black and twisted. There was a glint of gold and silver on the sideboards and tables.

Mrs. Bristow, pale-faced and nervous, with black, darting eyes and hands that moved like snakes' heads, greeted him with effusion.

"We were so hoping for a visit from your grandfather this afternoon. But dear Miss Handy sent me a sweet note to say that the old gentleman has a cold. I trust it's nothing serious. Oh, it's not? Good! One must be so careful at his age. I hardly like the idea that my uncle said he might drop in today. The dear man should look out for himself, particularly with this terrible Erie battle going on! And how are your distinguished parents? I should love to see them one day. Do you think they'd come? And what about dear Mr. and Mrs. Van Rensselaer?"

Selby, who knew that his grandfather had unexpected liberalities and was within the social reach of the Bristows, was also aware that his aunt Lily would not go to their house to ransom the life of a kidnapped child. But it was not kind to acknowledge such things, even by implication.

"I can't imagine why any member of my family wouldn't be tickled pink to be asked to a lovely party like this."

"Really? But Mrs. Van Rensselaer is supposed to be so exclusive!"

Selby's pleasant smile concealed his wince. How could the woman be so vulgar? And yet, though totally devoid of imagination or humor, she had a brain; she was not Vanderbilt's niece for nothing. Selby was sure that she could have drawn an inventory of every piece of tangible personal property in that house and given him the exact market value of each. Why had fate subjected her to the ignominy of playing the one game at which she could never succeed? And the one game her failure at which she would never comprehend?

"Well, I guess everybody likes to think of himself as exclusive," he observed mildly. "But it's only a kind of coyness, don't you think? Aunt Lily's probably wondering what she can have done not to be invited by the Bristows."

"If I believed *that*," exclaimed his literal-minded hostess, but then even she penetrated his game. "Oh, you young men! There's no getting you to take things seriously."

He took advantage of the amiability of her tone to turn his attention to her husband. Seth Bristow, sixty and bald, was much older than his wife. He had small, watery blue eyes, a crooked nose, thick, pale lips that seemed to be always parted, a soft, hollow voice and bad breath.

"We want you to go on the Erie sleeper to Buffalo," he told Selby, moving at once and without the least apology, to business. "I hear they're taking a substantial overload. And that they missed two stops on the Petauket run. Weren't you on that?"

Selby explained that he was not. Mr. Bristow never praised and never condemned; he simply pointed out deficiencies as he found them. He was the dryest man Selby had ever encountered; he seemed to regard the faintest intrusion of a non-business-related subject, at any time of the day or night, or in any place, as a lapse of taste, almost like a breaking of

wind. Selby, intrigued, had tried to see if there were not one
other subject on which Bristow could be drawn, but he had
found none. Man to him existed only to buy, sell and make a
profit. Seth Bristow was like a character in a restoration
comedy who had no qualities beyond those suggested by his
name; he might have been a "Mr. Shortsale" or a "Mr. Put-
call." And yet, for all of this, he was supposed to be financially shaky, and it was rumored that Vanderbilt knew that
he sometimes traded against him. It was only on the tenuous
relationship of marriage to a disliked niece, and possibly because treason amused the Commodore, that the broker was
tolerated at all.

Selby, who cared little for his job and less for his host,
moved away to the buffet, where he was disgusted to find
neither wine nor spirits, but only a pale lemon punch. He reflected how tough a religious prejudice must be when a social
ambition as strong as Mrs. Bristow's had to be thwarted by it.
Old Seth let his Presbyterian god slumber all week, but he
awakened him on Sunday, in time to mar his wife's festivi-
ties. Even the Commodore would not be able to get a drink!

And the Commodore had now arrived. The forty or more
guests in the chamber made no secret of what was almost
their obeisance when the great man, tall, broad-shouldered,
white-haired, imposing, appeared in the parlor doorway,
wearing what seemed to be the same frock coat whose marble replica adorned his famous statue by de Groot over the
portal to the Hudson River freight dock in St. John's Park.
All general conversation ceased as the hostess nervously led
her uncle among the guests, half of whom, Selby guessed,
were directly or indirectly his employees. The gossip at
Bristow & Mayer had been that Vanderbilt would go to Mrs.
Bristow's and to half a dozen other houses on Sunday after-

noon, to demonstrate his imperturbability in the midst of the
Erie crisis. Erie had hit 81 the day before, and the city was
close to panic.

What a tribe, Selby reflected, and what a prophet! These
be thy gods, O Israel! What could he do with this world in
which he found himself? He could not love it, like Fred. He
could not despise it, like his mother. He had made up his
mind he could not paint it. Could he write about it, satirize
it? Dickens had torn such a world apart in *Our Mutual
Friend*. But Dickens had hated the Veneerings, and Selby
could not find it in his heart to hate even the Bristows. He
thought that he might want, in some vague sentimental fashion, to "save" them, and it was perfectly manifest that they
had no desire to be saved.

Putting his hands in his pockets, he reviewed his situation.
He enjoyed his job well enough; he liked racketing about the
state, and he found time, as always, to talk to people in bars.
But the job was temporary. One could not spy on Erie forever. Indeed, if the Commodore won his stock battle, the
spy would be idle again. He supposed that he could always
sell stocks and bonds, like Fred, but he was sure he would
hate it. There was also his mother's suffrage work, or the
political reform movement starting up in Boston, but Selby
inclined to the opinion that the times were premature for
both. It seemed futile even to try to make a start until the
public mind, now sick of idealism and avid for industrial
expansion, should swing around a bit. Oh, a swing would
come; it was bound to come. But what could one do while
two-thirds of the nation seemed concentrated on hounding
out of office a President who was guilty of nothing but trying
to perform his constitutional duties?

"Do you remember this young man, Uncle Corneel?" Mrs.

Bristow was saying. The honored guest, to whose arm his hostess was clinging, had paused before Selby. "He's Fred Fairchild's brother."

Vanderbilt grunted and gave Selby an appraising stare. "You work for Bristow, too, young fella?"

"More or less, sir."

"I reckon that ain't quite enough."

"Or else too much. I was just thinking, Mr. Vanderbilt. What can a young man do to become quickly rich?"

"Really, Mr. Fairchild," Mrs. Bristow gasped. "I can't have my uncle bothered with such . . ."

"Oh, be quiet, Rosalinda. I like a young man to speak his mind. Tell me, sonny. You got any money?"

"A little, sir."

"Well, buy all the Central stock you can git your hands on. You can't go wrong."

"But isn't the profit pretty well out of that, sir? After all, *you* got there first."

Vanderbilt chuckled. "You're like all the young men. You ask for advice, and then you give it."

"No, sir, I'm sincerely humble. Do you mean the little guy can't do better than follow the great one?"

"Well, I'll tell you this, my friend. Half the fortunes in this world were made in businesses after the so-called smart investors thought it was too late to buy in. The big men don't take chances. It's the pioneer who goes broke. I didn't go into steam until I knew it was safe. Same thing in rails."

"But I suppose if one rides a great man's shoulders, one must know when to get off." Selby had deduced that Vanderbilt was the better type of bully, the kind that savored boldness.

"Yes, you must have a nose for Waterloo," the Commodore replied with another chuckle. "A lot of people thought mine had come yesterday. A lot of people were wrong."

"I'll buy Central tomorrow, sir."

"Never tell anyone what you're going to do. Just go ahead and do it. Come and see me any time, young man. You're a grandson of old Handy, ain't you? We'll try not to hold that against you!"

And with a high cackle the lord of Central moved on. Selby crossed the room now to join a young lady, some twenty years of age, who had been watching their colloquy. She had long, smooth dark hair, parted in the middle, and black, bright eyes in a pale face of almost too regular features. She was dressed in a sober dark red, like the room. It might have been protective coloration. But anyone could see that Elmira Bristow was a very determined young lady. What did she need to be protected against?

"I like your great-uncle, Ellie," Selby observed, when he was beside her. "And what's more, I think he liked me."

"What an honor!"

"You don't consider it one?"

"Should I?"

"You don't like your Uncle Corneel?"

"I hate him."

Selby, who always amused himself with Fred's passionate little goddess, was gratified to see that his afternoon was not going to be lost, in spite of the lemonade punch. "How can you say such a thing? Let alone mean it? Think how scandalized the people here would be if they could hear you. Pure sacrilege!"

"Oh, it's not *his* fault," she said impatiently. "It's not be-

cause of anything he's done. It's because they all fawn on
him so disgustingly. And he despises them for it! Particularly
my parents."

"But can you blame him for despising toadies?"

Ellie made no move to except her parents from his unflat-
tering classification. Her quick nod even approved it. "I don't
blame him. He's quite right. But I don't like being lumped in
the despised group. So I despise him right back!"

"Wouldn't it be more accurate to say that you envy him?"

"No! I don't envy him in the least. I care nothing for his
noisy steamboats or his rattling trains. Rushing people faster
and faster over land and water so they can make more
money. I find the whole business unutterably vulgar. Uncle
Corneel may charm you with his rough-and-tumble way, but
it's all just pose. He's much more literate than he lets on.
And, basically, he's cold as ice. He never respected his son,
Cousin Will, until the latter bested him in a contract over a
sale of manure!" Ellie looked even prettier as she wrinkled
her nose in distaste. "And that's what all these people worship!"

"What do you worship, Ellie?"

"Me? I don't worship anything."

"What do you admire, then?"

"What do you think I might admire?"

"Art? Music? Beautiful things?"

She laughed in surprise. "What makes you think that?"

"Because you're such a thing of beauty yourself."

She gave him a narrow glance. Was he overstepping the
role of younger brother? He looked her straight in the eye to
reassure her of his loyalty to Fred.

"Do beautiful things usually admire other beautiful
things?" she asked.

"In heaven don't the seraphim enjoy chanting to each other?"

Ellie's laugh brushed this off. "Some seraph here! No, Selby, a girl should never admit it, but I don't care that much for art. Oh, I have eye enough to see that everything in *this* house is bad, but that doesn't take much. And what's even worse is that the things don't go with Ma and Pa, the way your grandfather's bad pictures somehow go with him."

Selby smiled. "What about Daddy's pictures?"

"Oh, that's different again. They're good. But they're too good for *him*, don't you see? I shouldn't like that in my house. I shall want my house to set me off perfectly."

"You still haven't told me what you admire. Or even what you like."

"And yet I'm quite definite about it." Ellie turned and walked to a corner as she saw there was danger of their being joined by another couple. She did not even pretend to be helping her mother with the party. Selby followed her. "I like things to be secure and neat," she said, as she faced him again. He began to smile, but he stopped when he saw that she was serious. "I want to know just where I am. I want to have friends I can count on. I don't want to look up, and I don't want to look down. I want to live on a level. I want a stable place."

"But is that attainable?"

"Perhaps not. But some people come closer to it than others. Your family, for instance."

"Daddy and Mummie?"

"Well, your father, anyway."

"Not poor Mummie?"

"No. She had it, of course, but she seems bent on throwing

it away. I detest agitating in public. Almost as much as I detest railroads."

"You're not for women's rights?"

"Heavens no! What's it all for? So we can vote for a President who can be impeached if the Republicans don't like him? Or for state senators who are all in Uncle Corneel's pay? You should hear *him* on that subject. No, Selby, I see the future differently. In New York everything is left to the women but business and politics. I can make my peace with that. Particularly as I've told you what I think of business and politics."

"I see. You want to rule from the home."

"Oh, rule. You're going to be as vulgar as Uncle Corneel if you don't watch out. I simply want to live . . . well, decently, that's all."

"Like whom, for instance?"

She hesitated, as if doubtful as to how far she could go. "You'd really like to know?"

"Very much."

"Well, like your aunt. Like Miss Handy."

Had they been alone he would have whistled. "Like Aunt Jo! Well, I adore her, of course, but people have always felt sorry for her."

"*I* don't feel sorry for her at all. She knows just what she is and where she stands. She knows what she is going to do each day, to what houses she will go and who will come to her when she bids them. She is free to express herself on any topic. She has learned to dress quietly but perfectly. Her servants do her bidding exactly. Everyone respects her. To me she simply represents all that is best in old New York!"

Selby, listening to this strange outpouring, began to have

an uneasy feeling that Ellie might one day resent him for being the recipient of such confidences.

"Are you sure you want to tell me all this?"

"You think I'm a fool to do it? I am! But there's something compelling about you. And then I have nobody else to talk to. You see what my parents are. And the girls I know are all idiots. They can talk of nothing but men."

"What about Fred?"

"Ah, Fred." Her dark eyes were lit now with something like alarm. "There's no talking to Fred about such things." She laughed enigmatically. "One listens to Fred."

"I think he'd listen to you."

"Because he admires my mind?" she asked sarcastically.

"Because he adores you!"

"You're glib, Selby. You're glib." She shrugged impatiently as she turned away. "How do I know Fred can adore anybody?"

"If you were his brother, you'd know."

She swung back on him now, her eyes almost blazing. "If you ever tell Fred anything about our talks, I think I'll kill you, Selby! I really will!"

"Why should I tell him?"

"To deflect his attentions from a girl your family consider ineligible."

Selby shook his head slowly. "My parents have no such views."

"Well, then, from a girl whom *you* consider ineligible. A girl who cares about all the wrong things!"

"Why are they the wrong things?"

"You know perfectly well. Because they're the things girls care about and can't admit to. A girl is supposed to be idealis-

tic, ethereal!" She flung her arms in the air. "A girl is supposed to be soft and gentle and think her man a hero. That's
what Fred wants!"

"But it's not wrong to want a stable society. Or even to admit it. 'Uncle Corneel' just now was telling me that the time
to buy into a business was when the so-called smart folks said
the profit was out of it. Maybe you're buying 'old New York'
at just the right time."

"I'm sure of one thing, anyway. The Handys and Fairchilds will still be around when nobody's heard of the Bristows and Vanderbilts."

"Can't we all survive together? Anyway, I shan't quote you
to Fred. Not that it would make any difference. He'd buy
any opinion of yours."

"Do you care if he does?"

"Yes. Because I happen to think you're the girl for him.
Whatever happens, you're always going to feel strongly
about something. I envy you that. I can't seem to care that
much about anything."

"Fred cares only about New York Central."

"Yes, but that can change. You haven't seen Fred in his
down times. He was very down the first year after the war.
He kept saying all that slaughter had been in vain. And then
he discovered the stock market . . . well, say no more! Look
at him now!"

Fred was making his way towards them across the room,
splendidly handsome in black with a scarlet cravat. An un-
usual smile illuminated his long brown countenance.

"Have you heard the news?" he exclaimed.

"About the impeachment?"

Fred glanced at his brother impatiently. "The Erie man-

agement has fled to Jersey! Drew, Gould, Fisk, the whole
pack of hyenas. Taking everything they could put their
hands on except the printing press."

"The printing press?" Selby asked blankly.

"The one that's been printing the phony stock the Commodore's been buying! He swore out a warrant against them
yesterday, and they skipped."

"Does that mean you've *won?*" Ellie asked, clapping her
hands with a gesture of enthusiasm that Selby could only
silently admire.

"Not yet. But it means we hold the big trumps. They can't
come back to New York until they come to terms. And those
terms will certainly include, not only control of the Erie
board by Vanderbilt directors, but the repurchase of all that
watered stock."

"And will that make you rich, Fred?" Selby exclaimed.

"Hardly. It may bail me out. Most of us bought Erie too
high. But once it's all settled . . . well, let's say I may be on
my way to being . . . comfortable."

Fred's wink encouraged Selby to take his leave, and after
bidding farewell to his hosts, he walked home the short distance to Union Square. He knew that Elmira would not wish
him to watch her listening.

*   *   *

She remained with Fred in the library. There were only two
other couples there, both out of earshot. He continued to ex-
pand on details of the battle.

"When we first discovered the Erie crowd were printing
new stock certificates, not only in violation of Judge Barnard's injunction but in direct contravention of the law, there

was a moment of near panic. How many had already been issued? How many had we bought? We had driven Erie up to 81. Were we simply flinging gold to the enemy? Could we go on? If we stopped, the whole market would go to pieces. The Commodore might pull the house down, like Sampson, but wouldn't he be pulling it down on himself?"

Ellie's mind seemed to seethe and tumble behind her widened eyes and parted lips. She thought she had never seen anything as beautiful as that bronze face, flushed with battle frenzy. It was beyond the limits of hope and credulity that such a man might actually belong to her. And yet she was still capable of reflecting that she was actually bored, that, if talk made the man, she had rather listen to his brother. It all went to show how unimportant being bored was. If she could have taken the brain out of chubby, flabby Selby's head and put it into that nobler one, she would not have done so!

"And that is where your great-uncle showed himself a hero of the stature of Hannibal or Napoleon. He gave the order to go forward with the buying. Buying the fake stock, Ellie! At first we thought it was a kind of suicide, like the British cavalry charge at Balaclava. We didn't know the Commodore had already taken his measures to arrest the scoundrels and that he would only keep buying until he had his warrant. But even so it took magnificent courage. It made one think of Grant in the Wilderness. All through that terrible summer of '64 when he kept slugging, slugging, losing two of our men to every one of the rebels', until they were done for!"

No, Ellie reflected, Selby's brain would have spoiled Fred. If she wanted a hero, she had to take him as he was. But if she needed him, he was going to need her, too; heroes desperately needed women. Suppose, for example, he were to learn that his boss and future father-in-law had been hedging his position by selling Erie while allegedly going all out for his wife's uncle? Was that not the kind of arrow that could wreak havoc in the heel of the greatest warriors?

"The legal situation is complicated, of course, by the fact that the different supreme courts of New York State have concurrent jurisdiction. Barnard may give us an injunction here in Manhattan, and Drew can get it revoked upstate. But the Manhattan one is good in Manhattan, and those villains can't operate, or even breathe, really, until they're right back here on our skinny island!"

Ellie reflected that once she was Mrs. Fred Fairchild she would not have to see her mother and father very often. She knew more than enough about them to make them keep their distance. She would watch over Fred and his interests like a tigress — she did not evade the term. She would protect him not only from her family but from his. She would stand between him and his nervous, politicating mother. She would . . .

"All of which brings me to the point, dearest Ellie. When this is all over — with any luck — I should find myself financially in a position to marry. If that is the case, may I call upon your father and ask him to make our private engagement an official one?"

For answer she simply gave him her hand to hold and squeeze. She supposed this was perfect happiness.

30

The Appomattox, a fashionable new bar on Broadway and Fourteenth Street, was a favorite haunt of Selby's. He liked to stand at the long black mahogany counter and consume gin and oysters for half an hour before making his appearance at a dinner party. Sometimes he would fall into conversation with his neighbor; sometimes he would simply savor the sting of the dry liquor in his throat and contemplate the big painting behind the blue-frocked bartenders that depicted a Roman banquet in high decadence, with brown-limbed young men sprawled on divans drinking from golden goblets and talking to ivory-skinned, scantily clad young women. On the central divans, like an isolated goddess, was a splendid nude with a faraway gaze, presumably dreaming of an absent god. Selby found that he needed the Appomattox to anaesthetize himself against the fashionable New York dinner, but that, so prepared, he could almost enjoy even the most inane conversation.

On a freezing night that threatened snow he visited the bar before a party to be given by his aunt, Lily Van Rensselaer, promising himself a double gin as a bracer for that

occasion. At midnight he was to take the Erie sleeper for
Buffalo, which gave him a pleasant sense of mild, uninter-
rupted adventure. But he was startled to recognize the tall
figure of his older brother at the bar. It was not like Fred to
be drinking alone.

"I thought you might be here," Fred growled as Selby took
his stand beside him and picked up the iced gin that the bartender had poured as soon as he had spotted him in the
doorway.

"Are you too going to Aunt Lily's?"

"God no! That's one thing I've been spared today."

"What's happened? Have you had a row with Ellie?"

Fred looked surprised at so prompt an attribution of a romantic cause to his trouble. "No. Though that may be coming, too. I've had a bitch of a row with her father."

"Has he sacked you?"

"Or did I quit? I'm not sure which."

Selby whistled. "Things *have* been happening. But don't
worry. Ellie will forgive you a little thing like that."

"How do you know that?"

Selby reflected that it might not be wise, even now, to tell
Fred how strongly Ellie felt about her father. "Because she
loves you for yourself, poor girl."

Fred grunted. "Well, my poor self may be all the poor girl's
going to get. *If* she still wants it." He picked up his glass and
swallowed a gulp of whiskey.

"Don't keep me on pins and needles, man! What's happened?"

Fred seemed to consider for a moment how best to put it.
"Well, supposing, when Grant and Lee had met in that Court
House for which this bar is named, they'd mapped out an
armistice to suit themselves? Suppose, in return for a cease-

fire, Grant had authorized the continuance, for some period of time, of slavery in the South? Wouldn't we have felt awfully sold?"

"No doubt."

"Well, that's exactly how I felt when I saw and heard the drawing up of an armistice this morning between Mr. Vanderbilt and those two scoundrels, Gould and Fisk!"

"You mean the Commodore gave in?"

"I mean the Commodore compromised. Peace was made. The crooks will keep Erie, but they will have to take back their watered stock. At the prices the old man paid for it."

Selby shrugged. "So we're just back where we started. Is that the end of the world?"

"But it's a betrayal of every basic decency, don't you see, Selby?" Fred's face was drawn, and his eyes actually glittered. "Erie's been an open scandal for years. A road plucked to bits by ravens. The Commodore was going to clean it up and add it to his great network. It was going to be the brightest jewel in his crown! Does that sort of thing mean nothing to you?"

"To me! What have I to do with it?" But seeing Fred's bewildered look, he relented. "All right, tell me about it."

"Daniel Drew was the first to break. He's a fish out of water if he leaves Manhattan. So he came whimpering back and threw himself on Vanderbilt's mercy. Promised him this and that. Anything. He was perfectly happy, of course, to rat on his colleagues."

"But, surely the Commodore didn't trust *him!*"

"No, but Vanderbilt likes to see men on their knees. He sent word to the others that he was willing to listen, and they came right over, bright and early, the next morning. They went to Vanderbilt's house in Washington Place and barged into his bedroom while the old boy was still dressing. When I arrived for the day's stock market instructions, they were at it, hammer and tongs. You should have seen it, Selby! The old Commodore sitting on his bed, half-dressed, his white mane still mussed from the pillow, one shoe on and one shoe off, and Gould, his hands in his pockets, a little sardonic grin on his foxy face, and Fisk, puffing a big black cigar, cocky as the devil, striding about the room, laying down conditions and making insulting remarks! But do you know something? In that crowd they don't *mind* insults. Even old Vanderbilt chortled at some crack Fisk took at him. I had the sudden feeling that everyone in that room understood everyone else. Everyone but me!"

"You don't talk their language, Fred," Selby murmured ruefully. "And it's to your credit that you don't."

"Well, it didn't take them long to come to terms. All the Commodore seemed to care about was unloading the bogus stock he'd had to buy. Then I was sent off to round up Frank Work and Bristow and the other brokers, and Vanderbilt's lawyers, of course, and by the time I got back, the three of them had agreed on the terms of their unholy alliance. I tell you, Selby, it nauseated me!"

"And did you tell them so?"

"Not in so many words. But I told Mr. Vanderbilt that if he did business with crooks, he was no better than a crook himself."

"I see. And how did he take *that?*"

"Oh, he didn't really care. He growled something about my being a callow idiot. It was Bristow who really opened fire. He turned as red as a turkey cock and started shrieking about my insulting his 'family.' He said he never wanted to see me in his office again, and I told him his office was no place for an officer or a gentleman."

"Wow! That must have done it."

"And I told him, if he wanted to associate with swine like Gould and Fisk, he was welcome to their sty."

Selby looked at his brother wonderingly. "You called them swine? To their faces?"

"It was a pleasure."

"And how did they take it?"

"Gould didn't even seem to hear. What did he care for an insect like me? Fisk guffawed. He said he was going to tell P. T. Barnum he'd found an honest broker! I would have slapped his sassy face had Frank Work not got in between us."

"And then what happened? You left?"

"It was all I could do. Old Bristow followed me out into the street, still shrieking. I thought he'd taken leave of his senses. I didn't even turn around. I just walked off."

"So!" Selby glanced at his watch. "Something tells me I'm going to disappoint Aunt Lily tonight. She boasts she has never sat down to dinner without an even table of men and women. Tonight she may discover what it is to be short a man. Unless she asks her butler to join the guests." He scribbled a note on the counter and gave it to the bartender to be delivered by hand to Mrs. Van Rensselaer's.

"What are you going to do?" Fred demanded.

"I'm going to call on Miss Bristow. I, at least, may still be admitted in Madison Square."

"Bless you, Selby, boy. Tell her I adore her!"

"And don't stay here drinking all night. Go home and go to bed!"

At Madison Square, after some delay because of the lateness of the hour, Selby was ushered into the library where he found Elmira alone. She listened silently, her eyes intently upon him, as he told his tale.

"So that's what happened. I couldn't make out from Pa. He was almost incoherent."

"I'm afraid Fred let his anger get the better of him. He should have thought more of you before he was so rude to your father."

"I like him just as he is, thank you very much! I wanted him out of that world, and now he's out. I suppose he's lost everything he had in this business?"

"Probably."

"Well, I think I know a way that can be remedied. I'll go to Uncle Corneel."

"Uncle Corneel? Won't he listen to your father?"

"He loathes my father!"

"And what will Fred do when you've bailed him out?"

"Become a lawyer. As he should have been from the beginning. In your father's firm."

"You *have* thought it out."

"Somebody had to."

Selby, walking south to Union Square, found himself wondering if Fred would admire as much as he did the fiery passion that he had evoked in his beloved. He sighed. It was perhaps just as well for all of them that Ellie was too much obsessed with his brother to be even aware of other admirations.

He found his father alone in his study. His mother had gone to one of her meetings. Selby considered it characteristic of his father's departmentalized neatness that the room should contain no law books or paintings. Law was for the office; the seascapes were for the big, downstairs rooms. The little second floor chamber in back was for the personal life of Dexter Fairchild. The shelves that covered the walls were filled with the contemporary English fiction that he so loved — on the desk was an open volume of *The Last Chronicle of Barset* — and in the few wall spaces were watercolors executed by Fairchild aunts. The only large picture was a Mount portrait of Selby's priestly grandfather — the one who had absconded to Italy. Selby, as a boy, used to search for a forecast of adultery in the brooding eyes under those bushy eyebrows.

When he had related Fred's news, his father shook his head.

"Well, I can't really regret this if it takes Fred out of the brokerage mess. But poor boy! What a blow to his pride! How does the girl take it?"

"Like a brick. She wants him to be a lawyer."

Dexter looked up in surprise. "Does she really? By George! Maybe she's the right sort, in spite of her old man."

"She has quality. What she will ultimately do with it, one can't be sure. You'd like to have Fred become a lawyer, wouldn't you, Dad?"

"I confess it."

"You'd like to have him succeed you in the firm?"

"It would be a dream come true. A fourth generation of Fairchilds! Think of it, Selby."

"Poor Dad. You really ask so little of us. I'll bet you never even suggested that to Fred."

"Well, you know how your brother is."

"But even if he'd been different, you wouldn't have. You've always wanted us to be ourselves." Selby felt a small lump in his throat as he took in the furtive embarrassment of his father's roving eye. "I've always appreciated that. No matter what we wanted, well, that was what you wanted for us. You knew I wanted to be an artist, and you were afraid I wasn't good enough. But you always kept that to yourself."

"Not very successfully, it seems."

"Oh, you can't fool *me*. Remember, I'm a second son. A second son knows that his parents are only poor blokes like himself."

"A second son knows how to love."

"Oh, Fred loves you, too. In his own way. But you and I, Dad . . . well, we understand each other. But, as Hamlet said to Horatio, 'Something too much of this.' To change the subject. You're in a stew about Ma."

"And what should I do about it?"

"Back her up! Tell her you're with her."

"And if I'm not?"

"Say you are!"

"I can't, Selby!"

"It's like rape, Dad. Give in, and it's not so bad."

"Really, Selby! What about my principles?"

"How can you have a principle against women voting? You may think it's unwise, but you can't think it's immoral. God didn't decree that women shouldn't go to the polls, did he?"

"I'm not so sure. My father would have thought so."

Selby glanced up at the portrait and chuckled. "Well, look what a woman did to him!"

"Is a man to have nothing to say about what goes on in his own home?"

"Not if he wants peace and quiet."

"Cynic!" Dexter picked up a piece of note paper. "Maybe you think I should do this, too. It's a letter from Mr. Evarts. You know he's one of the five attorneys selected to defend the President?"

"I thought he was too much of a Republican."

"So many people thought. But he's a lawyer, first and foremost. He writes me that he's doing it for a nominal fee. He's made a list of half a dozen 'distinguished counselors' whose brains he would like to be able to pick. As a matter of public duty on their part."

"And you're one of them?"

"Yes. He would like me to come down to Washington and be available for strategy talks. Should I do it?"

"Do you believe the President's guilty?"

"I believe it would be a blessing to the nation if he were removed from office."

"That's not what I asked. Is he guilty?"

"Of high crimes and misdemeanors? For using intemperate language? For suspending Stanton as Secretary of War? For expressing doubts about the constitutionality of the Reconstruction Acts? No. Decidedly not. The whole thing's a farce. But a much graver issue is at stake . . ."

"Never mind the graver issue." Selby, in his sudden enthusiasm, did not hesitate to interrupt his parent. "If Johnson is charged unjustly, Johnson should be acquitted. Doesn't it *have* to be as simple as that?"

Dexter smiled ruefully. "And it doesn't matter to you that I'd ruin myself with the party? That I should be regarded as a traitor by a host of friends and relations? And that I should have ruled out forever the possibility of an appointment to the federal bench?"

Selby laughed in sheer delight. "You know as well as I do, Dad, that's your greatest temptation! To be the martyr of martyrs." He looked suddenly at his watch. "But now I've got to catch that sleeper!"

31

CHARLES HANDY was dressing for dinner in his bedroom, a large square chamber with gold and brown cloth-lined walls that overlooked Fifth Avenue on the third story of Number 417. He stood before a full-length mirror held in an Empire mahogany frame surmounted by two bronze eagles, attempting to adjust his white waistcoat without crumpling the stiff shirt front beneath. Sam, the young valet who Jo (she had grown quite bossy of late) had insisted should help him dress, was vigorously brushing down the back of his master's black coat.

The bureau and tables were covered with family daguerreotypes in red velvet frames with gilded mattings. The tan wallpaper above the cloth was almost concealed by dark prints of old New York. An oval portrait of Lafayette as an old man hung over the fireplace. Handy reached for a heavy gold chain lying on the stand by the mirror and stretched it across the center of his waistcoat.

"What do you think, Sam? Does it improve me?"

"It's very pretty, sir. A nice bit of joolry." Sam was an inscrutable Yankee youth. He agreed with everything his em-

ployer said, without the least alteration of tone, quietly resisting all efforts on the latter's part to establish any closer
relationship.

"I've had this chain for fifty years, Sam. I wore it when I
was in the Guard and rode beside the Marquis de Lafayette's
coach when he came to New York on his famous return visit.
You should have seen me in those days, Sam. I sat in my sad-
dle straight as a ramrod with my saber held so!" He raised
his cane to his shoulder to show how.

"You must have looked very fine, sir."

"That's the old man there." Handy jerked a thumb towards
the portrait of Lafayette.

"He was a Frenchy, sir?"

"Really, Sam, I'm surprised at you. Do you know who General Grant was?"

"Oh, yes, sir. He won the war."

"Well, Lafayette won the Revolution! Or helped to win it,
anyway. Yes, he was a Frenchman. A French nobleman who
believed in the rights of man." But what was the use? Handy
reflected with a sigh. What were they coming to with a
younger generation that had already forgotten the war that
had created the nation? And if the great were so soon forgotten, what would be the fate of the less great? Would anyone
in Manhattan in the year 1900 have possibly heard of the
man who had been president of the Bank of Commerce, ad-
viser in New York recruiting to President Lincoln and one of
the original commissioners of Central Park? Would even all
of his descendants recognize his name?

Ah, well, he thought now, sinking back in an armchair
while Sam polished his black leather slippers, at least there
was the dinner party to look forward to. He closed his eyes
to savor the sense of passing through a marble foyer to the

play of a little fountain, into a long chamber enlivened by
ladies with exposed white shoulders and necks partially concealed by large jewels, and then into a dim candlelit dining
hall with a long table glinting with silver and gold and with
a cluster of crystal wineglasses at each place. Ah, the ano-
dyne of wine and laughter and amiable flattering women! So
long as he had the dinner party in New York and his gardens
in Newport life was not all futile.

And tonight . . . but where was he going tonight? He
could not seem to remember. To the Aspinwalls? No, they
were in mourning. To the Clintons? Hadn't they gone to
Italy for the winter? To that nice, if rather stiff little Mrs.
William Astor? But, no, he had been there recently and
something had gone wrong. What? Oh, yes, the invitation
had come only the day before — very presumptuous — and
he had been seated too far down the table while Dexter
Fairchild had been on the hostess's right. Had people no
more respect for a man of his age and distinction in what
was still called society? But wait a minute. Perhaps Mrs.
Astor had been subtly honoring him by honoring his son-in-
law. One shouldn't be too suspicious. It was a fault of age.

"Do you recall where we're dining tonight, Sam? I wonder
if I should wear my ruby cuff links."

"I wasn't told, sir. Shall I ask Miss Joanna?"

"No, no. It doesn't matter. The moonstones go better with
the chain."

He recalled now that he had already asked Jo twice. He
did not wish her to imagine that his memory was entirely
gone. People her age never attributed their own memory
lapses to age, but the smallest slip after eighty was dubbed
senility. Still, it *was* worrying. For what was mind but memory? If one could not retain a fact for a day, an hour, a min-

ute, a second — what would that be but insanity? He shuddered as the icy feeling slid through his back and chest. And yet he could remember old Lafayette's head in the carriage window, gravely bobbing to the cheering crowd, as if it were yesterday! One could always live in the distant past, if need be. It was probably the best place to live.

The Bristows! Of course, they were going to the Bristows'! Relief pounded through him, but only for a moment. Then he remembered they had been to the Bristows' only the week before, and Jo had made the point that it would not be politic to go there more than once in a season, even for Fred's sake. It seemed that the Bristows were the kind of people who revised their estimate of one's social position downward the moment one appeared in their drawing room. Handy remembered now that Mrs. Bristow's attitude had changed in a single evening from the near hysteria of her initial greeting to an almost offhand farewell. Dreadful woman! Was New York society in the future to be made up of the likes of her?

He went downstairs to find Jo, in gray silk, patiently waiting for him in the hall. In the carriage he checked himself from asking her their destination. He would try to guess it from the route they took. The horses headed north up Fifth Avenue, so it would not be the Astors'.

"Why do you suppose Mrs. Astor put Dexter on her right the other evening?"

"Is that so surprising, Papa? He's a very prominent citizen."

"Of course. But I should have thought seniority alone would have entitled me to the place."

"Perhaps she was honoring him as her lawyer."

"But he isn't, really. He represents some of her family's

trusts. The Schermerhorns. That's a mere peppercorn compared to the Astor real estate."

"Then let's hope that one thing may lead to another."

"Don't be absurd, Jo," he retorted testily. "The Astors would never turn their tenements over to a trust lawyer in Wall Street. They wouldn't think him tough enough. No, all they'd ever allow Dexter to handle would be a couple of wills — of wives."

Jo was meditating. She seemed not at all put off by his impatience. "I suppose it's always possible that Caroline Astor wanted to show people that she took Rosalie's excuse for genuine. She may have wanted to protect Dexter from the reputation of having a wife who backs out of dinner parties at the last moment."

"What on earth are you talking about? Wasn't Rosalie there?"

"No, don't you remember? Elizabeth Cady Stanton was in town, and Rosalie went to meet her. Dexter had to send word that she had a sudden cold. But I don't think anybody believed that. Rosalie's done it too often."

Handy fumed with shame and irritation. Was there no limit to the humiliations to which his old age was to be subjected? And Jo accepted it all so serenely, so glibly! Sometimes he wondered if Jo believed in anything at all.

"I was brought up on the principle that if you accepted a dinner party, you either went or sent your coffin!"

"Then let us deem ourselves fortunate that poor Rosalie has not been driven to the latter extreme!"

"Do you countenance your sister in this, Jo?" he almost bellowed.

"She doesn't ask my advice, Papa."

"And if she did, what would it be?"

"I might tell her that I think she goes a bit far at times."

"A bit! That little Mrs. Astor is going to be ruling the roost one of these days. She's not somebody Rosalie can afford to offend."

"But Mrs. Astor *likes* Dexter. Rosalie's defection gave her a chance to do him honor. What's so bad about that?"

"Jo, I sometimes wonder if, deep down, you're not as radical as your sister."

"Oh, Papa, can't you try to accept people as they are?" Jo was at last showing signs of exasperation. "Rosalie's not going to change her ways for anything you or I can say to her."

Handy lapsed into a grumpy silence and gazed fretfully out the window. Jo never got really angry with him anymore; she treated him, he suspected darkly, like a stubborn child. But now the buildings to the west abruptly disappeared; they were passing Central Park. Who the devil did he know who lived this far north? Had he died, and were they headed towards eternity? And then, with a snort of indignation, he recalled a further outrage: the rape by the City of the park from the private commissioners. Well, the poor voters would see what they got for it! In ten years' time the lovely alleys, the rolling greenswards, the shady bosks, the silent, silvery ponds would be torn up and polluted by a rabble of Irish and Italian immigrants. Serve the public right for trusting its politicians!

They turned down a side street and stopped before a building on the south side. Handy could not at first make out its appearance in the darkness, but when he descended from the carriage he recognized, with a little stab of disappointment, the abbreviated French Renaissance façade that his daughter Lily had arbitrarily clapped on her new brown-stone. It was rather a sell to be going only to a family party, but he tried to console himself with the reminder that Rut-gers Van Rensselaer bought only the best champagne.

Lily's dinner party sat down promptly at eight in the Gothic dining room. Charley Fairchild was talking across the table, and Handy now realized that he was being addressed.

"I think everyone here will be interested to know, sir, of an appeal that your son-in-law received this morning at our office. It was nothing less than a communication from Wil-liam Maxwell Evarts asking him to come down to Washing-ton and assist him in defending the President!"

There was an immediate burst of comment around the table.

"Dexter act for Johnson!"

"Dexter join up with rebels!"

"Does Evarts think the whole world's gone crazy just be-cause he has?"

"This doesn't mean that Dexter would be acting directly for the President," Charley explained. "He would be working for Evarts."

"But the disgrace is in the cause, not the retainer!" Handy exclaimed roughly. "I am sure that my son-in-law will reject the proposition out of hand."

"I doubt that."

"How do you mean, sir, you doubt it? Do you presume to know my son-in-law better than I?"

"No, but perhaps as well, Mr. Handy." Charley had been fortified by the wine; he was grinning provokingly. "After all, he is not only my law partner. He is my brother-in-law and first cousin."

"He is also a loyal Republican, I'll thank you to remember, Charles Fairchild! And he has been as loud as any of us in his denunciations of Johnson's criminal policies."

"True. But Dexter is a hard man to pin down. There is something elusive about him, a kind of inner doubt. Just after he has banged his fist on the table, you see that little glint in his eye that seems to say, 'Could I be wrong?' Like Bishop Cauchon, he is always afraid he may have just burned a saint."

"Johnson a saint?" muttered Rutgers Van Rensselaer. "I never expected to hear that opinion expressed under my roof!"

"Nobody expressed it, Rutgers," Charley replied. "And nobody here, I trust, even thinks it. I was only observing that Dexter was a lawyer before anything else."

"Damn lawyers," his host muttered in a half whisper that everyone heard.

"And that you must always be prepared," Charley continued imperturbably, "to find him tomorrow regretting the thing he did yesterday."

"As you of all people should know, Charles!"

Handy was startled to realize, from the shocked silence around the table that followed this remark, that it was he who had made it. His words had obviously been taken as a direct reference to the old affair between Dexter and Annie.

"Has anyone heard any news about Erie?" Lily asked in a high, nervous quaver.

There was an instant, relieved spatter of comment.

"Oh, don't you know, Lily? The thieves have made it up."

"They're dividing the swag."

"Did anyone hear what Fisk said? That nothing is lost but honor!"

"I'm afraid I can't laugh at that. It's simply too shocking."

After dinner, when the gentlemen had joined the ladies in the parlor following their brandies and cigars, Lily rose at once to lead her father to two armchairs in a corner. As he had sat by her at dinner, her claiming him now made it perfectly evident that she did not trust him with anyone else.

"I'm getting old and waspish," he muttered apologetically. "It's probably high time I gave up going out to dinner parties."

"Stuff and nonsense! You're still the life of the party. And it was all Charley's fault, anyway. If he hadn't been such a toper, Annie might still be with him."

"I suppose Annie's nothing but a whore now. A fashionable French whore."

"Please, Papa! Be quiet! And you're quite wrong about Annie. She goes everywhere in Paris. She is even received by the Empress."

"Is that a guarantee of respectability? What was Eugenie but a little Spanish nobody that the old goat of an Emperor had to marry because her mother was smart enough to keep him out of her bed?"

"Papa! The Empress is supposed to be a saint!"

Lily was obviously relieved when Jo crossed the room to take him home.

That night Charles Handy slept only fitfully. He dreamed that he was in the White House with the Union Defense Committee and that President Lincoln, fixing his large, reproachful eyes upon him, kept saying over and over, "What is wrong, Mr. Handy? Not a single regiment has reached the capital! Yet each time that he went to Willard's Hotel to check his sources, he was told that three New York regiments had already arrived. He would keep waking up, bathed in sweat, but when he slept again the same dream would be repeated, with the martyred President sounding each time more anguished and more impatient.

The last time he awakened, it was after dawn, and he became aware of somebody sitting by his bed. It was Jo. She looked drawn and pale.

"Are you awake, Papa?"

"I am now," he grumbled. "What do you want?"

"I'm afraid I have some very bad news. There's been a terrible wreck on the Erie. The Buffalo Express. At Port Jervis." For a moment she seemed unable to go on. "It was a bad curve. Three sleepers went off the track. Selby was in one. They think he must have been killed instantly."

He stared at her stupidly. "Selby?"

"Selby Fairchild. Rosalie's boy." She paused again, and he could see now that she was weeping. "Your grandson, Papa."

"Do you think I'm an idiot? Do you think I don't know my own grandsons?"

"Of course you do, Papa. I'm sorry."

"It's a perfect scandal the way these railroads are run! I've said so again and again. It's murder, that's what it is. Men like Gould and Fisk should be strung up in public."

"I'm sure they're bad men. But that won't bring Selby back, will it?"

"Hmm." He stared, almost in embarrassment, at her bent head and shaking shoulders. "Has Rosalie been told?"

"Oh, yes, Papa."

"Will you send word to her and Dexter that I shall stand by to help them in every way I can?"

"Of course, Papa."

"And will you remind me after breakfast to write a letter

to the *Tribune* protesting the shocking mismanagement of our railroads?"

"I'll try to remember."

"And now perhaps you will let me have my room, so I can dress?"

"I'll send Sam in."

While he was dressing, aided by the silent Sam, Handy tried to assemble his agitated thoughts. Selby's death was like an oversized domino that would not fit in the case with the others. He recalled Selby, of course, with absolute clarity. He remembered the bright chubby face, the high, infectious laugh. And he took in perfectly the fact that this unfortunate young man was now presumably a mangled corpse. It was a bad thing. A very bad thing. Number 417 would become a house of mourning. There would be weeping and lamentation. The women would be particularly noisy. The Irish maids would be impossible. And there would be no more dinner parties that season. It was horrid of him, he supposed, to be thinking of dinner parties at such a time, but the years were precious at his age, and even the shortest period of mourning could be ill afforded.

Could he perhaps take the position that he didn't believe in mourning? That those with the deepest grief might be above the outward display? Might people not actually admire an old man who insisted on fulfilling his social obligations, even with dust and ashes in his heart? But he could not fool himself about Jo. It would certainly be difficult to induce *her* to accompany him on any renewed social round, and had he not reached the point where he was almost afraid to go out without her?

He had shaved and donned his underwear and shirt, and

was preparing, laboriously, to step into his trousers when Sam murmured something in his ear.

"What, what? Speak up, man!"

"Your tailor is outside, sir, with your new tweed suit. Might it not be easier to try it on now before you're fully dressed?"

"A good point, boy. Show him in."

Handy was almost cheered up, a few minutes later, as he contemplated his figure in the tall mirror, resplendent in fine Scottish tweed, while the tailor busily jotted down his fitting notes. There was nothing like new clothing to clear the mind. It was fortunate that gentlemen did not, like ladies, have to adopt total black. An armband would satisfy the strictest requirements of mourning, an armband and a black knitted tie, quite becoming, really . . .

"Who is it? Is that you, Jo? Can't you see I'm busy? I'll be right down."

"It's me, Rosalie, Papa. May I come in?"

"Oh, my dear, of course!"

And Rosalie came in, with her quick stride, pausing briefly to take in the scene.

"Oh, but I'm interrupting!"

"Not at all, not at all." Her father coughed in embarrassment and motioned abruptly to Sam to take the tailor away. Alone with Rosalie, he was shocked by her haggard look. "I was distressed beyond expression by your tragic news. My heart goes out to you and Dexter."

"We know it does, Papa."

"I told Jo that I should write the *Tribune* this very morning about the scandalous mismanagement of Erie. It is part and parcel of the unprincipled times we live in. And if I may say so, my dear, I hope this tragedy may have the effect of toning down some of your own public agitations."

As he heard himself say this, his eyes were fixed directly upon Rosalie's, and he made out, with a cutting clarity, that the pity in hers was not for herself, or even for poor dead Selby. And then the scene about him seemed to fall apart. There was no tweed suit, no Empire mirror, no four-poster bed, no portrait of Lafayette, no family mementos. There was only Rosalie, brokenhearted, battered, shattered Rosalie, who had lost her darling son. And there was nothing left of Charles Handy but the desperate need to reach out, to hug, to console . . . to cling to a remnant of heart.

"Oh, my girl, my poor little girl, what has happened to you? Come to me, Rosalie, poor little Rosalie."

She seemed to stagger into his outstretched arms, and they clasped each other in an embrace that lasted until Jo, wondering at the silence within, timidly opened the door.

32

IN THE FORTNIGHT following Selby's death Elmira Bristow saw Fred Fairchild only twice. Of course, she recognized that his time was necessarily taken up by his grief-stricken family, but she was also very keenly aware that this was not the real cause of his defection. Fred had been devastated by the catastrophe. He had moved out of Union Square to a boarding house in Rector Street, and he was spending his evenings mostly at Broadway bars. He refused to call at the Bristows', where he felt, correctly, that he would not be welcome to her parents, and he and she had had to meet, on those two occasions, in Central Park, where they had walked dismally past mounds of melting snow under a slaty sky, watching the pigeons peck for the crumbs that Fred languidly produced from his pocket.

He could really talk of nothing but his guilt. He had sent Selby to his death, he would morosely insist, as surely as if he had put a pistol to his head and pulled the trigger. His younger brother had been the innocent victim of his own perverse need to elevate a sordid scrap among bandits to the status of a crusade for a better America. He, Fred, was worse than a thief; he was a fool. He had no present, and he had no future. It would have been far better had he perished in the Wilderness Campaign. Selby would now be alive and proud of a dead soldier brother. Elmira must learn to forget him.

She had known that she had never understood him well; now she began to wonder if she had understood him at all. How could a man who had been a hero under hardships unimaginable to her go to pieces under difficulties so perfectly plausible? Of course it must have been horrid to feel even the smallest responsibility for a brother's death, but did it take an abnormally level head to recognize an accident? What made her, at last, after much inward fretting, decide that she must learn to tolerate her own sympathy for his self-pity, was her ultimate recognition that the intensification of her own passion for him in misfortune and despair was equally irrational.

She had had her own guilt feelings, too, about Selby. There had been a nasty little corner in her heart, a dusky spot where she had harbored something like relief at the elimination of Fred's brother from her scene. He had viewed her too clearly. He had comprehended too thoroughly that she was not the demure, conventional society virgin that his brother supposed — and that his brother wanted. Not that she was troubled about deceiving Fred or in the least concerned with the disillusionment that would inevitably follow their union. That, she was sure, would be a minor matter; Fred would be essentially content with his bargain — *after* he had made it. But it would not have been politic to thrust in so squeamish a bachelor's face such prickly facts as that she despised her father and thought Fred a fool for ever believing in him, or that she valued in Fred's family background all the things that he himself found most trivial.

Selby might never have given her away — but now he surely couldn't.

This sense of guilt, however, had been considerably lightened by her disgust at the attitude that her own father had taken as soon as he had heard of the accident. For he had simply uttered a solemn prayer that he should not be held liable to the Fairchilds for having dispatched Selby on his fatal trip! With a parent like that, could she blame herself too much for a minor meanness?

On their second walk in the park Ellie had tried to induce Fred to take a more sanguine view of his future.

"What can I do?" he asked gloomily. "I have no job, no money, no prospects. I refuse to go back to brokerage, and I'm trained for nothing else. Except killing. I might reenlist and go west to shoot Indians. That's about all I'm good for."

"Why not law? Your father would adore to have you in his firm."

"I'd have to go back to school. I've no money for that, Ellie!"

"He'd be only too happy to pay."

"But I wouldn't take it from him! How can I ask him to invest anything more in a son who has nothing to show for the last three years but an empty pocket and a murdered brother?"

Ellie resolved to take no note of his dramatics. "You wouldn't have to go to school. You could read law in his office."

"I'd still be his dependent!"

She turned to face him down. "Can't you stop thinking of yourself for a minute? Can't you think of me *once*?"

He seized her by the shoulders, gripping them until he

hurt her. "My dear girl, I *am* thinking of you! Don't you know that? I want you to be free. Free of me. My God, I'm nothing but a millstone around your neck!"

She reached up to place her hands on his gripping ones. "Then I think millstones must be all the fashion this season."

But he only glared at her as if he was actually angry at such insistence. Then, abruptly, he released her. "No, no, it's not fair to you," he muttered, turning away with what was almost a sob. "Let me take you home. I'm not fit for this. I'm not fit for anything!"

Ellie decided that under the circumstances she could do nothing but acquiesce. She went home and spent two hours alone in her bedroom, thinking hard. That evening, at dinner with her parents, she coolly made her first move in the hazardous campaign that she had just devised.

"I saw Fred Fairchild today."

"You know your father and I don't approve of that young man. Don't you think it would be kinder to him not to see him? He's completely ruined his business prospects."

"Not his prospects with me, anyway, Ma. I shall continue to see Fred whenever I choose. But that is not the topic I wanted to bring up. I wanted to tell you something else, namely that . . ."

"Highty-tighty, Miss!" her father interrupted. "Aren't you taking a rather grand tone to those who pay for every morsel you put in your mouth? Not to speak of every stitch you put on your back?"

"Hadn't you better wait, Pa, until you hear what I have to say?"

"I'll thank you, young lady, to keep a civil tongue in your mouth!"

"*My* tongue is perfectly civil."

"Elmira!" her mother cried. "Please remember you're speaking to your father!"

"Well, would he rather hear it from me or from Uncle Corneel?"

"What are you talking about?" her father demanded, his eyes instantly narrowing.

"Simply this: that I expect you to arrange that Fred be compensated for his losses in Erie. Just as all the other Vanderbilt brokers are."

Her father snorted in astonishment. "Losses? What losses? Fairchild wasn't buying on his own account."

"Oh, but he was. He put everything he had into Erie. And he should be made whole. As the rest of you expect to be."

"After what he said to Uncle Corneel at the conference?" her father cried. "You dream, young lady. You dream! The Commodore never forgets a thing like that!"

"It should be perfectly easy for you to explain that to him. Tell him that Fred's young and idealistic. Tell him he was Fred's hero. Like General Grant. Tell him Fred couldn't bear to see him lose even one battle. And now, with Selby's death on top of it all, Uncle Corneel's bound to relent."

"Even if all that were true, why should *I* intercede for a man who insulted me so grossly to my face?"

"Because I intend to marry him," Ellie responded firmly. "And I see no reason that my husband should not share with the rest of the family."

Her mother at this seemed to waver. "She has a point there, Seth."

"But you are forgetting, Rosalinda, how that young man reviled me. No, I can never do it. That's final!"

Ellie regarded him coldly. "What do you suppose he'd

have said if he'd known you were selling Erie while he was buying? Wouldn't he have really reviled you then?"

Her father's gaping face seemed to shrink and show more lines. It reminded her of an onion. "Whatever gave you such an idea?" he asked, almost in a whisper.

"Ma told me."

"Seth! I never did!"

"You're always shooting your big mouth off, Rosalinda!"

As Ellie took in the rasping hate in her father's tone, she realized with a shock what she had done. She had pulled up a floorboard in the creaking edifice of their family life and revealed the grubby little things that they had all known were underneath but which they had tacitly agreed to keep out of sight. In the shock of their sudden exposure to the light the creatures lay helplessly on their backs, their white shiny bellies exposed, their multitudinous legs waving. Glancing from her father to her mother, she read in the sudden pallor of each the effect of a similar recognition. And then a common impulse induced the three of them to shove that board back and stamp it down.

"I was only trying to hedge a bit for the financial security of my loved ones," Seth Bristow explained, almost with a whine. "One can't expect women to understand such things. But if you're so set on this young man, Elmira, I guess I'll have to see what can be done. I'll be calling on Uncle Corneel tomorrow. Maybe he'll view the matter as you say."

"Thank you, Papa," Ellie responded warmly. "Thank you very much indeed. I shall never forget that you did this for me. If Uncle Corneel gives you any trouble, tell him that Ma and I went after you like two furies. He'll understand. He has enough daughters of his own!"

She could not quite make out what her father mumbled

into his soup, but it seemed to be something about the Commodore at least knowing how to keep *his* "women folk" in line. Her mother now turned to her with the eye of the hostess who can never admit to an unpleasantness.

"We must ask Fred for dinner. Do you think his parents would come?"

"Hardly. They're in the deepest mourning."

"Oh, I mean just for a family evening."

Ellie did not bother to answer. She was wondering already how she would ever be able to persuade Fred to accept the reparation if offered. It seemed to her that the best plan would be to take him with her to call on her great-uncle on the excuse that the Commodore wanted to offer him personally his condolences on the death of Selby, a "casualty in the Erie war." This might be going a bit far, but in Fred's present despondency almost anything might work — or fail.

Fortunately, when she broached the matter to him the following afternoon, after her father had reported favorably of his visit to Uncle Corneel, Fred offered little resistance. Sitting in the dingy parlor of his boarding house, where she had boldly called upon him, he had simply stared at her apathetically and finally nodded.

"Well, if the old man has the decency to be sorry about it, I guess the least I can do is call upon him."

They walked to Washington Place where the Commodore lived in a plain square red brick house with a white Greek portal. It was handsome enough as New York residences went, but it was modest indeed compared to what the more newly rich were building farther uptown, and certainly modest compared to the Bristows' mansion in Madison Square. Ellie could only admire the self-assurance with which he so understated his wealth. But what might have been self-restraint without became something more like indifference within, where the whitewashed chambers were sparsely and inconsequentially furnished. They reminded Ellie of rooms in a doll's house; the pieces did not match, in size or in period. A vast Hudson River landscape might find itself hung over a miniature; a Hiram Powers caveman might be balanced by a frog.

Uncle Corneel, who was suffering from bronchitis, greeted them without rising from a Belter rococo divan upholstered in maroon. He was clad in a multicolored dressing gown and was smoking a pipe.

"You've had a blow, lad," he said to Fred when his guests were seated, "and I'm sorry for it. Someone should hang, and my choice would be Gould."

Fred nodded, a bit stiffly. "I had hoped we were going to change the Erie management, sir."

"We will, lad, we will. But Central, like Rome, can't be built in a day. We'll get hold of Erie in time, and then you'll see the difference!"

Fred remained discreetly silent.

"Tell him about the wreck you were in, Uncle Corneel," Ellie put in nervously.

"Oh, that. It must have been thirty-five years ago. It put me off railroads for a while, I'll tell you that." He chuckled at the vision of his own historical importance. "Yep, that wreck must have put the clock in rails back a dozen years."

Another silence fell, which Ellie again felt constrained to break. "Did you have another message for Fred today, Uncle Corneel? Papa said you might."

"A message? Oh, yes. If you have any of that bogus Erie

stock to unload, young man, just give me the figure, and I'll write you a check."

Fred looked startled. "You wish to make good my losses, sir?"

"Why not? It was in a good cause. I look after my people."

"I beg your pardon, sir, but may I ask if the check will be drawn against your personal funds?"

"You think it may bounce?"

"Hardly that. And if it did I should frame it. It would be a museum piece." Ellie, astonished, joined their laughter. Was Fred actually coming out of the slough? But his next words disheartened her. "I mean, will it be to you that I owe the restitution or to the Erie stockholders?"

"Oh, I'll be paid by Erie. Surely that's only right? They swindled me. Now they can cough up."

"If it was Gould or Fisk who had to do the coughing, sir, I'd agree with you. And heartily. But it won't be, surely? They'll just put their paws right back in the Erie till."

"What's it to me where they get the money?"

"But don't you care, sir, if it's the stockholders who are really paying?"

"Did God appoint me to look after the shareholders, young man? Let the shareholders look after themselves."

"If they only could! But they're helpless, the way things are. I'm sorry, sir. I can't take their money."

The old man shrugged. "Very well. I can't force it on you. Elmira tells me you may set up to be a lawyer. Sounds like it might be the right trade for you. I ain't got a very high opinion of lawyers or judges, but maybe you can help make things better. They sure as hell couldn't be much wuss!"

Ellie was almost without hope after this visit. Yet when

Fred took her back to Madison Square and asked her grimly on the threshold if she was ready to give him up *now*, she retorted "Never!" and then slammed the front door enigmatically in his face. What more could she say? What more could she appeal to? His obligation to her, created by the blackmailing of her own father? That would be moving indeed. She might have tried to induce herself to give him up, had it not been for his little joke about Uncle Corneel's check. If he had retained even a grain of humor in his depressed state, might it not be something to build upon, a tiny oasis in the swirling whirlwind of his self-hate?

Whom could she consult? Her family were out of the question. His father was in Washington. Miss Handy probably had a kind heart, but old maids were apt to be disappointing. In the last analysis they couldn't give enough of themselves. And as for Mrs. Fairchild, wasn't she a hopeless fanatic, roaring up and down the streets, shrieking about women's rights . . . ?

Or was she a possibility? She was at least detached from family matters. What was there to be lost?

The following afternoon at five Ellie presented herself at Union Square and was ushered into the library where Rosalie, in black, was seated at a desk writing letters. She rose at once to greet her visitor, and there was a momentary awkwardness as to whether they should kiss. Ellie then reached out her hand, which Rosalie clasped in both her own.

"My dear. How good of you to come."

"Oh, Mrs. Fairchild, I've thought and thought of you!" Suddenly, to her own surprise, Ellie found that her eyes were full of tears. "I loved Selby!"

Now they did kiss, and Rosalie led her to the sofa. "I'm

sorry my husband is not here. He's gone to Washington, you know, to help with the President's defense."

"Yes, I'd heard. It's very fine."

"I'm glad you think so. I wish more people did."

"Oh, people." Ellie was about to denounce her parents for their radical Republicanism, but then thought better of it. Mrs. Fairchild might not consider this consistent with filial piety. "Silly people," she finished vaguely.

"My poor Fred has taken his brother's death very hard," Rosalie continued. "I hope it hasn't made any difference between you two."

"With me, none at all. How could it? But he wants to break off. Or rather he wants to give me back what he calls my freedom. He says he's bust and out of a job and can't afford to marry."

"Not for just now, perhaps."

"That's what I keep telling him. I'll wait forever if need be."

Rosalie's expression seemed to mingle sympathy with a faint surprise. "Ah, my dear, you *do* love him."

"Did you think I didn't?"

"But, child, think how little I know you! And then there was all that terrible Erie business, and Fred's leaving your father's employ. I don't suppose your parents can have approved of that."

"And, of course, you don't like my parents." Ellie checked herself in time from adding, "Nobody does."

"I don't *know* your parents," Rosalie corrected her firmly. "I had to assume that your father's business was important to him."

"Well, it's not to me. I detest the brokerage business! And I'm glad Fred's out of it."

Rosalie's eyes gleamed a still surprised approval. "So am I. But what do you think he should do instead?"

"Be a lawyer. In his father's firm."

"Ah, my dear, how we agree! Do you think you could persuade him? His father would be only too proud and happy to stake him to it. After all, what have we left but him?"

"That's what I tell him. But he's so pigheaded about not wanting to owe anything to anyone. Dear Mrs. Fairchild, what can I do?"

Rosalie frowned as she reflected. "He won't do it for his wife-to-be?"

"He says I'm not his wife-to-be."

"But as you decline to release him . . . ?"

"I guess that just makes me his wife-to-be, indefinitely postponed. Not a very strong position."

Rosalie rose and walked slowly across the room and then back. When she spoke, it was with an artificial casualness.

"Suppose you were something more than his wife-to-be?"

"How do you mean?"

"Suppose you were . . . well . . ."

"His mistress?"

The two women stared at each other.

"Well, a mistress who's also engaged . . . wasn't she a wife under the common law?"

"You surprise me, Mrs. Fairchild."

"I'm sorry. You seemed so independent. So modern."

"I didn't say you had shocked me. You haven't. I said you surprised me. I hadn't thought a lady of your world would want her son to marry a girl who wasn't . . . pure."

"But you would be! To him."

"I see." Ellie rose and walked to the window. She was

very tense, but she thought she was beginning to see her way. "I suppose it's your work for women's rights that has liberated you from the old prejudices."

"Well, I hope it has! Why should we be ashamed of what our bodies want? Men aren't!"

Ellie turned to study this earnest woman who might one day be her mother-in-law. "Men certainly are not," she agreed tersely.

"My boy needs you desperately. Go to him! It's the only way to shake him out of this . . . this temporary madness. If you love him, you must want him! I know what that's like, old and staid as I must seem to you. I've known what it is to want to be loved by a man, and I'm not talking about my husband, either. I knew before I was married to him. And afterwards, too!" She paused as something less than sympathy flared in Ellie's eyes. "I'm not saying I gave in to it. I didn't. But with you it's different. You're going to marry Fred."

Ellie crossed the room to place her lips, the least bit coolly, on the older woman's cheek. "Thank you, Mrs. Fairchild. You've been wonderfully frank. I do appreciate it."

When she left the house in Union Square she had already made up her mind what she would do. She would call the next day at the boarding house in Rector Street and, instead of waiting in the parlor, she would go directly up to Fred's room. The landlady was not the sort who would object; five dollars would quickly smooth the furrows of her false frown. But Ellie had not told Mrs. Fairchild of her decision, and she resolved that she never would. For she was very certain that, if she was going to be the kind of woman who made love to a man out of wedlock — a fornicatress, as the Bible put it — she was never going to be the kind of woman who talked about it. She had found Mrs. Fairchild's frank avowal of her sexual urges distasteful in the extreme. It was Miss Handy, and not her younger sister, who was going to be Ellie's model in the future.

33

FRED FAIRCHILD sat with his grandfather Handy at the end of the picture gallery at Number 417 on a Sunday afternoon after a five-course lunch, when it was too cold and snowy outside for him and Ellie to take the walk that they had earlier planned. Ellie and Aunt Jo, arm in arm, were pacing the long chamber. When they reached the far end Fred could no longer hear even the murmur of their voices.

"I can't tell you, dear boy, how grateful I am that you have decided to go into law. And it will mean everything to your father. A fine firm like his — it would be the greatest pity to have it taken over by strangers. You will be the fourth generation of Fairchilds in it, isn't that so? Let me see. Your father and your uncle, that's one. And your father's uncle, that's two. And your great-grandfather Fairchild, wasn't he in it, as well?"

"I believe he was, sir."

"That must make it one of the oldest firms in the country. For we're still a young nation. Only a few years older than me, think of it! Unhappily, that doesn't make me a young man."

"You're young for your age, Grandpa."

"Thank you, dear boy, thank you. I believe I *do* look younger than most of my contemporaries. The few who are still around, anyway. But let me see . . . what were we discussing?"

"My going into Dad's firm. You were good enough to approve it."

"Ah, yes. The law. We need more law these days, Fred. Selby's terrible tragedy proves that. We have gone too far in letting these so-called financial wizards do things their own way. They're not gentlemen, Fred; they're not gentlemen. We need laws with teeth for their kind. I see you look surprised. You'll be calling me a share-the-wealther next! But I don't care. I've always prided myself on being ahead of the times."

"You certainly were, in the war, sir," Fred agreed politely. "Dad always says you were one of the first to realize how long and bitter the struggle would be."

Mr. Handy smiled and coughed with pleasure at such incense from a veteran. "What field of law will you specialize in? Estates and trusts, like your father?"

"No, I think I shall go in for business law. Corporations, and how they operate."

"You're right, my boy. That's where the future is. Your father has a fine practice, of course, but, between ourselves, there's a bit too much fussing over old women in it." Mr. Handy winked. "Holding hands and sympathizing." But now a disagreeable thought seemed suddenly to strike him. "Except I wish he were doing a bit more of that right now."

"You mean instead of defending the President?"

"Just so. What did he have to get into that mess for?

The President's got plenty of lawyers without him. Why must he throw away his reputation for a rascal like Johnson?"

"I feel differently, Grandpa. I'm proud of Dad for doing it. I look at this impeachment business as another example of the same lawlessness you were just talking about. We had to fight a shooting war to free the slaves. Now it appears we must fight a legal war to save the chief executive. We didn't ask if a slave was good or bad before we freed him. I think the same should be true of Presidents."

His grandfather appeared perplexed. Fred knew that the old man loved to feel that a grandson, particularly a decorated veteran, was on *his* side against a stuffy, set-in-their-ways, intermediate generation. But to find the two younger generations in sudden, unexpected alliance under a "liberal" banner was decidedly less rejuvenating. Mr. Handy scrambled to reassemble his position.

"I suppose that something may be said even in Mr. Lincoln's favor."

"Mr. Johnson's, you mean, sir."

"Mr. Johnson's, of course. Didn't I say Johnson?"

"Perhaps you did."

"Anyway, there are always going to be people who will claim that what a President is doing is unconstitutional. I had an uncle who maintained to his dying day that Mr. Jefferson should have been impeached for purchasing Louisiana from Bonaparte without an amendment!"

The ladies had turned and were approaching them. Ellie seemed totally absorbed in her conversation with his aunt. She appeared to be listening intently, her face turned up to that of the taller woman, and when she smiled and laughed in response, it was with an almost too girlish enthusiasm.

She was certainly making a great play for Aunt Jo's approval, and it wasn't necessary, either. Aunt Jo would have been automatically on the side of any sweetheart of her nephew. But what struck Fred particularly was the innocent, the virginal quality of Ellie's demeanor. It was hard to believe that only that morning, in his room at Rector Street, he had held her naked in his arms. Heaven was but three hours past!

"What are you ladies conspiring about?" he called out. "We feel excluded."

"Oh, you *are* excluded," Aunt Jo replied gaily. "We're having a women's talk."

Was it possible that she was telling Aunt Jo about *him?* Fred felt the back of his neck tingle excitedly at the idea that, behind the wall of female solidarity, there might exist a communion where a woman as pure as Aunt Jo and one as passionate as Ellie could share secrets never to be expressed to a world of jealous males.

"I hope you're not trying to persuade my granddaughter-to-be that women should have the vote," grumbled Mr. Handy.

Fred snorted to himself. As if a woman who could make love like Ellie needed a vote! She made him feel . . . how was it that that soldier had put it on the long night in the trench before Richmond, speaking of his girl back home? As if a flight of doves had burst from his ass when he came! Fred wondered if he wouldn't even vote against Grant if Ellie told him to. When he thought of all those awkward tales of his friends' wedding nights with sticky scared virgins . . .

"Nothing like that, Papa. If you must know, we were making wedding plans. We were discussing just how much could be done or not done with the family in mourning."

"Mourning doesn't seem to interrupt your sister Rosalie in *her* activities."

"Oh, Papa. Poor Rosalie. Her activities have not amounted to so much recently. There can't have been more than a hundred people at her big Brooklyn rally."

"Perhaps that will help her to see the light."

But Jo was not going to allow even the question of women's rights to spoil Ellie's visit. She addressed herself now to Fred. "Ellie has been telling me about Charley Fairchild's offer to you."

"Isn't it wonderful of him, Aunt Jo?"

"Indeed it is. Though, of course, he must rattle around in that big place by himself. Did you know, Papa, that Charley has offered the bride and groom an apartment in his house?"

"*His* house? You mean, Annie's house. My daughter's house. It seems to me that's the least he can do."

"And Dad's giving us an allowance until I can support myself," Fred intervened hurriedly to get his grandfather off an awkward topic. "I didn't want to accept it at first, but Ellie persuaded me it was the right thing."

"Ellie's a smart girl," Mr. Handy said approvingly. "Which should hardly come as a surprise in a niece of old Vanderbilt's. A chip off the old pirate, shall we say?" He seemed to have forgotten that Ellie was present. "More Vanderbilt than Bristow, let's hope," he added, giving Fred a knowing poke. "Egad, let's hope so!"

Aunt Jo gently propelled Ellie back to their promenade, but not so tactfully as wholly to conceal from the old gentleman his gaffe.

"Did I say something wrong?"

"Not really. I'm beginning to suspect that Ellie feels pretty much as you do about her family."

"That shows her perspicacity. But you spoke just now of an allowance from your father. That is all well and good, and I shall be happy to add my own small contribution to the kitty, but surely the Bristows are going to do something handsome for their daughter?"

"Not a thing."

His grandfather stared. "There's to be no *dot?*"

"Not a penny!" Fred let all the pride he felt vibrate in the last word.

"You mean they disapprove of the match? How extraordinary! There's no understanding these new people. But are you seriously telling me that a man who calls himself Seth Bristow, married to a nobody, of the humblest Dutch origin, possibly even Jewish — you will forgive me, dear boy, if I'm a bit free with your future in-laws; once that lovely girl has become your bride nobody will look behind *us* for her antecedents — but I repeat, a man like that dares not to feel honored when two families like the Handys and Fairchilds condescend to seek his alliance?"

Fred was amused. He had always suspected that his family must despise the Bristows, but he had not known how strongly. It seemed almost a pity to pour water on a fire as crackling as the one he had just ignited.

"No, sir, it's not as bad as that. Mr. and Mrs. Bristow are perfectly willing to accept me as a son-in-law. I've had my differences with Ellie's father, but they've been made up. The reason they can't give Ellie anything is that they haven't got it to give. Mr. Bristow, it turns out, has been financially shaky for some time."

"Ah, haven't I said so often enough!" Mr. Handy ex-

claimed, nodding vigorously. "These new people lack sub-
stance. It's façade, half the time, nothing but façade."

"And now, on top of some earlier investments that have
gone sour, he's stuck with a pile of invalidly issued Erie
stock."

"But I thought the Commodore had bailed out his brokers.
I know he did Frank Work. You're not going to tell me that
Bristow played the gentleman and turned him down the way
you did!"

Fred chuckled. "Quite the contrary. He pressed the Commodore as hard as he dared. But after I'd refused payment
at the expense of the Erie shareholders, Mr. Vanderbilt
decided to look a bit more closely into the propriety of
what he was doing. There was still a number of brokers
to be paid, including Bristow, and some of them panicked
when they heard he was talking to the lawyers. One of
Bristow's partners thought to ingratiate himself with the
Commodore by informing him that Bristow was a double
dealer. He'd been selling Erie one day and buying it the
next!"

"Those people are all crooks," Mr. Handy muttered in
disgust. "They even rob each other."

"Well, the Commodore wrote Bristow one of his famous
notes: 'Dear Seth, I have found you a cheat. Because you
married my niece, I shan't ruin you. I'll just leave you to
starve!'"

Mr. Handy cackled. "And is he bust?" He seemed to have
forgotten the consequent depreciation of his granddaughter-
in-law's dowry.

"Not quite that bad. But he's selling the house on Madison Square. And he won't be able to do anything for Ellie.
Which is just fine by me!"

"You're right, my boy. It's the best way. Your grandmother didn't bring me a penny when I married her."

Fred could have retorted; "But she brought you a small fortune when her father died a few years later!" Instead he rose to take his leave, embracing the old man with a warmth that was not feigned.

The weather had cleared when they left, and Fred walked with Ellie down to Madison Square. She tucked her arm snugly under his.

"Oh, Fred! I'm so happy I'm scared."

"Scared of what?"

"Scared of having so much. Why should we have all this and Selby so little?"

"He had more than the boys who died in the Wilderness. There's no fairness, sweetheart. We just have to enjoy what we get."

As he felt her grip on his arm he wondered, with a tightening in his throat, if they had time to go back to Rector Street before supper with her family.

"And of course it didn't just come to us," she said more soberly. "We took our gambles."

"What gambles did you take?"

"The greatest of all!" she exclaimed. "When I came to your room."

"Nonsense. You simply tossed your hook in the stream and I gobbled it."

"On the contrary. You might have thought me an abandoned woman. You might have used me and flung me away!"

"As if anyone could fling you away! You're an addiction, my love. And you know it."

"I didn't know it at all." She threw back her head and laughed. "But I gambled that I might be!"

"Darling! Shall we take a hansom cab to Rector Street? Have we time before dinner?"

"Really, Fred, you're insatiable! You're a beast!"

"Isn't that what you want me to be?"

"Not tonight, anyway. Not on Sunday night. Not after a visit to Number 417. I warn you that I greatly admire Aunt Jo. I want to be just like her."

"Isn't it a bit too late for you to start being like Aunt Jo?" he asked insinuatingly.

"What do you mean?"

"What do you think I mean?"

She burst into another laugh and then became suddenly grave. "You're very crude. And what is worse, you don't respect me anymore."

"Ellie!"

"You don't. All you want is . . . that."

"And *you* don't?"

"I want it in its time and place. As I want a great many other things. In their times and places. And right now I want to go home. And have you be as polite as possible to my parents." Her expression softened when she saw his dismay. "Don't worry, dearest. You will find that the things I want are perfectly nice things. You will find that you're going to want them, too."

She walked on more briskly now, and he followed, a half-step behind. For the first time since his enlistment in '63 he felt that the war was really over. The battle smoke had floated off the fields; the corpses had been removed; uniforms were for sale in old clothing shops, and peace, in shiny high heels, with a swish of satin skirts, was walking up Fifth Avenue. He sighed, but it was a sigh of considerable content.

34

DEXTER sat in the gallery of the Senate Chamber, which was somber despite its many gas jets, as he looked down on that hushed and expectant body. Chief Justice Chase, black-robed, presiding over the legislators sitting as a court, shiny bald, portly and splendid, was taking the verdict, senator by senator, on the eleventh article. It seemed to be generally agreed that if the Managing Committee of the House, as the prosecution, failed to obtain a conviction on this article of impeachment, it would fail on all the others. Nineteen votes of not guilty were needed to make up the third necessary for acquittal, and eighteen had been already obtained, but all the President's partisans, including the seven Republican "renegades" (or "heroes," depending on one's point of view) had now voted, and the tally was almost complete. Unless one waverer could be brought into the fold that morning, Ben Wade would be President of the United States. The heavy air of the chamber seemed fairly to throb with apprehension.

"Mr. Senator, how say you? Is the respondent, Andrew

Johnson, President of the United States, guilty or not guilty
of a high misdemeanor as charged in this article?"

"Guilty."

Dexter was not privileged to sit with the five official
attorneys for the defendant at the table facing the Chief
Justice and flanked by the House Managers. He could make
out the handsome, aristocratic, attentive profile of Evarts, a
model of controlled concern. At the Managers' table, his
opposite number, terrible old Thaddeus Stevens, ashen, mori-
bund, in a grotesque black wig, who had had to be carried
into the chamber in a chair borne by two negro boys, seemed
to be hanging on to life only to witness the final humiliation
of his mortal enemy. At the response "Guilty," Dexter saw
him turn to dart a sharp glance of satisfaction at Senator
Sumner, seated directly behind him. But the latter seemed
to regard the proceedings with the disdain of a Marcus
Aurelius. Bread and circuses were for the mob. Johnson had
already received the verdict of his inverted thumb.

Dexter, amid the general tension, felt curiously serene.
His work was done; there would be no appeal from this
court. He had prepared some half dozen memoranda for the
presidential counselors on jurisdictional questions that might
have arisen in the trial. He had been asked to concentrate
on the role of the Chief Justice, which triggered the larger
problem of whether the Senate was sitting as a legislative
body or as a court. As it had turned out, the Senate had
acted as little as possible like a court. There had been scant
opportunity for Dexter's questions to be asked, much less
answered. But all this had been anticipatable, and he had
had the diversion of a ringside seat for the only spectacle
in the nation that could have filled any part of the large area
in his mind now devoted to the memory of Selby.

He had reached for the distraction of this job with an almost desperate clutch. Selby's death had made him ashamed to have fussed so much over the political problems of the defeated South. When Evarts had said to him that no political objective could justify the impeachment of *any* federal officer, much less the chief executive, on so trumped-up a charge, it was as if the scales had fallen from his eyes. Evarts and Selby had been agreed. The President would have to be acquitted, and then, but not until then, could it be decided whether Congress or the White House should reconstruct the rebel states. If an acquittal should operate against the orderly return of those states to the union, even if it should result in the delay of universal suffrage and the continuance of some degree of racial injustice . . . well, that was unfortunate, nay, tragic. But the federal system had to be preserved. If that wasn't what the war had been about, what *had* it been about?

"Mr. Senator, how say you? Is the respondent, Andrew Johnson, President of the United States, guilty or not guilty of a high misdemeanor as charged in this article?"

"Guilty!"

Dexter had a sudden sense that Selby was there, somewhere close to him. The feeling was so strong that for a moment he actually looked around for him. Then he shook himself impatiently. Was he going to end up like old Vanderbilt, consulting mediums to get in touch with another world? Selby was there only because his memory of Selby was so vibrant. So as long as that was left to him, he would have a part of his son. Rosalie had said that Selby might have been destined for an unhappy life, lacking Fred's strength, in the world that was coming. But Dexter was less sure. Fred was not so strong as Rosalie supposed. His violent faith in battles bred disillusionment. Selby had lacked such faith, but he might have found his way without it.

In the suddenly intensified hush about him, Dexter sensed a crisis. A slight, pale-faced man of some forty years had just risen from his seat. It was Edward Ross, from Kansas, an undecided neophyte to the chamber over whose vote both factions had been struggling for weeks. Even his girl friend, it was rumored, had been besieged by distinguished callers.

"Mr. Senator, how say you? Is the respondent, Andrew Johnson . . . ?"

Dexter's heart bounded. It was going to be all right!

"Not guilty."

There were no cries, no calls, no sobs, only a vast low sibilant exhalation. Dexter rose and walked up the stairs in the aisle to the exit door. Only when he was outside in the corridor did he realize that he was being followed by a lady in black.

"It's all over?" Rosalie asked, as he paused to let her catch up.

"All over. I'm glad you didn't miss it." He tucked her arm under his and led her through the rotunda and out to the steps of the Capitol. "When did you come?"

"Last night. I got my ticket from Mr. Evarts."

"Would you like to walk a bit? It's a lovely day. As well as an historical one."

They strolled towards the greensward that swept away from the base of the Capitol.

"I hope you know, Dexter, that I'm very proud."

"Of the victory?"

"Of your part in the victory."

"It was nothing. Most of my memos were not even read.

But that's all right. They dealt with contingencies that didn't arise."

"But that might have arisen."

"Oh, yes. Any good defense team would have had someone doing what I did."

"So you're part of the victory," Rosalie insisted.

"Like a man with a fire hose when there isn't a fire. Sure. But you won't be reading about me in the histories of the great impeachment."

"I don't care!"

"Nor do I. For that matter, I don't think the acquittal was really the accomplishment of any of the President's counsel. Not that they didn't do a great job. They did. But I have a hunch that Mr. Johnson would have been acquitted even without a lawyer. The Managers made such a bloody mess of it! Anyone not blinded with hate could see the whole process was nothing but an attempted lynch."

"And even at that he got off by only one vote," Rosalie mused. "Two-thirds of our noble Senate — two-thirds less one — wanted to lynch him. Think of it!"

"Or think of it this way. That one vote may be our hope for the future. The Dutch boy's finger in the dike."

Rosalie paused to gaze up at the wheeling gulls that must have flown in from the Chesapeake. "Maybe it's not going to be so bad a world, after all. The world our Selby will miss."

"Do you want to hear a confession, dear? When I was looking down from the gallery at the men who had conspired to unseat Andrew Johnson: Stevens, emaciated, dying, eaten alive with hate; Sumner, smug, prissy, a megalomaniac; Ben Butler, vulgar, flippant, cynical, it suddenly struck me that a congress of women would have been incapable of such behavior."

Rosalie shook her head impatiently, as if embarrassed by his compunction. "You don't have to say that."

"But I do! I owe it to you. I don't say that women aren't as capable of evil as men, but I wonder if they're as capable of self-delusion. Of sheer folly."

"You can test that when you get to know Ellie's mother better."

"That horrible creature! Maybe she's the exception that proves my new rule. You're not going to talk me out of my apology, Rosalie. I've been wholly wrong about your work.

"Have you?" They were strolling now on the lawn by the Capitol. Rosalie unloosed the cords of her wide-brimmed hat and turned to face the mild breeze from the river. She seemed disheartened. "I wonder if it isn't all a waste of time. If I'm not up against the same old contrast between what *you* accomplish and what I do. In the war you could supply a whole regiment with medical equipment while I was changing a bed. And now, in peace, you can save a President's skin while I orate in some dingy hall to five snorers and one heckler. It sometimes seems to me the only way I can serve my fellow man — and woman — is to stay at home and make you comfortable."

"But don't you see the only reason I'm in a position to accomplish more than you is that men have had things their own way so long?"

She gave him a quick glance at this. "Oh, you're there, are you? You have come a way."

"I've done a lot of thinking on my lonely nights in Washington."

"Well, don't misunderstand me. I haven't changed my

position about the rights of women. Not a bit. I've simply begun to wonder if the time is ripe. So few people seem to care. And so few women! Is it really worthwhile for me to make a public spectacle of myself and upset you and Fred? And now Ellie? For she's a very conventional creature, you know."

"Is she? I guess I've seen too little of her as yet. But the beginning of every great cause must be full of discouragements. Think of the martyrs in the arena. Think of our early abolitionists."

"And think of the inquisition! Think of the war! Maybe violence only produces more violence. I've always been suspicious about the motives behind martyrs, and now I'm becoming suspicious about my own. How much is for women, and how much is resentment against you? For all your success . . ."

"That I owe to you," he interrupted firmly.

"Nonsense, Dexter! I'm trying to be serious. Any girl you'd married in our world could have given you what I've given you. What I'm attempting to say is there may be as much anger as idealism in my stand. Anger at Papa, at you, at that horrible Mr. Cranberry — maybe even at Fred, poor fellow. I want to break up your smug male world, smash the windows, pull down the curtains, make a mess of things! They say there are two kinds of revolutionaries: the wreckers and the builders. Maybe I'm just another wrecker."

"But you're *not* trying to wreck things," Dexter protested stubbornly. He was excited now with the idea that he might be breaking into a new plane in their marriage. "You're trying to bring women into a political system in which they presently have no place. To do that you have to preserve the system, not destroy it. I want you to go on just as you've been going, spreading the word, from street corner to street corner if need be. I don't want you to give it all up, just so I can be as cozy and stuffy as Rutgers Van Rensselaer. I've accepted enough sacrifices from you! I don't wish to accept any more."

Rosalie sighed. She might almost have been disappointed in him. "Well, I suppose you're basically right. Crusaders must expect slow starts. But I'm not as young as I was, and the light at the end of that tunnel seems very far away. I think I'm not going to embarrass my family for such small gains. I'll continue to write and organize, and raise money, but I'll leave the barricades to the younger generation."

"You're younger than many of the women engaged in this struggle," Dexter continued inexorably. "Whatever you decide to do or not do, I don't want it to be for my sake."

"It's really rather unkind of you not to give me an excuse, Dexter! I'm tired. And I miss Selby!"

But he knew that the issue was too important to be settled on a sentimental basis. "What do you think Selby would say?"

At this she shrugged and turned back towards the Capitol. "Don't you know? Selby would have agreed with both of us."

Epilogue

THE SUMMER of 1895 had been particularly brilliant, but no day had been lovelier than the one in August on which the governor's visit to Newport was celebrated by a garden party at Marble House. When Dexter arrived at four to hear the concert on the terrace under the Corinthian capitals, the neat rows of gilt chairs were almost filled. A young lady jumped up to offer him her seat.

"Oh, please, Mr. Fairchild, I was just going in, anyway," she whispered as he demurred. "I want to join my father on the porch."

He nodded, smiling, and seated himself in the vacated chair. One had to learn to accept the deference paid old age. It was better, after all, than if it had not been offered. The strains of a Saint-Saens concerto came to his ear, and he proceeded to arrange his reflections along comfortably irrelevant lines, as was his lifelong habit in listening to music.

The scene before him was relaxed and charming: the shimmering, quiet sea, the emerald lawn, the gently swaying elms, the box hedge, the large ladies in Irish lace, the broad-brimmed white hats. All Newport was there, as seemed to be the rule now at Vanderbilt parties. Mrs. "Willy K.," his hostess, her square, toadlike countenance and small black eyes directed from a kind of dais at the audience below, might have been a head mistress surveying her assembled school. And now she was nodding to him. He was much honored!

The Vanderbilts had certainly come a long way. Even Mr. Handy, who in the old days had always been one to favor bringing the new people along, had drawn the line at the Commodore. And now the wives of the latter's grandsons, Corneel and Willy, were practically running the summer community from the two most splendid palaces in Newport. And did not his own daughter-in-law, Ellie, a distant and unendowed cousin, owe more to this connection, carefully cultivated, than to all the Handys and Fairchilds of old New York? Such was social history. It did not even matter anymore that the owners of Marble House were about to be divorced, or that the great "Alva" was notoriously interested in women's suffrage.

But it was also true, Dexter reflected, that notoriety sometimes actually slowed a social ascent. There were families far less rich than the Vanderbilts, and even more newly so, who had come along even faster because, as they were more obscure, people did not remember the briefness of their pedigrees. Look at Dexter's own great-nephew, David Ullman, who had quietly changed his name to Fairchild, and who now, with the reddest cheeks, the curliest hair and the snowiest flannels in all Newport, was perched behind his hostess on her dais, the accepted court jester and *arbiter elegantiarum* of the summer community!

Dexter made out the stiff back of his son Fred seated beside Ellie in the front row. Fred had little ear for music; his rigid posture probably concealed an intense inner world of

planning for the administration of Fairchild, Stone, Dana
and LeRoy, the great corporation law firm of fifty attorneys
into which Fred's organizational genius had developed the
old family partnership. Fred and his wife now occupied Oaklawn, left by Mr. Handy to Rosalie and by her (at Dexter's
request) to their sole surviving son. Dexter had asked only
for the life use of the Gothic cottage in which he and Rosalie
had had their supper *à deux* half a century before. But he
was quite comfortable there with his old housekeeper to
cook and clean, and he was invited to the "big house" every
Sunday for lunch and to their larger dinner parties. Of
course, he had had to learn that Ellie did not relish his coming without an invitation, even to see the grandchildren. The
latter were sent, very punctiliously, to call on *him* at the cottage. Ellie as a daughter-in-law was just as correct as she was
as a wife and mother. He had learned not to look for a
warmth that she did not possess.

The piece was over now; people rose to stroll and chat.
Art in Newport was only the servant of social intercourse.
Dexter got to his feet as he saw Lily Van Rensselaer approach. His sister-in-law, at eighty-four, had come almost
comically to resemble her late father. Mr. Handy with a
parasol, in Irish lace.

"You're looking very fit, Dexter." Her tone rumbled, with
a mild condescension. Though she was seven years his senior,
everything about her proclaimed her faith in the physical superiority of the aging female. "I missed you yesterday when I
called at Oaklawn. You were out driving."

"I didn't know you were coming."

"Oh, I just popped in to see Ellie. The place looks as beautiful as ever. Papa would have been so pleased."

"I'm afraid it's rather old-fashioned compared to all this."

He waved a hand towards the gleaming facade of Marble House. "If your father were alive today, he'd probably be building a French château."

Lily's sniff was a sign that she, at least, was not yet prostrate before the new people. "Oh, I prefer the good old ways. People are getting altogether too fancy now. Too big for their boots, as my poor Rutgers used to say. But at least we have one of the real old guard coming today. Julia Ward Howe. Ah, there she is now." They turned to watch a little wisp of an old woman in gray, quaintly pretty in an old-fashioned closely tied bonnet, being greeted demonstratively by Mrs. Willy K. "I hear that Miss King is going to sing the 'Battle Hymn' in her honor."

"Will we be allowed to join in the stirring chorus?"

Lily ignored his sarcasm. "I should imagine so. It will make me think of poor Rosalie and her hospital ship. I never cease feeling proud of her."

"I don't think of her as 'poor Rosalie,'" he retorted, perfectly indifferent to the poor taste of taking her up on the use of an accepted adjective to describe the dead. "I think of her as having had a very happy and successful life."

"Well, of course, she did," Lily agreed hastily. "I was only referring to the tragedy of our losing her so early."

"She packed more into her fifty-four years than I have into my seventy-seven. And the last four were the best of all. Even after we lost Selby, and I thought her happiness gone forever. Not a bit of it! She had all those wonderful years organizing the Manhattan Nursing School."

"Really, dear Dexter, I never meant to imply anything to the contrary!"

But he was now rather enjoying his aggressiveness. "And

perhaps the greatest of her accomplishments was making her husband the happiest man in New York!"

"I quite agree."

He noted her tone of complacent reservation. To Lily's generation a single adultery stamped the marriage as a failure. All that "poor dear Rosalie" could do after that business with Annie had been to pick up the pieces. But to imply that such a patched-up marriage could ever be described as happy was simply ridiculous.

"Have you heard from Annie lately?" he asked bluntly.

"I had a letter from Paris last week." She looked taken aback by the crudeness of his showing that he had read her thoughts. "She's pretty well, considering her arthritis."

"Still running her salon?"

"Oh, she'll never give that up! Laura Garvan was there last spring and said she met some very strange people indeed. Of course, they're all artists and writers and that sort of thing."

"Yes. I don't suppose they get together to sing the 'Battle Hymn of the Republic.'"

"You seem to be in a rather critical mood today, my dear. I think I shall leave you to Fred."

She glided away, a galleon of white sail, as Fred Fairchild stepped up to take his father's elbow.

"How about a turn across the lawn, Pater? There's something I'd like to ask you."

Fred, at fifty, seemed older than his years, mostly because of his gray hair and walrus mustache. Like many leaders of the bar, he enjoyed and even affected the appearance of age. It had nothing to do with his perfect health and iron nerves. Everything had gone Fred's way. Having converted the family firm from a comfortable practice in trusts and estates to the lucrative service of mighty corporations, he was well on his way to making a fortune. Fred was gruff and practical and businesslike; he was always talking about the titans of oil and steel and the "natural destiny" of American industrial enterprise. But Dexter knew that he was afraid of his wife and secretly ashamed of the stiff way in which she treated her father-in-law.

"What can I do for you, my boy?" Something awkward was involved, for Fred was obviously constrained.

"At the partners' lunch last week the old question of the corner office came up again. It was felt that it should be occupied by someone who was more regularly there. That our principal clients shouldn't be led past the swellest room to do business in a smaller one."

Dexter, who went to Wall Street now only to open his mail, manage a few trusts and write his articles for The New-York Historical Society *Bulletin* (they were as near as he had ever come to that book on New York he had once planned) did occupy the corner office, but only at Fred's insistence. He strongly suspected that it was Ellie, and not the partners, who fumed at this special treatment of a fossil at her husband's expense.

"But haven't I always said so?" he protested. "Haven't I always insisted that you take that office? Let's make the change at once. Any room will do for me."

"Well, I thought we might put you in Tom Slater's old office. It's really very nice and has a window overlooking Trinity Church. That should inspire you in your articles!"

Dexter had to blush for his son. The late Tom Slater had not even been a partner! What was it that old King Lear had cried: "I gave you all!" True, but what had been the answer? "And in good time you gave it." Perhaps Goneril and Regan had been right. The only thing that was really sad about the whole silly business was that Fred had not initiated it of his own accord. Even if he became president of the Bar Association, even if he made as many millions as a minor Vanderbilt, he would still be Ellie's slave.

"Don't you know, my boy, that you're all I have left? What do I exist for but to do as you want?"

It wasn't true. It had never been true. Neither he nor Rosalie had ever loved Fred as they had loved Selby. But Fred, for all his timidity with his spouse, loved his old father and wanted to be loved in return. King Lear? Dexter reproached himself now for thinking only of the pathetic Lear, the driven, crazed old man. What about the awe-inspiring, the vituperatively cursing Lear? Was not the bath of blood in which his tragedy ended a tribute to the retributive power in even the oldest, feeblest parent? A power that Dexter Fairchild was certainly not going to make a fool of himself by using now.

"Actually, I prefer a smaller office," he told the still silent Fred. "I won't feel people are saying, 'What's that old fart doing with all that space?' "

As they turned back now to the reassembled musicians Dexter felt his hand suddenly gripped.

"You know how I care about you, Pater!"

"Yes, my son, yes. Of course, I do. And the Slater office will suit me to perfection. I've been embarrassed, occupying so grand a room when I'm really not practicing any law at all." He saw the next sentence in the wings of his mind about to rush in to ruin everything: "Ellie is quite right about that." But he repressed it. Oh, yes, he still had the strength for that!

"Dad!" Fred's voice changed as he reverted to the old address.

"Yes, Fred."

"You're going to keep your old office! I've just made up my mind."

"But, Fred, I don't want it. I really . . ."

"Then keep it for my sake!"

"This is ridiculous. I don't want the office. I don't want any office. I have my library in Union Square. That's more than enough for me."

"Dad, you've *got* to keep your old office! It is suddenly very important. To me. You must do it for *me!*"

Dexter decided that it would be ungracious, even unkind, to pretend that he didn't understand.

"I shall occupy any office you tell me to, Fred. Shall we resume our seats?"

Alva Vanderbilt was standing on the podium.

"Ladies and gentlemen, we are honored today not only by the presence of our governor but by that of a great patriot and a great artist, Mrs. Julia Ward Howe. You all know the story of how she composed her noble hymn after watching a review of the Grand Army of the Potomac. The words are as thrilling today as they were when Mrs. Howe penned them in an hour of inspiration, thirty-three years ago. I am going to ask Miss Gertrude King to sing the verses and invite you all to join her in the ringing chorus."

The high, reedy voice of a mature, demure damsel in white, who took her smiling stand by her hostess, was now raised in the hymn:

> Mine eyes have seen the glory of the coming
>   of the Lord;
> He is trampling out the vintage where the grapes
>   of wrath are stored;

He has loosed the fateful lightning of His terrible
    swift sword;
His truth is marching on.

The whole assembly rose with Mrs. Howe, who was over-
come and in tears, to join loudly in the "Glory, Glory, Hal-
lelujah." Dexter felt himself almost uncontrollably moved.
The tears jumped to his eyes too; his mind was a vision of
boys in blue marching to the sea. He heard, with a pounding heart, the trumpet that should never call retreat. All the
old feelings had returned in an ecstasy of exhilaration.

I have seen Him in the watchfires of a hundred
    circling camps;
They have builded Him an altar in the evening
    dews and damps;
I have read His righteous sentence by the dim and
    flaring lamps;
His day is marching on.

And then he suddenly recalled what Mrs. Vanderbilt had
said about the conception of the poem. In a carriage riding
back to Washington, had it not been? He thought now, less
comfortably, of his own ride to the capital after the disaster
at Bull Run. Looking around him, in altered mood, at the
splendor of the house and its gardens, at all the fine clothes
and shiny baubles, he had an eerie sense of that old retreat
somehow turned into a victory march, a rush over a pros-
trated enemy, a stampede from Atlanta to the sea, with the
parasols, the floppy hats, the Irish lace, the cutaways, the
gray waistcoats, the gleaming canes, the pearls and the diamonds, no longer abandoned by the wayside, but brandished
in triumphant, upstretched hands like the banners of con-
quering legions. Christ might have died to make men holy,
but had not Mrs. Vanderbilt and God won the war?

His vision had subjected him to a strain that was ill-advised for a heart that had already been the victim of one near-fatal attack, and he turned to go into the house and call his carriage. In the big hall an anxious Fred caught up with him.

"Are you all right, Dad?"

"Perfectly, my boy. Go back to the party. I'm just going home for a little rest before dinner."

But when his landau pulled up at the front door, he instructed his coachman to drive to the Island Cemetery. The man knew, without being told, that he should go directly to the Handy plot, and he waited as usual on his seat while Dexter pushed open the iron grille gate and went in.

On a vast marble slab a marble angel brooded over a huge urn. It was the tomb of Charles Handy, who had survived to his ninetieth year. To one side a modest headpiece denoted the final resting place of his daughter Joanna, subservient to her sire in death as in life. Dexter, seeing it, always recalled with satisfaction that, thanks to Rosalie, Joanna had at least escaped her father during the war.

He turned to the other side of Mr. Handy's memorial where Rosalie and Selby were buried. The latter had a thin piece of white marble marked with his dates and the words: "Given little, he gave much." Rosalie's slab, at her request, had only her name, her dates and the legend: "Wife of Dexter Fairchild."

Standing before it, uncovered, he bowed his head for several silent minutes. Then he chuckled aloud. "You're still helping to keep me from making a total ass of myself, both of you," he murmured. "Keep it up, my darlings! It shouldn't be too much longer."